"All great legends, whether of Britain's King Arthur, Greece's Trojan War or Europe's Charlemagne cycle contain stories of minor characters begging to be elaborated on. In *Quest of the Warrior Maiden* Linda McCabe has picked up the lesser known tale of Ruggiero and Bradamante, this last being the warrior maiden of the title. Classic in its theme of young, idealistic lovers from opposing camps, it sheds a bright light on the culture, history and legends of a time and place too little explored by most western readers." ~ Persia Woolley, author of the internationally acclaimed Guinevere Trilogy

"McCabe paints a vivid portrait of Medieval France whose vestiges can still be found in the streets of modern Paris." ~ Cara Black, award winning author of the Aimée Leduc mystery series and *Murder in the Lanterne Rouge*

"Amidst opposing armies of an ancient holy war, debut novelist Linda C. McCabe adds fresh interest to the tale of the star-crossed lovers, Bradamante and Ruggiero, in *Quest of the Warrior Maiden*. Rich in detail of the period, fans of the genre will truly appreciate McCabe's intelligence in detailing for her readers the events behind and leading up to the poignant love story between this lesser known couple from legend." ~ bestselling author, Patricia V. Davis

"A grand and engaging re-telling of the original 'star crossed lovers' epic with everything Orlando – chivalry, romance, fights to the death, hippogriffs, madness, and beauty! As engaging a story as I have read this year, I couldn't put it down and I urge you to pick it up today." ~ John Granger, author of *Unlocking Harry Potter*

"In many ways *Quest of the Warrior Maiden* is a distant mirror of our present day passions: both political and personal." ~ Rob Loughran, author of *Tantric Zoo*

"I read the story in one sitting and was devastated to find out what I had in my hands was only volume one! I look forward to volume two." ~ Ibrahim Al-Marashi, professor of History at IE University in Spain

"This tantalizing love story is based on the Italian romantic epic poems of *Orlando furioso* and *Orlando innamorato* written in the Italian Renaissance about medieval legendary events. Yet the author retells this tale to highlight the Maid, Bradamante, a Christian warrior fighting for Charlemagne, and her love for Ruggiero, a Saracen knight and her sworn enemy.

Weaving fantasy and history in a complex plot with many characters, the author uses Bradamante's love for Ruggiero as the single thread pulling the action forward. When Bradamante learns of her noble destiny, her love for Ruggiero is elevated into a quest to save her religion and country.

Fraught with obstacles, trickery, and magic, Bradamante is entangled in a web, but is she caught? At the book's fast paced ending, madness and conflicts are at every turn. A well written and exciting adventure, fueled by passion and revenge, this is the stuff of great literature. Compelling and entertaining!" ~ Kate Farrell, author of *Wisdom Has a Voice: Every Daughter's Memories of Mother*

"This is an original approach to the story of Bradamante and Ruggiero. Historically accurate, with a clever sense of plot and with an incredible cast of characters. Once you start you simply can't stop!" ~ José Lúcio, professor of Economic Development at New University of Lisbon-Portugal

"*Quest of the Warrior Maiden* captures the feeling of the old epic poems from which they are adapted. The main characters, Bradamante and Ruggiero, are strong, endearing characters who go through numerous struggles of separation and conflict in their quests for love. This story is about love at first sight between two people who cannot, on the surface, be together because of their positions in opposing armies (Muslim and Christian). This religious barrier and the physical separation between the characters create constant tension that makes the story a page-turner." ~ medieval blogger Steven Till.

Mary,
May all of your quests be filled
with honor and victory!

Quest of the Warrior Maiden

Bradamante and Ruggiero Series

I enjoy schmoozing about writing
with you!

Volume One

Linda C. McCabe

LINDA C. McCABE

Destrier Books

Windsor, California

Quest of the Warrior Maiden

Bradamante and Ruggiero series, Volume One

Destrier Books
P.O. Box 2344
Windsor, California 95492
www.destrierbooks.com

Cover art design by Iain R. Morris

Author photo by Cindy A. Pavlinac / CAPavlinac.com

This novel is a work of fiction. Names, characters, and events are either products of the author's imagination or used fictitiously.

ISBN 978-0-9836362-1-2

To the heroes of my own lifestory, Scott and Ian. Thank you for supporting
me in this magical journey.

CONTENTS

Part I:

Love, War and Faith

CHAPTER 1

Summer Solstice in the Year 802

A low moan emanated from a pile of corpses on the battlefield. Ruggiero turned in the direction of the sound. *Did someone call my name?* The opposing army had fled, leaving a bloodied plain covered with dead bodies as far as the eye could see.

The knights he was riding with were the last group of soldiers who had not yet returned to camp. His friend Danifort had smears of blood on his face and was regaling the others about his various kills earlier in the day. No one else appeared to have heard the sound that bothered Ruggiero. His victorious flush evaporated as he realized his guardian was not among the riders. When had his mentor left his side?

"Danifort, have you seen Atallah?"

"Was it my turn to watch the old sorcerer?"

"Watch out Danifort or Atallah will send a jinn your way," said another knight.

"This is no matter for jest. He could be dead or injured." Ruggiero's face burned. Atallah was a mystic and not a sorcerer, but this was not the time to quibble over the difference.

"The surgeons will be out soon. It is their job to care for the wounded." Danifort cocked his head toward the city towers bearing plumes of billowing black smoke. "The sacking of Toulouse has already begun. Tonight, we shall take you on your first pillage. Fame and glory are won on the battlefield, but a warrior such as yourself will only amass wealth through plundering."

Ruggiero hated the reminder of his poverty. He was riding alongside wealthy governors and powerful nobles, yet his only valuables were his armor, sword, and horse, which had all been given to him. He had no lands or title and needed to acquire goods in order to support himself, lest he continue depending upon his guardian to provide for him. The sound of two vultures fighting over a corpse brought him to his senses.

"No," said Ruggiero. "I owe it to Atallah to find and help him if I can. Or save his body from desecration."

Danifort shrugged. "If he died, means more for me in the looting."

"Take my share as well. I would rather miss out on a few trinkets than spend the rest of my life regretting what I might have done for a loyal friend."

"Enjoy yourself looking at the dead!" another knight called out. "We shall amuse ourselves with Frankish maids instead."

They galloped off. Ruggiero turned his attention to the search for his guardian while their laughter rang in his ears.

"Atallah!" he called out.

In the midst of the plain stood a large oak tree whose shade had offered the only reprieve that day from the hot summer sun. He remembered the landmark for he had fought the famous Frankish warrior Orlando near the tree. Orlando had ducked to avoid hitting his head on one of the lower branches. Ruggiero recognized the warrior from the shield he bore with red and white quartering. The day's battle had been so intense that the white portions of Orlando's shield were hard to see under splatters of blood.

Atallah had shouted, "Do not advance against Orlando!" But avoiding a fight was not within Ruggiero. Their duel had been fierce and short-lived. For some unknown reason, Orlando broke off and galloped away, as if the paladin had responded to a command only he could hear.

Ruggiero urged his horse, Frontino, to walk toward the massive oak, taking care to avoid stepping on any scattered limbs in their path. He repeated his guardian's name while making his way across a tableau of death. In the morning the plain had been a wheat field, but now the only harvest would be weapons, armor, and valuables from the dead. Thousands of bodies were scattered about and severed heads dotted the ground in grotesque patterns. An oppressive calm hung in the air intensifying Ruggiero's feeling of dread.

His spirits were lifted somewhat when he did not see any sign of Atallah near the tree. Then, the ominous sound that drew him on the search rose again. Ruggiero turned and urged his horse toward it. As he came near the source, he realized that it was a dying man's incoherent murmurs. The fallen man's legs were broken and splayed at awkward angles. Ruggiero was uncertain if he was an enemy or a comrade in arms for there were no signifiers of his allegiance. The man wore a simple coat of mail and had lost his helmet and shield. Ruggiero felt this very anonymity gave him an air of dignity; as he represented all warriors brave enough to sacrifice their lives for a cause greater than themselves.

He made a move to dismount when the man pointed a finger at him. There was a look in his eyes that made Ruggiero remain on horseback. He was unsure if the gesture was a silent accusation or a signal of the man's desire for forgiveness of sins. Maybe it was a longing for compassion before death.

Was I the one who did this to him? Ruggiero had no idea, for the day had been a blur of blood and carnage. He had quickly lost count of the number of men he had felled with his sword since joining the war a week before. Slashing his way through throngs of men, he never paid attention to the destruction caused by his blade. This man could have been one of them.

The man's lips twitched into a smile as his chest fell, never to rise again and his eyes took on the vacant glassy stare of the dead. Ruggiero closed his own eyes as the reality of war crystallized for him: it bore no resemblance to the tales of glory sung by poets. Atallah had warned him about the world of men and war, but Ruggiero had clung tenaciously to the idealized images wrought by Homer and Virgil. He was saddened to see that his mentor was right yet again.

A funeral would be performed for the dead later, but Ruggiero felt the need to mark the passing of this man's soul into the afterlife. Turning in the direction of Mecca, he bowed his head and tried remembering what he could of the *Salat al-Janazah*. The imams led those prayers. He had said responses with the other warriors, but never had a reason to give such a prayer before.

"*Allahu Akbar.* Forgive me for not being cleansed for prayer, and for not knowing the proper words. I seek your blessing for the soul of this man and for the souls of all those who died in battle today. All men belong to you, and upon their deaths will return to you. May they be cleansed of all their sins and be permitted to walk in your glory." His throat tightened and he paused before continuing. "Allah, I ask that you keep Atallah safe and bring me once again to his side. Amen."

As he lifted his head, he noticed a new smell in the air. It was different from the mixture of blood, sweat, and stale urine from the battlefield. The aroma of roasting mutton made his stomach rumble with hunger. This day marked the joining of Amir Akramont's armies with the advance forces, bringing about their first major victory in the war against the Franks. Ruggiero smiled as he imagined the celebration awaiting him in the royal tent; the amir treated him not as a neophyte knight, but as a valued member of his inner circle of advisors. Perhaps Atallah was there already and this search was all in vain. *After all,* Ruggiero reminded himself, *Sufi mystics are harder to kill than ordinary men.*

Ruggiero was ready to return to camp when he heard the clinking sound of a sword fight. In the distance, two mounted warriors were engaged in combat.

Why are they still fighting? The battle is over.

Upon approaching them, he did not recognize either combatant, but it was clear that neither was Atallah. He waited to hail them until there was a pause in their fighting.

As one warrior turned his horse to charge at his opponent, Ruggiero called out. "If one of you is a Christian knight, bear that you hear me out. Charlemagne has fled, taking his forces with him. If you wish to follow your emperor, make haste lest you be left behind."

The warrior bearing a shield and plume all of white said, in a youthful muffled voice, "Please sir, allow me to follow my sovereign. If I am to die this day, I would rather it be with him."

"The answer to your request is no," the opposing warrior said. "I was about to kill Orlando when you interfered! I shall not quit this duel until one of us is dead. You wish to leave now? You must kill me first."

As that man turned, Ruggiero saw a banner hanging limply on the back of his horse. It was a scarlet flag with a lion rampant and guarded the face of a beautiful woman. Ruggiero then realized who this man likely was as well as his notorious reputation.

"We fought valiantly today," said Ruggiero, "but the battle is over. Let this man withdraw, so he may return to his forces. That is the way of the knight." Ruggiero turned his attention to the Christian warrior and gestured toward the horizon. "They left yonder in full retreat. If you leave now, you might catch them before darkness falls. Since this man still desires an opponent, I shall take your place."

The knight gave him a gracious bow and galloped away.

"Are you a bastard son of a swineherd?" said the remaining warrior. "Do you not know who I am?"

Ruggiero fought back the anger rising inside of him as he remembered the words of his mentor, *"Anger unbalances and kills faster than swords."* He struggled to keep his face impassive as he looked the scowling commander directly in the eye.

"We have not met before, but by your dragon-hide armor and your standard, I believe you must be Governor Rodomont of Sarza."

The man's eyes narrowed. "You knew me and yet you dared question my honor? You shall pay for this insult. Give me your name, so that I may tell Amir Akramont who was foolish enough to die for a Christian soldier out of a misplaced idea about chivalry."

"I am Ruggiero Tazeem."

Rodomont laughed. A mirthless laugh rooted in malice. "Do you expect me to bow down to you? Kiss your noble feet? I am legend, while you are merely a child. My forces began this invasion months ago while Akramont dithered in the Maghreb. I will not stand for you, of all people, trying to teach me manners. Instead you shall be taught the last lesson of your charmed short life."

Ruggiero was surprised at the intensity of Rodomont's reaction. He forced himself to breathe evenly and not respond to the insults clearly intended to provoke him.

Rodomont brandished his sword. "There is no place for mercy on the battlefield. To show mercy is to be weak, and I despise weakness in all its forms."

"I cannot question your honor," said Ruggiero, "because you have none."

"You disrespectful little whelp."

Ruggiero raised his sword and gripped his shield as Rodomont's horse charged at him. Their swords clashed in midair echoing the two warriors' tempers.

CHAPTER 2

Bradamante paused at the crest of a hill and scowled at the empty road stretching before her. The rear guard of Charlemagne's retreating army was still not in sight. She shook her head in frustration and took a long drink of water from her flask.

How much longer until I catch up with them?

Returning her flask to a saddlebag, she turned behind. As she watched the two warriors in the distance, Rodomont made a wild swing of his sword at the other knight. She was relieved to see him miss, but then guilt tore through her.

What have I done? How could I relinquish a duel for a Saracen to finish? I took over that fight when Rodomont was about to deliver a deathblow to my kinsman Orlando. What if that Saracen knight dies in my stead? Rodomont will likely boast that Orlando and I were cowardly and abandoned our fights with him.

Bradamante's face burned as she imagined the humiliation she would face. All because she had grown weary of fighting and wanted to rejoin Charlemagne's army. Her reputation and that of her famed cousin depended on an unknown knight being victorious over a ruthless enemy.

"May Rodomont rot in Hell."

Bradamante tugged the reins on her horse, prodding him to return to the battlefield. The horse was pulling hard on clumps of grass and resisted.

"I know you are hungry, Erebus, so am I. When our duty is finished, we shall both find something to eat."

The promise was as much to herself as to her pure black companion. She was tired, sore and hungry and wanted nothing more than to eat and sleep. Returning to fight Rodomont was an obligation. Needing to gird herself to face her enemy, she actively purged any thoughts of defeat. However, she was distracted by questions about the courteous Saracen knight and various pretenses she might have for speaking with him.

The setting sun gave the plain an orange-red hue over patches of black bloodstains. Despite herself, even from a distance she enjoyed watching the spectacle of two well-trained combatants exchanging blows. Rodomont was becoming erratic while the younger knight appeared to be gaining the upper hand. As Bradamante drew near, she was surprised to realize her champion was using the flat side of his blade, rather than its edge.

This is not a tournament, this is war. Rodomont will kill you if given the chance.

Bradamante held her tongue lest she interrupt the young knight's concentration and provide Rodomont an advantage. She did not want to witness the death of a chivalrous knight at her enemy's hands.

A sense of relief came over her as the younger knight pummeled Rodomont. He slung his shield over his own back and delivered a two handed strike to Rodomont's helmet. Bradamante smiled as the arrogant commander slumped forward onto his horse's neck. His sword fell to the ground with a resounding clatter. Lowering his blade, the victor watched Rodomont dangle in the saddle. Courtesy and mercy being extended to such an unworthy recipient amazed her.

"Pardon me sir," Bradamante called out.

He turned and bore a look of surprise on his face.

"I appreciate your championing my cause," she said. "However, I was wrong accepting your generous offer. The duel was not yours to finish and you should not fight with a fellow soldier. Should Rodomont recover and wish to continue, please allow me the honor of ending this fight."

Smiling at her, he nodded his assent. Rodomont began stirring. His eyes appeared unfocused as he rose in his saddle, but when he saw his empty right hand he emitted a curse.

"Your courtesy is the victor today," he said. "But you failed. You should have killed me when you had the chance. I admit defeat and will leave, but mark my words: I will get my revenge for your insolence."

Rodomont retrieved his sword from the dusty plain. His face convulsed with anger before he rode toward the Saracen encampment. Bradamante faced the young knight feeling unsure how to proceed.

"As you said, the battle is over for the day, so…" She replaced her sword in its scabbard.

"It is," he agreed, sheathing his sword.

There was silence as they exchanged nervous smiles. The conical helmet covered his browridge and the nosepiece obscured the center of his face. From what Bradamante could see he appeared handsome, but she wanted to see his full face.

"I admire your prowess," she said.

"Your skills are impressive as well."

"Thank you." She felt the heat of a blush forming on her cheeks. "Why did you hold back against Rodomont? He would have killed you then gloated about it."

"I saw no honor in killing him."

"Yes, well, you should be wary. He might murder you during the chaos of a battle to cover up the crime of killing a fellow soldier."

"Tell me what you know of him."

"He is ruthless and cruel. I battled him once before. When Rodomont could not defeat me, he attacked my horse. I was trapped under its body. Thankfully there was a depression in the ground beneath me or I would have been crushed to death. I was not found until the next morning."

"Attacking horses," he said gritting his teeth. "Rodomont is worse than I thought."

"There is no one I hate more."

"I would show no mercy if anyone dared harm Frontino." He patted the neck of his dun colored stallion.

"Why were you still on the battlefield to even come upon my duel?" asked Bradamante.

"I was searching for someone. I fear he may have died or been injured. I checked the areas where we fought today, but did not find him. Now I wonder if he is waiting for me back at the camp."

"Let us hope that is the case."

"Allow me to escort you. There are bandits who lie in wait to attack lone riders."

"I would be grateful for your company." Rejoining Charlemagne's army had become secondary to Bradamante's desire to learn more about this knight. "Tell me what he looks like and I will help you search for him on our way."

"Atallah is old with white hair and a long beard," he said as they traveled slowly back to the ridge. "You must think me foolish for searching amongst the dead."

"On the contrary. I prayed during that long, cold night when I laid on a battlefield that one of my brothers or a kinsman would come looking for me."

He fixed his eyes upon hers. "Thank you. My friends were not as understanding as you. They thought I was mad for passing up the chance to sack Toulouse."

Bradamante broke his gaze. She had never felt nervous around a man before. Being with this young knight was intoxicating. Casting her eyes over the ground, she avoided focusing on the shield designs. She did not want to put a name on any of the dead. In the distance, near the Saracen encampment, a small contingent of surgeons and plunderers emerged beginning their own search among the fallen.

"Tell me about Atallah."

"He is all the family I have and has been my guardian since I was born."

"What happened to your parents?"

"My father was murdered. My mother died in childbirth."

Bradamante's heart ached at the thought. Her family provided her with a sense of strength; she could not imagine being an orphan.

"I am sorry for the loss of your family," she said, feeling woefully inadequate.

He nodded and then turned away from her, though not before she noticed a glistening in his eyes.

"Atallah," he called out, after clearing his throat.

She added her voice to his. Together they repeatedly called out Atallah's name. Night would soon be upon them and Bradamante was no closer in finding Charlemagne's army. Logic told her she should be galloping away while there was still some light left, but her heart overruled. How could she leave the side of the only man who had ever stirred passion in her without knowing his name? How would she ever find him again?

Bradamante brought her horse to a halt as she spied a white haired man lying face down. "Could that be him?"

The young knight dismounted and walked over to the man. Kneeling, he carefully turned the body over and gave a sigh of relief. "Praise Allah."

As the knight moved, Bradamante saw the dead man's face clearly. The first thing she noticed was the man's lack of a beard. Then she fixated on his full white moustache and blue eyes. Eyes she recognized. Eyes that laughed at her the first time she ever wielded a practice sword. It was his scorn that lit her inner fire at the tender age of three. He was the one who christened her "the Maid." He had meant it as an insult, but it quickly became her nickname. She proved to him time and again that women warriors were no laughing matter.

And now he was dead.

Her throat tightened as she bowed her head and made the sign of the cross.

"Do you know him?" asked the knight.

"Yes. That is – or was – Duke Guillaume of Orléans."

The young knight folded the man's hands upon his chest and then closed the man's eyes. "I am sorry for your loss."

Bradamante fought back tears. His sentiment was simple and heartfelt, as was the gesture of respect he made to the dead. Coming from an enemy soldier made it all the more overwhelming to her.

She took a few deep breaths trying to recover her composure. Warriors did not cry on the battlefield, no matter the circumstances. It was then she realized they were not far from the crest of the hill where she had first paused before returning to her fight with Rodomont. The idea of parting from him caused her pain. A wild thought crossed her mind. *What if I asked him to come away with me? Would he?*

"Was he dear to you?" the knight asked as he remounted his horse.

His question startled her. "No, I – I..."

"What is it that vexes you?"

"You have been kind to me, more than I deserve. Your courtesy is greater than anything I have ever seen demonstrated by Christian warriors, even Charlemagne. I am upset because had we met in battle earlier, I might have killed you. I would never have met you or known how honorable you are. That thought gives me pain as well as the idea of someone as noble as you dying in battle. It would be a tragedy. I must know your name and your family."

He gave her a warm smile as their horses began walking again. "I share your feelings. In this short time I feel a greater kinship with you than with my comrades. I hope to never cross swords with you. I would hate myself if I were to harm you in any way. You asked of my family. I must start with my noble ancestor Hector of Troy. My sense of honor comes from him. I strive to live up to his image as the perfect knight. It is his standard that adorns my shield."

Bradamante felt her breath catch in her throat. She had grown up hearing many tales of that legendary hero's prowess and valor. The young knight held up his shield for her inspection. Its leather covering bore a hand-painted design of a silver eagle on a field of blue.

"Hector of Troy is your ancestor? I thought his only son died in the fall of Troy."

"*The Iliad* is wrong. Hector's widow Andromache spirited their son Astyanax out of the city with a trusted friend. The Greeks murdered Andromache and another Trojan child, which led them to think they ended Hector's bloodline. Astyanax grew up on Sicily, and as a young man slew a giant while rescuing the warrior queen of Siracusa. They later married."

"A warrior queen? What was her name?" asked Bradamante, awed that her companion had clearly read an epic poem she had only heard about.

"I wish I knew. Her name has been lost to history. She was as brave as Astyanax, perhaps braver. Their life together was short. He was betrayed and slain by the Greek villain Aegisthus. The warrior queen was heavy with child and fled for her life in a small boat barely escaping the clutches of the Greek army. She landed safely in a cove in Reggio, where she bore Astyanax's son Polidoro."

Bradamante was pleased to hear pride in his voice at being descended from a female warrior, but her thoughts quickly shifted to the plight of the nameless queen. She imagined the terror an expectant mother must have felt fleeing for her life in a boat. Not knowing where she would land, as well as worrying about when and where she would go into labor.

The young knight described succeeding generations of his ancestors captivating Bradamante by a verbal weaving of his family's tapestry. It was when the names Charles the Hammer, Pepin the Short, and Charles the Great were mentioned that she came out of her reverie.

"Pardon," she interrupted, "did you say Charles the Great?"

"I did. Floviano of Rome brought forth two famed lines of descendants; one line includes Charlemagne and I am descended from the other."

Bradamante was awestruck. She was distantly related to him, because her mother was one of Charlemagne's sisters. This young man was not her enemy; he was a kinsman. A *distant* kinsman, but he was still a kinsman. It also meant her family was descended from royal Trojan blood. That new knowledge made her swell with pride.

He stopped his horse after reaching the top of the ridge. "My grandfather, Duke Rampaldo, was a kind, honorable man, and a wise ruler of Reggio. He had two sons, my father was named Ruggiero the second, the other son was Beltramo, my uncle. My father married Galiziella, a warrior he met in battle."

"Your mother was a warrior?"

"Yes, an accomplished warrior in the Muslim army. I do not know how my parents met, but it was during a war in Italy. She was baptized a Christian and they married."

Bradamante's heart leapt. *Might he follow in his mother's footsteps and convert his faith for love? For my love?* She almost laughed out loud realizing he most likely did not even know he was talking with a woman.

Tendrils of fog crept over the hillside. She knew they would need to find someplace safe to spend the night, before darkness descended. *But how to bring up such a subject?*

"My uncle was jealous and wanted my mother for himself," the knight said. "He betrayed my father and grandfather, which led to their murders. My mother escaped Reggio while it was being pillaged. She died giving birth to me. I am Ruggiero the third, named after my father."

"Ruggiero of Reggio," she said, turning the sound of his name over in her mind. "Tell me where you were raised."

"On the summit of Mount Carena in Tunisia. It was just Atallah and me, no one else for miles around. He taught me to hunt as well as the art of the joust and sword play."

"How did you learn to speak Frankish so well?"

"Atallah insisted that I become a man of letters like my father. He taught me several languages including yours."

"I am impressed. I have a passing knowledge of Arabic. A few phrases I picked up on the battlefield. The one thing in life that gives me difficulty is the Greek language. That is my bane."

Ruggiero laughed. "Greek was difficult to master."

"Tell me how you came to serve Akramont," she pressed. "I remember hearing of your father's admirable service to Charlemagne. Why are you his enemy?"

"Akramont made me a knight."

"And you are a Saracen?"

"I am a Muslim," Ruggiero corrected her. "That is how my guardian raised me. Please, tell me of your name and family."

Bradamante was overcome hearing Ruggiero's tale of his family's history of valor and tragedy. The request for her name was a simple enough return courtesy, except she hoped by revealing her identity she might stir passion within his heart to match hers. Then perhaps he would run away with her and join Charlemagne's forces.

"That I will answer happily. I am from the house of Lyon. My father is Duke Aymon of Dordogne; his most famous son is the celebrated Count Renaud of Montauban, and I…" she paused as she removed her helmet and pulled at the tether in her hair, "…am Renaud's sister Bradamante."

~~~

Ruggiero was stunned. He had assumed the sweet voice of his companion was that of a youthful male whose voice had not yet changed. He stared as her golden tresses cascaded over her shoulders catching the last gleams of light from the setting sun. He wondered how he had ever been so blind to think he was talking with a male soldier and had never considered he might be in the company of a woman. *No,* he corrected himself, *he was in the company of a beautiful woman.* His feelings of being drawn to her were not out of a sense of kinship with an honorable warrior, but out of attraction.

As he looked into her eyes, he imagined his father reacting similarly when he met Galiziella or how Paris felt upon meeting Helen of Sparta. Ruggiero then understood why the Trojan War was fought over the love of a woman. If necessary, he would kill a thousand men for her. Defending her earlier from Rodomont he originally thought had been about idealism. Now he realized its true significance. Fate had meant for him to come upon that duel and to protect her from harm. Bradamante had suddenly become the most important thing in his life.

"Please, Ruggiero, remove your helmet," she said.

He quickly complied. Bradamante gave him a smile, showing that she shared his feelings. The Greek god Eros could not have invoked a more powerful response in two people. Ruggiero was afraid of saying anything lest he break the magic of the moment. He was barely aware that the hills were turning a dark purple, and the air filling with thick fog. A crash behind him made Ruggiero jump.

A voice called out, "There is one now, and it is the Maid! Get her!"

A horse galloped up the hill. Ruggiero turned as a mounted soldier's sword hit Bradamante squarely in the back of her unprotected head.

CHAPTER 3

"No!" Ruggiero roared. "Leave her to me!"

He slammed on his helmet, drew out his sword and waved it at three Muslim soldiers threatening Bradamante. Anger coursed through him as he charged after her attackers, when another knight's horse blocked him.

"Stop, Ruggiero! That is Martisino."

The words hung in the air as Ruggiero glared at the person in front of him. The rage in his eyes prevented him from immediately recognizing his friend Danifort.

"He hurt her," said Ruggiero.

"She killed his brother."

"In battle."

"Yes and we are at war with the Christians," said Danifort.

"The fight is over for the day," said Ruggiero. "She was *with me*. He should not have attacked her."

~~~

Bradamante used this time to recover. She had fallen forward onto her horse's neck. Spitting his mane out of her mouth, she sat up in the saddle and touched the back of her head. Warm blood slicked her hair. She grabbed a pennant from a discarded spear stuck in the ground, pulled up her hair and wrapped the banner loosely around her head to absorb blood, and replaced her helmet.

Martisino was my attacker. I know that bastard. He will die for this!

Fury gave her newfound vigor. Raising her shield, she drew her sword and assessed her surroundings. More knights bellowed as they charged up the small hill in response to Martisino's call about a straggling Christian. Amidst the chaos, a knight attacked Ruggiero from behind by landing a two-handed blow upon his helmet.

"No!" yelled Bradamante as she sprang to his defense. With a single stroke of her sword she sent the villain's head soaring across the field.

Ruggiero, momentarily dazed, was almost hit by the headless body as it fell forward. His horse jumped abruptly to avoid tripping on the corpse. Ruggiero turned around and locked eyes briefly with Bradamante. He gave her a nod, acknowledging her aid before he resumed his fighting.

Bradamante was now surrounded by enemies and began striking down man after man with her sword. There was no time to parry or thrust. Slashing her blade through their necks, slicing open their chests, she quickly winnowed down their numbers.

Ruggiero killed her attackers as well. Soon the ground was soaked with blood and littered with freshly dead bodies and severed limbs. As the mêlée brought more men, she lost sight of Ruggiero.

Bradamante then saw a soldier with a red shield bearing a gryphon's head, neck and claws. She knew that design belonged to Martisino and had been watching for it. He smiled at her before turning his back and riding over the crest of the hill. She wanted to follow him, but three warriors stood in her way. After dispatching them, she left in the direction she saw Martisino go. Bradamante was unconcerned that he might be luring her into an ambush. She wanted revenge.

Riding down the backside of the ridge she came upon a small wood. Hearing movement within, she urged her horse forward. The dense fog made it difficult to see, making the uneven ground treacherous. Before long Erebus stepped into an animal hole near a dry creek bed and tumbled onto the ground, throwing Bradamante off his back. The horse tried standing, but crumpled with a loud whinny.

Bradamante rolled onto her back. The pain was excruciating. She struggled to breathe.

The sound of a twig snapping reminded her Martisino was nearby. She froze and listened as her enemy walked toward her on foot. Out of the corner of her eye she saw him stop, bend over and pick up something. The sound of a sword being sheathed was followed by a whoosh. Inwardly Bradamante cursed her enemy for daring to touch her beloved sword. *I must remain still.*

Martisino renewed walking, but stopped a few feet away from her. She held her breath and kept her eyes wide open, taking care not to blink. He stepped forward, his boot connecting solidly with her ribs. She remained motionless, feigning death and refused to allow any sound to escape her lips even though inwardly she screamed with pain.

Satisfied she was dead, he chuckled before uttering something in Arabic. Then he leaned downward and lifted Bradamante's sword in the air intent on chopping off her head. At the last moment she sprang to life, reaching upward and plunged a dagger deep into his throat. Martisino staggered around struggling to remove the weapon lodged in his windpipe and then fell onto his back. His death was marked by a gurgling sound as his lungs filled with blood.

Bradamante watched a large pool of blood form under his neck. Once she was assured her enemy was dead and not merely wounded, she stepped toward him. Wrenching her dagger free, she wiped the blade clean on the man's leggings.

"This also belongs to me," she said as she picked up her sword from the ground nearby.

The crisis had passed. It was then her head throbbed. Her arms, shoulders and back ached from swinging a sword all day. Every step she took brought a new symphony of pain. The image of taking a hot bath, eating a warm meal and sleeping in a soft bed floated before her eyes. They were as likely that night as flying to the moon.

"Ruggiero," she said. "I must find Ruggiero."

Her wounds needed tending. She knew he would see to them. Or if Death should claim her, Ruggiero would see she was buried properly. No longer did she yearn to be with Charlemagne's army. If she were to die that night, she wanted to die by Ruggiero's side. At the least she wanted to gaze upon his face one more time. Each step became more difficult for her as she grew progressively weaker.

Bradamante knelt next to Erebus assessing his injuries. The horse whimpered as she touched his mangled front leg. Tears filled her eyes while she stroked his head.

"I am sorry Erebus. I promised my brother I would take good care of you and I failed." Tears ran down her cheeks. "Your suffering will be over soon."

Bradamante stood on Erebus' right side. Her hands trembled as she drew her sword across the horse's throat, releasing a torrent of blood. The horse convulsed before slumping to the ground lifeless. She used Martisino's leggings again to wipe her sword clean of blood.

She then sat down, rested her head on her knees and sobbed. Never before had she taken an animal's life. Killing men in battle was easy compared to killing animals. Erebus had trusted her, yet he died because she wanted revenge.

"You cannot stay here," she said to herself. She wiped away tears as she fought to regain her composure. "Nor can you die next to that infidel."

She retrieved some bare provisions from the saddlebags and headed for the woods. Listening for sounds while walking through the fog, she closed her eyes and concentrated on the soft munching of a horse eating grass. Following those sounds she made her way to Martisino's horse tied to a tree. She stashed her meager stores into its bags, untied the horse, and mounted it. Wrapping the reins around her forearms, she steadied herself in the saddle and slung her shield on her back.

Fatigue was claiming her. Her eyelids were getting heavier, but she struggled against resting. She needed to find Ruggiero. The dense fog made it difficult to see more than a few feet ahead. Bradamante no longer knew which direction to go to find her way back to him.

"Ruggiero," she mumbled before passing out.

The horse continued walking steadily into the night without guidance from its rider, as if responding to an invisible hand.

CHAPTER 4

After his last opponent fell, Ruggiero looked for Bradamante. Fear struck his heart when he did not find her and assumed the worst.

"Bradamante!" he called.

Silence greeted him.

He briefly dismounted and grabbed a discarded spear. Using the long weapon he could remain on horseback while checking shields on the ground. Closing his eyes, he saw Bradamante's lovely face once more. Though he had only known her for a short while, her likeness was permanently etched in his heart.

A lump rose in his throat as he recognized his friend Danifort on the ground. Uncertain whether he or Bradamante was responsible for the man's death, he felt a twinge of guilt. The soldiers had been discourteous, Ruggiero reminded himself. Bradamante had set aside her arms and was unhelmeted when they attacked her – without warning – an unforgivable act of villainy. Had she been allowed to defend herself before they attacked, he would have persuaded them she posed no danger to him. Then they would still be alive. Because they were unchivalrous, he killed fellow soldiers to protect the woman he loved. His only regret was allowing himself to lose track of Bradamante.

No longer did the concern about his guardian's safety and whereabouts have the same sense of urgency as before. Atallah represented his past, whereas Bradamante represented his future. Atallah might be waiting for him back at camp while Bradamante was injured, of that he was certain. He needed to find her before it was too late.

"Bradamante!" he called. "Bradamante!"

Ruggiero made an ambling journey searching for her. The fog prevented him from seeing where he was going. He continued through the night, not wanting to rest until he found her. At the sound of clattering hoof beats his spirits lifted in the hope it was Bradamante.

CHAPTER 5

Two knights on horseback emerged from the fog. Due to their large builds, Ruggiero's hopes that he had found Bradamante were dashed.

"What brings you out on this lonely road in the dead of night?" one hailed him in Arabic.

"I am searching for a wounded soldier," Ruggiero said. "During the fight we were separated."

"You were in battle today? Tell us, are you sworn to Akramont?"

"Yes, he is my commander."

"Wonderful. My name is Gradasso," said the first knight. "This is Mandricardo. We are on our way to join his campaign, but we were surprised how quickly the accursed fog rolled in."

"We should have stopped at the last village," said Mandricardo, "but we were anxious to join the fray and there was still plenty of light then. Let us save you time in your search; your friend is not on the road behind us for we have not passed anyone for miles. He is most likely down on the valley floor."

A moment later Mandricardo bellowed in anger and began cursing in a foreign tongue.

"Damned tree! That branch nearly took my head off," he said as he dismounted. "I am not riding any further lest I be blinded in this darkness."

"We should pitch camp," agreed Gradasso. "It is folly to continue traveling this night."

Ruggiero wanted to resume his search for Bradamante, but he knew they were right; he was lost and without sense of direction. They came upon a small clearing where they tethered their horses to nearby trees. Scouring the ground for wood and kindling, they soon built a small fire.

Ruggiero shared food stores from his saddlebags with his companions. Sitting on a hilltop and gnawing on dried mutton with two strangers was not the celebratory feast he had imagined earlier in the night.

"You have not told us your name," said Gradasso, as his teeth tore into a leathery strip of meat. "Nor what territory you rule."

"My name is Ruggiero Tazeem, but I am only a knight and not a ruler. I grew up on Mount Carena in Tunisia. From where do you two hail?"

"I am King of Sericana," said Gradasso. "Mandricardo is Khan of Tartary."

"Pardon my ignorance, but where is Sericana?" asked Ruggiero.

"It is a vast kingdom east of India, stretching to the ocean that marks the end of the earth," said Gradasso.

"And Tartary is north of Persia," said Mandricardo.

"What brought you to Francia? And why are important monarchs such as yourselves not commanding armies?" asked Ruggiero.

"I am on a mission to avenge my father's death," said Mandricardo. "Orlando killed him last year in Cathay. I am not here to conquer lands, only to vanquish a foe. Therefore, I need no army to command." The Tartar turned to Gradasso and smirked. "The great King of Sericana returns here in the hopes of fulfilling a quest he could not accomplish when he led over one hundred thousand men."

"You were here before?" asked Ruggiero.

"Yes," said Gradasso. "A year ago I invaded al-Andalus. I knew of the longstanding rivalry between Amir Marsilio and Charlemagne. I hoped to draw out the Frankish army by putting their neighbor to the south in jeopardy. The emperor dispatched Count Renaud of Montauban with fifty thousand troops to aid Marsilio. Charlemagne hoped to stop my war of conquest before it spilled over into his empire."

"Why did you wish to draw out the Franks?"

"He did not care about the Franks, dear boy," said Mandricardo as he stood. "Gradasso has the largest and wealthiest kingdom in the world, but that is not good enough for him. He traveled thousands of miles with tens of thousands of troops spending a fortune all because he coveted an animal. However, just as he was about to get his hands on the wretched beast, he lost a joust to a fool. He could not have been more humiliated if he had been caught in the act with a goat. I cannot bear to hear this story again. Instead, I will go search for more firewood while he bores you with his infernal tale."

The flames reflected orange on Gradasso's face. His eyes were closed and his jaw clenched.

"Unless the subject is about finding and plowing women, Mandricardo is not interested in what anyone else has to say," said Gradasso. "He has never once heard my full story. I did not risk my life and fortune over a mere animal. I came to the west to seize the best warhorse and the best sword of knighthood. Both are held by paladins of Charlemagne. I will not rest until I have Renaud's horse Bayard, and Orlando's sword Durindana."

"What is so special about them?" asked Ruggiero. "Is Durindana anything like Ali's famous sword?"

Gradasso sat up and grasped Ruggiero by the neck. "What do you know of the Dhul Fiqar? Do you know who has it?"

Ruggiero had been taken by surprise and was pinned against a boulder. He could not reach his dagger. His throat was being squeezed. "I only know the legends," he rasped. "Nothing more. There is no hero like Ali and there is no sword like the Dhul Fiqar. I have no idea where it is or who has it."

Gradasso seemed satisfied and released Ruggiero. "Of course I would prefer Ali's sword that brought so much glory to Islam, but as you said its whereabouts are unknown." He sat back down as Ruggiero massaged his own neck. "Instead, I have set my sites on Durindana, which once belonged to Hector of Troy. It is said to be the most powerful sword ever made next to King Arthur's Excalibur and Ali's Dhul Fiqar. As for the other prize I am after, the destrier Bayard, is not a mere animal as Mandricardo suggests. It is said that this horse is enchanted with near human intelligence, which is more than I can say for Mandricardo."

Ruggiero stifled a laugh. He did not want to risk doing anything that might cause Gradasso's temper to flare again.

"Bayard and Durindana are the two most coveted accoutrements of knighthood. I must have them." Gradasso poked the embers of the fire stirring sparks into the air. "I fought Renaud outside Barcelona. He was the fiercest opponent I have ever faced. I would have beaten him, but he had the advantage of a superior mount. I challenged him to a proper duel – on foot. I promised to end the war, release all my prisoners, and leave the west. The ownership of Bayard hung in the balance."

"Did he agree?" asked Ruggiero.

"Of course. Had he not accepted, he would have been seen as a coward. We were to meet on shore the next morning alone, armed only with our swords and shields. I showed up and fought with what I thought was Renaud. Just as I was about to deliver the death blow, my opponent disappeared like a puff of smoke."

"Sorcery?"

"That is my belief. Some men swore they saw Renaud onboard a ship sailing away. After his abrupt disappearance, the cowardly Franks abandoned Marsilio's cause. The amir surrendered to me that very day. I forced him and his army to join my campaign against Charlemagne. We journeyed northward and overwhelmed Paris, taking the emperor prisoner. I made the mistake of extending mercy to Charlemagne for I did not want his empire. All I wanted were Durindana and Bayard. He gave me his word and sent messengers eastward to Orlando demanding surrender of the sword. Count Orlando of Anglant had abandoned his emperor and was defending Angelica against Mandricardo's father, the late Agrikhan of Tartary. Charlemagne also commanded that Bayard be given to me."

Mandricardo dropped an armload of wood on the ground. "Is he still yammering about that accursed horse?"

Gradasso kept his eyes fixed upon Ruggiero, ignoring Mandricardo's outburst.

"Charlemagne's vassals are unworthy of respect. The paladin holding the prized destrier ignored his emperor's orders. He refused his emperor! This insolent man challenged me to a duel rather than relinquish what was mine by right of conquest."

Mandricardo snorted as he threw another log onto the fire. "Tales of his shameful defeat in the joust reached my shores before I left on my journey. The mighty Gradasso felled in one pass by the court's jester." Mandricardo covered himself with a blanket. "He and his forces left Paris that same day. Now a year later he has returned desperate to reclaim his honor."

"Tell me about Akramont," said Gradasso. "What is he like and who are the governors serving him?"

"He is young, bold, and fearless," said Ruggiero. "He patterns himself after his noble ancestor Alexander the Great as well as his late father, the renowned Amir Troiano. He commands thirty-two governors from the Maghreb as well as Amir Marsilio."

Mandricardo laughed. "Marsilio will be pleased to hear Gradasso will once again be fighting by his side."

Ruggiero cleared his throat. "Akramont's goal is to spread Islam throughout the Frankish Empire and to further the glory of Muhammad, peace be upon him."

"Perhaps he will make you a governor over some of these lands after the conquest," said Gradasso.

Ruggiero's face burned. "That is for him to decide. Akramont is also seeking vengeance against Orlando for killing his father."

"Was Orlando in the battle yesterday?" asked Mandricardo.

"Yes," said Ruggiero. "We dueled."

"Is he still alive?" asked Gradasso.

"He is, as is Renaud," said Ruggiero. "I fought both famed knights today, but thankfully our duels were interrupted."

"Why?" asked Mandricardo. "Afraid you might have died at their hands?"

Both of his companions had an eager, almost predatory look upon their faces at the mention of the two Frankish paladins.

"No, because I might have deprived you of your heart's desire," Ruggiero said as he took a drink of water from his flask.

Mandricardo laughed. Ruggiero sensed that either of his companions might have slit his throat in anger had they missed their opportunity to challenge Renaud and Orlando. He was grateful his duels had been interrupted; had he killed any of Bradamante's kinsmen, she might never forgive him.

"Both paladins have returned to Charlemagne's service," murmured Gradasso as he leaned against a boulder.

While Ruggiero spoke to Gradasso of the other commanders in the campaign, Mandricardo rolled over and drifted off to sleep. Gradasso questioned Ruggiero relentlessly through the night. He wanted to know the reputation of every governor. They talked until the filtered light of the rising sun through the fog allowed Ruggiero to see Gradasso's face properly for the first time. There was a cruel countenance about his eyes and several ragged scars on his face. As Ruggiero turned to their other companion, he was surprised to see red hair on a man from Asia.

Mandricardo stretched as he woke and blinked. His eyes grew wide as he stared at Ruggiero's shield and jumped to his feet. His face contorted with rage. "You dare carry a silver eagle on a field of blue. That is my standard! Renounce it or die!"

CHAPTER 6

Shocked by the outburst, Ruggiero examined Mandricardo's armor. He bore an ancient bronze cuirass and matching shield with a design of a silver screaming eagle on a blue background. The major difference between their shields was that Mandricardo's was made of metallic inlay and Ruggiero's wooden shield was covered with hand-painted leather.

"Sir!" said Ruggiero as he scrambled to his feet grabbing his shield. "This standard was borne by my father, and his father before him. It belonged to our noble ancestor, Hector of Troy. Pray tell me, do you also claim him as your forebear?"

"No, and I care not of your claim of ancestry," Mandricardo growled. "I bear the *very armor* worn by Hector. I won it by force. No one else shall bear this standard."

"Where and under what circumstances did you come upon the armor of my ancestor?" said Ruggiero, his face burning.

"Anatolia. It had been held there for centuries by magic. Hundreds of warriors and kings had been ensnared over the years in that enchanted realm. None were deemed worthy until I came." Mandricardo cast a sideways glance at Gradasso. "With my victory all the failed knights still alive were freed. This eagle is mine now. Either renounce it or pay with your life!"

Ruggiero drew his sword and held his shield, then stared in amazement as he realized Mandricardo was unarmed. "How can I fight you when you have no weapon?"

"That has never stopped me," said Mandricardo. "I shall fight you with a rock, a club, my bare hands, or with a weapon that I shall steal from you. I swore an oath to the sorceress who awarded me this armor that I would not bind a sword to my side until I secure Durindana and reunite Hector's sword with his armor."

35

"What is that?" said Gradasso as he scrambled to his feet. "You are on a quest for Durindana? Stand in line, knave. I have had my sights on that blade longer than you. I have risked my life and my fortune for Durindana and for Bayard. I shall not allow you or anyone else to wield *my* sword."

"I have beaten you once," said Mandricardo. "You wish to lose again? Fine. Only this time, we fight to the death."

Mandricardo snapped a limb from a nearby tree and began stripping it of leaves and smaller branches. Gradasso hacked at another tree with his scimitar making his own wooden weapon. Soon both men bore crude lances and charged their horses at one another. Ruggiero stayed clear of the duel, shaking his head at the spectacle. He could not understand why two men would fight to the death over a sword that neither one possessed. He was grateful that Gradasso had released him so quickly the previous night over the unknown whereabouts of Ali's sword.

Mandricardo and Gradasso's jousting splintered their makeshift lances. The warriors then swung the jagged wooden shafts as crude swords. Their anger increased as their poles decreased in size. Ruggiero wondered how long it would take them to strip the hilltop of trees, and if they would resort to using their bare hands against one another. The two kings had been fighting for a good portion of the morning when Ruggiero noticed, through the thinning fog, a knight progressing up the slope toward them.

He hoped it might be Bradamante, but as the rider came closer it was the strange standard of a dwarf named Brunello, the governor of Tingitana. Brunello's shield bore a golden goose with its wings and tail extended over an egg upon a field of red.

Gradasso was preparing for another charge at Mandricardo when Brunello rode around the bend. His horse spooked and toppled Brunello backwards. One of Brunello's feet became entangled in the reins and he dangled off the side of the horse. His helmet scraped the ground as his hands frantically groped the air.

Mandricardo laughed at the small upside-down man. Gradasso aimed his weapon at his rival's head, but his blow was deflected by Mandricardo's shield.

"Thought I was distracted, eh?" said Mandricardo.

"Will you stop this senseless duel?" bellowed Ruggiero. "Help me save this man's life."

Ruggiero ignored the look of contempt the two monarchs gave him. He had shamed them and he knew they did not like being chastised by anyone, let alone a mere knight. Nonetheless the two rulers dismounted and secured their steeds before joining Ruggiero in an attempt to calm the horse and free Brunello. Once the diminutive man was placed safely on the ground, he wept.

"Thank you, thank you my lords, for coming to my aid," the man said, bowing at their feet. "I am Brunello, governor of Tingitana and now your humble servant."

Brunello raised his head and a look of recognition came over his face. "King Gradasso, it is my honor to serve you. And Khan Mandricardo, may you live up to the noble reputation of your late father."

They nodded at him.

"Ruggiero," Brunello said as he struggled to stand, "Amir Akramont sent me to find you. He was displeased by your absence last night from the celebration in the royal tent."

"I went searching for Atallah rather than join Danifort in the looting of Toulouse. I became lost when the fog rolled in."

Gradasso frowned. "I thought he was a minor knight, of no real importance. Tell me why the amir would allow such a man in the royal tent and why his absence warranted a search for him."

Brunello stammered, "Akramont favors Ruggiero."

"Why? Is he a bedmate?" asked Mandricardo.

"No," said Ruggiero as anger rose inside him.

Brunello fidgeted with a golden ring. "Uh, his skills are praiseworthy."

Gradasso and Mandricardo fixed their eyes upon Ruggiero who felt his cheeks begin to burn for the second time that morning.

"I have been the amir's favorite ever since being named tournament champion," said Ruggiero. "That was the day he knighted me."

Mandricardo gave a crooked smile as he looked Ruggiero over from head to toe.

"Tournament champion," repeated Gradasso, appearing satisfied with that answer.

Brunello cleared his throat. "This morning we discovered a massacre of at least two dozen of our bravest men last night, including Danifort. They were sent to patrol the area to make sure Charlemagne's forces did not double back on us under cover of darkness. It is feared this treachery may have been the work of Orlando or Renaud."

Gradasso and Mandricardo perked up at the news, their eyes filled with anticipation. Ruggiero, meanwhile, felt guilty about his role in the carnage. Bradamante had been right when she said he should not fight with his fellow soldiers. Killing them was worse, but they had left him no choice when they attacked her.

"Was Atallah at the celebration last night?" asked Ruggiero.

"No."

Ruggiero swallowed hard. "Was his body found on the battlefield?"

Brunello shook his head. "No. We searched for you, and would have noticed if he was among the dead. I would not worry about him. Most likely Atallah left during the battle to gather magical reinforcements when it looked like the Franks were winning. Come," he said as he gestured to the valley floor, "you can see our forces have already begun their move toward Bordeaux and Aquitaine."

The fog had lifted and they could see thousands of people amassing in a slow moving convoy. From this vantage point they looked like tiny ants moving about on the plains east of Toulouse. Dozens of men turned up the reddish brown soil for graves. Some of the corpses had already been washed and placed in white shrouds. By the end of the day, the ground would appear blanketed with white petals when in reality it would be covered with dead soldiers awaiting burial.

"If we start now," said Brunello, "it will not take us long to reach them." He turned to Mandricardo and Gradasso. "The amir will be honored to have such renowned monarchs join his campaign."

Mandricardo and Gradasso nodded, and mounted their horses.

Ruggiero took one step toward Frontino when he stopped. "*As-Salat!* We have not performed our morning prayer."

He kneeled on the ground and said, "*Bismillah,*" announcing his intention to begin *Wudu*, a ceremony to cleanse and purify before prayer. Having grown up in a desert area he was accustomed to not having adequate water to use for this ritual and instead used the dust from the ground to rub his hands clean.

Ruggiero was penitent because his prayer life had been altered dramatically by the war. No longer was he able to leisurely pray five times a day, feeling the connection with the Divine in a peaceful setting. Instead, there had been many times of late that the Muslim army had resorted to using "the prayer of fear" where they did not have to bow their heads, nor face Mecca. This was done to avoid being in a vulnerable position while facing their enemies. Ruggiero felt shame because he realized he had neglected to perform the previous day's evening and night prayers.

He noticed Mandricardo and Gradasso exchange a glance with each other before they reluctantly knelt. Ruggiero sensed they were only praying because he shamed them into it. He suppressed a smile, having gotten the true measure of those kings. His suspicions were reinforced as they awkwardly performed *Wudu*, as if they were unfamiliar with the requirements of the ceremony and were interested only in giving an outward impression of following the requirements of the Muslim faith.

The four men turned in the direction of Mecca, and audibly chanted their prayers. Ruggiero's voice was strong and clear, leading the foursome. Soon after he joined Akramont's army, Atallah pointed out to him the telltale signs of fake piety: men mumbling or speaking their prayers overly loud. Both of those examples were displayed by Ruggiero's three companions. Faith to them was something like fine clothes that they donned for the sake of appearances, but did nothing to change the man inside.

After audibly reciting his required prayers or *Rakat*, Ruggiero kept his head bowed and silently added, *Allah, I beseech you to look after your daughter Bradamante. See that she is cared for and is safe. I also ask that you care for Atallah as well. Amen.*

CHAPTER 7

Namphaise was confused by the ecstatic vision he had that morning. He rarely had visions, but when he did they consumed his mind and body for days. As he lay on the bottom of his cave with his arms wrapped around his legs, he could barely hear the sounds of the forest. There was the familiar sound of songbirds, but in the distance he could hear a new sound approaching him. It was a rhythmic sound.

Like a heartbeat.

Or hoofbeats. The sound ended as a horse clopped to a halt at the opening of his small cave.

What is this? I live in this forsaken place as a refuge from the sins of the world. What, dear Lord, does this intrusion portend?

Namphaise had not spoken aloud for several years, having taken a vow of silence. He had lived in the woods longer than that, with no real idea of how long it had been. In less than a month of living in the wild, he had lost track of time. He knew the seasons and had a vague idea of the months, but did not know the specific day. Every day was a day of devotion for him, but he set aside one day a week as a day of rest. He refrained from gathering wood, water, food or anything to assist his austere existence because that was the day he dedicated for prayer and fasting. To help him remember, Namphaise had collected seven rocks and rotated them each morning. When the single white rock was placed in the carved out shelf, he treated that day as his Sunday regardless of how it actually fell on the calendar.

He crawled out of his small hand-dug cave and saw an unconscious soldier slumped forward with arms around the horse's neck.

A wounded soldier, why must you tempt me Lord by sending a sinner my way?

He untangled the reins from around the soldier's arms and worked to lift him off the horse's back. Namphaise laid the young man gently on the ground and removed the helmet, revealing a blood stained cloth wound loosely around the warrior's head.

Retrieving a few roughly hewn wooden bowls, Namphaise went off in search of fresh water and herbs. Kneeling in front of a spring, he stared at the blue-green water. A torrent of images rippled across the still pond, erasing the reflection of fallen trees and replacing it with a portrait of death. Memories of his own time on the battlefield assaulted his senses. The scent of pine and moss was replaced with the smell of blood, urine, and excrement. Cries of agony rang in his ears from soldiers as they were stabbed and slashed along with the mournful sound of death rattles. He wept while gathering the herb dittany. Years of isolation and deprivation did not allow Namphaise to forget the horrors of war.

He was uncertain if the wounded soldier was Christian or Saracen for the armor was plain and indistinguishable. The saddle and the tapestry covering the horse's back appeared to belong to a Saracen, but many horses were claimed as spoils of war so those indicators were no guarantee of the rider's allegiance. This man did not stumble upon Namphaise. This man was brought to him for a reason. It was either the work of God and His angels or that of the Devil and his minions.

Namphaise returned to the wounded man and carefully unwound the banner to find long hair matted with clots of blood. Shaking his head, he grabbed the dull knife from his belt and began hacking the hair to better address the wound.

Why does this man have such long hair? Was he a member or follower of the deposed Merovingian dynasty? Had he challenged the Carolingians for the throne? Or did this soldier consider himself to be a latter day Samson whose strength was held in unshorn locks? Either way, it is a shame for someone so young to be engaged in war.

He tore the banner into strips. Wetting a piece of fabric in the fresh spring water, he did his best to clean the wound. The water in the bowl soon turned a deep scarlet with flecks of black. Using rocks to crush the dittany, he collected the precious liquid expressed from the herb in another bowl. He finished by applying a poultice of dittany to the wound to stanch the flow of blood and wrapped a piece of cloth about the soldier's head.

Namphaise propped the youth up against a boulder, and lifted a cup of fresh water to the soldier's lips. As the water entered his mouth, the young man sputtered and regained consciousness.

"Wh-where am I?"

"In the wood," Namphaise croaked. He tried clearing his throat; his years of silence left it exceedingly hoarse. "The Lord brought you to me."

The warrior reflexively felt the back of his head and moaned.

"I changed your dressing and cut your hair," Namphaise said. "Tell me, my child, whom do you serve?"

"Charlemagne is my sovereign."

Namphaise closed his eyes, and sighed. *Christian. A Christian soldier.*

"Charlemagne," repeated Namphaise his mind going elsewhere. "King Charles *the Great.*"

He had once served in Charlemagne's army. Namphaise had loved his king, but it was the love of one the king's daughters that drove him from the royal court. King Charles would never have consented to any of his daughters marrying someone of Namphaise's meager stature. After only one incident, he realized he had to leave to save his immortal soul from temptation.

Monastery life had given him the needed reprieve. Construction of the abbey near the *Gouffre de Lantouy* in the Lot River Valley kept him busy from dawn to dusk with no time to think of his past sins. However, once construction was complete, he found that life in a monastery did not provide the solitude and deprivation he needed. He set out again in search of a place where he could be with God and devoid of human companionship. The forest had been his sanctuary, until the intrusion of a wounded man brought back memories of his prior life to haunt him.

Namphaise rummaged around in his small cave retrieving roots, pine nuts, and dried berries and offered them to the soldier. The youth gratefully accepted the food, eating in silence. This suited Namphaise, for he did not want to know what was happening in the outside world. He wanted only to demonstrate penitence and beg God's forgiveness for his sins of lust and violence.

"Thank you for your kindness." The young man stood and winced in pain.

"Do you have another wound?"

"I was kicked in my side last night," the soldier said through gritted teeth. "I do not know if anything is broken or just bruised."

"Let me have a look," said Namphaise as he helped remove the chain armor.

He lifted the thick padding and saw, not the tight abdominal muscles of a male, but the soft belly and gentle curves of a young woman. The armor had been heavy enough to flatten her breasts, but once it was off, it was apparent his patient was not a young man. His hands trembled as he examined her. There was extensive bruising, but the skin remained intact. He felt her ribcage, trying to avoid touching the curve of her breast. Namphaise closed his eyes and remembered a stolen embrace long ago where he had groped the bare skin of a princess in a fit of passion. Once again he was overcome with shame.

"No bones are broken," he said through tears of despair and turned his back on her. "Who brought you here? Are you a demon sent to tempt me?"

42

"I am not a demon! I am a follower of Christ, and a soldier for Charlemagne. I do not know how I came here, but I am thankful for your help."

"You must leave for I cannot trust you. I have had many visions sent to torture me. Just this morning, I saw a ship with lost souls on board flying through the air. The Devil laughed at me and said the valiant Ruggiero was with him and had almost turned to Christ, but was now beyond reach. Ruggiero is a valorous young man who would have been a fine Christian and servant of God, but he is no longer on the road to baptism and salvation. I cried at that vision. And now the Devil in the shape of a woman stands before me, testing my dedication to the True Way. Be gone! Off with you!"

Namphaise fell to the ground weeping while begging for God's forgiveness. He vowed to find a new place to worship in isolation. He would leave that day and return northward in hopes of finding a more secluded area where no demon could ever reach him again.

~~~

Bradamante stared at the hermit as she reluctantly put her armor back on. She was still sore from her wounds and would have preferred to rest longer, but it was unsafe in his company, for the hermit was clearly mad. She did not know which direction to turn, and merely hoped she would find a way out of the ancient forest. Remounting Martisino's horse, she traveled until coming upon the banks of a river. There she allowed the horse and herself to drink freely.

It had startled her to hear the hermit speak Ruggiero's name. The idea of Ruggiero converting to Christianity filled her heart with hope. Her meeting him the previous night must have influenced the hermit's visions. She did not worry about Ruggiero's soul being beyond salvation; God could not refuse entry to Paradise to someone so honorable. She refused to consider his fate as being one of eternal damnation.

They would meet again; of that she was certain. She had almost asked Ruggiero to come away with her, but she was attacked before she had the chance. Had she not left his side, perhaps he would be with her right now. She smiled at that thought. He *would* convert to Christianity out of love for her. They could not be married otherwise. She could never renounce her family, and her father would never accept her marrying outside their faith. Ruggiero's conversion was their only hope of a life together. She would also be heralded for recruiting a powerful new knight for Christendom.

Bradamante tied the horse to a tree on the riverbank, and laid down to rest in the shade of a large oak. Removing her helmet, she closed her eyes and recalled Ruggiero's handsome face. It had reminded her of marble statues, flawless in their beauty. She imagined touching the curls of his dark hair and tracing the contours of his face. Smiling as exhaustion once again overcame her, she fell into a deep sleep.

CHAPTER 8

Ruggiero rode next to Brunello down a rocky path leading to the valley floor. Gradasso and Mandricardo rode behind them in silence. The two kings had come to an uncomfortable truce, one that could end at any provocation.

It had been two days since Ruggiero had slept and his eyes were becoming unfocused. A single tree in the distance would dance and then split into two. As he continued to stare, the trees would reunite just as the ground appeared to roll. He needed rest, but he knew he could not ask the others to delay meeting Akramont's forces. Ruggiero's heart was not in their journey, nor in rejoining his liege. He wanted to resume searching for Bradamante because he worried about her safety. His only solace was that his heart told him she had not died, and that they would meet again.

"How do you like the sword I gave you?" Brunello asked.

"It has served me well," said Ruggiero. "I doubt there is one finer anywhere."

Brunello smiled at him, exposing the large gaps between his remaining teeth. Ruggiero tried shaking the unsettled feeling he had about his companion by reminding himself that Brunello had shown nothing but kindness and generosity toward him.

"Your horse also seems to suit you," said Brunello.

"I agree." Ruggiero gave Frontino's neck an affectionate pat. "Thank you again. He is a wonderful steed. I cannot imagine a better destrier."

Ruggiero thought Gradasso's obsession over Bayard and Durindana was pure vanity. He hoped his subtle digs about his own horse and sword would serve as a reproach. Sneaking a glance backward at the king, Gradasso gave him a satisfied nod. Clearly the king of Sericana had not felt insulted, but instead was happy to learn Ruggiero was not another rival for his coveted objects.

As they passed a copse of trees, a knight on foot could be seen in the distance wailing in Frankish.

"Baron," hailed Ruggiero as they approached him. "Why do you weep?"

"It is my lady," the man replied. "She was stolen from me. I do not know how to get her back."

"Another man?" Mandricardo leered.

The knight had anguish in his eyes. "You will think I am mad, but this truly happened. Yesterday, we were traveling on this very road. She was riding next to me on her horse. Then without warning, from out of the sky came a man on a flying horse."

Mandricardo laughed.

"The old man snatched her in his arms and flew away," said the man.

"You were attacked from the sky?" said Ruggiero frowning.

"Yes, it was over quickly. I tried pursuing the villain, but a flash of light blinded me. I woke up later and night had fallen. Dear Sirs, if you have any compassion I beg of you to help me recover my lady."

"Brothers, I recognize the coat of arms he carries," said Brunello in Arabic. "A white falcon on a field of blue is from the house of Maganza. They are known for their wealth as well as their treachery. This may be a trap. Then again, since there are four of us, and only one of him, I say we take him hostage for Akramont. He should fetch a fair ransom."

The Maganzan looked nervously at the four men surrounding him. His hand touched the pommel of his sword.

"He is already a prisoner!" said Ruggiero. "A prisoner of love. It would be discourteous to make him suffer more. We cannot continue on our journey now. A fiend is abducting women from the midst of knightly protectors. Can you be certain none of the women in our camp were taken last night?"

Brunello, cowed at Ruggiero's outburst, shook his head. "No, I cannot say that."

The man's tale made Ruggiero worry about Bradamante suffering a similar fate. He could not bear the thought of her being held hostage and what could happen to her safety and virtue.

"We cannot risk having a madman target Akramont's sister or wives who are traveling with him, since they are only a fair bit up the road," Ruggiero said. "We must help this man by finding the villain responsible and release all his captives."

"Find another lover," Mandricardo said under his breath. He gathered his reins and announced, "I am leaving to help Akramont in his quest against Charlemagne. I will not be deterred, and certainly not on behalf of an infidel."

His horse galloped off in the direction of the Akramont's army.

Gradasso watched his rival ride away and appeared torn about whether to stay or follow. The more he stared the more his face darkened. Turning back to the Maganzan he asked in Frankish, "Which direction was your lady taken?"

"Toward the mountains," the man said. "Thank you, Sirs, for agreeing to help me." He bowed as he mounted his horse. They turned toward the Pyrenees.

"Ruggiero," Brunello pleaded. "We cannot do this. Akramont is expecting your return."

"I will not turn my back on this man," said Ruggiero. "You may return to Akramont if you wish."

"No. I cannot return without you. We shall remain together."

They rode quietly along the riverbank in the heat of the day, when a large cloud momentarily blocked the sun's rays. Ruggiero looked skyward and realized it was not a cloud, but a flying beast. He tried blocking the glaring rays of the sun with his shield, but still had trouble seeing clearly. He urged Frontino forward to position himself better to fend off an attack. As the flying creature bore down on him, he recognized its rider.

Not you.

A blinding flash of light caused him to fall out of his saddle. He watched his helmet roll on the riverbed before all turned black.

CHAPTER 9

Fiordespina enjoyed the bright sunshine. It was a glorious summer day and she was engaged in her favorite pastime of hunting with hounds and falcons. The day was successful, for her party had brought down a large stag. The expedition set out early in the morning with the high hopes of seeing a battle. War, when viewed from a safe distance, was grand entertainment. She was disappointed to learn they had missed the hostilities by a single day, and that the invading forces broke camp prior to her party's approach.

Searching for a suitable spot near the river to have their midday meal, Fiordespina spied the form of a sleeping soldier. She coaxed her horse to walk nearer the youth. Gazing in wonderment, she decided that she had never seen a lovelier face on a man.

"This is where we shall have our meal," she announced as she dismounted.

"My lady," sputtered her chief attendant Neron, "there is a soldier nearby."

"We have plenty of food to share with him as well."

Neron shook his head. "This is not safe. Where there is one soldier, there may be more. I cannot risk our party being ambushed. You are far too important to your father."

She gestured at the soldier. "Look at his countenance. He is incapable of such discourtesy. He has a noble mien."

"My lady," he warned, "you are far too trusting. You do not understand the ways of men."

Fiordespina ignored him and daintily brushed her scarf over the face of the sleeping soldier.

~~~

Bradamante woke with a start, and was surprised to find herself surrounded. A beautiful dark haired young woman knelt before her. Behind the maiden stood ten soldiers, three white haired women, and a stern looking elderly man.

"We were about to have our dinner when I spied you," said the young woman. "Would you care to join us?"

"Yes I would," said Bradamante as she struggled to sit up and get her bearings.

The lady clapped her hands and her elderly female attendants quickly spread a linen cloth upon the ground that was soon covered with breads, cheeses, cherries, and smoked fish. Bradamante marveled at the events of the last day and how she had awoken to two dramatically different people offering her nourishment. She much preferred the company of a well-dressed maiden offering a sumptuous meal rather than a filthy, louse-ridden old man offering roots, nuts, and dried berries.

As the two young women ate in silence, something nagged at Bradamante. She recognized her companion, but could not remember who she was. Bradamante stared at the maiden and her richly embroidered scarlet dress. It was only when their eyes met and the young woman blushed, that Bradamante recognized her companion. She was Fiordespina, the daughter of Marsilio, Amir of Hispania, an area the Muslims called al-Andalus. Bradamante had seen her the previous year when she had helped defend Marsilio's realm from Gradasso's invading army. Once Bradamante realized whom she was with, she worried about her own safety. Hispania was controlled by Muslims and would be a natural ally of Akramont. Indeed, Amir Marsilio's massive army joined Rodomont's forces in the early battles against the Franks. Bradamante's kinship to Charlemagne, if discovered, might lead to her being taken hostage.

The soldiers were taking turns eating near the wagon, but watched Fiordespina the entire time. Bradamante had killed far more men the previous night, but she was weakened by her wounds. She was uncertain if she would emerge victorious should she battle with them.

"Tell me, sir knight," Fiordespina said, "how did you come to this lonely riverbank? It is far from any town."

Bradamante realized Fiordespina had mistaken her for a man. Not knowing how to delicately disabuse the noblewoman of this misconception, she lowered her voice slightly to sound masculine.

"On horseback."

"Where is your horse then?"

"Tied to that tree," Bradamante said gesturing behind her. She turned and was horrified to see the horse's bridle dangling from the trunk.

Bradamante felt tears well in her eyes and she covered her face with her hands. Being exhausted and distracted by thoughts of Ruggiero, Bradamante made a careless mistake. The horse had not been secured properly and had freed himself. There was no telling how long ago that occurred or where the horse had gone. She was without a horse and had few prospects of getting another. She had little coin with her, and without being in active battle it was doubtful she would come across another rider-less horse. Trying to overpower her dining companion for a mount would be discourteous, and unlikely to succeed given the number of soldiers protecting her. Frustration overwhelmed Bradamante.

Fiordespina touched her on the shoulder. "Do not worry, dear sir. I have a steed you may use."

"Thank you," Bradamante said bowing her head.

"My lady," said the stern looking man, "we should be leaving. It is a long journey back, and we should not travel after dark."

"Yes, Neron," Fiordespina said as she motioned for her servants to clean up the remains of their meal. She then turned to Bradamante, "Sir, I could not help but notice you are wounded. I insist that you recuperate in my home before continuing on your way. Far too many men die in war. I cannot bear the thought of you falling in battle because you were unable to defend yourself properly."

Bradamante smiled and nodded. She had resolved to allow Fate to help her. Right now, Fiordespina's offer of hospitality and the use of her horse sounded far more promising than remaining near the isolated banks of the Tarn River without a horse or food. Nevertheless, she would remain on her guard.

Fiordespina handed Bradamante the reins to a fine Andalusian stallion, gray with dark legs and a black mane and tail. Fiordespina mounted another horse while the displaced soldier rode in the back of a cart with the women attendants and the trussed stag.

Neron glared at Bradamante as he took the lead. Two soldiers followed him while the rest provided protection as rear guards. The procession climbed up mountainous roads outlined by emerald green hillsides punctuated with outcroppings of white rock. Bradamante had expected they would turn south toward the Pyrenees, and was surprised when they headed northward. After a few hours, a town loomed above them in the sky.

The stones of the ramparts took on a yellowish-orange cast from the light of the setting sun. The steep incline in the road slowed their ascent as they approached the gates guarding the town's perimeter. The guards recognized the hunting party, signaled the raising of the portcullis.

The horses' hooves clopped over flagstones as they made their way through the heart of the hilltop village lined by wooden buildings with thatched roofs. Soon eyes peered at them from behind shutters. Murmurs from the villagers reached Bradamante's ears. She was an outsider in their midst and she resolved to keep her head held high even as she felt their suspicious stares following her every move.

A large stone fountain occupied the center of the village square. At the summit of the town were gates leading to a grand old Roman villa with Doric columns that dominated the town. Soldiers guarded its entrance and patrolled the wall that surrounded the estate. They moved aside at a signal from Neron and the party was admitted to the inner courtyard. Neron lost no time issuing orders to the domestic servants while Bradamante dismounted.

Fiordespina urged Bradamante to follow her through the south facing garden that was lined with fountains, fruit trees and hanging baskets of flowers. Ivy covered large sections of the wall surrounding the estate. The wall seemed less of a defensive structure and more like a barrier from the noisy village to this tranquil setting. After walking past several stone benches, they entered the brightly colored villa whose entrance way was painted terra cotta. Bradamante was ushered inside a small chamber.

"Please sit here so that I may tend your wound." Fiordespina gestured toward a chair at a table.

An elderly woman followed them into the room. "My lady, it is not proper for you to be alone with a man."

"And it is not proper for wounds to fester," retorted Fiordespina. "Fetch me some fresh water and clean linen."

"Perhaps I should call for someone else so that I may remain with you," said the woman.

"Perhaps you should do as you are commanded."

The woman kept her eye on Bradamante as she bowed and then left the room.

"Tell me how you were wounded," said Fiordespina.

"Last night, after the battle ended, I removed my helmet to speak properly with another soldier. I was attacked from behind without warning."

"Villains," Fiordespina declared as she slowly unwound the fabric wrapped around Bradamante's head.

Feeling warm breath on the back of her neck, Bradamante was startled when Fiordespina leaned forward and kissed her squarely on the mouth.

CHAPTER 10

Bradamante froze. Fiordespina drew back when her kiss was not returned. The maiden's cheeks quickly became as scarlet as her dress.

"My dear lady," said Bradamante, "I do not wish you to think I am unfeeling, but I fear my appearance has deceived you. I beg your forgiveness for not revealing the truth about myself earlier. Only a man with a heart of stone could be unmoved by affections from someone with your beauty and grace. However, I am not a man, but a maid, as you are."

Fiordespina stared at her and after a long pause said, "A maid?"

"Yes, until this morning I had locks rivaling yours in length, but they were cut to tend my wound."

"Who *are* you?"

"My name is Bradamante."

Fiordespina's eyes widened. "The Maid. You are Renaud of Montauban's famed sister."

Immediately Bradamante knew she had made a mistake. "I should not have told you my real name."

Fiordespina grasped Bradamante's hands. "You are my guest. The customs of hospitality are clear and they will not be violated. I will not allow any harm to befall you."

"It is too dangerous for me here, I must leave."

"No. You have traveled too far today. I insist that you stay and recuperate."

"No one can know who I am," whispered Bradamante.

"You are worried about Neron," said Fiordespina. "You are right to be concerned with him. He is a creature of my stepmother and is always spying on me."

"You cannot use my name. He will know who I am and recognize my value as a hostage right away."

"That will not happen to you," said Fiordespina as she peeked out the doorway. A broad smile crossed her face when she came back in the room. "I shall call you Juana. It is a common enough name and one that shall not give you away."

"As being an enemy?"

"As being a Frank. My father and your emperor may be adversaries, but you and I shall never be enemies," insisted Fiordespina. "Our dialects are not *that* different. If Neron does not hear you speak much, you can pass as one of us."

"That is a dangerous plan. Surely he will ask me questions about where I am from, and who my commanders are –"

"And I shall not allow that snake to question you. I have always disliked him and I now have a good reason to treat him imperiously."

"You thought I was a man; perhaps everyone else did as well. I think it would be safer for me to continue that ruse," suggested Bradamante.

"No." Fiordespina began to pace. "I want you close to me. We cannot be together if you are thought to be a man. It is a miracle that I have been allowed to be alone with you for even this length of time. We will say that you disguised yourself as a man to serve in my father's army."

Bradamante heard something in the hallway and put her finger to her lips. Fiordespina stopped talking as footsteps were heard approaching them. The servant returned carrying a pitcher of water and a bowl and placed them on the table.

"Thank you," said Fiordespina. "Now I want you to draw a hot bath for my guest. You will also bring me a tall gown and a pair of large women's shoes."

The servant appeared puzzled, but left on the assigned tasks.

Fiordespina soaked the clean linen in water and wrung it out. "Where were you hurt?"

Bradamante was confused. The wound was large and should be obvious to see. She felt the back of her head and was surprised to feel only hair and scalp. There was not even a scab.

"That is most strange."

She picked up the bloodied rags that had been wrapped around her head to prove to herself that she had indeed been wounded. "I was hurt. I cannot explain what happened."

"Who tended your wound?" asked Fiordespina.

"An old man in the woods. A hermit. The horse brought me to him. The hermit must have healed me with his touch." Bradamante stood and felt her ribcage. "My side has been healed as well."

She stood there, her mouth agape, wondering what it all meant. Was God truly looking out for her? Was that why she was brought to this place as well?

Fiordespina rummaged through a cupboard. She returned with a comb, a pair of scissors and draped a cloth around Bradamante's shoulders. "The hermit may have healed your wounds, but he did you a grave disservice when it comes to your appearance. Allow me to improve your haircut."

Fiordespina dipped the comb in water and hummed a tune while trimming Bradamante's hair. Bradamante could not help but laugh at how happy her new friend was at performing such a mundane task.

"There!" Fiordespina announced when she finished and handed Bradamante a small hand mirror.

Bradamante was shocked at the image staring back at her. She appeared boyish with a cropped hairstyle whose ends curled upward at the nape of her neck. It was no wonder that she had been mistaken as a young man.

The servant had returned again and was now holding a long blue gown with white sleeves. "The bath is ready, milady."

"Thank you," said Fiordespina as she took the offered gown and shoes. "Please sweep up this hair, while I show my friend to the bath."

Bradamante followed Fiordespina down the hall, while the old woman bustled behind them. "It is not proper for a lady...your father would not approve..."

Fiordespina seemed to ignore the protests until the three of them walked into a small chamber holding a large wooden bathtub. "Close the door."

The servant stared at her.

"Well then, I shall do it," said Fiordespina as she closed the door. She placed the dress on a railing and the shoes on the floor. "Help me lift this armor off my friend."

The old woman swallowed hard, but came forward and assisted Fiordespina in lifting the armor above Bradamante's head. Bradamante removed her boots and then her thick woolen gambeson. The servant's eyes bulged as she stared at Bradamante's feminine curves showing plainly through the thin linen tunic and breeches.

"He's a she," said the woman dumbly.

"The *proper* thing would be to allow our guest privacy as she takes her bath," said Fiordespina. "You will sweep up that other room as I asked."

"Y-yes, milady." The woman bowed as she left.

Fiordespina laughed. "Soon the entire household will know that you are a maid and not a man. Enjoy your bath. I will be waiting for you in the other room."

The door closed on Bradamante. Her teeth chattered from the chilled stone floor beneath her feet. She became alarmed to discover there was no way to bolt or lock the door. Bradamante felt vulnerable at the prospect of being naked in a house surrounded by armed enemy soldiers. She placed a wooden bucket in front of the door, so that at least she would be warned if anyone tried entering the room.

Bradamante placed her sword and her dagger upon the top step leading to the bathtub before removing the rest of her clothing and climbing into the bath. The water was uncomfortably hot at first, but she soon grew used to its temperature. Just the night before she had yearned for a hot bath and a warm meal; now they were both being offered to her from an unexpected source. Wasting no time, she scrubbed herself clean. She toweled off quickly before donning her breeches and linen tunic again. If she were to stay here a few days, she would ask for those items to be laundered on the morrow.

Bradamante put on sandals made of cracked leather. They scratched her feet, but she would not complain for they were better suited to wear with a gown than her boots. She lifted the dress over her head and pulled it downward. It fit well enough, even if it was made for a woman of girth.

Kneeling, she said her prayers for Vespers, feeling guilt at having missed the other prayers during the day and previous night.

"Thank you, dear lord, for saving my life, for finding someone to heal my wounds, and for bringing me to a safe place to recover. I ask for your continued guidance and that you protect Ruggiero from harm."

After finishing her prayer, she picked up her weapons and wondered what best to do with them. It was doubtful that Neron would allow her to keep her sword with her while she was near Fiordespina, but perhaps she could hide her dagger.

Lifting the skirt of the dress, she fastened her belt around her waist, and attached the scabbard of her dagger. Bradamante then rearranged the folds of her skirt hoping that the bulge would not be too obvious. Picking up her armor and sword, she returned to the chamber where Fiordespina waited.

Bradamante set down her hauberk and sword on the table. Fiordespina was kneeling on a small rug and a scarf covered her head. She bowed and used many hand motions corresponding with spoken Arabic words. Bradamante was fascinated for she had never seen or heard an Islamic prayer up close before.

Fiordespina finished and smiled at Bradamante as she stood. "Let me help you with your dress." She pulled the drawstrings closed in the back. "There. Now let us go eat."

Bradamante felt the loose fabric on the bodice. "At least I fill out the shoulders."

Fiordespina laughed and linked an arm around Bradamante's. As they left the room, Bradamante collided into Neron.

CHAPTER 11

Neron stopped Bradamante from falling on him by grabbing her upper arms. His hands gripped her firmly and did not let go of her. Bradamante moved her right hand to cover the bulge of the dagger under her skirts. She then realized how difficult it would be to retrieve the weapon, and how it would spell her death if she was discovered to be armed. His black eyes bored into hers while she did her best to appear calm.

"It is true then," he said. "The soldier you brought back is a woman."

"Yes, she is," said Fiordespina. "She is my guest and will stay with me as long as I see fit. Tonight I wish to dine alone with her."

"She must be —"

"Hungry. As am I," said Fiordespina with a touch of defiance in her voice.

"Not so quick. I have heard of a woman warrior in Charlemagne's army."

"Her name is Juana and she is on our side," said Fiordespina.

Neron moved his hands up and down feeling the muscles on Bradamante's upper arms. "She is not a new recruit."

"No she is not. She wanted to serve in the war and dressed in her late brother's armor. No one knew they had a woman in their ranks."

"Can she not speak for herself?"

"Of course I can," said Bradamante.

"Where are you from?"

"She is from Lapurdum," said Fiordespina. "And you will take your hands off my guest. Now I must insist that we be allowed to eat before the cock crows."

Fiordespina took Bradamante by the hand and strolled out of the antechamber with Neron at their heels. They entered the main hall which was decorated with a large mosaic of a woman being borne away on the back of a bull. In the middle of the room a large table was set with three place settings. Neron pulled out a chair for Fiordespina.

"As I said, I wish to dine alone with my guest. You may join the rest of the staff in the kitchens."

Neron's face twisted as he picked up his trencher and left them. A servant came and placed fresh greens with vinegar and oil in their coarse bread bowls and filled goblets with fresh water. They spoke in hushed tones so their voices would not carry, but their laughter rang out with more clarity than the bell Fiordespina used to announce their readiness for the next course.

"Where is your family?" asked Bradamante.

"My brother Matalista is off in the war with our father. Our mother died in childbirth when I was only five. My father was heartbroken and did not remarry for five years. His new wife does not like me or my brother because we were born of a different woman, a woman whom my father still loves and speaks of with affection. When his new wife gave birth, she began treating me as if I were a scullery maid because she thought I took attention away from her own daughter. My father moved me to another palace far away from her."

"That is horrible."

"It is the way things are," Fiordespina said with a shrug. "My fondest memories from childhood are of my father taking me hunting, and letting me ride with him on his horse. I felt safe with his strong arms wrapped around me. Now, I rarely see him. Instead of family, I am surrounded by servants and no one is my age. The soldiers guarding this villa are not allowed anywhere inside these walls, only in the garrisons outside, and I cannot speak with them at all. You do not know what this evening and your companionship means to me." Fiordespina patted Bradamante's hand before ringing the bell.

The servant returned and ladled a hearty lamb stew into their trenchers.

"Our supper was postponed due to our late arrival, so it is not as lavish as I would like to share with you. On the morrow we shall have a proper dinner feast with roast venison."

Bradamante waited until the kitchen door closed behind the servant to whisper, "I regret that I cannot partake in such a repast."

"Why? Do you have troubles with game?"

"No. I enjoy venison, but tomorrow is a fast day. Christians are forbidden to consume meat, fowl, and dairy on Wednesdays, Fridays, and Saturdays."

"That is odd. We Muslims cannot eat pork, birds of prey or drink wine, and we must fast from sun up until sun down during the holy month of Ramadan. Why is it that Christians cannot eat meat, chicken or even cheese for three days of every week?"

Bradamante was dumbstruck. "I do not know the reasons why. It is Church law. I was taught not to question, but to simply accept the teachings of our faith. We can however, eat fruit of the sea on fast days."

"Well then, tomorrow we shall have eel. You will not leave my side until Monday morning at the earliest. For you should not travel on your Sabbath day. Even if your wounds were healed by that holy man, you should rest and regain your strength. On Sunday we shall have our venison dinner. I shall instruct the kitchen to smoke the deer and serve it on that day instead."

They finished their meal with cherry pudding. Afterward, Fiordespina led Bradamante and two hounds up a spiral staircase to her private chambers.

"You will stay with me. We can continue our talks where no one will overhear us."

Fiordespina opened the door to a spacious chamber with a large canopy bed hung with red fabric. Bradamante could not help but compare this opulent home with the austere fortress where she grew up. Her relative poverty came from her family's financing of armor and horses for five children. There simply was not the money to spend on lavishing their castle.

Closing the door behind them, Fiordespina stroked the dogs and urged them to fall asleep in front of the door. The two young women walked onto a balcony bathed in moonlight and gazed at the pastoral lands in the valley below. The parcels resembled a large patchwork quilt surrounded by mountains with a narrow winding road on a neighboring hillside and a stone tower that peeked out over the treetops.

"How long have you lived here?" asked Bradamante.

"A few weeks. I had been traveling with my father's forces, but his wife complained about my presence. So once this village was captured, he claimed the villa and stationed a battalion of soldiers here for my protection. Since he is not here, I chose the master chamber for myself."

"How have the villagers treated you?" asked Bradamante.

"They have been gracious, with no sign of rebellion. Then again, these people are used to having different overlords. My grandfather ruled this area before your grandfather did. Over the years, these lands have been ruled by Romans, Visigoths, Muslims, and Franks. People will swear fealty to whoever allows them to live with dignity and without oppression. The previous lord of this manor was taken hostage and is being held for ransom, but my father gave strict orders that the villagers were not to be harmed or the village sacked. He did not want to give them any reason to resent my presence." Fiordespina absentmindedly played with a bird shaped pendant hanging around her neck.

"That is a beautiful necklace," Bradamante said.

"Thank you. My stepmother hates it because this is a Visigothic eagle; it serves as a visible reminder of my mixed heritage through my mother."

"Visigoth. My grandmother on my father's side was Visigothic as well."

Fiordespina opened her mouth to say something when one of the dogs snarled. The two young women returned inside and found both dogs barking at the door leading to the hall.

"Whoever is spying on me should leave before I unleash my hounds on you," Fiordespina called out.

Lifting her skirts, Bradamante retrieved her dagger. Holding it low in front of her, she waited for the door to open. A bead of sweat trickled down her face as she wondered how many men would be attacking. Bradamante allowed herself to breathe again when she heard the muffled sound of retreating footsteps. The dogs yawned and snuggled together on the floor, each head resting on the other's back.

Bradamante turned and saw Fiordespina staring at her knife. "I would never use this against you. I kept it with me because I am surrounded by enemy soldiers. If I have upset you, I will leave."

"No, please stay. I was just surprised. I am unaccustomed to women displaying such bravery. I play at hunting, but I am no match for your courage."

Bradamante felt foolish holding her knife in front of her and lifted her skirts to replace it in her scabbard.

"Perhaps we should change for bed," said Fiordespina as she walked to a trunk and removed two simple linen tunics. They changed into the garments. Bradamante was careful to avoid watching her companion undress. Fiordespina washed her face and hands then knelt to perform another prayer. Bradamante placed her weapon on the floor near the bed and said her prayers for Compline.

Afterward, Fiordespina sat down in front of a small dressing table and brushed her long black hair. Bradamante stood next to her and studied their reflections in a mirror made of polished metal. Fiordespina was curvaceous with dark eyes and sultry good looks. Bradamante frowned at her own tall athletic build and felt inadequate by comparison. She would never be considered buxom, and the one feature of femininity she had cherished had been severed earlier that day.

"My mother wanted a daughter like you," said Bradamante. "Had I been petite like you are, I could never have been a warrior. I fear that I am not womanly."

"There is nothing wrong with you," Fiordespina protested. "Do not dare think otherwise. You are fair and your features are angelic."

"Thank you for your kind words, but my height has made it difficult for my father to find suitors for me. Many of the noblemen he considered as marital prospects were wealthy, elderly widowers in the market for a young wife, but none wanted a bride taller than they were. The younger noblemen are intimidated by my fame on the battlefield, because few measure up to my skill."

"I have faith that your father will find a husband for you soon."

A week ago Bradamante would have said that she was destined to serve Charlemagne as a soldier for the rest of her life, but now thoughts of Ruggiero filled her heart.

"Are you betrothed?" asked Bradamante hoping to shift attention away from herself.

"Not yet, but my father is sure to find someone to my liking," Fiordespina said as she resumed brushing her hair.

"It is better to remain happily unmarried than to be married unhappily. For your sake, I pray your father takes your wishes into account before arranging your marriage."

"My father adores me. Why would he not find someone to make me happy?"

"Marriages are for political alliances," said Bradamante, "especially in royal families. Your father could marry you off to an elderly nobleman if he thought it would strengthen his political power."

Fiordespina looked horrified. "My father would never do such a thing to me."

"Do you know Doralice of Granada?"

"Yes. We played together as children at royal banquets. I have not seen her for years, but we were friends. Why do you ask?"

"I have never met her," said Bradamante, "but I have seen her likeness on the standard of one of the cruelest men alive. She is betrothed to him, and they will soon be married."

"Who is he?"

"Rodomont, Governor of Sarza. Your father could, in the heat of battle, decide he needed to reward someone like Rodomont and offer him your hand in marriage."

Tears welled in Fiordespina's eyes.

Bradamante had to finish her thought, even though she knew it would cause her friend great pain. "And, since Muslims are allowed to have up to four wives…"

"I might also have to marry Rodomont," said Fiordespina. She dabbed her eyes with a handkerchief. "Do you know of any decent Muslim soldiers? Perhaps if I sent word to my father, he would arrange my marriage with one of them. At least I could try to sway him before he promises me to some horrible man."

Bradamante blanched. The only Muslim she knew who was worthy of Fiordespina was Ruggiero. The thought of Fiordespina betrothed to him terrified her. Marsilio could not find a more honorable husband for his daughter and since they were all Muslims there would be no religious barrier to their marriage. She also knew Ruggiero was human and would likely be compelled by an offer to marry such a beautiful and charming maiden. Indeed, he would be foolish to turn down such a match; Fiordespina was the daughter of a powerful and wealthy monarch, and would undoubtedly come with a large dowry. Whereas, Bradamante was the daughter of a duke with limited financial means; her dowry would pale in comparison. Besides that, she and Ruggiero were still considered to be enemies.

She could not bear the thought of another woman in Ruggiero's arms, and could not imagine herself converting to Islam nor sharing him with another wife. No, she wanted to keep alive the dream of marrying Ruggiero in a Christian ceremony. She could not risk losing the only man who stirred passion in her heart.

"I know few Muslims," Bradamante said shaking her head. "They are my adversaries therefore I am not a good source for recommendations."

"Of course, sorry for my asking," said Fiordespina. She climbed into bed and crawled under the covers. "Tell me, have you ever been in love?"

"Me?" said Bradamante. "I - I..."

"I was in love once," interrupted Fiordespina. "At least, I was enamored with a young man once. I was eleven and he, fifteen. He was a handsome stable boy. I made many excuses to visit the horses, just so I could see him. We never so much as shared a kiss, when my affections were discovered."

"What happened?" Bradamante asked as she joined her friend in bed.

"Neron saw me and my chambermaid giggling over the boy. He told my father that my reputation was endangered. My father was furious and banished the boy. Since that time, to avoid any risks with my virtue, he has surrounded me with old women and eunuchs. I am a prisoner here, and fear I shall never fall in love."

"You are far too young for such bleak thoughts," said Bradamante.

"What if my father marries me off to a toothless old man? What then? Shall I embrace being with a man whose very touch I dread? Or worse, my father could force me to marry a brutal man such as Rodomont. I would rather die than suffer such a fate."

Bradamante silently agreed. She closed her eyes and tried sleeping, but her own worries about love kept her awake for hours.

The next few days were a pleasant reprieve from war, but her worries about Neron discovering her identity kept her from feeling at peace. He tried on several occasions to question her, but Fiordespina did not allow Bradamante to answer him. Bradamante spent her days strolling about the lush gardens laughing at Fiordespina's stories which earned her amused looks by the female attendants and glares from Neron. She was careful to not speak above hushed tones lest her accent or word choice reveal her Frankish identity.

On Monday morning, Bradamante readied herself for her long trip to Montauban. After a hearty breakfast, Fiordespina assisted dressing Bradamante in armor and gave her an embroidered surcoat to wear. The Andalusian stallion was brought forth; its saddlebags filled with provisions for the journey.

Fiordespina pressed something into Bradamante's hand. "Take this as a token of our enduring friendship. You will always be welcome in my heart and in my home."

Bradamante opened her hand and saw the Visigothic eagle pendant. She searched Fiordespina's eyes for reason for giving her such a gift. "This is an heirloom."

"I know, but my late mother's heritage is the past. My future depends upon my father. My stepmother has taken great pains at making that impression upon me over the years. This pendant has been a source of antagonism. I want you to have it. I know that you will appreciate it."

Bradamante nodded and felt her throat tighten. "I shall treasure this always."

Fiordespina fastened the necklace about Bradamante's neck. They gave a tearful embrace before Bradamante mounted her horse.

She left the village by the northern gate and went slowly down a steep road. As she passed by a neighboring castle at a confluence of several roads, she glanced back at the hilltop village of Cordes. The rooftops emerged above a layer of clouds clinging to the base of the town. It was as if the town floated on air with an ethereal glow.

By midday Bradamante recognized the benefits of wearing a surcoat. The white fabric reflected the harsh rays of the sun keeping her cooler than if she had worn only her iron armor. She stopped by the banks of a brook on the outskirts of the vast Gresigne Forest for her midday meal. As she sat in the shade of a moss covered oak tree and ate bread and cheese, she thought about Ruggiero.

"Where are you Ruggiero," she wondered aloud. "Are you thinking of me?"

She hoped she made a lasting impression on him and that he also thought of their meeting as magical. She supposed he was with Akramont's forces. Her stop at Montauban would allow her to learn where Charlemagne's forces were headed before she left the next morning. Her liege needed the help of all his warriors so she could not remain away from battle for long, even if it meant fighting against her beloved.

After resuming her journey, Bradamante rode past rolling hills turning from green to golden in the summer heat. As the familiar sight of Montauban's white stone tower loomed in the distance, she grew excited and urged her horse to go faster. Approaching the gate in the middle of the wooden palisade, she held up her hand to hail the guard when an arrow whizzed through the air narrowly missing her head.

CHAPTER 12

"Are you trying to kill your sister?" Bradamante called out.

The blond youth from the guard tower poked his head over the wall. "Bradamante?"

"Thank heavens it was only you, little brother. Had any of our other brothers shot at me, I would be dead."

"It is you!" Richardet shouted. "Open the gate. The Maid is home!"

A commotion went up inside the castle walls as news of Bradamante's return quickly spread. A horn was sounded and loud voices shouted as people rushed about. Soon the heavy wooden portcullis rose allowing her to enter. She had barely dismounted her horse when she was surrounded by her family.

"My daughter, you have come home," said Beatrice as she smothered Bradamante in a hug.

"Daughter," said Duke Aymon. "What an unexpected pleasure."

She reached out to embrace her silver-haired father when his head bumped against her helmet. Smiling sheepishly, she removed it.

"What happened to your hair?" Beatrice asked, her lips pursed.

"I cut it off," said Bradamante. "I was roasting under the hot sun in my iron casque. It is cooler with shorn locks."

"Scandalous!" said her mother. She tucked a stray lock of graying hair into her hat and shook a finger at Duke Aymon. "This is your fault. You encouraged this martial attitude in her since she was a small child. The girl will die an old maid. What man would want a wife who looks like a boy?"

"Go to the kitchens my dear," he replied. "Be sure there is a proper feast to celebrate our daughter's return."

Beatrice glowered at him before she turned her back.

Bradamante's older brother, Alard, embraced her. "You discovered a new way to annoy Mother. Well done."

A small boy ran at them. "Auntie, take that," he said as he swung a wooden sword at her.

Bradamante grabbed her shield, dodged a few of his blows, and felt the muscles in his upper arm. "Bernard, you are getting as strong as your father. Before long, you shall be a page."

He grinned and pulled her hand. "Come see baby Aymon."

Renaud's wife Clarice came forward holding an infant.

Bradamante felt uncomfortable with anything that was considered part of women's sphere of influence. She had no maternal instincts, so while most women cooed when shown a baby, Bradamante fought to keep from flinching. Unsure of what was expected of her; she awkwardly kissed the baby's forehead.

"I cannot believe how much he has grown."

"I know," smiled Clarice. "Every morning I swear angels have stretched him during the night."

Then Bradamante's younger brother came running and gave her a bone crushing hug and whirled her about.

"Put me down, Richardet," she said laughing.

"Certainly, sister," he said as he spun her around another two more times. "Sorry I shot at you, but you charged the gate. I did not recognize you."

"Did you not see my shield?"

"I saw a soldier in a surcoat riding an unfamiliar horse. I did not notice your standard. Tell me, where is Erebus?"

Bradamante hooked her arm around Richardet's and excused herself to the rest of her family. She turned to her twin and said quietly, "I am sorry brother, Erebus is dead."

Richardet's face fell. "He was my horse."

"I know. I promised I would be careful, but his leg broke in battle. I had to put him down. To make amends I am giving you this destrier as a replacement; his name is Cyllarus." She handed him the reins of the stallion.

Richardet's eyes lit up. "Where did you get such a fine horse?"

"Let us go inside and I shall tell you."

They walked into the small castle and climbed the spiral staircase to the second floor where the sleeping quarters were. As she passed by her parents' room, she remembered how spacious Fiordespina's was in comparison. Three of her parents' chambers could have fit in her friend's room. As it was, there were only three bedrooms in the whole castle in Montauban. Her parents slept in one, her brothers in another, and she shared one with Clarice and the young boys, while the servants slept on mats in the dining hall.

Nothing had changed since the last time she was home. There was one large bed, a crib for the baby, a mirror on the wall, and four trunks stacked against the wall.

"Tell me about the battle of Toulouse," said Richardet.

Bradamante closed the door. "It was by far the worst battle I have ever been in. Our forces were overwhelmed as wave after wave of enemy soldiers washed upon the battle plain. The momentum kept shifting during the day. At times we were winning, but then they would rally and force us to retreat."

"Were there a lot of casualties?"

"Thousands died. On both sides. It was a sea of corpses."

Richardet gulped. "Do you know the names of anyone important who died?"

"I do not know how many dignitaries perished, but I saw the bodies of the duke of Arles and the duke of Orléans on the battlefield."

"Duke Guillaume is dead? Father will be saddened about that," said Richardet.

Bradamante then told him of her duel with Rodomont, but not how her fight was taken over by Ruggiero. She had decided against telling her family anything about Ruggiero at this point in time.

"So what is the truth about your hair?" asked Richardet.

Bradamante sat on her trunk and sighed. "I was wounded on the back of my head. I dared not say anything in front of Mother, for fear she would forbid me from returning to battle."

"Your helmet seems fine," he noted as he turned it over in his hands.

"I took it off for a moment to speak with another soldier and was attacked without warning."

"That was foolish of you," said Richardet. "But you are right about Mother. She has been a nightmare of late. She swears the Saracens are lying in wait to burn our castle to the ground, even though they should be well on their way to Paris by now. I wish I had been allowed to continue serving as Namo's squire instead of being sent back here to guard Renaud's home. I feel like a prisoner in this castle."

"Perhaps you will have new orders soon," she replied.

He snorted. "I do not expect anyone will remember the plight of a lowly squire. So, are you going to tell me how you acquired that magnificent horse or must I guess?"

"Do you remember a maiden named Fiordespina?"

"Marsilio's daughter? How could I forget a face like hers?" said Richardet. "What does she have to do with this?"

"She was my gracious benefactor."

"H-how did that happen?"

Bradamante relayed to him the story of Fiordespina finding her unconscious near the Tarn River and mistaking her for a man. "At first I was afraid to correct her, for I worried about being taken hostage should my true identity become known. Later, I was forced to admit to her that I was a maid for she had become enamored of me. I had to let her know that I was not equipped to satisfy her needs."

"Sister!" he said with his mouth agape. "I have never known you to be bawdy."

"Blame it on Renaud," she laughed. "He has made much merriment about the girls in our village who giggle as you ride by, hoping you will deign to cast your eyes upon them."

Richardet ignored her teasing. "So where did you stay with Fiordespina?"

"In her chamber."

"Indeed? But surely you did not travel all the way to Saragossa?"

"No, it was in the town of Cordes. The Saracens captured it recently and Amir Marsilio claimed the villa for his daughter."

Richardet nodded. "So that is how you were able to make it home in one day. Still, I am amazed she gave you such a fine horse. She could have given you a simple palfrey to see you safely on your way."

"She could have, but she is kind and generous. Fiordespina said I was welcome in her home anytime. We swore that, even though our fathers are at war with one another, we would always be friends and never enemies."

Richardet touched the embroidered sleeves on Bradamante's surcoat. "This is remarkable workmanship."

"She has the talent for the domestic arts, an area where I am sorely lacking. It was to be a gift for her brother Matalista, but she gave it to me instead. I should change for supper. Will you serve as my squire little brother?" she said as she stood.

"If you will stop calling me 'little brother,'" he said while untying the fastenings. "I am an inch taller than you."

"Yes, but you are the shortest male in our family, the runt of the litter," she teased. "Besides, I am older than you."

"I was born right after you," he protested.

"I am still older and therefore wiser than you."

He pulled the surcoat roughly over her head.

"Careful!" she said. "With an attitude like yours, it may be years before Charlemagne makes you a knight."

"It is not fair," said Richardet. "You serve him as if you were a knight, and yet you have never gone through the knighting ceremony."

"And I never will. He dares not bestow that honor upon me because I am a woman. It is enough for me that he allows me to use my talents to serve him."

Richardet lifted the armor up and over her shoulders. "I understand all that, sister. We are the same age and yet I am still regarded as too young to be a knight while you are a commander. I cannot help feeling jealous."

Bradamante felt compassion for her brother and contemplated asking him to come with her the next day to serve as her squire, but then decided against it. He had his orders and she could not overrule them.

Richardet held her armor in his hands, surveying its links. "Would you like me to polish this for you? A few rings are beginning to show rust."

"I would appreciate that."

"By the way, Eos is ready for you. The farrier fit her with a new set of shoes the day after you took Erebus," Richardet said. "I shall have your armor ready by morning and hang it in your horse's stall. Will you be staying here long?"

"No. I am leaving at dawn," she said, "but do not tell Mother. You may keep the surcoat if you like, for while I can manage my hauberk alone, the surcoat is far too difficult without a squire."

"Thank you. Do you think Cyllarus will recognize the difference between us?"

"Of course," she said grinning. "I have better horsemanship."

CHAPTER 13

Bradamante lifted the top dress from her trunk and held it against her body. The dark green gown no longer fit since her most recent growth spurt.

"That will never do." Clarice clucked her disapproval as she walked into the room. "Your hair is bad enough, but you cannot walk about showing your ankles."

She laid the sleeping baby in the crib and rummaged through Renaud's trunk. "Try this. I made it for your brother to sleep in, but it has never been worn." She pulled out a long sleeved, full-length white linen tunic. A note of anger had crept into Clarice's voice at the mention of Renaud, even if she did not use his name. Bradamante had never heard Clarice say anything against Renaud, but there were times when undercurrents of her displeasure were evident. Renaud had not been home in over a year and this clearly made Clarice unhappy.

Bradamante tried on the tunic and found that it brushed the ground. Clarice then laced the back of Bradamante's dress.

"It is the best I can manage for today," Clarice muttered. "On the morrow we shall sew on a border at the sleeves and hem."

Bradamante pulled at the sleeves on her dress, but they would not extend the full length of her arms. The white tunic showed underneath near her wrists and at her ankles.

"Now, about your hair." Clarice scowled at Bradamante.

Clarice searched through the contents of her own trunk and produced a dark green matron's hat. Bradamante put on the hat and studied her reflection in the mirror. She thought she resembled a pine tree. Bradamante hated wearing the color green, yet her opinion was never consulted on such matters. Clarice made clothes that suited her own fair complexion – black hair and green eyes – and did not care if they drained all the color from Bradamante's face. Giving Clarice a gracious smile, Bradamante thanked her for her assistance and headed downstairs.

As she entered the great hall, Bradamante inhaled deeply to capture the smells of baked bread, almond-milk soup, and grilled quail. There were two long tables set apart from each other joining the high table at the front of the room. The U shape allowed for servants to walk about and serve meals to the noble family.

Duke Aymon took his daughter by the hand and escorted her to a side table.

"A messenger came Saturday with a letter from your brother Guichard. I became worried about you," Aymon said quietly. "He said you were missing and feared dead after the dreadful battle near Toulouse. Tell me what happened."

"I was wounded and became separated from our forces. Fortunately, a kind woman allowed me to recover in her home. Has the battlefront moved to Paris?"

He nodded.

"As I thought," she said. "I came here to restock for the long journey."

"Of course, my dear," he said patting her hand. "Take what you need. You are safe, and for that I am grateful. I wish I could still take part in war, but my back no longer allows it. Guichard also wrote about Renaud. He has returned to the west and Charlemagne sent him to Britain to secure reinforcements. I know my brother, King Odo, will send a favorable word to the leaders of the other tribes and to the Scots as well."

"Praise to God that Renaud has returned to us," she said. "Father, how fares the construction of your castle?"

Duke Aymon sighed. "Before the invasion it was doing well, but I had to leave to oversee this castle's protection. I shall soon return to see if any workers remain or if they have all fled in advance of the Saracen army. I will also see if your mother's worst fears have been realized."

Aymon kissed her cheek, walked up to the high table and sat down in the chair of honor next to his wife. Bradamante stood there wondering what her father meant, when Alard cleared his throat announcing his presence. She accepted his outstretched hand and grumbled as her skirts snagged on a rough edge of the wooden trestle bench.

Alard was five years older than she and Richardet, and had been knighted the year before. He had the familial blond hair and blue eyes of their parents, and his face now bore the angular lines of manhood with a full moustache whereas Richardet still appeared boyish, his facial hair sparse and irregular.

Bradamante sat down and whispered, "What did Father mean by 'Mother's worst fears'?"

"That their new castle will be burned to the ground," said Alard. "Truth to tell, she resents that he has chosen to forego using stone as the primary building material. She hates that it will be made of wood and makes disparaging comments at every opportunity. While she was happy that her brother finally made her a duchess, she does not want to move into an inferior castle to her station in life, even if it will be larger than this one."

"But it would take many years for a stone castle to be built," protested Bradamante. "They would have to quarry the stone and…"

"I know," he said. "Father cannot simply condemn a villa from a conquered foe then steal its stone as our Grandfather Pepin did to build this castle. Quercy has been under Frankish rule for over thirty years. Its *castellas* are now all held by loyalists to Charlemagne. Mother cannot in fairness compare a duke's castle to the palace of the emperor."

Richardet sat down on Bradamante's right. "Are you talking about Mother and the wooden castle?"

Alard and Bradamante nodded.

Richardet shook his head in disgust. "She seems to have forgotten the decades of construction in Aachen. Even if Father started building a stone castle on the morrow, it is doubtful they would live long enough to move in. Of course if Father was a Maganza, he would simply evict or," he lowered his voice, "*murder* noblemen from a manor he coveted."

Alard glared at him as servants delivered platters of food. "Do not speak of that accursed house over dinner, lest I lose my appetite."

Richardet blanched at the reproval, and a lull in the conversation followed. Bradamante sipped her soup and reflected on the guilt she felt about Richardet being in the shadow of her and Renaud's glory. She then had to admit that he was not the only one in their family to pale in such a comparison. Guichard and Alard were competent soldiers, but they excelled in archery rather than sword play and had not garnered the acclaim Bradamante felt they deserved. Nor had they earned the same level of confidence from Charlemagne as she and Renaud had.

Bradamante closed her eyes to better savor the taste of quail in verjuice. Her mother could be annoying, but she had made sure that Bradamante's favorite game was served for supper. The temporary pall between her brothers lifted when Alard began spinning tales about their parents squabbling. She laughed, but her mind could not stay focused on the conversation. Her thoughts drifted away to the battle of Toulouse and the image of Ruggiero's handsome face. Once the trenchers were removed, Bradamante rose to excuse herself from the table.

"Have some more wine," Alard begged while grabbing her hand. "I want to sing a song in your honor."

She smiled and nodded as a servant refilled her goblet. Richardet snuck outside when Alard's back was turned. The older brother retrieved a lute and strolled in the center between the two long tables and sang in a loud clear voice.

"My garden is lush and green
Surrounded by a mist of uncertainty
Many marvel at it, but few understand
Its true beauty
In my wild and lovely garden
Things grow untamed, but in harmony
Through the mists I see you
In your bright crystal palace…beckoning me
I come closer and am in awe

Of its beauty
Of its beauty
Of its sheer beauty

For you show to me what others never see
And I love you
I go inside and you see in me
What others never cared to see
And you love me
Our worlds are open for all to see
And understand
But no one knows

Of their beauty
Of their beauty
Of their sheer beauty"

"That was lovely." Bradamante wiped away a tear.

"Thank you," he said as he bowed. "I hope one day to sing that song to a fair maiden who will consider marrying the third son of a nobleman with no lands and little inheritance."

Her parents seated at the high table were in deep conversation with Clarice. They would not have heard Alard complain about his lack of financial stature, and for that Bradamante felt relieved. Duke Aymon's limited means was a sore subject with their mother. Beatrice expected a higher lifestyle than her husband was able to afford and she hated living far from the royal court. Similarly, Beatrice bitterly resented knowing her favorite son, Renaud, had the widespread reputation of being not only one of Charlemagne's best paladins but also the poorest.

Bradamante lifted her goblet when she saw her favorite serving girl bearing a pitcher of wine.

"Hippalca," she whispered. "I would like a bath drawn for me tonight, but I must speak with you alone first. Excuse yourself from your kitchen duty and meet me outdoors in the park."

"Yes, milady."

Bradamante excused herself from the table while Alard sang another song. It was evening, but the sun had only begun setting and sunlight still illuminated the interior of the castle. She walked outside into a small grassy courtyard and waved to Richardet as he rode on his new horse and practiced his jousting skills against a quintain. She shook her head as the training tool spun wildly after being struck, its sand bag almost hitting her brother in the back of his head. Clearly his technique needed improvement. Strolling near the raised flower beds holding aromatic and medicinal herbs, she plucked a white rose from a nearby bush and smiled as she inhaled its perfume.

"You needed me, milady?" asked Hippalca.

Bradamante turned and embraced her handmaiden. Hippalca was a pleasant, but plain-looking girl who had been orphaned as a young child. She grew up serving the needs of another girl her same age, but never appeared to resent that her own prospects were significantly less. She benefited from having close contact with an educated noblewoman, for her own vocabulary became superior to that of the other servants.

Over the years they had become as close as sisters. Hippalca was Bradamante's only confidant. She dared not tell her insecurities to her mother or brothers and would certainly never allow her father to know she harbored any self-doubts.

"Hippalca, I have yearned to speak with you. I have so much to confide, and you are the only one whom I can trust."

The two young women sat down on a stone bench; they were alone in the garden. The sounds of merriment and clapping drifted out from the open door of the castle, while Richardet had taken his horse to the stables.

"I am in love," said Bradamante.

"Oh, milady that is wonderful news. Who is he?"

"His name is Ruggiero. He is young, strong, handsome, and the ideal knight. I saw him level a two-handed stroke of his sword that was miraculous. He comes from a long and distinguished noble family for he is descended from Hector of Troy."

"He sounds like a wonderful man. Will he be speaking with your father about betrothal?"

Bradamante grimaced.

"What is it milady? I fear there is something you are not telling me."

Bradamante nodded and covered her face with her hands. "He is a Sara – a Muslim."

She peeked through her fingers to see her handmaid's reaction. Hippalca's eyes were wide.

"Are you mad?"

"I am in love. I am in love with a sworn enemy of our emperor."

She gave a nervous laugh which quickly turned into sobbing.

"Oh my lady, my lady," Hippalca said and took Bradamante in her arms. "He must be a remarkable man. He has brought out in this fierce warrior something that I thought I would never see: the beating heart of a woman."

Bradamante dried her eyes and told Hippalca of how she met Ruggiero and the chivalrous act he performed on her behalf; then how they had been alone with one another.

"We gazed at each other for what seemed like an eternity, but it was only a few moments. I know we would have kissed if it had not been for villains who attacked me without warning."

"You were hurt? What happened?"

Bradamante touched the back of her hat. "I was wounded, hence my new hairstyle. Ruggiero defied his own sovereign by killing his fellow soldiers in my defense."

"He killed for you?" Hippalca's jaw dropped.

"I defended him as well."

"Did you two speak afterward?"

"No," said Bradamante. "We became separated."

"And you have not seen him since?"

Bradamante shook her head.

"Milady, forgive me," said Hippalca, "but I wonder how you can be so certain of your feelings of love for a man you met only once, and for so short a time."

"No man has ever stirred passion in my heart before. The most I have ever felt was respect and admiration, but never have I yearned for the touch of a man. I had thought my heart was made of stone."

"Your father will never consent to you marrying a Saracen. Do you think Ruggiero will agree to be baptized as a Christian?"

"I do. After the battle, I was somehow brought to a hermit who healed my wounds. This holy man told me of a vision he had earlier that morning in which Ruggiero appeared. The hermit's words gave me hope, because he confirmed what I felt the moment I met Ruggiero – that we are destined for one another." Bradamante stood with confidence. "I shall leave at sunrise. Please have a large breakfast ready before my journey. I need more than wine and a sop of bread on the morrow. I also need my saddlebags packed with as much dried meat and fish as it can carry. I shall take my horse Eos and do not know when I will return. I wish to depart before the bells ring for the morning prayers."

Hippalca nodded. "Yes milady. I am sad you cannot stay longer, but I understand you serve the emperor. Let us see if your bath is ready."

They walked into a small chamber on the main floor where a large bathtub was set up. Heated water in buckets were far too heavy to carry upstairs, and so the family bathed in a room near the hearth. Hippalca added rose petals and dried lavender to the water. Bradamante enjoyed soaking in warm water and cleansing all the sweat and grime off her body. She did not know when she would have another opportunity to bathe, and hoped that the next time she saw Ruggiero the scent of flowers might still cling to her.

As Bradamante fell asleep next to Clarice, she dreamt of Ruggiero. However, this dream was different from her previous dreams reliving the night they met. He was dressed in a tunic and breeches rather than armor. The expression on his face was one of love and longing.

"My love," he said. "Do not return to the war. Come to me instead. I am being held prisoner in the Pyrenees."

Part II

Bradamante's Call to Adventure

CHAPTER 14

Bradamante woke before dawn. She had difficulty sleeping and had constant images of Ruggiero in her dreams. Slipping out of bed, she took care not to wake Clarice or Bernard. Hippalca was waiting for her in the small bath chamber. Bradamante handed Hippalca a long piece of cloth.

"I need you to help me bind my breasts down."

"Why is that milady?"

"I have always traveled with legions of soldiers and everyone knew that Charlemagne valued my service. Therefore no one ever dared treat me with anything less than respect and reverence. Today I am setting off on a solitary quest without even a single squire for company. I think it would be wise to keep my identity as a woman secret at all times."

Bradamante put on tights and a fresh tunic that reached the top of her thighs. She felt her flattened chest approvingly. That, along with her closely cropped hair should allow her to pass unquestioned as a man, she thought. She had only to remember to lower her voice to sound the part as well. Thick padded doublets came next before she wrapped herself in a dressing gown. She hoped to disguise her intent of leaving should she encounter anyone inside the castle.

Bradamante ate a large meal of sausages, bread, and cheese behind the stables in an area not visible from the castle. After eating, Bradamante performed her morning prayers before entering the stables. Her armor hung in her horse's stall just as Richardet had promised. She was pleased to see it had been cleaned, oiled, and the few spots of rust removed. Hippalca struggled to lift the shirt of mail over Bradamante's shoulders and assisted attaching the metal leggings as well.

"I have packed your saddlebags with as much food as they would hold, milady," said Hippalca. "There are two skins filled with water as well."

"Thank you for that, and for saddling my horse."

"That was Richardet's doing, milady," said Hippalca. "He readied Eos because he knew you were leaving. He left earlier for a long ride on his new horse."

Bradamante silently wished Cyllarus might bring Richardet some modicum of happiness. She then noticed her handmaiden was blushing. "Hippalca, do you fancy my little brother?"

"He is a handsome lad, but he will never notice someone like me."

Bradamante knew that her maid spoke the truth. Richardet had an eye for beauty and would not be interested in someone as plain as Hippalca. Words failed Bradamante as she embraced her friend.

"May God be with you, and may He bring you safely back to us bearing good news," Hippalca said.

The young woman handed Bradamante her dagger and sword to fasten onto her belt. Bradamante slung her shield over her back and mounted her horse while Hippalca held open the stable door to the courtyard. Bradamante waved to the sentry raising the portcullis.

The pink tint in the morning sky mirrored Eos; her pure white coat was underlay with a pale pinkness. The mare had been a gift from Charlemagne as a token of gratitude after Rodomont killed her previous horse. He chose a white destrier to match her shield and plume of white. Bradamante had just received Eos when the mare lost a shoe and she was forced to bring Erebus to battle instead. Taking a deep breath, she drank in the crisp morning air.

"Are you ready for an adventure my dear?" Bradamante asked her horse.

Eos nodded as if she understood, and they rode down to the village of Montauban. Beatrice regarded their castle and village as small and insignificant, but Bradamante loved everything about her home and surroundings. She loved the colored brick of the larger buildings, especially at dawn when it reflected pink hues from the sky. Church bells rang signifying the Prime prayers filled Bradamante with inner warmth. The town of Montauban had not been harmed by the invading army. She assumed the Muslim army chose the old Roman roads from Toulouse through Auch, a good fifty miles south of Montauban. If they had chosen that route, as she speculated, they would soon be approaching Bordeaux on their journey up the *Aquitania Caesari* to Paris.

Bradamante rode at a comfortable pace. She used the extended daylight to ride longer than she ordinarily would. To compensate, she gave her horse extra rest breaks and enjoyed a leisurely meal along the shady banks of the Garonne River.

Clouds began gathering in the late afternoon cooling the air. Along with them, gloom descended on Bradamante. Normally the road to Toulouse was heavily traveled by merchants transporting their wares, but instead it was eerily devoid of anyone save for herself.

There were smaller towns than Toulouse where she could have stopped and spent the night, but she considered it too risky. A solitary traveler with an expensive horse and a set of armor would be a source of incredible wealth to a poor peasant family. The temptation to murder a knight to steal his horse and armor might cause even the most devout family to commit a grievous sin.

Bradamante paced herself to make it to Toulouse before nightfall. Inns earned their livelihood by providing safe accommodations for travelers. There might be petty thefts, but horses and persons would be safe from assault. Otherwise, innkeepers would soon find themselves locked up by local magistrates and put out of business.

A knot of apprehension stuck in Bradamante's throat as she saw the red brick city in the distance. It was on the plains outside this city where she last saw Ruggiero. Fresh graves dotted the area bearing witness to the battle only the week before. Bradamante shook her head to purge these horrific images from her mind as she turned toward the city itself.

The walls surrounding Toulouse had been breached in several places and their repair had not yet begun. After entering through the city gates, scorch marks were visible everywhere as well as destroyed buildings. A smattering of people walked down the normally busy streets.

Bradamante made her way down the *Rue du Taur* following the path where the patron saint of Toulouse, Saint Sernin, had died. After refusing to sacrifice a bull to the Roman gods, he was dragged to his death behind the animal. She bowed her head and made a sign of the cross as she passed by the brick church housing the martyr's remains. Farther down the street she came upon a tavern and inquired about room and board for the night.

"You are my first customer since this city was pillaged," said the innkeeper as he handed her a bowl of stew. "I cannot decide which was worse: cleaning up the city after being sacked or burying the dead from the battle."

"How many were buried?" asked Bradamante.

"Thousands. And the damned infidels stripped the dead of all valuables before we could get to them. At least they buried their own which is more than I can say for our emperor. He left that unpleasant task for the count of Toulouse."

"Has Count Ottino rejoined Charlemagne's forces?"

The innkeeper shook his head. "No, he was badly injured in the battle for his city. I doubt he will ever make war again."

Bradamante ate the rest of her meal in silence remembering the night when she and Ruggiero scanned the plain searching for Atallah. There were bodies everywhere. They would have needed multitudes of grave diggers to bury all the war dead. The heat of the summer would speed rotting, leading to smells worse than the normal battlefield stench. She pushed the bowl away, having lost her appetite.

Leaving the tavern behind, she walked up the staircase to the sleeping quarters. She stowed the saddlebags with her provisions on a beam above the bed, hoping no rats or other vermin would find it while she slept. Her armor and sword were placed under the bed, but she left her dagger on her belt. After looking at the straw mattress, she decided to sleep on top of the thin woolen blanket in hope it might serve as a protective barrier from bedbugs. The only sound during the night was the distant snore of the innkeeper.

That night she again dreamed Ruggiero was calling her. "Not much farther, my love. We shall soon be together. Beware though, danger surrounds you."

Bradamante woke with a start and instinctively reached for the scabbard on her belt. It was still there. Sunlight streamed through gaps in the roof alerting her that it was now morning. She left on her journey southward after eating a breakfast of porridge.

The plains south of Toulouse gave way to rolling hills dotted with trees on their ridgelines. Strong winds made it difficult for her horse to walk unimpeded. The second day of not seeing any fellow travelers on the roadway was more unsettling for her. This area had not suffered from the invasion. She could not think of a logical reason why the road was devoid of merchant traffic.

By evening the sky was overcast. In the town of Frédélas all the doors and windows were shuttered and no person stirred in the streets. She secured lodging for the night at the largest inn and once again she was the only lodger.

"Why is there no one traveling these roads?" Bradamante asked the innkeeper as he handed her a bowl of white bean soup and brown bread.

"There is a curse about the land," he whispered. "No one is safe out of doors, especially at dusk. That is when the monster strikes."

"Monster?"

The man shuddered. "Best not speak of it, lest you bring the curse down upon yourself."

"If I am to avoid the monster, what am I to look for?" she said.

"It is not safe to travel, especially near Foix," he whispered again.

The man turned his back and Bradamante knew that he had spoken his last word on the subject. She ate the rest of her meal in silence and slept fitfully that night. Every creak or groan from the rafters sounded malevolent.

The next morning she stared at the snow-capped Pyrenees looming on the horizon. She sensed that somewhere in the mountains was the answer to what had become of Ruggiero. Once again she was the lone traveler on the road, and had developed an uneasy expectation of not seeing anyone else. So it came as a surprise when she saw a knight off the road. His helmet and shield were hung on a nearby oak tree and he was openly weeping. She scanned the area for places accomplices might be hiding. Seeing none she felt assured this man was alone and in true anguish.

CHAPTER 15

"Sir," Bradamante hailed, "why do you weep?"

The man lifted his head. Tears had stained his cheeks and his eyes were bloodshot. His nose was hooked and his black hair showed off a prominent widow's peak. He would not have been considered handsome under normal circumstances, but being grief stricken made him even more unattractive. Bradamante nonetheless felt moved by his emotional display.

"A week ago, my lady was stolen from me by a monster. I do not know what has become of her. I am driven mad by visions of her being ravished by that foul creature."

"Tell me what happened," Bradamante said as she dismounted.

"Are you a Christian?"

"Yes."

He gave a sigh of relief. "I was traveling last week when it happened. I was leading a procession of troops as reinforcements for our emperor. My lady was by my side, as I could not bear the thought of being without her for any length of time."

Bradamante understood. Charlemagne brought his daughters with him when he went to battle. They were kept in the rear guard and closely protected.

"We saw the battle raging in the distance," he continued, "when a large cloud covered the sky. Except it was not a cloud. A man swooped down taking my lady in his arms and flew away with her."

Bradamante was puzzled. "A man was flying in the sky?"

"He rode on the back of a flying horse. I tried following him, but the villain used magic on me. I woke up after night had fallen with a broken heart. I would be of no use on the battlefield. I sent my men onward, hoping they would be of some service to Charlemagne." He paced under the tree. "That contemptible piece of filth who abducted my wife terrorizes this area every night as the sun sets. He snatches up any woman who is fair of face and brave knights as well. The townspeople are afraid to leave their houses for fear they might be his next victim. Those needing to venture outside disguise themselves to look wretched in the hopes of avoiding attack."

"This must be the curse the innkeeper refused to talk about," she mused.

The man nodded.

"Has no one tried recovering the captives?" she asked.

"No one in the town of Foix or Frédélas has come to my aid. Two Saracens tried helping me last week, the day after my lady's abduction, but they were also taken prisoner." He paused and then whispered, "One of them was the horrible Gradasso."

"Gradasso?" said Bradamante. "King of Sericana?"

"Yes, he has returned to Francia. I did not know who he was at first. Gradasso would never have offered to help me if it had not been for the bold and courageous youth who was with him."

Bradamante's heart began beating faster. "Do you recall the youth's name?"

"Ruggiero. He heard my plight and vowed to find and release my wife. Alas, shortly afterward we were once again attacked by that monster and his magic. This time after I awoke I discovered those two brave warriors and their horses had been carried off. I was left with a companion of theirs, a foul and loathsome insignificant little beast of a man who wailed about his loss of Ruggiero. He acted as if he had lost a lover."

"Tell me," said Bradamante, "do you have any idea where they are being held? I should like to try my luck in releasing them."

"I have found it," he said brightening. "It is a castle created and beset by sorcery. I do not know how you will enter, but let us set off at once. There are still a few hours of daylight left."

The sound of thundering hoof beats reached Bradamante's ears. A rider was coming from Frédélas. The horseman saw her shield and drew his horse to a halt.

"Bradamante!" he hailed. "Thank heavens, I found you at last. I have an urgent message for you."

"What is it?"

"The people of Marseille beg for your return," said the messenger. "They are in danger of falling to the infidels."

Bradamante's heart was torn between duty to Charlemagne and her love for Ruggiero. She had been charged with the defense of Marseille, but had left when ordered to help in the battle of Toulouse. Ruggiero was being held prisoner nearby and could be in grave danger. Duty required that she turn her back on his plight and return to Marseille. However, if she did that, there might never be another opportunity to rescue him. She could die in battle, dooming Ruggiero to spend the rest of his life in a magical prison. The snow-capped mountains in the distance beckoned her.

"I shall return to Marseille," said Bradamante, "but not today. I have heard this baron's plight and I cannot ignore it." She turned to the knight, "Tell me your name sir, so the messenger may relay it."

"Call me Orpheus," he said. "Until my lady is returned to me, I shall sing dirges. I am too ashamed to admit my real name, for I was unable to protect the most precious of all of my possessions. What good is a knight if he cannot safeguard his own lady?"

Bradamante noticed the man's shield hanging on a tree limb. It was draped in black. Assuming it signified mourning, she returned her attention to the messenger.

"The Ariège is being terrorized by a madman attacking women and soldiers. Should I leave without helping, I too could fall prey to this fiend. Instead, I shall aid these people by challenging the knave responsible. Afterward, I will report to Marseille."

The messenger nodded before his horse took off in a full gallop back toward Frédélas. As Bradamante turned, the grief-stricken man was on horseback and waiting for her. She mounted Eos and held her shield tightly in her left hand. There would be no turning back.

They rode in silence while climbing a mountainous path northwest of Foix. Bradamante was apprehensive once again about not seeing another person on the road, but now understood the reason people avoided traveling.

The two rode side by side until coming to a narrow mountain pass where they were forced to ride single file. As they approached a blind curve, he signaled for her to remain behind.

"This area is prone to rockslides," he said. "Stay here until I tell you it is safe."

A few moments later she heard his desperate cry. "Bradamante, come quickly!"

She rode around the bend. He was kneeling beside a thicket of trees.

"There is a child trapped at the bottom of this cave," he said. "I heard a cry for help, but it has stopped. There is no one else around. If we do not rescue her, she will perish."

Bradamante dismounted and peered into the mouth of the cave. The opening was barely large enough for her to enter. She poked her head inside the dark hole and did not see or hear anything from within its depths. Drawing her sword, she hacked at a long branch from one of the nearby trees.

"Hold onto this branch tightly, and help lower me," she said.

"Yes, my lady."

Bradamante slowly descended into the cavern and was plunged into darkness. As her eyes adjusted, she realized the floor of the cave was empty.

"Sir!" she called. "Bring me up. There is no child in this cave."

"There is now!" he laughed. "You asked my name: I am Pinabel of the house of Maganza. I cannot accept your help because no Maganzan can ever be indebted to the house of Lyon. May death and destruction rain down on your family!"

Pinabel let go of the limb and Bradamante fell to the bottom of the cave.

CHAPTER 16

Nestled in a narrow valley in the Pyrenees was a castle that appeared to be made of polished silver. By midday there was a blinding glare as the sun's rays reflected off its metallic surface. It was perched on a butte in the center of that slender valley. One would have to scale fifty feet of an almost vertical incline to reach its lowest level, but the sole entrance was a door on the roof, which could only be accessed from the sky. Any observer would conclude this castle had been created by magic.

The fortress had many large windows allowing sunlight to flood the interior. The walls were covered with ornate tapestries and the furnishings, with silk cushions. Every convenience and comfort was provided for, including Roman-styled baths and elaborate fountains. Beautiful ladies lounged about wearing silk gowns in bright colors of peacock blue, poppy red and gold. The necklines of their gowns revealed ample cleavage, which was unheard of for proper ladies. To accentuate their décolletage, they wore elaborate necklaces adorned with sparkling emeralds, sapphires, and rubies. Girls were the only ones in society allowed to go without hats and wear their hair down, but many of the captive women flaunted that convention by deliberately brushing and styling their long hair in front of men.

A dozen brave knights entertained themselves with jousting in an indoor arena. The knights displayed their prowess before the ladies by day in hopes of earning their favor and in turn be bestowed with the ladies' favors by night.

Each meal was a time of feasting and revelry with plentiful food and wine. Roasted peacocks were served with their feathers reattached, as well as trout appearing to swim in a suspension of aspic, delighting the men and women. They soon forgot or no longer cared how they had come to being held captive, for all their wants and needs were accommodated. It seemed that everyone was satisfied, except the one person the castle was built for and designed to protect.

"Release me *Ustadh* Atallah," Ruggiero pleaded. "I sense she is in danger, I must go to her."

"Forget about her my child," said Atallah. "That is a dangerous path for you to follow. You would be betrayed and killed in the prime of your life by her family's enemies. You would die far too young, just like your father, just like Hector, and Hector's son Astyanax – all for the love of a woman. I will not let that same fate befall you."

Ruggiero grew angry as he stared at his mentor's lined face. The old man had dismissed his concerns, *again*. He wanted to shake him and cause the turban to fall from his head, but he restrained himself. Atallah had raised him from infancy and had served as his guardian and teacher or *Ustadh*. Ruggiero used the title *Ustadh* before Atallah's name as a sign of respect for the mystic. Atallah was the closest thing to family Ruggiero had ever known. Now he chafed at his guardian's over-protectiveness.

"You would rather I live the life of a coward and be unloved," said Ruggiero, "than allow me to face my destiny and experience love before I die."

"You can love another," said Atallah. "There are many beautiful women in the world. Do none of the women I have provided please your eye?"

"I love Bradamante. All other women pale in comparison. She is not only beautiful, but brave and courteous. No other woman will ever capture my heart."

Atallah crossed the room and stroked his long white beard as he gazed down at the banquet main floor. "Tell me what color hair you prefer. I shall try again tonight to find another beauty for you, one that is more to your liking."

"Did you not understand me?" Ruggiero demanded. "I want no one but Bradamante. Swear to me that you will not cast a spell to remove her from my heart or mind."

Atallah looked wounded. "Ruggiero, I am hurt that you think I would cast a spell on you."

"Then you should have no problem swearing you will not do that to me or to Bradamante. Swear it!"

Atallah hung his head and said softly, "I swear I shall not cast direct spells on either you or Bradamante."

Ruggiero gave a sigh of relief and then changed tack. *"Ustadh* Atallah, I do not trust fortune telling, but if I should perish after loving her then my life will have had some purpose. I almost died due to Bardulasto's treachery at the tournament on Mount Carena. If I had died that day, my life would have amounted to nothing."

"Had I not healed your wounds that day, you would have died," said Atallah. He gave Ruggiero a look filled with tenderness before shaking his head. "I am sorry, but you are not ready for the world of war."

"I ended Bardulasto's evil reign, just as Bradamante ended the life of his cousin, the vile Barigano. She acted boldly and swiftly on my behalf when he attacked me from behind."

"She did. I saved your life that day as well. Did you not wonder how you survived duels with both Orlando and Renaud? Without my magic intervening on your behalf, you would have been just one more Muslim knight felled by their mighty swords."

"I do not believe you."

"It is true, my child. After saving your life twice that day, I knew you were not ready for war. I left your side after those two warriors quit the field. I created this castle to keep you safe and secure. I realized it had been unfair of me keeping you isolated for so long on Mount Carena, so this time you have company. You have beautiful women for your amusement and brave knights with whom to practice jousting and sword play. Come, stop your sulking. You have yet to try your skills against the mighty Gradasso."

"I have no heart for mindless games," said Ruggiero.

Atallah stroked the curls on Ruggiero's head. "I cannot bear to see you die, therefore I must keep you here under my protection."

"Meanwhile, my heart is broken and my love is in danger. For the hundredth time, I beg of you to use your magic to see where she is and tell me if she is safe."

"I will not. You must forget about her."

"Tell me *Ustadh,* were you ever in love?" asked Ruggiero.

Atallah looked at him coldly.

"Forget about her," he repeated as he left the room.

CHAPTER 17

Pinabel's wicked laugh echoed through the cavern as he threw Bradamante's shield into the black hole. Looking up at the bright opening to the outside world, Bradamante silently berated herself. She had let down her guard and unwittingly trusted a Maganzan. That mistake meant her certain death. She heard Eos' whinny and neigh as the mare was led away by the traitor who clearly meant to leave no trace of her.

Bradamante stared vacantly at the opening as if waiting for some signal to tell her what to do. Tears trickled down her cheeks. Even if she was able to claw her way back to the top, she would still be without food, water, or a horse in the middle of a mountain wilderness far from the nearest town.

She said a silent prayer asking for God's forgiveness and for His guidance. As she opened her eyes, she noticed the opening to the cave had become smaller. At first she thought it was a trick of light, but as she stared the hole continued closing. The light became no larger than a pinhole, and then she was left in total darkness. Bradamante then realized she should be wracked with pain from her fall, but had no injuries whatsoever. Touching the ground beneath her, she felt a thick bed of soft loam rather than cold, hard rock.

An eerie otherworldly sound began emanating from deep within the recesses of the cave as an ethereal light emerged from the wall of the cavern. Bradamante sat up and squinted as the light intensified and the outline of an open door appeared. Curious, she stood and cautiously walked through the opening into a chamber with high ceilings. The room was enshrined with alabaster columns. A white marble altar gleamed with light from a single oil lamp. Bradamante walked toward the altar, removed her helmet and bowed as she knelt in fervent supplication before the Lord.

A barefoot, elderly woman entered from a neighboring passageway. She wore a long white robe without a belt. Her gray tresses were disheveled, but she appeared jubilant.

"Bradamante, I have been expecting you."

"Who are you and how do you know my name?"

"I am Melissa, an enchantress here to aid you in your quest. Fear not, dear child, the love you feel toward Ruggiero is because your souls are destined for one another."

Bradamante stared at the woman.

Melissa smiled. "Do not worry about the differences of your faith keeping you apart. Those things will fall away. There are forces however, which must be dealt with as they are attempting to alter your destiny. Should they prevail the world will suffer by never having known the future generations who would have been born of your union with Ruggiero."

Melissa took the bewildered Bradamante by the hand and led her into another chamber. In the center lay a tomb made of intricately carved stone bearing a glowing light from within. This had been the source of the sound she had heard. There was a low reverberation intoning an undeniable reverence. Bradamante saw mysterious words in an unfamiliar language carved on the crypt. On its lid was the image of an old wizened man.

"This is the tomb of Merlin," Melissa said. "He was betrayed in this very cavern years ago by the Lady of the Lake. His soul is trapped here and he will answer any question set before him. It was on your behalf that I came here to ask his advice. Merlin predicted you would come into his domain on this day. I have been waiting here patiently for your arrival."

Bradamante was confused. She wondered if she had struck her head when she fell and this was all a vivid dream. Then the casket ceased humming. She jumped as words came from within its depths.

"Blessed are you noble and chaste maiden, daughter of Aymon from the house of Lyon," intoned the deep voice of Merlin. "The two purest lines of royal Trojan blood shall combine in your womb and the pride of Italy shall be born. Future generations of emperors, dukes and princes shall spring forth. Italy will be restored to her former glory as in the golden days of yore, all due to the acts of valor from your progeny. You must not tarry, nor allow yourself to be deflected from a path that has been destined for you before your birth. You have the requisite courage and the strength to bring about liberty for Ruggiero the valiant."

The voice fell silent, and the humming sound resumed. Melissa walked over to a stone pedestal in a corner holding a pool of water. Touching a finger to its still surface, an image emerged. It was the face of a baby. Bradamante watched in wonder as she recognized Ruggiero's facial contours on the child and who bore eyes like her own. Their features had commingled and created a beautiful child. Tears filled Bradamante's eyes as her arms ached to hold the infant. The image changed and the face turned from a baby to a child and then into a handsome young man.

"That is the face of your future son you will name Ruggiero," Melissa said. "Such a son would make any parent proud. He is destined to help defeat another uprising by the Lombards, and for that he will be richly rewarded."

Melissa swirled her fingers and new faces emerged. The enchantress told a story of future generations who would come from Bradamante's son and the noble deeds they would perform. Bradamante heard Melissa speaking, but she could not concentrate on anything further than the face of the child she was destined to bear. She had never considered becoming a mother. Now she felt an overwhelming desire to nurture a child who was nothing more than an image in water.

Bradamante took a deep breath and looked directly at Melissa. "Tell me what I must do, and tell me why anyone would want to keep Ruggiero and me apart."

CHAPTER 18

"Atallah is your biggest obstacle," said Melissa. "He has served as Ruggiero's guardian since birth."

Melissa dipped her fingers in the water and a new image emerged, that of an elderly man with a long flowing beard and long white hair. "Atallah is determined to protect Ruggiero from the consequences of your marriage."

"I do not understand," said Bradamante.

"Ruggiero has two possible fates. Should he become a Christian and marry you, he is destined to be cut down in the prime of his life, just as his ancestors Hector and Astyanax, as well as his own father. Ruggiero shall never live to see the birth of his own son. He will be betrayed and killed by your family's enemies."

"The Maganzas," Bradamante whispered.

"Yes," said Melissa. "Their house is filled with hatred and bad blood, but nothing can be done to change the tragic loss of his life."

"You are telling me that should I marry Ruggiero he will die soon after?" Bradamante's eyes stung. "Perhaps it would be better for him to marry another, if he would live a longer life."

"That is what Atallah is hoping for. However, Ruggiero would still die young at the hands of another, but he will only beget a child with you. Without you, this noble bloodline will end with his untimely death."

Melissa dipped her fingers in the water again and the image changed back to the face of the young child. "Your son Ruggiero will avenge his father's murder, but you must not dwell on that unpleasantness. Right now, you must set your mind upon the task of securing your future husband's freedom."

Bradamante remembered hearing Ruggiero's family history and the sacrifices made by the mothers of Astyanax and Polidoro. Her throat tightened as she thought of Ruggiero's own mother. Each woman suffered to secure the safety of a child. She realized that she was being asked to demonstrate the same strength and courage.

"You will see your son grow tall and live up to the honored name of his father," Melissa promised.

"You said he had two possible fates. What is the other?"

"Should Ruggiero remain a Saracen, he shall bring about the defeat of Charlemagne and the fall of the Frankish Empire."

Bradamante could not breathe. If she tried denying her own heart in the hope that Ruggiero would live a longer life, it would devastate Christendom and likely mean the execution of her own family, possibly herself as well. She gripped the edge of the pool's pedestal. Tears fell onto the water, their ripples destroyed the image of her son's face. There was only one choice she could make.

Wiping the tears from her cheeks, she said with a steady voice, "Tell me what I must do."

Melissa's fingers swirled the water again and a shining castle appeared.

"Pinabel spoke the truth when he told you Ruggiero is being held nearby in a castle made of magic. Once Pinabel learned your identity he thought only to kill you. Had he not brought you here to me, you would have failed in your rescue attempt. You would not have the tools necessary to earn Ruggiero's freedom. The castle walls cannot be scaled, nor can you hope to gain admittance through ordinary means. You must first obtain a ring that protects its wearer from all enchantments. Only then can you face this wizard on your own terms."

"How can I obtain this ring?" she asked.

A new face emerged from the pool of a dark and ugly man.

"The ring is worn by a thief known as Brunello," said Melissa. "He is now Governor of Tingitana. Akramont sent him to the kingdom of Cathay to steal the ring from a woman named Angelica. It was the only way Akramont found the otherwise invisible castle that had held Ruggiero in the mountains of Tunisia. The amir heard a prophecy that his victory over the Franks depended upon the valorous deeds of Ruggiero, and he postponed his invasion until he found the youth and made him his knight."

"Does Akramont know of my part in the prophecy?" asked Bradamante.

Melissa shook her head and the face in the water changed to a handsome, dark-haired young man.

"That is Amir Akramont," said Melissa. "He heard only one part of the prophecy, because the old governor of Garamanta was not as skilled in divination as I am. He could only see the impact for the Saracen army if Ruggiero was in the war, but nothing else. Atallah tried warning Akramont of Ruggiero's possible fate of becoming a Christian, but the amir would not listen. He does not know of your part in the prophecy."

The image changed to a tournament of knights in a mêlée. Bradamante recognized Ruggiero among the men. He was surrounded by knights, but Ruggiero stood out from the rest with the moves of a victor.

"Once Akramont had the magic ring, the invisible castle on Mount Carena was revealed to him. A tournament was held underneath, luring Ruggiero out of his protective confines. Brunello was the first person to see Ruggiero. He gave the youth a sword, armor and a horse so that he could enter the tournament. Ruggiero distinguished himself on the field. Then one knight who was unwilling to lose, used lethal rather than tournament strokes of his sword."

Bradamante was horrified as she watched a man stab Ruggiero's side. Blood coursed from the wound as the phantom image turned in anger. With a fierce two-handed stroke of his sword, Ruggiero split the villain in two.

"Atallah healed his wounds, and Akramont was infuriated to learn there was a death in his tournament. Once all the circumstances were revealed he forgave Ruggiero. The amir knighted him and proclaimed him tournament champion. The next day Akramont's army set sail for Francia." The watery image changed back to Brunello's ugly face.

"I will lead you to the inn where this dwarf is staying," said Melissa. "You will let it be known you want to challenge the evil residing inside the enchanted fortress. Beware of Brunello, for he is untrustworthy. Do not let him learn anything about you. Not your name, nor your sex. Keep your identity as well guarded as your purse. He is bound to Akramont and fears returning to his commander's service without Ruggiero. Brunello will lead you to the castle, but you must take heed and plan carefully. By force you must deprive that thief of his life and steal the ring."

"You want me to kill him?" asked Bradamante.

"Do not feel compassion toward this man, nor lose your strength of purpose," assured Melissa. "If he senses your intent, he shall place the ring in his mouth and its powers will allow him to disappear. Should that happen, all will be lost. Dispatch the knave, wear the ring and then use this horn to call out the necromancer." Melissa handed Bradamante an ivory horn carved with images of warriors in battle. "When you blow upon this horn, your enemies will know fear and it will serve to strengthen your purpose and resolve. Atallah will stop all that he is doing and respond to your challenge without delay."

"How will the ring guarantee my victory?"

"Atallah has a shield with magical powers. He keeps it covered with a veil until he wishes the fight to be over. Once revealed, every living thing that looks into its reflective rays falls into a deep sleep. The ring will spare you, but do not allow the wizard to realize you are not under his power. You must treat him as you did with Martisino that night in Toulouse. Entrap him and then kill him. Be strong my dear. All has been foretold and should you hesitate at any point, you will surely regret it."

Bradamante had killed many men before, but always in battle. Never had she plotted to commit murder.

CHAPTER 19

Melissa led Bradamante away from Merlin's tomb. The enchantress picked up a long narrow stick. As she touched its tip, a light illuminated their surroundings. She navigated their way through a maze of narrow passageways so quickly that it would have been impossible for Bradamante to retrace her steps to find the hidden chapel. Melissa continued forward until they emerged upon the banks of a subterranean river where a small boat awaited them. After they climbed into the vessel, Melissa raised her branch into the air as an unnatural breeze suddenly propelled them forward.

Bradamante marveled at the shadows cast by the light onto the strange rock formations in the underground cave. A few times the women were forced to lower their heads to their knees to clear the low passages of the cave. While riding in silence, she reflected on the mission that lay before her. It was difficult for her to believe that her life had been preordained before birth. However, she could not deny the powerful reaction she felt upon meeting Ruggiero, nor the enduring passion the mere thought of him stirred in her heart. That feeling was enough to convince her they were destined for one another, and that she had a leading role in this cosmic play.

Finally the boat came to a stop. Melissa stepped out and gestured for Bradamante to follow. They clambered upon the rocky banks and made their way to a smooth boulder. The enchantress closed her eyes and made a small upward motion with one hand. The rock slowly grew and lifted the two women skyward to a small opening to the outside. As she breathed in the cool air, Bradamante was surprised to find that the sun had already set. A crescent moon cast its silvery rays upon the rocky ground as she walked toward an inn.

"Brunello will be awake even at this late hour," said Melissa. "He has become despondent because he does not know how to rescue Ruggiero. The fruit of the vine is Brunello's only solace. Alcohol is prohibited by his religion, but he does not care because he has no faith or beliefs. His religious acts are based upon convenience rather than conviction. He says and does whatever he thinks will please those in his presence."

Bradamante thanked Melissa and walked alone through the narrow streets. The large castle perched on a massive rock cast its long shadow over the town. Once again she felt an oppressive sense of gloom hanging in the air. Opening the door to the inn, all talk ceased as the tavern full of men turned their eyes upon her. Undaunted, she strode toward the innkeeper and announced she wanted a meal and accommodations for the night.

"Traveling alone?" he asked.

"Yes," she replied. "I am hungry and tired. I do not wish for conversation."

"Let me call my son to secure your horse in my stable," he said.

"Not necessary. I have no steed at this time."

The innkeeper stared at her as the buzz of conversation from his patrons started up again. She heard the words "stranger," "madness," "without a horse," and "dangerous" bandied about. The innkeeper set a bowl of stew, some brown bread and a cup of wine before Bradamante. She ate her meal in silence, waiting for Brunello to appear.

Soon a small dark man emerged from the crowd. He stumbled as he grabbed the chair next to Bradamante.

"I heard you say you came here without a horse," Brunello said. "How can that be? This is far from any other town, too far to walk."

Bradamante recoiled from Brunello's stench of dirt, sweat and alcohol. She glanced at his hands and saw fat, stubby fingers, with dirty fingernails and a single gold band.

"I came here on horseback, but it was stolen from me," she said fixing him with a piercing gaze. "The villain will pay for his treachery."

Brunello gave a faltering smile. "Why are you here?"

"I came to vanquish the plague of the Ariège."

He spilled his wine at the pronouncement as others crowded around her.

"The curse?" an old man interjected. "You are going to challenge the curse?"

"A madman has attacked villages throughout this land," said another. "No one has stopped him."

"Has anyone tried?" she asked.

"The Count of Foix and a few of his soldiers tried, but they were taken prisoner as well," said the old man.

"Why are you not in your homes tonight?" she asked. "I have traveled many miles and this is the first time I have seen a crowd of men."

"Night is the only safe time from this monster," said the innkeeper. "These men have lost women in their family and seek comfort from one another and from my wine. You came here to help us?"

Expectation filled the eyes of the men surrounding her.

"God willing, I shall lift this curse on the morrow," she said. "All I lack is a guide to direct me to the source of the evil."

"Brunello can show you the way," said the innkeeper. "He saw some of the first people taken."

The dwarf nodded and gave her a toothy grin.

"You witnessed abductions?" she asked. "Why were you not taken as well?"

The room exploded in laughter.

"*This* villain has taste. He takes only brave knights and beautiful women. Who would want an ugly, broken down dwarf?"

Brunello, unfazed by the ridicule, leaned forward to Bradamante. "I have seen the castle where they are being kept. I will lead you there."

"We leave in the morning," she said.

"What is the name of the baron bold who would embark on such a quest?" asked the innkeeper.

"I come not for fame or personal glory, only to conquer evil. May the morrow bring the liberation of all the captives and may *their* names and stories be on everyone's lips. I shall let my accomplishment speak for itself or my name will die with my failure."

Admiration adorned the faces of the men in the room, and with it came the promise of hope.

CHAPTER 20

The sleeping quarters at the inn were eight beds in a row in the rafters above the tavern. Bradamante slept closest to the window giving her several empty beds between herself and Brunello who was the only other lodger.

A nightingale serenaded Bradamante throughout the night. The melody was a welcome diversion from Brunello's deep throated snoring. As Bradamante listened to the warbling, she was reminded that animals were not bothered by things that vex Mankind. The idea of wars, invasions, and service to one's sovereign were all concepts which meant nothing to God's lesser creatures. Animals would continue to live their lives as they had from the time of Creation, and would do so whether or not Charlemagne was victorious in this current war. No, this little bird simply sang his songs and mocked those who worried about things beyond their control.

Bradamante discarded her fear of Ruggiero's prophesied untimely death for she hoped that if she could save him now, she could save him in the future. After finally drifting off to sleep, she dreamt of a life with Ruggiero.

In the morning she woke with a new determination and confidence. She was a warrior and had never shied away from confrontation on the battlefield. By day's end she would encounter a new type of opponent, one who used magic and guile as weapons. Bradamante was aware of Atallah's scheme, and she trusted that the magic ring would nullify the wizard's tricks. Her duel would then become a matter of prowess and skill. She harbored no doubts that in a fair fight, she would emerge the victor.

Bradamante bent over and put her arms and head through the hauberk. As she stood, the metal armor slid into place. After strapping the dagger and sword to her belt, she turned to Brunello who was fast asleep. A line of drool hung from his open mouth and his right hand dangled over the side of the bed. It would be easy to slip the ring off the drunken man's finger, but she would then be without a guide to Atallah's castle.

Leaving the little man to sleep off the effects of the night before, she went downstairs and found the innkeeper. "As I said last night, I came to vanquish the plague of the Ariège, but my horse was stolen yesterday. I cannot accomplish my task without a horse. Do you have one that I might purchase?"

The man wiped his hand over his face and nodded. "Follow me."

He led her to a stall in the stables where a dappled gray gelding stood. "He has a fine temperament, not too willful."

Bradamante ran her hands along the horse's side. She felt the musculature over his bones. The horse appeared to have good strength and not undernourished.

"You are willing to risk your life for others," said the innkeeper. "People you do not know. It is more likely you will be taken hostage than it is that you will succeed."

"I am willing to take that chance." She lifted the hooves and examined them for rot or signs of disease. The eyes were clear, no signs of cloudiness. "This horse will work. I can offer you one solidus."

The man snorted. "This is not a cow. Three solidii is the going rate."

Bradamante knew he was right, but her purse did not contain enough to cover that cost. "He is a gelding, not a stallion. One solidus and six denarii."

"Not enough," said the innkeeper. "Perhaps someone else in town will sell you a horse."

She pulled at the chain around her neck and brought forth the eagle pendant. "I cannot tarry looking for a steed. Reluctantly, I offer this heirloom in place of two additional solidii."

The man's face turned red. "That is too precious." He turned his back to her and brushed the horse. "Every man in the tavern last night knows someone who was taken by that monster."

"Every man? Does that include you as well?" asked Bradamante.

The innkeeper nodded. "My daughter. I have had no rest since she was taken. Everyday I hear of new abductions, but nothing to give me hope of her return. Not until you showed up." He pulled burrs from the horse's mane. "It is not the money for the horse that I care about. It is Marie. She loved this horse," his voice cracked. "If I lose it as well…"

"I will do my best to rescue her."

He saddled the horse. "Bring Marie back to me and the horse is yours to keep. I will return your money as a reward. She named him Nikephoros. It means to bear victory. May he live up to his name."

"Should I be taken hostage, I will have no need for money." Bradamante handed him her purse. "Please hold this for me until my return. I shall also need some rope."

Once her business was concluded, she returned with the innkeeper to the tavern where she encountered Brunello. He held his head up with one hand, while drinking porridge from a bowl.

"Morning Brunello!" barked the innkeeper.

The thief winced at the greeting, before he turned his bloodshot eyes upon Bradamante. "This is the day. We shall make history together."

Bradamante said nothing. Instead, she closed her eyes and turned all her thoughts toward her upcoming fight with Atallah for it promised to be the most important duel of her life.

CHAPTER 21

Bradamante and Brunello left the town of Foix while there was still a dense layer of fog. It had rolled in late the night before and appeared to be the kind which refused to burn off until midday. She was grateful not only that it was cooler than riding under a blazing sun, but it also provided a level of secrecy to her mission.

"How did you hear about the curse of the Ariège?" asked Brunello. "And why risk your life on behalf of strangers?"

Bradamante kept her face impassive. She did not want to carry on a conversation with him, and thought it best to not respond to his attempts at idle chatter.

"Where did you say you were from?" Brunello asked a short while later.

He was greeted again with silence and soon stopped trying to enliven their journey.

They rode throughout the morning southward up steep and narrow mountain paths. As they reached the summit and rode over its crest, Brunello pointed toward a shimmering castle in the valley floor below. It appeared to be floating on a cloud as a layer of fog stubbornly clung to its base. Since there was no path leading to the castle, they would have to blaze their own trail over rocky terrain to get near it.

Brunello bounced in his saddle upon seeing the fortress. "Once you get near it and look at a certain angle, you can see inside. You can see people eating at banquet and the knights jousting. You can even watch them bathing and coupling."

Bradamante did not react, even though she was filled with disgust. Most men would share his interest in voyeurism, so she could not afford to show any outward reaction lest Brunello start to have suspicions about her.

"I wonder how many wish to be free of such arduous captivity," he said with a lecherous grin.

She surveyed the emerald green hillside populated with trees growing out of the side of gray rock. Urging her horse near a clump of pine trees, she dismounted.

"What is this?" she exclaimed loudly. "Could *this* be the source of the enchantment?"

Brunello rode over to Bradamante. She hid the rope behind her back. Creeping around a large rock she cried "Ha!" in a loud voice.

Brunello leapt from his horse onto the ground. Bradamante jumped him and bound his arms to his sides. She tied the dwarf to the trunk of a large pine tree.

"Release me, I beg of you," said Brunello.

Bradamante ignored his pleas. Turning her attention to his hands, she removed his ring before slipping it on one of her own fingers.

"I am showing mercy by not killing you," she said. "I see no reason to stain the ground with your blood. But I will leave you where you cannot harm me."

"Why are you doing this to me?" asked Brunello with tears in his eyes.

"Your reputation as a thief and a liar precedes you. You would betray me at the first opportunity. I am preventing that from happening."

Brunello struggled to free himself, but was unable to do so. His cries turned to whimpers as Bradamante tied both horses to nearby trees. Removing the magic ring from her finger, she examined it closely. It was made of fine gold and had markings of a foreign language she was unfamiliar with on its exterior. She wiped it clean on her doublet before placing it in her mouth. She looked down and could not see her body. Bradamante was invisible, just as Melissa had promised. This filled her with a sense of invulnerability.

Bradamante walked down the hill to get a better view of the castle. Its base was perched on glassy but jagged black rock, making it impossible to scale. The castle itself was at least forty feet in the air, too tall for any ladder. Not that she had time or tools to build a ladder. True to Brunello's word, there was an angle at which the occupants could be clearly seen. The men and women walked about in courtyards filled with flowering trees, reminding her of the royal court in Aachen. They did not appear to be mistreated prisoners.

Knights jousted in tournament play while well-dressed ladies sat in risers watching the spectacle. Bradamante searched in vain to find Ruggiero among those competing. On another floor, a couple was engaging in lewd acts. Bradamante blushed and quickly averted her eyes. It was then she discovered Ruggiero. He was sitting alone in a room and wore a simple white tunic and breeches. She was startled when he looked up and seemed to stare directly at her. She glanced down to reassure herself that she was still invisible. The haunting words of Alard's song came back to her:

Through the mists I see you
In your bright crystal palace...beckoning me
I come closer and am in awe

Of its beauty
Of its beauty
Of its sheer beauty

Bradamante shook her head. She could not wait any longer. The morning fog had finally burned away and there was not a cloud in the bright blue sky. Walking back to her new gray horse, she untied and mounted him. She took the ring from her mouth, placed it on her left hand and grasped her shield. As she rode down to a plateau, she blew her horn loudly, announcing her challenge.

CHAPTER 22

Bradamante waited patiently, but nothing seemed to happen. She counted to ten and blew her horn again. By the third blast shadowy forms gathered within the castle around the windows. Movement on the rooftop caught her eye. She raised her shield and drew her sword as a winged beast took to the sky.

She marveled at the fantastic beast flying through the air bearing the wizard Atallah. Bradamante had assumed from the stories told at the inn that Atallah rode on the back of a flying horse similar to Pegasus. She never dreamt it would be a creature with the head, wings, and forelegs of an eagle atop the body of a horse. The animal was yellow, but its beak, talons and wings bore a visage of pure gold.

Bradamante raised her sword high into the air; its blade reflected a beam of sunlight. Atallah winced and turned his head, having been temporarily blinded. Clutching her shield with her left hand, she said a silent prayer. As the wizard flew closer, she realized his left hand clutched a shield covered by a red silken drape, while his right hand held no weapons, but instead an open book. She knew that only the magic ring she wore afforded her to see things as they truly were.

As Atallah swooped downward he threw a spear at her. Bradamante urged her horse to jump sideways avoiding the projectile. The wizard threw spear after spear and she repeatedly dodged the attacks. The spent weapons stood upright in the ground and a pattern quickly emerged; he was surrounding her in a cage of spears. She leaned downward, yanked one from the ground, and hurled it into the air narrowly missing him.

"Coward!" she yelled. "Come fight me on a horse. My steed is bound to this earth, while yours takes to the sky. That is an unfair match. Only cowards who know they cannot win in a fair fight resort to such deplorable tactics."

Atallah's face grew red.

"Are you going to stay aloft? Or are you going to fight me on equal terms?" shouted Bradamante.

Atallah hurled another spear, but she stood her ground using her shield and deflected the weapon with a backhanded swing. Her arm exploded with pain, but her rage would not allow her to stop the fight. She dismounted and challenged Atallah from the ground.

"My horse is no match for your flying beast; therefore, I renounce it entirely. Meet me on the ground if you dare test your skills against mine."

She wrenched the spears loose, stacking them in a pile while never taking her eye off her foe. The wizard tucked his magic book under his hauberk and unsheathed his sword. Flying downward he delivered a fierce blow against Bradamante. Their swords clashed in midair. Her arm stung from the impact. Atallah had the motions of a skillful warrior, but lacked the strength to execute his strokes with any power. His animal flew high into the air. Bradamante watched him massage his arm and catch his breath. The look on his face changed to one of determination as he fingered the red veil. The beast swooped downward again as Atallah removed the cover from his shield.

Bradamante fell to the ground and feigned unconsciousness when she saw the light reflected off the mirror like shield. She heard Atallah dismount and walk to her side. She bided her time as she had with Martisino. The wizard bent down and barely touched her when Bradamante sprang forward and knocked him to the ground. She grabbed the chain that had been intended for her and wrapped it around him, pinning his arms to his side.

She was surprised in the act of subduing him at how frail he was. His bones felt brittle and he had little musculature left. Her fury was soon replaced with pity as she looked into the eyes of a broken old man. From the deeply etched lines in his face, she guessed he must be at least seventy years of age.

"Kill me," said Atallah, "for my life is no longer worth living. You were right to chastise me, for I did not fight fairly."

"Release your prisoners," Bradamante commanded, "and I may show mercy and spare your life."

"I do not deserve mercy, only scorn. I will grant the freedom of all those in the castle, bar one," said Atallah, as tears trickled down his cheeks. "There is one I cannot release, for his protection is my sole purpose in life. Nowhere is there a finer youth than the brave Ruggiero whom I raised from birth. I have divined that without interference he would become a Christian and murdered in the prime of his life. I cannot allow that to happen."

Bradamante was conflicted. Melissa had instructed her to kill Atallah because he might pose further threats, but she could not bring herself to commit such an unholy act. Ruggiero valued loyalty and he might never forgive her if she murdered his mentor.

"You have kept Ruggiero prisoner. Why will you not allow him to live his own life?" she challenged.

"Lords and ladies keep him company. He wants for nothing."

"Except liberty," spat Bradamante. "You deny him his destiny. Instead you keep him locked up inside a den of iniquity."

"Take my shield and my hippogriff, and I will release the others, but leave me Ruggiero."

"Your mount and your shield are mine by right of conquest. They are not yours as a means to bargain." Bradamante forced the wizard to his feet. "You will set your captives free."

Atallah groaned with pain as he walked forward tightly bound by the chain Bradamante held. He led her to a rocky crag and struggled with the chain to lift his fingertips to a round stone. Steps magically appeared spiraling upward. They climbed the stairs until they were beneath the base of the castle.

"Only I can break this spell," said Atallah. "The *jinn* who I have enslaved would likely kill or possess you should you be the one to lift the enchantments. Then the people inside the castle would fall to their deaths."

Bradamante felt dizzy as she looked down at the valley floor below. Reluctantly, she loosened the chain about the wizard. Atallah lifted the heavy stone threshold revealing urns emanating smoke. He smashed the urns along with the tablet. The castle walls melted away and the people who had been held inside suddenly appeared standing on the valley floor.

Suddenly Bradamante realized that she was alone on the spiral steps. She searched frantically for Atallah. Scanning the area she saw a multitude of men and women wandering about the hillside, but not the elderly wizard.

Her anger was displaced when she saw Ruggiero riding toward her on the back of Frontino. She descended the steps taking care not to fall. He had removed his helmet and was standing at the bottom waiting for her. As she drew near him, Bradamante felt nervous for the first time that day. She gave a shaky smile while removing her own helmet. Ruggiero took their helmets and gauntlets, and placed them on the ground.

"Your hair is...shorn," he said.

"Because of my head wound," she said, casting her eyes to the side.

He stood directly in front of her, and touched the nape of her neck. "There is no trace of it."

"It has healed," she said feeling her cheeks burn.

Her heart pounded in her ears as she felt his warm breath upon her face.

"I feared for your safety," he said, as his hands moved to cup her face and caress her cheeks.

"I am fine," she said, still avoiding his gaze.

"You rescued me."

"I rescued my heart for it was locked up with you," she said and forced herself to look him directly in the eye.

Ruggiero leaned forward and kissed her. A shock went through her body as their lips touched. Their arms encircled each other, and Bradamante felt an overwhelming desire to find a quiet place where they could spend the rest of their day together without a word being spoken.

A loud screeching noise caused them to turn, as Atallah's magical steed reared on its hind legs and nearly crashed into them. Bradamante raised her arms in self-defense and the beast flew a short distance away. She followed, intent on claiming the creature, but it flew away again as she came near. Other knights, including Gradasso, whom Bradamante recognized from his invasion of Hispania the year before, joined in the chase to subdue it. Gradasso nearly captured the animal, but its talons sliced through the air and he faltered. After several attempts, Ruggiero finally seized the rope around the creature's neck and mounted it.

He smiled and waved at Bradamante. "I captured the steed for you."

As she walked over to claim her prize, the strange bird-horse creature flapped its powerful wings and took off in flight with Ruggiero still in its saddle. Ruggiero called out in vain to Bradamante. She stared in horror as her beloved flew off in the sky on the back of the magical beast and disappeared from view.

CHAPTER 23

Bradamante's heart was pierced as surely as if one of Atallah's spears had punctured her chest. The farther the beast rose into the sky, the more the phantom blade twisted. She thought of how the Greek hero Bellerophon had been thrown from the back of Pegasus when he had flown too near Mount Olympus, and she worried a similar fate might befall Ruggiero. It was her fault for not guarding Atallah properly. Whatever hesitation she had felt about following Melissa's orders to end the old man's wretched life was now gone. Bradamante glimpsed the wizard as he galloped over the top of the mountain on a black horse whose hooves appeared as if they were made of smoke. Pursuit would be futile, and her hands shook with anger.

Feeling a gentle nudge at her back, she turned to see Frontino. She threw her arms around the horse's neck, drawing strength from him. Ruggiero valued Frontino, and by caring for his prized destrier she would maintain a connection to the brave knight.

Bradamante turned and faced the crowd of people. A dozen knights were mounted upon various steeds while scores of women stumbled about looking confused. A few knights allowed women to ride upon their horses, while others appeared oblivious to any needs but their own.

Climbing on Frontino's back, Bradamante raised her horn and blew a fierce blast that drew everyone's attention to her. "How many knights here are sworn to Charlemagne?"

All the men save Gradasso and two others raised their hands.

"You now are under my command," she announced. "Muslims are free to choose your destiny. You may return to your home country or leave to join Akramont. Follow your conscience, for your way shall not be blocked. This was a rescue mission, and this hillside is not a battlefield. We will not make war with you today."

Gradasso paused from releasing Brunello and looked respectfully at her. "As for the Christian knights, our first duty is to assure the ladies are returned safely to their homes. Two knights will ride ahead to the town of Foix, and bring back wagons for transport. The roads will not accommodate wagons to come the entire way, but bring them as far as you can. No one should have to walk the entire journey. The innkeeper will send messengers to surrounding towns to alert them the prisoners have been released. On the morrow we shall depart on a mission for Charlemagne."

Knowing that Gradasso and the enemy knights were still nearby, she decided against giving any details of her destination. Her silence on the matter might lead them to think she was bound for Paris rather than Marseille.

The Christian knights nodded their assent.

"Tell us your name, so that we may know our liberator and commander," one asked.

The time had come to announce her identity. The faces of the Christian soldiers were unfamiliar, that was a troubling thought. They might not recognize her name, but they would certainly recognize her famous male relatives and understand the implied threat if anything less than deference and respect was shown to her.

"I am Bradamante, sister to Count Renaud of Montauban, daughter of Duke Aymon of Dordogne, and niece to Emperor Charlemagne."

The men kneeled and bowed their heads with their swords before them. The sight gratified her. Her command would not be questioned.

In the distance, Gradasso's knife finally cut through the rope binding Brunello. "You were bested by the Maid," he laughed. "She had better sense than the rest of us by dispatching you when she did. Otherwise we would all still be prisoners."

Brunello grumbled as he mounted his horse. "We should leave for Frédélas now."

The four foreign soldiers left in advance of the Christians. Bradamante rode toward a girl with plaited hair pinned on the top of her head. She was stroking the nose of the dappled gray charger.

"He looks like my father's horse," she said, tears welled in her eyes.

"Are you Marie of Foix?" Bradamante asked.

"Yes."

"Your father will be overjoyed at your return. Please, the horse is yours to ride."

The girl nodded as she mounted Nikephoros, while Bradamante led the procession over the mountain.

That night the tavern was a raucous place, but Bradamante was in no mood to join in the revelry. She ate her supper, graciously accepted the expressions of gratitude from the townspeople as well as their gifts, including the gray horse from the innkeeper. As soon as she deemed it polite, she left the crowd in search of solitude in the sleeping quarters. Once again, she claimed the bed nearest the window. She entered a fitful sleep as various images haunted her dreams. Melissa's disappointed face melted into Atallah's mocking leer and was finally replaced by Ruggiero's terror stricken grimace. Bradamante woke to an overcast sky, and a pillow drenched with tears.

Part III

Alcina's Island

CHAPTER 24

Ruggiero clung to the back of the hippogriff as they flew eastward at breakneck speed. He closed his eyes as the wind slapped his face. They flew throughout the day, into the night, and into the next day. The beast finally slowed as it came upon a verdant island. The creature circled over a gleaming three-story white marble palace surrounded by lush hanging gardens bursting with flowers and fruit trees. They landed in a meadow beyond the palace grounds. Ruggiero dismounted while holding tightly upon the reins. He feared the winged charger might fly off, stranding him on the island.

His legs wobbled as he tied the rope around its neck securely to a nearby myrtle tree. Once he felt steady, he left in search of water to slake his incredible thirst. He had only taken a few steps when the hippogriff uttered an ear-splitting screech and reared upon its hind legs. Its talons repeatedly tore at the myrtle until only a trunk was left standing. Ruggiero was shocked when a piercing wail emanated from the tree.

"Stop hurting me," the tree said in Frankish.

"Can I help you?" asked Ruggiero, feeling foolish talking to a stump and fearing he was hallucinating.

"I beg of you, kind sir, remove this creature from my side. I am in enough misery having been turned into a tree, without a beast attacking me."

Ruggiero rubbed his eyes, wondering if the oppressive heat along with his tremendous hunger and thirst were playing tricks on his mind. Nevertheless, he untied the hippogriff and held the rope.

"Forgive me for the acts of this animal," said Ruggiero. "Pray tell me who you are, and how your spirit became locked inside a tree."

"I am ashamed to reveal my name, for I have disgraced my family. However, many others also succumbed to the wiles of the fay Alcina. Look around you, every rock, every tree, and every statue was once a bold and brave knight. She captures men, seduces them with her charms. Later when she tires of them, they are transformed into ornaments. I warn you, so you may avoid this same fate."

Ruggiero had a hard time believing that the beauteous palace he had passed in the air was evil and that the trees surrounding him at every turn were men in enchanted form. He shook his head, and decided that he was hallucinating.

"You asked my name, and I shall answer. I am Aistulf, once a paladin to Charlemagne. I grew up in the royal court jousting with my cousin Renaud. Just last year I earned the emperor's admiration by ridding the Frankish Empire from the scourge of Gradasso. Now I am reduced to this shameful existence."

Ruggiero remembered Mandricardo taunting Gradasso over losing a joust in Paris. Here could be the man who not only humbled that mighty king, but was also a kinsman of Renaud and Bradamante. That is if the tree were truly talking and not just a product of his exhausted mind.

"Please tell me how you bested the king of Sericana," said Ruggiero, as he sat down near the stump.

"Gradasso terrorized Hispania before conquering Paris. He took Charlemagne hostage, but all Gradasso wanted was Renaud's horse Bayard and Orlando's sword Durindana. The emperor agreed to Gradasso's demands and commanded Bayard be surrendered. However, I was guarding the steed in my cousin's absence, and I knew Renaud would never relinquish his horse without a fight. Therefore, I issued a challenge on his behalf. Gradasso and Charlemagne were furious with me for not complying with the command, but my terms were met."

"How did you win?"

"We jousted and with one pass Gradasso was flat on his back. He was humiliated and left Paris immediately. Once the enemy was gone, there were celebrations," said the tree-man with a hint of happiness. "That was my finest hour. Banquets were held in my honor. I then left on a mission to find and bring my lost kinsmen back to Francia. There had been rumors Renaud had gone eastward and joined Orlando. I traveled for several months until I found him and returned Bayard. Alas, it was shortly after that when we came near these shores and Alcina spied us. She captured me by magic, and I was deceived by her guile. Once I was in her arms I lost all sense and willingly became her servant."

"What did she do to you?" asked Ruggiero.

"She is a beautiful sorceress. I became her lover and experienced many joys in her bed. Alcina was not my first lover, but there are none who can compare to her in that arena. That is, until her desire for variety wins out and she yearns for another's touch. She turns her old lovers into silent souvenirs of her evil deeds. It is only because your steed ripped apart my trunk that I am able to warn you. I beg of you to avoid her at all costs. You should fly away now, before she knows you are here."

Ruggiero shook his head. "Alas, I do not know how to control this beast and am wary of climbing on his back again. Tell me, is there no one who could break her spells and release you?"

"There is another sorceress named Logistilla who opposes Alcina. She lives on the other side of this island, but the road to her palace goes through a small isthmus guarded by Alcina's grotesque army. To get there, you must follow the path through the forest. You might also try commandeering a boat from the marina, but those are also heavily guarded. Should you make it to Logistilla's domain, you will be safe."

"Thank you for your warning, Aistulf," said Ruggiero. "I shall remember your words and endeavor to release you. You come from a noble family, and they deserve your return."

The tree stump gave a small sigh as Ruggiero led the hippogriff onto the road leading to the forest. He had not walked far when he came upon a golden fountain with sparkling water. His lips were parched and his throat on fire. He was in sore need of food and rest, but above all he needed water. The hippogriff dipped its beak into the fountain and began drinking. A goblet sat perched nearby, as though waiting for him. He filled it with cool water, drank his fill and splashed some on his face. While relaxing, he noticed a sign engraved near the base of the fountain:

For the weary traveler
Drink and forget all your worries

He smiled as he read the inscription for he had no worries; in fact the water had not only quenched his thirst, but gave him a sense of serenity. Standing there holding the rope to the hippogriff, he vaguely wondered what he had been doing before he stopped for a drink.

"Hello, dear sir."

Turning, two beautiful young women approached him. They were attired in dresses of brightly colored orange, red, and yellow silk.

"You must be tired and hungry. Please come with us," said the first beauty. "Our lady offers her hospitality."

He smiled and nodded. He could think of no reason to turn down such a gracious offer.

"What is your lady's name?" he asked.
"Alcina," they said in unison.

CHAPTER 25

He passed through the gates into a vast courtyard of white marble and elaborate fountains. The extensive gardens surrounded a tall labyrinth made of trimmed hedges. Dozens of lifelike marble statues of handsome courtiers adorned every corner. Trees laden with tropical fruit were sprinkled throughout the garden, and a large pool beckoned with its promise of cool water. The two ladies brought him to a patio where a table was spread with food.

"Enjoy a repast after your long travels," said one of the women. "Once you are finished, we shall see to your other needs."

"Where is your lady?" he asked.

"You will meet her tonight, after you have rested."

Sitting down, he sampled food from the platters heaped with smoked fish, flat breads with honey for dipping and a wide variety of unfamiliar fruit. He used a knife to cut through a brown spiny peel and was rewarded with sweet, yellow flesh. He had not realized how famished he was until he started eating and devoured everything that had been set out.

Once finished, the two women took him inside the palace. The walls were made of the finest marble and the floors were covered with inlaid mosaic tiles patterned with intricate geometric designs. Paintings of beautiful men and women adorned the walls in golden frames. They brought him to a spacious room with a large sunken bath, and he was left alone to luxuriate in the warm scented water.

Later, when the two young women returned, he tried deciding which was the prettiest. One had curly black hair with skin the color of rich honey. The other had a mane of long straight black hair with dark brown skin. Both were petite with curvaceous figures and pleasing smiles. He decided after much consideration they were equally beautiful.

"We took your armor away," said the dark-skinned beauty as she handed him a towel, "You will not need it. We do not make war here."

He stood in front her and allowed the water to pour off his body before wrapping himself with the towel.

"What is your name?" he asked.

"I am Rangada, and this is Malha."

"Come over here," said Malha. "And we shall ease your aching limbs."

He climbed upon a padded table as both women massaged perfumed oil upon his body, gently removing the soreness from his back and limbs. Enjoying every moment of their attention, his mind drifted into scenes of pleasure involving the three of them. As the massage ended, he sat up and pulled the closest one to his bare chest and tried kissing her.

"No, dear sir," said Malha as she blocked him with her hands. "Our lady forbids us to do such things with her favored guests."

Rangada nodded. "We shall take you to your room where you shall rest. You will meet her tonight, and then you shall surely find all your needs satisfied."

Swinging his legs off the table, his towel dropped to the floor as he stood naked before them. Neither woman blushed, but they retained their distance from him. Reluctantly he dressed in the silken tunic and breeches set out for him and followed them upstairs. They showed him to a bedroom with a large four poster bed adorned with a golden silk canopy. Climbing under the silk covers of the feather bed, he immediately fell into a deep slumber.

It was night when the two young women woke him for supper. He wondered why they always came in pairs, but then he realized that if only one had come he might have pulled her into the bed, which would have violated Alcina's orders. He smiled at the thought and once again wondered what their mysterious lady looked like.

He was brought to a large dining hall decorated in red and gold. The long tables seated many pairs of beautiful women and handsome men who were deep in conversation with each other. Seated at the head of the table next to the white marble throne, he waited anxiously for Alcina to appear. Malha and Rangada had spoken of her beauty, but he could not imagine how any woman would outshine either of those two.

Voices stopped abruptly when Alcina entered the room. She seemed as if she were gliding across the floor. Her hair was the color of white gold and styled high upon her head with long tendrils framing her beautiful face. Her eyes were emerald green, her complexion as white as alabaster, and her full red lips showcased perfect pearl white teeth. The red silk gown clung to her womanly curves in a most flattering manner and a ruby necklace directed his attention to her ample cleavage.

"I trust my hospitality has been pleasing to you?" she asked, extending her hand for him to kiss.

"In every way."

"I have been waiting all day for this moment," she said, handing him a large tankard as they sat down.

He picked up the strange glass. "What is this made of?"

"The horn of a rhinoceros."

He lifted the vessel and drank, a warming sensation ran down his throat.

"Do you like it?" she asked.

"I think so, what is it?"

"My finest wine. Here taste this." A servant carving a roast pig brought over a small place with sliced meat. Her eyes gleamed as she watched him taste the pork and take another sip of wine. "Tell me your name, dear sir, and what brings you to my island."

He frowned. "I do not know what brought me here. All I remember is drinking from a fountain earlier today and being invited inside your palace." He shook his head in frustration. "I cannot even remember my own name."

She gave him a broad smile as her fingertips brushed the muscles on one of his arms. "You are welcome to stay here as long as you like and since you cannot remember your name, I shall call you Adonis."

Alcina popped an oyster into his mouth, as she nibbled on a vegetable spear. They ate their fill of dinner and later dessert – platters of fruit, figs and honey-dipped pastries.

She clapped her hands signaling the start of the entertainment. Musicians with drums and stringed instruments played a melody he found intensely erotic. A man and woman stepped forward and danced in the center of the room. As the music progressed the dancers removed layers of their clothing while touching each other intimately.

Alcina motioned to him to feed her dessert. He placed a sweet triangle shaped pastry on her tongue and she slowly licked the honey off each of his fingers. There was desire in her eyes. He moved forward to kiss her but was taken aback when she pushed him away.

"Not in front of the others," she said, with a half smile.

He was frustrated. Only a few couples remained in the room and no one was paying attention to them because everyone else was focused on their own dining companion. The woman dancer now wore only a thin layer of sheer silk billowing in the air. Her partner had stripped down to a loincloth and ground himself against her while his hands touched her bare bottom.

Alcina squeezed his inner thigh and breathed into his ear, "I shall see you later tonight."

He watched as she turned her back on him and left the table. He felt the urge to follow, but knew it would displease her. Walking back to his room, he heard moans of ecstasy coming from behind the numerous doors he passed. Once he entered his room, he was struck by the heady scent of jasmine filling the night air. He walked out onto his balcony and saw the dancers in the pool. They were naked and finishing the intimate dance they had begun indoors. He went back inside and paced the floor wondering why Alcina was keeping him waiting.

Just as he resolved to go searching for her, Alcina walked in through a secret passage. Her hair had been let down and the lustrous tresses extended past her waist. She now wore a gown made of sheer red silk revealing every nuance of her body. He rushed to her side, embracing and kissing her.

Alcina pushed him away gently. "Slow down my love, otherwise you will be finished before we even get started."

She handed him a cup of tea. "Drink this. It is made from the ginseng root and will help you relax and improve your stamina. We have all the time in the world, my darling. You shall know every inch of my body and I shall know every inch of yours."

He drank the tea as she kissed him on the back of his neck. Her hands tugged at his tunic and breeches. He returned the favor by lifting her thin gown over her shoulders. After that, no barrier kept them from fulfilling their desires.

CHAPTER 26

Bradamante had stopped dreaming of Ruggiero the night he flew helplessly on the back of the winged creature. It troubled her that their spiritual connection had been severed. She was afraid that something terrible had happened to him, but refused to consider his possible death. She felt that she would know intuitively if such a tragedy occurred.

Originally, her intentions were to leave the following day for Marseille, but it took another day to acquire adequate supplies for her soldiers. Geoffroi, Count of Foix, had been one of the prisoners. He sent word to her that he was gathering knights, squires, and a farrier. She was in charge of the mission, but he was a count and therefore outranked her in many aspects. Delaying their departure was something she disliked, but soon the expedition swelled to two dozen men and was a true battalion on a mission. Reinforcements were always welcomed, and she hoped they would not come too late for the fate of Marseille.

Bradamante had known of Geoffroi's reputation as an honorable, well respected man, as well as a widower, but she had never met him before. He was the type of man her father had long sought as a husband for her. Her first real opportunity to speak with him was as they rode side by side leaving the town of Foix.

"I do not believe that I properly thanked you for rescuing me and my men," said Geoffroi.

At first she thought nothing of his remark, but then he gave her a small smile as if he had said something funny. Bradamante wondered what he meant because he had shaken her hand as had all the men on the hillside after being released from Atallah's palace. Then she remembered that she and Ruggiero shared a kiss in the open. Had Geoffroi seen that? If he had seen that display of intimacy, perhaps he considered it as a token of gratitude and not an exchange of affection between two lovers.

She did not regret kissing Ruggiero for it was the most magical moment of her life, but there would be dire consequences to her reputation if it became known she had embraced an enemy soldier. All it would take was one of the nine Christian knights who rode with her to have seen them together and begin gossiping for the word to spread. It was a subject she dared not broach lest she call attention to something that might not have been noticed in the chaos surrounding the dissolution of the magical palace.

Feeling a bit queasy, she gave Geoffroi a weak smile to acknowledge his attempt at thanking her. She hoped there was no deeper meaning to his statement for she did not want him attempting to kiss her in gratitude either.

"You should feel proud," he added. "Your adventure in Foix rivals the heroic exploits by your brother Renaud and your cousin Orlando. Songs will be sung in your honor."

"Thank you," she said. Bradamante was surprised. No one had ever made such a suggestion to her before. Geoffroi, unlike other men, did not appear to be intimidated by her prowess. She studied his appearance. He was twice her age with fair looks, unruly brown hair, and clear blue eyes. Had she not fallen in love already, she might have been content with marriage to such a man.

"It was probably expected that I throw a banquet after you lifted the scourge," he said, "but I thought it more appropriate to postpone a celebration until we expel these invaders from our lands. That is the greatest threat to our way of life."

"I agree," she said. "You should feel grateful because I heard no grumbles of disappointment about your actions. The people seemed happy enough to gather together at the inn where I was staying."

"That is fortunate. Being the daughter of a duke, you must understand there are times when peasants resent the nobility because they cannot fathom the larger landscape at work. I thought it wiser to dedicate the food stores for our contingent during our time guarding the coastline rather than a single feast for the masses."

"As someone who will benefit from such a decision, I want to thank you," said Bradamante. "If you do not mind my asking, could you tell me why you were not a part of the battle in Toulouse."

"I do not mind at all. I was assigned the task of guarding the nearby passes in the Pyrenees. I doubted Akramont would choose such an arduous route, but Charlemagne developed a newfound respect for mountainous roads after his terrible defeat in Roncevaux over twenty years ago. He insisted that my men monitor the area. As I suspected, the infidels landed off Narbonne and made their way to Toulouse. I had learned about those events and was about to order my men to leave the Ariège when that wizard took me prisoner."

There was a certain familiarity and comfort in traveling with a group of soldiers. They knew of her identity as Charlemagne's niece, so she had no need to disguise her sex or worries about her safety with them. No one would dare ravish her without risk of certain death. However, she did not have the customary excitement of going to war, instead, Bradamante felt as though her heart had been placed on ice. They passed fields of lavender in bloom but its beauty was lost on her; they could have been crossing a barren desert for all that she cared.

One evening as they camped, Geoffroi offered her armfuls of the fragrant purple flowers. "You appear dour. I hope this might lift your spirits. My late wife, Avelina, adored lavender."

She thanked him, but her voice offered no enthusiasm. His attempt at lifting her spirits failed just as she had failed to free Ruggiero from Atallah's magical influence.

Bradamante could not even muster any sense of awe as they passed the colorful salt marshes of the Camargue which took on varying hues of pinks, blues, reds, and oranges depending on the angle of the sun. Nor did she smile while flamingos took off in flight. Some of the squires could not stop talking about those dramatic sights, and she wistfully remembered how she had been previously captivated by the land's beauty.

By the time they reached Marseille, Bradamante decided to put Ruggiero out of her mind. She rejoined Guy, Duke of Burgundy, in leading the defense of the city. Day after day she directed soldiers in pouring boiling sea water on those daring to scale the walls, and sent fiery arrows at enemy ships. Rumors spread that the invading army had grown weary at the prolonged effort in Marseille and that they were considering moving their forces to concentrate defeating the fortified city of Arles.

Bradamante rode Frontino even when he deserved a rest, because being near Ruggiero's horse felt like the only thing keeping her love for him alive. One day as she saddled up Frontino, she was disheartened to find one of his shoes needed replacing. It was like a nail in her heart, for she was forcibly reminded of Eos losing a shoe before the battle of Toulouse. She reflected on her recent spate of bad luck when it came to horses. She thought of her horse killed by Rodomont, Erebus breaking his leg, Martisino's horse wandering away, and Eos being stolen by Pinabel. Tears welled in her eyes to think of herself as being cursed. Fearing for Frontino's safety, she decided that the safest place for him would be at the stables in Montauban. That night she wrote a letter.

To the honorable Duke and Duchess of Dordogne from their daughter Bradamante
May this letter be delivered to you with all deliberate speed. It is my hope that my recent unannounced departure did not cause undue worry. I was honor bound to return to war and fulfill my obligation to defend the city of Marseille. The defense of this port city is a constant struggle. There are rumors that the enemy may give up their challenge here. Until they abandon this effort I shall harass our persecutors daily. Along with this letter I am sending a destrier for Hippalca to care for. The horse's name is Frontino and I look at him with much favor. I also ask that she embroider a surcoat for him before my return as I admire surcoats on horses. If Richardet is still awaiting new orders have him join me in Marseille. I could always use another squire.
Your devoted daughter Bradamante

A messenger was dispatched the next morning to Montauban with her letter and Frontino. Bradamante said a prayer for the safe deliverance of the horse and for word on the whereabouts of Ruggiero. That night while in her private quarters, a guard came to her door.

"An old woman wishes an audience with you. She said it regards your family."

"Send her in."

She sat on a wooden chair nervously tapping her foot. Bradamante froze when Melissa crossed her threshold.

CHAPTER 27

Melissa embraced Bradamante who shook violently.

"Tell me," Bradamante said, "does he live?"

"Yes. He is in good health, but he is in danger. It took me a long time to divine where he went. That is because his soul lost its markers."

"I do not understand."

"He is physically the same, but spiritually his soul has changed."

Bradamante trembled as she sunk into a chair. "Where is he?"

"He is in the clutches of an evil sorceress named Alcina on an island east of India. I used my divination skills to search all of Europe for him, but to no avail. Then I searched in vain throughout Africa and Asia. It was after searching the enchanted realms that I found him at last, but I hardly recognized him. You must know the truth of what this evil woman has done to Ruggiero."

Melissa wrapped a blanket around Bradamante's shoulders. "She raped him in a most hideous manner. He was stripped of his mind, his memory, and his conscience. After he had no idea who he was and could no longer tell right from wrong she seduced him. He has become a creature of licentiousness, but you must not blame him. He is not responsible. All blame lies with Atallah. He was the one who sent Ruggiero to her."

"And I spared Atallah's life," said Bradamante, as tears rolled down her cheeks.

"You showed mercy to an undeserving man," said Melissa. "He is obsessed with Ruggiero, and yet he deliberately placed that young man in the care of an evil old hag."

"Ruggiero was seduced by an ugly, old woman?" asked Bradamante.

"She does not appear that way. She uses powerful enchantments to look as young and as beautiful as you. Many men have been lured to her realm over the years, but this time she has committed a far more grievous sin. She wiped away Ruggiero's memory and tainted his soul."

"How can I get him back?"

"This is a battle he must fight himself," replied Melissa. "Otherwise, he will never forgive himself or regain his sense of self. However, he does require one thing from you. The magical ring you wear will reveal the truth he has been prevented from seeing. He must see Alcina's true nature and be protected from her spells which might otherwise entrap him on her island forever."

Bradamante slipped the ring off her finger, handing it to the enchantress.

"Thank you my child. I shall take my leave. My first stop will be Greece to obtain water from the spring of Mnemosyne. That will restore his memory. Only then will he fully understand how completely he was violated by the acts of his mentor and Alcina. Afterward he will be able to fight to regain his life, his soul, and his self- respect." Melissa placed a hand on Bradamante's shoulder. "Ruggiero will soon return to your dreams."

CHAPTER 28

"You were incredible, my love," said Alcina. "You are by far the best lover I have ever had, Adonis."

He rolled over and rested his head on a feather pillow.

And I have had a lot of lovers to compare you with.

He gave her a smile and closed his eyes. Alcina watched her lover's breathing become regular as he drifted off to sleep. She waved a hand over his face and placed a spell on him to stay in a deep sleep.

"Now to deal with that annoying wizard." She climbed out of bed and gave a charm for a breeze to calmly dry off her sweat soaked body. "Much better."

Alcina entered into a large private chamber where all her clothes were hung. She chose a white silken gown; one that was not too revealing. There was no point in showing off her figure to this man. If anything, she wanted to mollify him so that he would never bother her again.

A slight pinging sound came from her full length mirror. He was still waiting.

She ran a brush through her long hair and adjusted her dress until she felt her appearance was suitable for the occasion. The slightest touch to the mirror changed the image from herself to that of an old wizard.

"What can I do for you Atallah?"

"I wanted a report on Ruggiero."

"I have done all that you asked of me," said Alcina. "He is blissfully happy here. All his wants and needs are satisfied."

"So he has forgotten about Bradamante?" asked Atallah.

"Yes. He has no desire to return to her or to your war. His only desire is for me."

"May I see him?"

Alcina put a hand over her heart. "That is a dangerous request. He has forgotten about his former life. Should he see you, his memories might come back. Is that what you want?"

A look of terror came over his face. "No! No, I just…I miss him. I long to see him again." He paused. "Perhaps you could cast a spell on him to fall asleep, so that there would be no risk of him seeing me."

"Cast a direct spell on him? I am loath to do such a thing."

"Please?"

She paused. "Very well, but just this once. This will be the last time I ever grant you such a request. It will take me a few moments; then you will see him through my hand mirror."

Alcina walked out of her secret chamber and closed the door. She pulled the sheet up over Ruggiero's body to cover his nakedness. After she counted to thirty, she picked up a silver hand mirror and touched its surface.

"Here he is." Alcina held the mirror over Ruggiero's sleeping form. "Are you happy now?"

She looked into the mirror and saw tears streaming down the old man's face.

"Thank you," he said, his voice thick with emotion.

"I cannot risk doing such a thing again."

"I understand. I will contact you once this war is over to arrange his return."

"Do not contact me until such time," said Alcina.

"Agreed. Thank you again for coming to my aid." With that, the wizard's image melted away. Alcina was left looking at her own beautiful reflection.

"No. Thank *you*, Atallah." She sat down on the bed, drew back the sheet and gazed upon Ruggiero's nude body. "I had never considered removing someone's memory. It has worked wonders for compliance. There were no bad habits to break. He simply does as he is told." Her fingers lazily worked their way down his chest. "You have been an extraordinary lover, but I do love variety."

She stood and walked to her balcony. Looking out at her terraced gardens she smiled as she studied the various male statues bathed in the glow of moonlight.

"Never again will I search for a new lover. I can lift the spells bringing them back to life and then remove their memory as I did with Ruggiero." She ran her hands over her body. "They will have forgotten their anger with me for casting them aside and satisfy me once again. I can rotate my paramours as often as I wish." She gave a throaty laugh. "I knew keeping old lovers as souvenirs would one day be useful."

She returned to her bed and climbed in next to Ruggiero.

"I am not ready to turn you to stone just yet, but soon." She waved her hand and lifted the sleeping spell. Alcina woke him with a kiss.

CHAPTER 29

Once Melissa left Bradamante's side she placed the magic ring in her mouth. Rendered invisible, she could go anywhere unchecked and unquestioned. Leaving the walled city of Marseille, she journeyed a few miles away until she found a field of roses and lavender. She cut ten white roses and placed them into a magical bag. Inside a small wooden shed were bundles of dried lavender. She picked up ten bundles that were tied with white ribbons. Placing these in her bag, she left a denarius on the farmer's doorstep as payment.

Leaving the farm, she made her way to the seashore. The Mediterranean Sea was calmly lapping on the rocky shore. Melissa threw a biscuit near a seagull. The bird gobbled the food before others could get near it. Immediately the bird began growing until it was the size of an albatross with a six foot wing span. She carefully slipped a bridle over the bird's head, a harness around its massive wings, and mounted the newly gigantic beast. The animal not only gained in size, but also in strength and endurance. She whispered a suggestion into the bird's ear, and it took off into the sky.

Melissa needed to guide the bird to their destination so she could not fall asleep. They flew throughout the night. Knowing that if she slumbered she might fall to her death helped her fight against the strong urge to close her eyes and rest. In the morning, they landed outside Livadia in Greece.

Melissa dismounted, removed the harness and bridle, and then fed another biscuit to the animal. The spell reversed; the bird shrank to its normal size and flew away. Melissa removed the ring from her mouth and placed it on a finger. She slapped her face to help drive away any drowsy thoughts, took a quick drink of water from a leather bag, and climbed a steep rocky hill toward an ancient temple.

In the dawn's light the white Doric columns appeared slightly pink. Melissa hoped the words she had rehearsed and the gifts she brought would be enough. She bowed before entering the temple, walked to the northern side, and bowed again. Removing the roses from her magic bag, she raised them above her head.

"I call upon the Titaness Mnemosyne, the goddess of memory, and the mother of the nine muses. I bring you freshly picked roses from Provence."

Melissa walked in a circle, first toward the east, then to the south, then to the west, and ended at the north altar where she set down the white flowers. She reached again into her bag pulling out the bundles of lavender which now appeared as if freshly picked.

"I ask for permission for water from the sacred spring of Mnemosyne, the spring of memory. I ask not for myself, but to restore the memory of someone who unknowingly drank water from the River Lethe. I bring you lavender from Provence."

She repeated walking in the circle, showing the flowers to the four sides of the temple, and set the ten purple bouquets before the altar. Then she brought out ten necklaces made of mother of pearl and held them in the air.

"Water from the River Lethe is for sacred purposes and initiations. A virtuous man was tricked into drinking the water so he would be unable to resist committing unholy acts. I ask for your help to restore his memory and his soul. I bring ten necklaces made of mother of pearl."

Melissa once again walked in the circle, stopping at each of the four sides of the temple, and then laid the necklaces upon the altar. She bowed her head, closed her eyes and waited. Time passed. Melissa patiently waited, not moving or saying anything else. A cold breeze made her shiver. She was no longer alone, but Melissa remained in the respectful position.

"Rise, tell me your name, and the name of the man of which you spoke," said a melodious voice.

Melissa rose slowly. Standing before her was Mnemosyne, a beautiful woman with a regal bearing and a large mane of auburn hair. She wore a long white tunic embroidered with gold.

"I am the enchantress Melissa. I have pledged to use my powers only for the good of mankind, and not for personal gain. I seek your help on behalf of Ruggiero. He is the only son of the late Ruggiero of Reggio and Galiziella. He, and Bradamante, daughter to the Duke of Dordogne, have both been struck by the arrows of love."

Melissa told Mnemosyne of Ruggiero's destiny with Bradamante as well as Atallah's determination to change their fate by keeping them apart, then how Alcina tricked the young knight into drinking the magical waters of forgetfulness.

Mnemosyne clapped her hands and her nine beautiful daughters appeared. Melissa was amazed to see in one place the muses who inspired poets, writers, and artists throughout the ages. Each woman had long beautiful hair ranging in color from pale blonde to ebony. They retrieved their gifts from the altar, and listened as their mother relayed Melissa's story. After a few moments of solemn discussion, Mnemosyne turned to Melissa.

"Your wish shall be granted, but we must learn more about Alcina. Calliope will bring Nemesis and the Furies here to insure her crimes will be punished severely."

CHAPTER 30

Melissa gave Mnemosyne a respectful nod. She was grateful to know Alcina would soon receive the punishment she deserved. It was not long before Calliope returned, bringing seven women back; three more than expected. Melissa needed no introduction for she recognized them from legend. These seven goddesses were the most feared of all the deities in the ancient Greek pantheon.

Nemesis, the goddess of retribution and vengeance, was a beautiful red haired woman bearing a large pair of wings, while carrying a whip and a sword on her belt. Her beauty was overshadowed by the overwhelming fear she instilled in people as she was tireless in persecuting those whose crimes angered the gods.

Next were the Avenging Furies. These three women also bore wings, but they were not remotely attractive. Dressed in black robes with whips on their belts, their eyes dripped with blood, and their scalps had writhing serpents instead of hair. These goddesses punished those who committed evil acts, hounding them both in life and after death.

The last three women were small in stature, appearing frail and elderly. Their hair was thin and as white as their plain tunics, but they were the most feared of all the immortals. They brought with them an elaborate tapestry in progress denoting their sacred duty: they were the Fates and they determined when mortal lives were over. The first sister, Clotho, spun the thread of life, the second sister, Lachesis, measured the length of a strand, and the third sister, Atropos, was the smallest and by far the most feared because she cut the thread of life. They came at Calliope's invitation, but did not pause in their work of weaving threads into a pattern only they understood.

The small temple had without any ceremony, enlarged itself to accommodate the addition of the new goddesses. Melissa retold her story to the Fates, the Erinyes, and Nemesis.

"I fear if that fountain remains on her island, she may misuse those sacred waters again in the future," Melissa warned.

Nemesis removed the sword from her belt, running its blade against a sharpening stone. "Where can we find Alcina? And how has she managed to escape our attention?"

"I am gratified to have such an august assembly gather to hear my pleadings," said Melissa. "I ask only that you give me three days before you begin her punishment. The goddess Mnemosyne has graciously granted me permission to bring sacred water from the spring of memory to Ruggiero, but he must be allowed to restore his own sense of dignity. He must fight his way off Alcina's island, after that I would welcome all of your attentions upon this evil woman."

"Let us examine our tapestry. Here is Ruggiero's golden thread. Such a noble life as his never lasts long," Clotho said, shaking her head sadly. "His thread has twice crossed Bradamante's silver one, and is now entwined with Alcina's scarlet thread."

Melissa squinted as she looked at the tapestry. Alcina's scarlet thread encircled many threads over an extensive area. She did not know how to interpret the pattern, but it seemed aberrant. Looking closer, Melissa saw the thread was not taut like the others.

"How much longer will that scarlet thread last?" asked Melissa.

"Alcina's?" said Lachesis. "It is not yet time for her life to be ended. Clotho still has more to spin before it has reached its full measure."

"Are you quite certain?" asked Melissa, gently. "For in my acts of divination, she appears to be several hundred years old, far longer than a normal life span. Pardon me, but it looks as if her thread has been woven differently into your fabric than the others."

The old women studied that portion of the tapestry of life, and Lachesis gave a grunt of indignation.

"This thread somehow snagged, and is bunched up on the back, and in many places. Here let me pull it through so we may see it properly."

Lachesis tugged gently at the tapestry and repeated the process over and over until the scarlet thread showed its true length. The three Fates stared in amazement.

"Our work has been tampered with," said Lachesis, her face reddening. "No one has done that before."

As Atropos pulled out her scissors Melissa thrust one hand in front of the tapestry.

"Please, I beg of you, let her live a few days longer," said Melissa. "Allow Ruggiero the chance to redeem himself. Then it shall be up to you seven goddesses to determine her fate on this earth as well as her punishment in the afterlife. She stole sacred waters for profane purposes, meddled with your sacred tapestry, and hid her numerous sins away from your watchful eyes as well. Alcina deserves all your wrath and fury. I ask only for three days on behalf of Ruggiero."

"Very well," said Atropos. "I shall refrain for now. I do not believe that any mortal has ever tricked us before; she shall be punished."

Lachesis looked curiously at Melissa. "Hmmm, I wonder how much longer *your* thread will be?"

Melissa felt chilled. "Please do not tell me. I do not wish to know. I have had a long life, and I know I do not have much longer on this plane of existence. However, I am on a Divine mission to assure that Bradamante and Ruggiero fulfill their destiny to marry and beget a child together. Until they are safely wed, I humbly ask that you not cut my thread. After their wedding, I shall be ready and willing to leave this life. I ask this not for myself, but for the generations of noble men and women destined to be born of these two virtuous warriors."

Atropos gave a small smile. "I do not recall anyone, god or mortal, swaying our decision before. Yet we shall grant your request because you are not arguing for yourself, but on behalf of glorious lives yet to be spun by Clotho."

The first Fury bared her hideous fangs. "Does Alcina feel her age?"

Melissa shook her head. "No, she uses many enchantments to make herself appear and feel as if she is still a young woman."

"Then our first act will be to remove her charms, one by one. She will slowly begin to know all the individual aches and pains of age that she has avoided all these years. Each new pain will magnify and intensify the accumulated pain of a mortal body living far longer than is allowed. She will remain in that pain-filled body for all eternity."

"We should collect the shrieks of horror from those around her when they see her true form," said the second sister. "Those terrifying sounds will echo in her ears forever, never allowing her a moment of rest."

"Since this woman has lived a lust-filled life," began the third, "we shall make sure that she never feels a warm touch again. She will be placed naked in her own cave in the deepest part of Tartarus with her old pain-filled body, and have only a small scrap of a lice and flea infested blanket. Never enough to wrap around any part of her body, and in a cave so cold she cannot refuse the blanket's feeble promise of warmth."

The three Furies laughed like hyenas. One laughed so hard that tears of blood ran down her cheeks. Melissa shivered as she listened to their inhuman sounds of mirth.

"She shall forever be cold, alone, forced to hear screams of horror, and suffer the bites of fleas and lice," laughed the first one. "Her only reprieve will be when she is forced out of her cave to be whipped by us."

The three gruesome sisters erupted again into fits of laughter.

"Now," Mnemosyne said, turning to Melissa, "we must give you some water, and send you on your way."

CHAPTER 31

Mnemosyne linked arms with Melissa, guiding her from the temple, past a river, deep into the forest and to her sacred spring. A sign was posted warning anyone from drinking the water.

The goddess handed Melissa a large golden chalice decorated with an intricate design. The outside of the goblet was ringed by naked men and women holding hands. A winged serpent graced the inside bowl. The stem was in the shape of an egg with a snake entwined around it. Melissa dipped the chalice into the spring and filled it halfway with the magical water. She did not want to fill the vessel too far, fearing that she might anger the gods by wasting any of it. Mnemosyne ushered her to a dark cave whose entry was obscured, and would not have been found without a guide.

"You will walk inside the cave of Trophonius and take one hundred paces forward," said Mnemosyne. "Do not turn back, nor turn to the right, nor to the left. After walking one hundred paces, close your eyes and picture your destination with the person you seek. Open your eyes then walk another one hundred paces and repeat the process. After you have taken three hundred paces you will stop, as you open your eyes you will be at your destination. Be careful that you do not spill even a drop of water. If you do, you will raise the ire of the Furies."

"What would you have me do with this chalice after Ruggiero is finished drinking?" asked Melissa.

"Place it in the fountain filled with water from the River Lethe. While the other goddesses may wait three days before acting, I shall not. That fountain will be removed today, so no one else will fall victim to it."

Melissa nodded.

"Your journey begins with your next step," said Mnemosyne.

Melissa took a deep breath, and heard her stomach rumble. She had not eaten for hours, but fasting had always been a part of sacred rituals, so she purposefully had not packed any food with her. She focused her mind on the task at hand, avoiding thoughts of thirst, hunger, or anything else.

"One, two, three…"

The stones beneath her feet were cold and damp. She carefully placed one foot in front of the other, gingerly feeling the ground. As she came upon large rocks, she gently felt around with her feet to discover a way around them. She knew that the distance traveled was not important, but rather invoking the magic through the journey in the cave.

She paused at her hundredth step, closed her eyes, and imagined Ruggiero's face.

"Ruggiero," Melissa called out. "Find a place where you can be alone with your thoughts. A place where no one will see you. Go there now."

Melissa visualized Alcina's gardens, which she had viewed while scrying in a pool of water. The hedges in the labyrinth were as tall as men. She imagined Ruggiero walking toward the center of the labyrinth.

Melissa opened her eyes and saw nothing. She was deep within the recesses of the cave with no source of light. Her feet were numb and her heart raced with fear while she concentrated on holding the chalice steady.

"One hundred and one, one hundred and two," she said as she continued onward.

She repeated her visualizing of Alcina's garden and her plea to Ruggiero at her two hundredth step. After Melissa took her three hundredth step she stopped. Once again she imagined Ruggiero sitting among tall hedges in the center of the labyrinth in Alcina's garden. Then she felt warm sunlight on her face. Her feet tingled as if stabbed by hundreds of needles.

She smiled as she opened her eyes and saw Ruggiero sitting on the ground with his back to her. He was alone, as she had hoped. She closed her eyes again and concentrated on changing her appearance. Within a few moments she resembled Atallah complete with long flowing beard and dark violet robes.

CHAPTER 32

"Ruggiero, my child, let me see what has become of you," said a deep voice.

He turned and was surprised to discover an elderly man wearing a full-length dark robe who was staring at him. He did not recognize the man, nor did he understand why he would be addressed by that strange name.

The old man scowled as he looked him over from head to toe. "I am shocked to see you this way, Ruggiero. Warriors do not drape themselves in silk clothing, nor do they wear necklaces, bracelets, and earrings. You are living a life of idleness, where lust rather than honor rules your mind and body."

"Who are you, and why are you insulting me?" he asked as he stood.

"I am Atallah, the man who rescued you as a baby. I raised you as if you were my own son, and yet you stare at me as if you had never seen me before. I fed you the meat and marrow from lions to help you grow strong, but now your most strenuous activity is raising a cup of wine to your lips. I gave you defanged serpents to wrestle, but now all you wrestle is a whore. You are wasting your strength! Have you no dignity?"

His cheeks burned. "I am sorry, but I do not know you."

"No, you know me, but you do not *remember* me. You do not even remember your own self. Drink of this chalice," said Atallah. "Regain what was stolen from you. Remember your life."

A small voice in his head told him to take the cup, but his gut overruled. This man was a stranger who might be untrustworthy. Shaking his head, he refused to take it.

"You prefer remaining ignorant of your noble ancestors and of the honorable life you once lived? This water is from the magical spring of Mnemosyne, it will restore your memory."

Taking the chalice, he stared at the strange markings on its side. Before Atallah challenged him, he had only vague questions about his past when he first met Alcina. Those questions were soon forgotten after falling for her charms. Now with Atallah's urgings, those dormant questions erupted in his mind. He needed to know who he was. The risk of being poisoned was worth taking for he could no longer exist in a cloud of ignorance. He lifted the goblet to his lips and drank until the last drop of water was gone. A strange feeling came over him. Images flooded his senses causing him to drop to his knees and close his eyes.

He saw himself as a baby in Atallah's arms. Playing hide and seek and laughing. Being mad and pounding on Atallah's chest with his little fists, sobbing in his arms. Being taught to pray. Hunting wild animals in the jungle. Wrestling serpents. Learning to write Latin, Greek and Arabic. Learning swordplay. Riding on horseback and jousting with the mystic. Watching the tournament on Mount Carena. Meeting Brunello and being given Balisarda and Frontino. Engaging in a tournament mêlée with dozens of Muslim knights. Being stabbed by Bardalasto. Seeking revenge and killing the villain. Atallah tending to the wounds on his side. Akramont's fury when he found Bardalasto's corpse. Telling the amir what happened and being forgiven. Akramont dubbing him a knight. Crossing the Mediterranean Sea. Invading Francia. Fighting the Franks. Searching for Atallah. Fighting Rodomont. Meeting Bradamante.

The memories stopped flowing at the sight of Bradamante and her beauty. Ruggiero had felt embarrassed as he recalled being a Muslim because during his time with Alcina he had repeatedly violated the tenets and obligations of his faith. Those current and past memories colliding together made him feel sick to his stomach. However, once he saw Bradamante's face he felt shame. He had unknowingly betrayed the woman he loved.

Tears filled his eyes as more images flooded his mind. He watched helplessly as Bradamante was attacked by Martisino. Rage coursed through him as he relived killing his fellow soldiers followed by anguish at his separation from the Maid. His emotions were as powerful as they were when the events occurred.

Gradasso. Mandricardo. Brunello. Pinabel. Being taken captive. Arguing with Atallah about Bradamante.

The stream of memory slowed as Atallah's words rang in his ears.

"I swear I shall not cast direct spells on either you or Bradamante."

Ruggiero's head throbbed in pain as his eyesight blurred with the color red. Atallah had circumvented his vow by having someone else, Alcina, remove Bradamante from his heart and mind. He shook his head in anger, and the memories started again.

The duel between Bradamante and Atallah. Standing before Bradamante. Kissing her.

Ruggiero's heart, mind, and soul reacted strongly to the memory of her and of kissing her lips.

Attack by the hippogriff. The chase for the flying beast. Climbing on the creature's back. Taking off into the sky. The look of horror on Bradamante's face. She grew smaller and smaller and disappeared from view.

Tears streamed down Ruggiero's cheeks.

The mad flight over land and sea. Landing on the island. Tethering the hippogriff to a tree. The beast nearly destroying a myrtle tree. Aistulf's warning. Walking on a path towards the woods. Stopping at the fountain and drinking.

Ruggiero's memory was now restored. He removed his hands from his face and blinked at the harsh sunlight. He stood and glared at the old man.

"How could you do this to me?" Ruggiero demanded.

"That is a good question." Atallah's features faded away into that of an elderly woman. "Do not be alarmed Ruggiero, I chose the guise of Atallah because he is the closest thing to family you have ever known. Your anger at him is justified, for he betrayed your trust. My name is Melissa and I am here to help you."

Ruggiero released his fists.

"This time you must fight your own battles," she said. "No one else can do that for you, but I have tools to help you in this task. First is this ring."

He took the golden bank offered to him and examined it carefully. "Is this magical?"

"Yes. It protects its wearer from magical spells. You will then see things as they truly are here. Bradamante wore that ring when she battled Atallah. That is how she was not blinded by his magic shield."

"You know Bradamante? Tell me, how does she fare?"

Melissa gave him a comforting smile. "Her heart is wounded and she longs for your safe return."

"Does she know about…?"

"She knows Alcina took advantage of you. She also knows that when you had your wits about you and were faced with temptation that you remained faithful to her love."

He gave a sigh of relief as he clutched the ring in his hand, but still felt guilt over his infidelity.

"You must go to the stables without raising any suspicion," said Melissa. "There is a cabinet holding armor. Take both your shield and Atallah's enchanted shield, for you will want both after you leave this island. Leave the hippogriff behind, as he is too dangerous for you at this time. Select Rabican, a horse as black as pitch, for he was born of magic spells in Baghdad and there is no swifter horse. His mother was fire and his father the wind; he does not graze or eat grains but gains sustenance from air alone. Alcina recognized the steed's worth and did not turn him into a statue as she has so many others. Saddle him up and go to the gates. Kill the guards if you must. Otherwise they will alert Alcina to your escape. You must leave this place as quickly as possible."

As her fingertips brushed the ground, blades of grass sprung up in the dirt creating a map.

"After going through the woods, you will come upon a marina. If you can, commandeer a vessel and go northward. There you will be safe. Otherwise you will have to fight your way through a heavily guarded pass separating this island between Alcina and Logistilla's domains. However, I must warn you against seeking revenge. That ring will protect you from Alcina casting spells upon you, but she can still harm you with her magic. She could cause a tree to fall and crush you, or launch hundreds of arrows at you. Trust that her crimes will be dealt with in due time."

"Melissa, can you free others?" asked Ruggiero. "There is a paladin named Aistulf, a kinsman of Bradamante. He is imprisoned as a myrtle tree outside her gates, although his form is now nothing more than a stump. I spoke with him when I first landed on the island. He told me that there are hundreds of men being held prisoner here. They all deserve freedom."

She smiled. "I shall work to release them from their magical bonds. Aistulf will be the first. They will be your reinforcements in the battle against Alcina's army."

Ruggiero put the ring on a finger on his left hand. Everything around him changed.

CHAPTER 33

Bradamante had difficulty falling asleep after speaking with Melissa. She willed herself to see Ruggiero again. In her dreams she saw him sleeping peacefully covered lightly by a sheet. Her desire to be held in his arms grew stronger at the sight of his bare chest. Jealousy, however, reared her ugly head as a blonde woman crawled in bed next to Ruggiero. The woman kissed him and ran her hands over his body.

Bradamante forced herself awake. "Was that just a dream? Or is that the witch Melissa told me about?" She sat up and cradled her knees next to her chest. "How can I compete for his heart when I cannot give him that?"

She rocked slowly back and forth as she tried to comfort herself. Insecurities about her own beauty gnawed at her. Bradamante did not wish to sleep again for fear of witnessing carnal acts between Alcina and Ruggiero. Morning came and she had not slept.

During breakfast she tried listening to a report by Guy, Duke of Burgundy. Her eyelids grew heavy as she heard about the previous day's casualties. Bradamante began drowsing with her head propped on one hand when Ruggiero's face appeared in her mind's eye. The shock of seeing his image jolted her out of her dreamlike state and she knocked over her goblet.

"Bradamante, are you ill?" asked Guy, as he helped clean the spill.

"No, I - I...did not sleep well last night."

"Did that old woman upset you?"

"She had news about my family," said Bradamante. "Should you see her again, please send her to me directly. I may have to leave for home, depending on further events."

"Is there anything you would like to tell me?" he asked as he placed a hand on hers.

She took comfort from his gesture and regarded him with the same respect she held for her father. "Not at this time."

Guy nodded. "Do you feel up to hearing from the Count of Foix? He says that he may have a weapon which might end this siege once and for all."

"Certainly, just give me a few moments."

Walking over to a basin on a nearby table, she splashed her face with cold water to hide the tears that had welled in her eyes. She hoped the sudden appearance of Ruggiero's face foretold his imminent return.

CHAPTER 34

The labyrinth surrounding Ruggiero was adorned with dozens of men frozen in time. He had expected the lifelike male statues decorating the palace to be enchanted, but he was surprised at how many men were spread throughout her garden. The magnitude of her evil reign shocked him.

The men were all young and handsome; clearly Aistulf had told him the truth about the fate of Alcina's former lovers. Ruggiero wondered how long it would have been before he was treated to a similar fate. His anger toward Atallah flared again. His guardian sent him into the arms of a wicked whore. *Why? Did Atallah think I needed protection from the love of a beautiful and virtuous Christian woman?* He cursed Atallah under his breath, momentarily losing his concentration and stumbled into the hedges. Ruggiero closed his eyes to calm himself. He would confront Atallah one day, but first he must escape this island. Giving a sigh of relief, he picked up his pace as he came upon the last row of hedges with the exit in sight. The smile on his face vanished when he nearly collided with a frail old woman who had entered the maze.

"I was wondering where you had gone, my love," she said.

Ruggiero shook his head. He was disoriented to hear Alcina's voice coming from the hideous hag standing before him. Melissa had not prepared him as to how the evil sorceress would appear stripped of all spells and enchantments. Alcina was ancient and withered. Her skin was gray, paper-thin, and lined with wrinkles and dark brown age spots. Her bosom, which had the illusion of being bounteous and perfectly shaped, was actually two sacks of shriveled flesh hanging near her abdomen. The numerous moles on her chin sprouted far more hairs than those remaining on her scabbed over scalp. Thick cataracts obscured whatever color her eyes had once been.

Ruggiero sneezed uncontrollably. This was not something he feigned; it was a reaction to the overpowering stench of rotting flesh emanating from the old harpy. He knew that she bathed daily, and perfumed oils were applied to her skin, but none of her spells reversed the ravages of time on her body. Her wispy eyebrows knitted in response to his sneezing, she then moved her hand slowly in a small circle. He sneezed once again with more violence.

"Forgive me," he said, wiping his face. He walked farther away from the maze. "I think it may be your perfume. I fear that I cannot stop sneezing. Could you take another bath and choose a different scent?"

"I wear this perfume frequently and you have never had a problem before," she said. "I shall bathe again if that is what you require, however I am afraid that our dinner will be delayed."

Ruggiero waved one hand in front of his face. "It is of no consequence as I am not hungry yet. I shall entertain myself by exploring your grounds while awaiting your return."

"Of course," she said, smiling to reveal one remaining tooth perched on cracked and bleeding gums. A drop of spittle trickled down her chin. "Everything here is for your pleasure."

Ruggiero turned his back and walked away from her, fighting the urge to vomit. He glanced over his shoulder and saw Alcina enter her palace. She did not appear to be suspicious of his true intentions or aware that he saw through her enchantments.

Wasting no time, Ruggiero went in the direction of the stables. He had seen the building, but had never visited. As he neared the entrance he retched violently. Alcina was a vile woman, and her true form reflected the ugliness of her soul. He could not believe he had been repeatedly intimate with that foul being, and that Atallah had arranged it. Wiping his mouth, he walked into the barn and took a deep breath. The smell of straw, manure, and horses was far more appealing to him than Alcina's mixed scent of decay and cloying perfume. There were many fine horses in the stalls, but he continued searching until he found one black as pitch with a fierce demeanor.

"Are you in need of anything?" asked a sweet voice.

Ruggiero jumped at the familiar sight of Rangada and Malha. He assumed Alcina sent them on a mission to monitor his whereabouts and actions.

"I fancied going on a ride," Ruggiero said, recovering his confidence. "Alcina said everything here was for my pleasure, and I would like to go exploring a bit. Saddle this horse for me."

The two women exchanged a look with each other, but then prepared the horse.

"Now bring forth the arms you took from me," Ruggiero commanded.

"Why is that?" asked Rangada. "Those are weapons of war. We do not practice war here, only love."

His stomach turned at those words for there was no love practiced in Alcina's compound, only lust.

"It is my armor. I command its return."

Rangada bowed and led him to a room where many sets of armor were stored. She unlocked the cabinet while he removed his silken tunic and all the golden jewelry Alcina had bestowed upon him. Ruggiero retrieved his armor and weapons and selected replacement gloves and a helmet since his had been left on a hillside in the Pyrenees. He donned thick padded doublets, his hauberk, and then attached his dagger and sword to his belt. The more armor he put on, the more agitated Rangada appeared.

"You will not need a sword to ride on the grounds," she insisted.

"I should like to explore the island," he said. "I wish to be prepared for whatever I might come across."

Ruggiero found his shield bearing the standard of his ancestor, and slung it over his shoulder. Then he pulled out Atallah's shield covered with crimson silk. Ruggiero knew Rangada and Malha could complicate his escape and it would be unforgivable for him to kill unarmed women.

"But my lord, my lady will soon be finished with her massage," Rangada insisted. "She does not like to be kept waiting."

"Alcina is many things," Ruggiero said coldly, "but a lady she is not."

He removed the silken cover from Atallah's shield and Rangada fell to the ground. He grabbed a spear from the cabinet and headed back to the horses. Malha also succumbed to the magic of his uncovered shield. Ruggiero hurriedly replaced the silken covering, mounted Rabican, and headed for the gate. It was only a matter of time before Alcina came looking for him. The two burly men who were standing guard broke off their conversation with each other at his approach.

"Raise the portcullis," Ruggiero commanded.

The larger of the two men stepped forward. "We only take orders from Alcina. She has not authorized anyone to leave today."

Ruggiero lost no time as he plunged his spear into the man's chest. Just as swiftly he drew Balisarda and in one stroke beheaded the second guard. The soldier's body thudded on the ground, as Ruggiero scanned the area for others who might block his path.

Melissa emerged from the shadows, yanked the bloodied spear out of the first guard's body and handed it to Ruggiero along with a leather flask. "This is water from Provence. You must not drink anything else until you arrive safely in Logistilla's realm. Godspeed." She turned the crank and raised the heavy metal bars allowing his exit.

Ruggiero nodded in appreciation toward the enchantress as he urged Rabican to a full gallop. They traveled several miles on a dirt path through a dense forest. The farther he got from Alcina, the lighter his heart felt. That brief exhilaration ended as he rounded a bend and a horrific dwelling appeared. Human skulls decorated the fence posts, with leg bones sticking out of the ground. The road ahead was limited to a narrow bridge over a ravine that appeared at least thirty feet across. He knew instinctively that the bridge would be guarded by whoever lived inside the gruesome hut.

Indeed, within moments, a large gray wolf ran out and snarled, causing Rabican to rear on his hind legs. A massive bull with vicious looking horns followed with an ogress riding on its back. The giant woman bore a necklace strung with the bones from human thumbs. Her mammoth shield had an image of a poisonous toad adorning its front and the background was painted reddish black. It took Ruggiero a moment to realize that it was likely painted with blood. In her right hand she bore a large tree limb as a crude lance. She smiled at him revealing blackened and broken teeth.

"What do we have here?" said the ogress. "You looks like an escapee and no escapee ever made it past Erifilla before. Mmmm, I loves fresh meat."

The wolf bore its fangs as the bull snorted and pawed the ground preparing to charge.

CHAPTER 35

Melissa followed Ruggiero outside the palace grounds and found the golden fountain. It was dry, indicating that Mnemosyne had reclaimed the sacred water. Placing the golden chalice in the bowl of the fountain, Melissa smiled as the structure faded away leaving behind a dry patch of ground. She crept into the woods and found a secluded spot to hide and wait. It was time for patience.

~~~

"A-DON-sis," Alcina sang. "Where are you, my love?"

She was surprised that her lover was not waiting for her on the terrace. She had changed her attire from earlier and now wore her favorite white silk gown with a plunging neckline secured by a large ruby brooch. Her hemline brushed the ground, but slits on each side revealed her shapely legs. She had chosen this dress because Ruggiero struggled to keep his hands off her in public whenever she wore it.

Earlier events in the day bothered her, bringing about her decision to stop postponing the inevitable and turn Ruggiero into a permanent fixture in her bedroom. This would be their last night together and she wanted it to be memorable.

Where is he?

Something was not right. During her second bath of the day she wracked her brain trying to understand his reaction to her scent and why the spell she cast upon him did not resolve the problem. Using her hands to shield the harsh rays of the sun, she scanned the grounds. It was then she saw the open portcullis and a man running toward her.

"My lady," he began, out of breath. "The guards…"

150

"What about the guards?"

"They have…been…killed," he said, grasping his side.

"WHAT?" she shrieked. "Where is Adonis? Search the grounds for him!"

Alcina strode over to a large bell and angrily swung its clapper. Servants ran from all parts of her palace and grounds, some hastily rearranging their clothing.

"We are at risk. Either we have an intruder or someone has left without permission. Search the grounds for anything unusual and report to me at once."

Alcina paced. Something went wrong with Ruggiero. If he was the one responsible for killing her guards, it meant someone had meddled with her magic. No one had ever succeeded in doing that before, and the thought terrified her.

Did Logistilla find a way to overcome the magical barrier? Or is Atallah behind this?

She pulled out fistfuls of hair. There was no reason why Ruggiero should want to escape. Only troublesome slaves tried to escape. Ruggiero had been the model of compliance. He had never shown interest in anything other than the pursuit of pleasure.

A young woman ran to her. "My lady, Malha and Rangada were attacked in the stables."

Alcina felt fire burn in her eyes. She had sent them to follow Ruggiero.

"And a horse is missing," the woman said nervously.

"Sound the alarm," Alcina ordered. "Everyone is to set off immediately in pursuit of Adonis. He is not to leave my realm."

A man blew a large horn whose sound could be heard throughout the island. All of her servants, human and nonhuman, would hear the call and be put on high alert. Alcina whistled and three large ravens instantly appeared. She spoke to them in a magical tongue filled with the sound of clicks, before they flew off to deliver her message not to harm Ruggiero. He was to be captured, but not killed. Atallah must not have just cause to seek vengeance. Erifilla was her greatest concern for Ruggiero would first come across the ogress and no one had ever made it past her garden.

Alcina ran to the stables and saw slaves saddling up horses as they donned armor. She was grateful to see the hippogriff tethered in its stall, for it meant that at the very least, Ruggiero was bound to the earth. She was momentarily tempted to grab the winged charger, but stepped back as it reared on its hind legs and screeched at her. Ruggiero had occupied too much of her attention and Alcina had not learned how to control the beast. This was not the time to risk riding a temperamental animal. She needed something she could dominate without question. Her eyes fell upon a statue of a horse with its front legs raised high in the air. Searching the ground near the base of the statue, she uncovered a small bit of clay decorated with a whorl.

Alcina touched one hand to the statue's back and crumbled the piece of clay in her other hand. The enchantment broke and the horse snorted as its hooves fell upon the earth. With a second touch, the animal stilled, allowing her to leap upon its bare back.

"Follow me!" she commanded her slaves as she rode off into the forest.

CHAPTER 36

Ruggiero heard a bell ring in the distance, followed a few moments later by a horn being blown. His absence had been discovered.

"I was right. You *are* an escapee," said Erifilla, licking her lips. "She will be coming after you; a pity she will be too late."

Ruggiero considered the large club the ogress wielded, the menacing horns of her bull, and the teeth on the snarling wolf. He decided her mount represented the greatest threat to Rabican, and he could not risk his horse being gored. He threw the spear at the bull, penetrating the animal's back. The beast bellowed and staggered as blood gushed from the wound.

"Filthy coward!" howled Erifilla as she fell from her saddle.

Ruggiero jumped from his horse, bracing himself in a crouch as the wolf leapt into his arms. The fierce canine's jaws snapped as it attempted to sink its teeth into him, but Ruggiero was quicker. He wrapped an arm around the feral dog's neck and squeezed. His childhood spent wrestling wild beasts in Tunisia had prepared him for this day. The wolf's legs flailed as the life was forced out of its body.

Erifilla's face was purple with rage. She towered over Ruggiero at her full seven foot height. Lifting her tremendous cudgel, she aimed for his head. He watched her looming shadow approach and rolled away just as her heavy club crashed to the ground. There was a crunching sound as the weapon cracked the wolf's skull.

Ruggiero released the dead beast and yanked hard on the shaft of the club. Erifilla lost her balance, collapsing on the ground. He jumped behind the ogress and grabbed her in a headlock. The monstrous woman gasped for breath and clawed at his forearm trying desperately to loosen his grip upon her throat. She thrashed about, but Ruggiero would not let up until her breath stopped and her body grew slack. Shifting his arms slightly, he crushed her windpipe with one hand and then bit an ear; when she did not flinch he knew she was dead. He dropped her corpse upon the ground and withdrew Balisarda. Next he cut off her head and placed the gruesome trophy on a fence post as the last addition to her collection of human skulls.

A sound behind him made him turn. The wounded bull had staggered to its feet. Ruggiero could not risk crossing the bridge until it was dead; if the beast followed him, its weight and unpredictable actions might destroy the structure while he was still on it.

The bull charged at him in an erratic path swaying from side to side. Ruggiero nimbly scaled a large flat boulder. Just before the creature crashed headlong into the rock, Ruggiero grabbed a large branch of a nearby tree. He swung out of danger and propelled himself away onto the ground. Surprised by the sudden movement, the beast swerved, lost its balance and tumbled over the edge into the ravine.

A large black raven landed on the fencepost near Erifilla's head and cawed loudly as Rabican emerged from behind a tree. Ruggiero grabbed a discarded rusty spear, mounted the horse, and crossed the bridge. Once on the other side of the ravine, Rabican was in a full gallop as the sound of the raven's cry rang in Ruggiero's ears.

CHAPTER 37

Alcina was out of breath when she arrived at Erifilla's forest. She had hoped to find Ruggiero being held by the ogress and was shocked to find Erifilla's hideous head adorning a fence post. Alcina buried her face in her hands. Her carefully constructed world was unraveling. The raven cawed, bringing her back to her senses.

Shortly afterward her slaves arrived on their mounts. Alcina had composed herself enough to give off the appearance of being in command of the situation.

"We must cross and continue on our way," she ordered.

She could not risk letting them know how desperate and terrified she was. For if they revolted against her while she was so distracted, she might not have the power to subdue all of them with her magic.

As she led the procession across the bridge she spied the corpse of Erifilla's bull at the bottom of the ravine. Never before had the ogress failed. Alcina was oddly pleased to discover Ruggiero was still alive, but what else would she discover in his wake? She now regretted coming to an accord with Atallah; she should have known better than to trust a wizard.

Alcina urged her horse onward hoping that Ruggiero had not yet boarded a ship and left the island. She could punish the sailors easily enough, but retrieving Ruggiero once out at sea would be a challenge. The ogress had failed, but Alcina had confidence that Erifilla's mate Caligorant, her loyal servant overseeing the sailors, would overpower her wayward lover. Now, she had only to hope the giant Cyclops would subdue Ruggiero without killing him.

CHAPTER 38

Melissa waited until she no longer heard any sounds from the palace grounds. Alcina, in her haste, left her compound unprotected. There was no one to defend it from the army of soldiers Melissa was about to bring back to life.

Upon touching a tree, a bush or a rock Melissa could feel a heartbeat pulsing if there was the spirit of a man trapped inside. She walked swiftly toward the damaged myrtle tree, examining the ground around its base. The source of the enchantment was a knot hidden beneath a stone nearby. After untying the cord Aistulf stood before her. His eyes blinked fiercely under the hot sun. He was unharmed even though his enchanted form had been torn apart by the hippogriff. Aistulf had a medium build, wavy light brown hair and bore a rakish grin on his face. He shook his head in wonderment and surveyed his body as he realized that he was human once again.

"Welcome back to your life, Aistulf. My name is Melissa. I need your help in liberating the others. Then you shall lead them in battle against Alcina and her evil minions."

"With pleasure, my lady."

The two worked quickly to convert the enchanted menagerie into an army of men. Alcina's spells had been fixed by knots, whorls and seals. Once they located a few of the charms, their task became easier; the witch was predictable in her hiding places. In a short while they released two hundred men, a sizable army. Many of the knights were in full dress armor while some still had their horses.

"I shall release the rest of the men later," said Melissa. "Come with me to the stables."

There they gathered armor from the unlocked and unguarded cupboards. Aistulf hastily donned some of the left over armor and smiled as he picked up a gold-dipped lance. He left as other men dressed in what armor remained.

Melissa saw Aistulf approaching the stall containing the hippogriff. "Do not ride that mount," she warned. "Only someone skilled in magic can ride him until he is trained properly. I shall teach Ruggiero how to control this beast once we are all safely in Logistilla's realm. For now, please choose a normal horse."

He nodded, mounting the nearest charger.

"My work is not done here," she said. "You must lead these men by taking the road north to the other side of the island. Alcina has summoned all her forces together to capture and punish Ruggiero. He will need your help in fighting her dreadful army."

Aistulf raised a shield and readied his golden lance. Once outside the stable he gave a short blast of his horn.

"Men, tonight we shall have our revenge against the evil witch who ruined our lives. Alcina is in pursuit of a brave knight named Ruggiero. We shall aid him in his quest for freedom and liberty. In so doing, we will secure our own."

A cheer rose up from the men as they readied themselves for battle.

Melissa returned to her task of releasing men still held in captivity. She finished the grounds outside and searched the palace for statues and other objects containing the spirits of men. Once finished, she gave orders to one soldier to lead the newly created army as reinforcements in battle. These men lacked horses, and were thus foot soldiers. Now that all the former prisoners had been released and were on their way, Melissa began a new mission to find and destroy the source of Alcina's power.

CHAPTER 39

Ruggiero rode hard for another three miles and eased up as the road neared a marina. All the docks were empty, but the cove was filled with ships of many sizes. He continued onward and was startled when an eight foot tall Cyclops emerged out of the shadows blocking his path. A raven perched on the giant's shoulder gave a plaintive caw.

"Going somewhere?" bellowed the monster.

The man had legs the size of tree trunks, a neck as thick as a barrel, and a single eye the size of an ostrich egg. Ruggiero knew it would be impossible to choke him to death, or to even think of engaging in a battle of strength against someone that much larger than himself. He surveyed his surroundings, quickly devising a plan.

"Alcina wants you back, my little man," taunted the giant, as he leaned forward and tried grabbing Ruggiero off his horse.

Rabican bolted forward in the nick of time and the giant merely took an empty swipe in the air with his hands. The monster snarled and took another step forward. Ruggiero hoisted the rusted spear on his arm and hurled it with all his might. The projectile landed squarely in the middle of the Cyclops' eye causing him to howl with fury and pain. Blood cascaded onto the ground as the giant struggled to pull out the weapon.

Urging Rabican forward, Ruggiero grabbed a length of chain attached to a post. He encircled the giant, who stood roaring in agony, and draped the chain at the height of the colossal man's knees. Ruggiero circled him three times as the Cyclops lost his balance and crashed to the earth. The man rolled onto his back and continued pulling on the spear in his wounded eye.

Ruggiero stepped forward intent on slitting the monster's neck with his sword, when the creature seized his legs and pulled him toward its chest. Ruggiero raised Balisarda above his head as the giant's other hand came at him. The blade pierced the center of the massive palm causing the Cyclops to scream yet again. Ruggiero wrenched his sword from between the bones in the giant's hand and then turned it downward. Both his hands were on the jeweled pommel as he drove it deep into the monster's chest. Ribs splintered as the blade punctured his enemy's heart. Blood gushed in torrents and showered Ruggiero in its sticky warmth as the monster's grip on him ended. He had to struggle to remove his sword and had barely stepped away from the corpse when a small band of sailors wearing leather collars threw a large fishing net over his head.

"No one has ever challenged Caligorant before," said one man in awe. "He has literally bitten the heads off men who did not follow Alcina's orders."

"Release me," said Ruggiero.

"We cannot for fear of what she will do to us."

"We are all prisoners of that evil witch," said Ruggiero. "I trust none of you serve her on your own accord."

"True," said another sailor pointing to his collar, "but we cannot defy her. She could kill us all with a single spell."

"Life spent serving someone like her would not be worth living," said Ruggiero. "I was under her spell, but it has been broken. I see her for what she is and I would rather die than live another day in the company of someone so vile. I swear if you release me I will not forget your plight. I will find a way to sever the bonds tethering you to that witch. I give you my word as a knight."

The men exchanged looks with one another.

"We cannot help you directly," one man said, "but we will not stop you from releasing yourself and leaving our grounds."

Ruggiero used Balisarda to slash through the rough nets. His blade cut through the rope as if it was made of silken spider webs. He mounted Rabican and paused to salute the sailors before pressing onward. As his horse galloped down the road, he heard another horn being blown in the distance. It had a different quality than the previous one. This time he felt encouraged.

CHAPTER 40

Alcina kicked her horse, urging it to go faster. She was close to the marina and would soon see Ruggiero captured, or so she hoped. Caligorant surely would have stopped him. The sound of a horn being blown from her palace alarmed her.

Who blew that horn? And why? It must be an enemy.

She realized her mistake at leaving her compound unguarded and cursed under her breath. Perhaps Atallah sent Ruggiero to her in a plot to destroy her and her island. Random accusations of deception and betrayal consumed her. Sensing her lover was only a short distance ahead, she continued onward. Her plan was to subdue Ruggiero and force him to be her soldier against Atallah, even if it meant casting harmful spells upon the young knight. She was determined to not turn around and see what lay behind her.

Slowing her horse as the road dipped down to the marina, Alcina was horrified at the sea of blood blanketing an expansive area. The gigantic corpse of Caligorant lay in the middle of the road, a spear sticking out of his eye. His chest was scarlet. Ten sailors were lying on the ground covered in blood. She closed her eyes while fighting the urge to vomit.

Her slaves finally caught up with her and murmured as they came upon the horrific scene. She could no longer contain her emotions as she shook with rage.

"I trust you heard a horn being blown," Alcina said, trying to sound undaunted. "I suspect the sound came from my palace. I am sending half of you back to defend my home."

The slaves cast furtive glances at one another. A few failed to suppress smiles at her misfortune.

CHAPTER 41

Melissa walked through the empty palace searching for the secret place Alcina kept her cauldrons and magic ingredients. She wandered through the halls until she found her way to the numerous bedrooms. They seemed uniform in size and none were extravagant enough to be Alcina's. After searching over a dozen rooms, she made her way to the third floor and discovered a spacious bedroom extensively decorated in red and gold. Images of naked men and women in various acts of copulation adorned the walls and ceiling. An oversized bed covered in red silk dominated the room. A large sunken bathtub with golden faucets occupied one corner with a padded table nearby for Alcina's daily massage. A nearby cabinet overflowed with various oils and perfumes in multicolored bottles.

The room reeked of Alcina's rotting flesh and cloying perfume. Thinking that magical objects in the room might be attuned to only respond to the witch's image, Melissa concentrated and changed her form to mimic the beautiful exterior Alcina used to beguile everyone. Closing her eyes, she felt a strong magical pull and walked toward its source. When she opened her eyes she stood in front of an unadorned stretch of wall. She ran her hands over it until a handle magically appeared. She pulled on it and the wall opened to reveal a hidden chamber containing hundreds of silk gowns and shelves covered with expensive jewelry. At the back of the room stood a piece of highly polished metal serving as a full length mirror. Melissa examined its frame closely before she discerned the hinges.

She pushed and prodded a few times until the mirror swung outward revealing a hidden staircase descending to a subterranean chamber. As soon as Melissa touched the railing, torches burst into flame on the walls. She walked down a long spiral staircase to the bottom of a dark, damp cellar.

In the center of the room a half dozen cauldrons filled with potions were simmering by the heat of magical flames that required no tending or venting. On the walls hung hundreds of amulets near shelves filled with jars containing magical ingredients, including dried herbs and the heads of animals suspended in green liquid.

Melissa closed her eyes again and took a deep breath. She knew what she sought was nearby for she could feel magical vibrations. After a few moments of concentration an image floated into her mind. Once again she walked slowly forward with her eyes closed. This time when she opened them she stood before the smallest cauldron containing a murky gray liquid with gray flames licking its base. Finding an empty jar, she lifted her hands suggesting the potion to transfer itself to the new vessel.

When she touched the outside of the cauldron with the back of her hand, she discovered the iron was cold. Melissa smiled as she investigated the inside of the container and saw it was surprisingly shallow. Focusing her mind, she drew a circle around the false bottom. Her magic cut the metal and she carefully lifted up the thick black iron circle revealing a bi-colored cord made of black and white wool, tied in at least a thousand knots. She turned the tangled mass over in her hands a few times, but it was impossible to find the ends.

Melissa placed the knotted cord into her bag, and climbed to the top of the stairs. Closing her eyes to concentrate, she waved her arms and muttered a few words; the room burst into flame. Only then did she throw off Alcina's image, resuming her own true form.

She ran out of the burning palace to the stables and to the stall where the hippogriff was tethered by a thick chain to the wall. As she drew near, the creature reared on its hind legs, screeching at her as its talons sliced the air. Melissa stepped back, pulled out an herb from her magic bag and held it before her.

"I will not harm you."

The creature warily sniffed the leaf, nibbled and then ate the entire offering.

"There you go. Let me ride you to safety." She stroked its beak while she attached a bit and bridle. She untied the animal, opened the gate, and mounted its back. The winged steed trotted out of the stables and with a little prodding took off to the skies. Melissa looked over her shoulder at Alcina's palace, now fully engulfed in flames.

CHAPTER 42

Aistulf smiled broadly as he led the charge of the newly freed knights. He felt exhilarated leading an army of men who came from all over Asia. Bearing his golden lance aloft with confidence, he was ready to face anyone or anything. He had his life back and felt it would be impossible to lose on such a glorious day. Neither defeat nor harm would befall Ruggiero. Aistulf would bestow his gratitude to the knight who had kept his word and remembered the plight of those imprisoned by Alcina's spells.

He slowed his horse as they turned a corner and was shocked at the sight of a decapitated body and a dead wolf in the forest. Clearly Ruggiero had made it through here alive. They had no time to waste. Leading his men across the bridge, they traveled another mile when they were met by dozens of Alcina's forces.

Aistulf surveyed the scantily armed slaves. A few bore swords and a few others had lances, but many were without armor or weapons.

"Get out of our way," Aistulf commanded, "or be taken prisoner."

"We cannot surrender the path," said the leading man of the group. "We are under orders from our lady."

"Steady yourself then," said Aistulf, "for I shall test our right to travel on this road by force of arms."

Aistulf's horse charged. His lance struck a direct blow on his opponent's shield as the man was thrown on the ground.

"Does anyone else wish to defend this road?" asked Aistulf as he turned his horse around.

Two more men reluctantly came forward. Within a few moments they were likewise defeated by Aistulf's golden lance. After that, the field surrendered. Aistulf ordered several of his knights to hold them prisoner in the hovel they passed on the other side of the bridge. One woman burst into tears.

"Please do not make us stay in that hut," she wailed. "Erifilla was a cannibal. Her place will be filled with horrors."

"We are at war with Alcina," said Aistulf. "Until she is utterly defeated, we must use whatever tools are available. That dwelling is the only place nearby to house prisoners."

A tall knight stepped forward. "I shall take twenty-five men and carry out your orders. We shall guard the road to Alcina's palace."

"Resume your advance," Aistulf ordered the rest of his soldiers. They soon came upon a marina. He held his hand over his mouth while passing a large corpse being pecked at by birds. He led his troops onward without delay in pursuit of Ruggiero and Alcina.

CHAPTER 43

Melissa flew on a path she hoped would be invisible to Alcina. Landing in Logistilla's garden, she was greeted by a bevy of beautiful young women. They led the hippogriff away as she was brought to the mistress of this domain. Logistilla was dressed all in white with golden cords adorning her waist. Her long tresses were as white as her gown, and she radiated a sense of serenity.

"Welcome Melissa," said Logistilla. "We have been waiting for you. Come inside."

The women linked arms and entered an ornate palace rivaling Alcina's. Logistilla's halls elicited feelings of peace and tranquility whereas Alcina's halls inflamed passions and lust. They walked down a long hallway and arrived at Logistilla's private room. Nemesis was sitting at a table and staring intently at a basin filled with water.

The goddess of retribution looked up and smiled at Melissa. "You have done well. It appears that I shall not have to wait the three days you requested. The worst should be over by nightfall."

"Come see what has transpired," urged Logistilla, as she led Melissa to the pool of water. "We have followed your progress by scrying."

Logistilla touched the water with her crystal wand. The image showed Ruggiero riding on Rabican. She touched the water a few more times in quick succession to show Ruggiero battling with an ogress and later a Cyclops.

"Ruggiero has proven his worth by defeating hideous monsters," said Logistilla. "He is approaching his greatest test. Soon he will be surrounded by multitudes of horrific creatures as well as Alcina herself. She has made many mistakes and will soon pay the price for her hubris. Half of her troops have been taken prisoner and Aistulf's army is gaining on her. Their forces will soon collide."

"I watched you with great interest in Alcina's palace," said Nemesis. "I want what you took from her dungeon."

Melissa pulled the black and white bundle of knots from her bag. The goddess took the tangled mass and turned it over in her hands.

"I could use my sword and treat this like the Gordian Knot," mused Nemesis, "but that would destroy too much too soon. I would force Atropos to cut Alcina's life thread by such an action, and the Fates would not look kindly at that. Instead, I should like to slowly cause the destruction of these knots undermining her power. Logistilla, please bring me some lye."

CHAPTER 44

As Ruggiero rode over a large crest the road abruptly ended in the middle of a dense forest. Gathered in a small clearing was a vast array of bizarre creatures; some bore the heads of animals but had the bodies of men; there were also centaurs and satyrs as well as two-headed men and Cyclopes. Some were clothed in animal skins while others were naked. These beasts surrounded Ruggiero, threatening him with rocks and clubs. He was outnumbered at least fifty to one.

A raven cawed from atop a nearby tree.

The monsters bore only crude weapons and lacked armor. Ruggiero fingered the drape on his mirrored shield, but decided against it. Using the magical device in this situation would be cowardly. He had felt no guilt over using the enchanted shield against Rangada and Malha because they were unarmed women and he did not intend to fight or harm them. However, these beasts were armed, and he would rather die a noble death, outnumbered and overpowered, than resort to trickery to save his life.

Ruggiero drew out Balisarda and with a sweep of his arm beheaded a satyr who lunged at him. Rabican snorted in anger as the beasts grabbed the horse with their filthy hands. Rocks pelted his shield as he hacked his way through the terrible throng.

CHAPTER 45

Alcina galloped up the hill followed by her armed slaves. She was startled to see Ruggiero as a warrior covered in blood with a fierce countenance. Somehow she still expected to find a pleasant young man whose only concern was satisfying his lover. Dozens of corpses were strewn about the ground surrounding him as he hacked away at Erifilla's brood. She could not depend on any of her minions; she would have to take command of Ruggiero or risk losing everything.

Later, she would ascertain what had brought about his change and seek revenge against the responsible party. After Atallah or Logistilla suffered, she would turn Ruggiero into a naked statue in the middle of a fountain to serve as a constant reminder for all to recognize her supreme command of the realm. Any rebellion to her rule would be punished with death.

"Adonis, what is the meaning of all this?" asked Alcina. She surreptitiously cast a spell hoping to change him back to being her compliant lover. "Have you no gratitude for all the kindness and hospitality I have shown you?"

"Kindness? Hospitality?" snorted Ruggiero. "You used me like a pawn. Everything you did was for you, not for me, but all that is over now. I know who I am, and I know *what* you are."

A murmur arose among her slaves, leaving her without any doubt that her spell had no effect on him.

"My name is Ruggiero. I am descended from a long line of noble warriors and proud of my heritage. I am ashamed that for even a moment I was beguiled by you. Against my will you made me your sex slave, but you no longer have any claim or power over me. Deception is your art, because you are foul, evil, and thoroughly unlovable. Without enchantments no man would be your lover for he would shrivel at your true, hideous nature. You disgust me!"

He spat on the ground.

"No one had ever dared insult me before," Alcina shrieked.

She raised her arms and concentrated with all of her might in casting a spell to kill Ruggiero instantly. The curse ricocheted off his shield and struck and killed a centaur. Her heart pounded wildly, as she frantically tried to understand why her intended target was protected from her curse.

"You have no power over me," Ruggiero repeated. "You bring slaves who are nothing more than courtesans to a battle? They are not trained for war, and yet you conscript them for such?"

"Kill him," she commanded.

"You will have to go through us first," announced Aistulf, riding over the crest with an army of nearly two hundred knights behind him.

CHAPTER 46

Malha and Rangada were awakened by the smell of smoke. The two young women groggily raised their heads and staggered to their feet. Leaving the stables, they were shocked at the sight of the palace fully engulfed in flames. No one replied to their repeated calls.

"Where has everyone gone?" Malha said to Rangada.

"I do not know. Why is there no one trying to put out the fire?"

The two women ran to the scorched terrace, furiously rang Alcina's large bell, and fled through the open gates away from the inferno.

~~~

The lye slowly dissolved the woolen fibers of Alcina's knots. Nemesis watched with a growing smile on her face as the harsh chemical seeped its way through the tangled mass. As the yarn fell apart so did Alcina's myriad spells.

Soon, the sailors noticed their collars becoming loose, as the leather disintegrated. One brave soul wrenched his off, and waved the remnants in the air.

"Freedom!" he declared.

The other men followed his lead and shouted as they celebrated their liberation.

~~~

Alcina heard the sound of a bell ringing in the distance followed by a loud cheer from another part of her island. Both sounds disturbed her, as well as the sight of hundreds of her former lovers alive again and glaring at her with murderous intent. She was unsure who had wrought this destruction to her carefully orchestrated world, and wondered how she would be able to change everything back to the way they had been that morning.

Alcina was struck with waves of intense pain. Her shoulders hunched as she doubled over. She concentrated on her breathing, since her vision had become blurred. Her slaves shrieked in horror as they stared at her. Lifting her hands, she was shocked to see they were gnarled with age. Fearfully she touched her face and let out a piercing wail as she felt folds of skin.

Capturing Ruggiero no longer mattered. Something horrible was happening to her magic and she needed to salvage whatever she could. Alcina drew upon her remaining powers, turned herself into a vulture, and flew back to her palace to see what remained.

~~~

A cheer rang out from the knights as the woman who destroyed their lives left in utter disgrace. The remaining beasts turned and ran into the forest, abandoning their challenge to the warriors. Alcina's slaves put down their weapons and surrendered.

The leader of the knights rode over to Ruggiero. "I am your humble servant Aistulf. For the rest of my life it shall be my honor to be in your service."

"We must go forward," Ruggiero said, suddenly fatigued. "We are not safe here."

Aistulf nodded. "We shall take Alcina's slaves with us, and send for the others who were taken prisoner. Melissa was going to free more soldiers from their magical bonds after I left her side. She and Logistilla will know what we should do next."

"There are sailors," said Ruggiero. "They deserve freedom as well."

The two new friends led the soldiers and Alcina's former slaves through the forest, down a steep embankment, across a narrow sandy isthmus and into Logistilla's realm.

CHAPTER 47

Bradamante stood on a rampart gazing down at the clear blue water surrounding Marseille, but her mind was thousands of miles away. She was desperate to learn about the events surrounding Ruggiero. Her heart was not in waging war, but she had no choice; this was her duty.

She walked up the spiral staircase leading to a small room at the top of the highest tower. The view overlooked the marina as well as the city itself and provided the best vantage point in the whole fortified city of Marseille. It also afforded great privacy since the room was small and no one would overhear their discussion.

Guy, Duke of Burgundy, was waiting for her as she entered the small room. Her heart was pounding from the steep climb and she took the opportunity to catch her breath and survey the armada of enemy ships blockading the harbor. The island where the Muslim fleet docked at night could be seen plainly in the distance.

"He will be with us shortly," said Guy. "I have noticed that he appears enamored of you."

"Have you?" Bradamante struggled to keep her face impassive at the thought.

The sound of footsteps coming up the stairway announced the impending arrival of Geoffroi, Count of Foix. As he walked into the tower room, the hair on his forehead was slicked with sweat.

"I hear that you have news of a weapon to share with us," said Bradamante as he stood before them.

"Yes, I have been waiting for years for this day," he said, panting slightly. "As a child, my grandmother told me stories about a weapon so fearful it destroyed an entire army in one night."

"Go on," said Bradamante.

"She called it liquid fire, and when she was a girl in Constantinople, an entire fleet of Saracen ships were consumed by flames." Geoffroi had a gleam in his eye. "The formula is a closely guarded secret and known only by a select few. I have tried for years to discover how to make such a weapon. Last night, I, and a foot soldier from Auch, may have stumbled upon the answer."

"How does it work?" asked Bradamante.

"We will take a small rowboat and get near their fleet. The weapon is a thick and sticky liquid held in a barrel and will be sprayed on their ships with a hose. Ignition occurs upon contact with water."

Bradamante shuddered. "So this fire cannot be put out with water?"

He shook his head slowly, his eyes fixed on hers. "Any attempt to use water to douse the flames will only cause it to spread."

She swallowed hard. "I see how that would decimate our enemy. It sounds dangerous though."

"That is why I am volunteering," he said. "It has been my life's mission to uncover this formula and, should anything go awry, my life should be the one at risk. However, if this works the way my grandmother described, I believe it will drive the infidels from our coast and our lands. It would be my honor to present such a weapon to Charlemagne, who would only use it for the noble purpose of defending and extending Christendom."

The enemy ships surrounded the barricaded entrance to the harbor. They were numerous and it seemed as if new arrivals of enemy soldiers would never end. Marseille was the last Frankish holdout along the *Côte d'Azur*, and Bradamante worried about the city's dwindling provisions.

She hated the idea of this weapon; fires were difficult to control. They spread easily past their intended targets, with infernos sometimes lasting for days. Yet she could not allow fear to prevent her from using a potentially effective weapon, especially if it might change the outcome of the war in her sovereign's favor. There could be no weakness or indecision in the face of a brutal enemy. She turned to Guy and saw his nod of approval.

"We shall need as much stealth as possible," she said. "There will be a new moon next week. We shall wait until then, or earlier should we have a cloud filled night to cloak your mission."

Geoffroi smiled as he kissed her hand in gratitude.

CHAPTER 48

Nemesis idly stroked her coiled whip while watching Alcina's humiliation at the hands of Ruggiero. As the evil sorceress turned herself into a scavenger bird, the goddess of retribution stretched her own wings and flew off to torment Alcina. Nemesis wanted to arrive in advance of the Furies, for she hated competing with them over the living. The three gruesome sisters had the solemn task of torturing sinners after they died, and would persecute Alcina for eternity. Nemesis only had a short while before the Fates would send that miserable wretch to the Underworld.

~~~

As soon as Ruggiero entered Logistilla's side of the island, he dismounted Rabican. He splashed ocean water upon himself to perform *Wudu* and turned westward to pray. His armor was still covered with blood, but he could wait no longer to express his profound gratitude to God. Dozens of other knights followed suit, kneeling towards Mecca as they said their prayers. Hindu soldiers dismounted and stood with their heads bowed quietly offering their own prayers of thanks, while others kneeled. Aistulf held the reins for both his horse and Rabican while Ruggiero prostrated himself before God. Ruggiero returned the favor and held the reins for the two horses as Aistulf kneeled and silently prayed. After the prayers concluded, the two knights looked at each other and smiles broke across their faces.

"Come," said Aistulf, "Let us find Logistilla."

Ruggiero nodded as he led his horse on the path towards the palace.

"How was Rabican?" asked Aistulf. "He can be temperamental."

"Is he yours?" asked Ruggiero, suddenly feeling as if he had done something wrong. "Melissa bade me ride him."

"As well she should. You were in dire need of a swift horse and none can compare with Rabican."

Ruggiero relaxed. "He is a fine mount, and I freely return him to you."

He handed the reins over to Aistulf, taking the other horse's reins in return.

"Melissa stopped me from taking your winged steed," said Aistulf. "She said only someone magical could control that beast right now, but she did speak of teaching you how to ride it properly."

"Did she?" Ruggiero said brightening. His mind instantly flew to Francia where his life and his love were waiting for him. If he were to ride on the hippogriff, his journey back might last only a few days.

As their procession rounded a bend in the road, they saw Melissa waiting for them. Her hair was disheveled, but she bore a large smile. She stood near an elderly woman with long white hair clad in robes of white.

"Both of you have done well," she said. "I want you to meet Logistilla."

Ruggiero felt a sense of peace and calm wash over him. He had been assured of his safety on Logistilla's island, and now he was certain. He still wore the magic ring Melissa gave him. Had Logistilla been as deceptive as Alcina, the ring would have exposed her lies.

"Welcome," said Logistilla. "You both showed incredible bravery today in the face of evil. Melissa will oversee the safe passage of the remaining soldiers, as well as the rest of the men, women, and children from Alcina's side of the island."

Ruggiero closed his eyes. He could not bear to think of what the children raised to serve Alcina had endured.

"There are sailors as well," he said, remembering his promise.

Logistilla smiled. "Yes, and they will be of great assistance to us. They shall help ferry the people here. The next few days I shall help everyone plan their futures now that they are free of Alcina's bondage."

Ruggiero was exhausted and dripped blood upon her white marble terrace. An attendant took him to a room with a drawn bath where he relaxed in solitude. His armor was taken away to be cleaned and oiled. After bathing and dressing in the linen tunic and breeches that were provided for him, Ruggiero said another prayer. He asked for Allah's forgiveness for having committed sins when he did not know his own name or conscience.

Feeling serene knowing he would soon be returning to his beloved, he walked outdoors and came upon multitudes of people milling about. Musicians played drums, flutes, and stringed instruments while hundreds of knights talked and laughed with one another. Many of the soldiers were in deep conversation with Alcina's former female slaves, and began pairing up with them. Some couples openly embraced and kissed one another, while others left in search of trysting spots.

Logistilla's attendants feverishly cooked to provide enough food for everyone. Several large simmering cauldrons contained curried rice, chana dal beans, and fish stew making Ruggiero's mouth water. Aistulf joined him in line where they patiently waited their turn and watched the celebration unfold before them.

Another shipload of people arrived bearing dozens of children of varying ages. They spilled onto the grounds and were greeted with joyful shouts and embraces from some of the women. Other women who had been engaged in intimate conversation with knights deliberately turned their backs when the children arrived. Ruggiero was disturbed to witness this shunning. Many of the children were too young to understand the meaning or significance of the evening. They played with one another and danced to the music without being disciplined.

Ruggiero and Aistulf sat down on the grass and ate their supper of warm rice, beans, and stew. They continued watching the interaction of the recent arrivals. Many of the newly freed female slaves ignored their former lovers. The women also avoided the sailors, concentrating their attention on the knights instead.

As the meal ended, the attendants brought out hundreds of pillows and blankets, setting them on the ground.

"Ruggiero, you and Aistulf are welcome to sleep inside my palace tonight," said Logistilla.

He shook his head. "That is generous of you, but such comforts should be reserved for women who will soon give birth or new mothers with their babies. Soldiers can sleep outdoors without any hardship."

"Very well," she said. "I shall take my leave from you for the night. On the morrow the plans for the mass exodus from this island will begin."

After Logistilla left, the sailors came over to Ruggiero and apologized for their attempt to stop him. They congratulated him for bringing about everyone's liberation. Soon tiring of the revelry and wanting solitude, Ruggiero sat down next to Aistulf and sipped some tea.

"Every woman has their eye on you," said Aistulf. "Yet you ignore them all."

"All these women are tainted by Alcina," Ruggiero said. "They may be beautiful, but they lack morality. They have no love for me, nor any man here. They are desperate and are seeking any man they think will support them. However, they would abandon him in a heartbeat should they receive a better offer. That is not a marriage I want."

"Marriage." Aistulf coughed. "Yes, you are right on that score. None of these women would make a proper bride. I am once again, thanks to you, the heir to the throne in Essex. My father would force me to put any such woman away were I to bring her home with me."

"Essex? You are from Britain? I remember you saying you were kinsmen with the famous Renaud, but he is from Francia."

"We are kinsmen. My father married the maiden queen of Essex. It was thought to be a good political marriage as he was the eldest son of Bernard of Lyon, a powerful Frankish nobleman."

"Tell me how you came to be this far from your home."

"That story began over a year ago," said Aistulf leaning back. "Charlemagne wanted to celebrate being crowned Emperor of the Western Roman Empire. He announced a great tournament starting with a feast on Pentecost. Hundreds of knights, Christian and Saracen alike, came from distant lands to take part. It was a joyous occasion until Angelica arrived and everything was thrown into turmoil."

"Who is Angelica?" asked Ruggiero.

"A beautiful woman with a heart as cold as ice. She is the princess of Cathay, a kingdom not too far from here. Her brother Argalia and four giants accompanied her. A challenge was issued to all those in attendance. Anyone who could best her brother in a joust would win her as their prize, but the losers would become her prisoner and brought back to Cathay. Her beauty was so powerful that no man could resist a chance to possess her, even at the risk of losing their own freedom. Every man burned for her."

Ruggiero shuddered, for he realized there must have been sorcery involved.

"Lots were drawn," said Aistulf. "I was the envy of all for my name was drawn first. I lost the joust and was taken to the prison tent under guard. The second knight was Feraguto."

Ruggiero sat up. He heard of Feraguto from the short time he had been with Akramont's army. Feraguto was a fierce warrior and nephew to Amir Marsilio.

"He was likewise unhorsed, but Feraguto would not honor the terms of the engagement," said Aistulf. "Refusing to surrender, he challenged Argalia on foot, killing him treacherously."

"Treacherously?"

"Feraguto attacked an area unguarded by armor." Aistulf gave him a knowing smile and crossed his legs.

"Indeed," said Ruggiero as he realized Aistulf's meaning. He was then amazed at Feraguto's ruthlessness. He wondered whether Rodomont had ever stooped as low during a fight.

"Argalia's death led to many knights attacking Feraguto, and during that madness I escaped. Since I needed a lance and Argalia no longer lived, I took his golden one."

"But all that happened in Francia. What brought you here?" asked Ruggiero.

"Angelica drove men mad with passion and lust," Aistulf said, shaking his head. "She escaped in the chaos and headed back to Cathay. Many knights pursued her, forgetting all about Charlemagne's tournament. Orlando abandoned our emperor in search of that bewitching woman, but I stayed in Francia and was there when Gradasso invaded Europe.

"After humiliating Gradasso," Aistulf continued, "I set off in search of Renaud to return his prized horse to him. Rumors circulated about him being in Cathay. By the time I found him there, his fame had increased with more heroic adventures. He was grateful to have Bayard again, and gave me Rabican as my reward. We started back to Francia when we came near these shores. Alcina captured me and my horse. I was her prisoner until today."

Ruggiero stared at the stars in the sky. He did not want to hear anything more about Alcina. It was then Rangada and Malha appeared among the newest arrivals. He stood and smiled as they walked over to him.

"I am glad you are both safe," he said. "I apologize if my actions earlier caused you harm, but I had to escape."

Malha threw her arms around Ruggiero and began kissing him passionately. She pressed her bosom against his chest and ground her hips into his pelvis. His body responded, but his resolve was stronger. Yanking her hands from his neck, he pushed her away.

"I cannot give you what you seek."

"I - I do not understand," she said, her eyes filling with tears. "You tried kissing me before. I thought you desired me, Adonis."

"My name is Ruggiero. I am not the same man I was on that day. I cannot provide you anything other than your freedom from servitude."

She hung her head and turned away. The two young women were soon surrounded by handsome knights. Ruggiero was grateful that temptation was over. He sat back down next to Aistulf.

"I do not think I have ever met a knight with your integrity or self control," said Aistulf. "If only I had been able to withstand Alcina's charms in such a manner."

"Let us not talk about that witch anymore. She is in our past. Tell me," he paused, "does your kinsman Renaud have a sister-in-arms?"

"Ah, my fair cousin, Bradamante," Aistulf said brightening. "Have you met her?"

"Briefly although I have never fought against her."

"You are fortunate then, for she is formidable on the battlefield. Bradamante is by far the finest lady in all of Christendom. She has no equal in skill, courage, beauty or grace. I would marry her except there are four good reasons why I cannot."

"And those are?" Ruggiero said, trying to keep his voice even.

"Her four strong brothers," Aistulf laughed.

Ruggiero, realizing Aistulf was poking fun at himself, joined in the laughter.

"Especially Renaud," Aistulf said. "We trained as pages and squires together and Renaud knows full well I am not worthy of such a fine maiden. He would string me up from the nearest tree if he thought I had anything but fraternal interest in his fair sister. He is quite protective of her. I doubt she would marry anyone who did not earn his approval. Besides, Charlemagne would never permit it. His laws prohibit marriage between men and women closer than seven degrees of kinship."

Ruggiero was relieved to know Aistulf was not a rival for her heart, and reflected on his short lived duel with Renaud in Toulouse. He realized how fortunate it ended without incident. Had he been responsible for harming or killing Renaud, there would be little chance he could ever marry Bradamante.

"Do you fancy her?" asked Aistulf, eyeing Ruggiero carefully.

"I wondered about her being a soldier," Ruggiero said quickly. "My mother was also a warrior, but she died giving birth so I never knew her. Female warriors are uncommon. I thought perhaps if you told me about your cousin, I might understand my own mother a little better."

Aistulf leaned back again, seemingly satisfied with that explanation. Ruggiero enjoyed Aistulf's companionship, but he thought it unwise to divulge his love for Bradamante. He was unsure how Aistulf would react to the idea of a Muslim knight sworn to Akramont being in love with his cousin. Rather than risk everything by confiding in a member of her extended family, Ruggiero kept his love for the Maid a secret.

The smoke from the fire destroying Alcina's palace finally reached into Logistilla's realm. Its smell served as a reminder of unfinished business with the evil sorceress. Ruggiero heard strange sounds coming from that side of the island. He did not understand its meaning, but the sound of hyena-like laughter caused the hair on the back of his neck to stand on end.

CHAPTER 49

Orlando, the Count of Anglant, was slowly going mad. He had wandered aimlessly throughout Francia for a month searching for Angelica after she went missing during the battle of Toulouse. The most powerful warrior in the world was vanquished not by the stroke of any sword, but by the face of a woman. Orlando had been conquered by love.

He stared at his reflection in the pool of water and hardly recognized himself. It had been weeks since he had combed or washed his hair and it had become unkempt and unruly. He had not shaved since the day she went missing and he now had a full beard. Angelica would be frightened if she saw him looking like this, but he had no energy to change his appearance. He splashed his face and set off again.

Ambling along the countryside, Orlando's horse Brigliodoro walked behind him. At the sight of a few wafts of smoke coming from a small house, he brightened slightly. Perhaps these people would know what happened to his beloved.

He approached the modest wattle and daub house and knocked. A young woman cautiously opened the door, and stared at the tall knight towering over her.

"My lord," she said, "what brings you here?"

"I am searching for my lady. She is as beautiful as the rising sun. Her name is Angelica, for her face looks like she was created by angels."

The woman opened the door wider. "Come inside and sit down. We have little to offer, but please allow me to serve you some pottage."

He ducked to enter the dwelling. Sunlight streamed in onto the dirt floor from an open window frame. The corners of the single room were still cloaked in shadows. The woman shooed her son off a three-legged stool.

"Fetch our guest some beer," she said, as she ladled a thick liquid into a bowl.

"Have you seen her?" he asked. "Her hair is the color of gold, and her eyes are as blue as the summer sky."

The woman shook her head. "You are the first stranger I have seen in months."

Orlando sat down at the table, holding his head in his hands. "I do not know what has become of her," he said, his eyes welling with tears. "I fear for her safety."

"Go find your father," the woman said to the boy. "Tell him that we have a warrior in the house." She placed the food and drink on the table. "Perhaps my husband can help you. Please eat, you look hungry."

He nodded and drank the gruel in a few swallows. It had been days since he had eaten anything. As he downed the beer, he stared off in the distance. "I had never felt love before. Ladies never showed interest in me for I am not handsome, nor do I speak poetry. Other knights dally with women, but no woman has allowed me to be alone with her before." Fear crossed the woman's eyes. He waved his hand for her not to worry. "My mother arranged a marriage for me. The lady is fair of face, gentle, and comes from a fine, noble family. She was everything I could ask for. We were to be married once the tournament was over and my mother hoped I would be champion again," he said, his voice trailing away. "Then I saw Angelica. She came to the royal court, offering herself to any knight who could best her brother in the joust. By right, I should have been the first to try for I have been Charlemagne's champion since before I was knighted. But the emperor insisted on lots being drawn. Thirty men's lots were chosen before mine."

His hand pounded the table, causing the woman to jump. She stood as her husband entered the house.

"This baron is searching for a beautiful blonde woman named Angelica," she said crossing the room to stand near her husband.

He handed her his straw hat. "I have not seen her."

"I would have won that day, if Feraguto had been honorable. The villain lost, but he refused to yield. Feraguto killed her bodyguards as well, leaving my lady defenseless," said Orlando, his voice choking. "She ran, and I followed, as did dozens of other knights. I wanted to protect her, while they wanted to ravish her. I traveled to her homeland and found her in Cathay, where she tried to return to her father's side while his castle was under siege."

Orlando motioned for more beer. The woman shared a look with her husband, who nodded at her.

"Agrikhan of Tartary wanted Angelica. He used his army to force the issue. Angelica refused to marry him and begged me to save her from such a fate." Orlando finished the beer as soon as it was set before him and gestured for another. "I dueled with Agrikhan and killed him. I thought Angelica and I would be together then, but she sent me on a mission. She wanted more proof that I was the most valorous knight alive and deserving of her hand. She sent me to destroy the sorceress Falerina's enchanted garden." He closed his eyes as images of dragons and other beasts ran through his tangled memory. "I did the impossible for her. I was then welcomed back to her castle with open arms."

"What happened then?" asked the woman as she gave him another mug of beer.

"New enemies surrounded her. The fierce Queen Marfisa switched sides after being insulted by King Sacripant of Circassia. Marfisa swore to kill my lady. Then Renaud joined the warrior queen's side." He shook his head with disgust before downing the beer. "Messengers from Charlemagne came bearing dire news. Spies warned of Saracen forces in Africa gathering to invade the Frankish Empire. Angelica begged me to bring her back to Francia, and swore she would be my bride."

"So you married her?" asked the woman.

"No," choked Orlando. "I offered countless times during our journey to baptize her, but she refused. She wanted Archbishop Turpin to perform her baptism and our marriage. It took all my strength of purpose to be so near a woman of her beauty and not lie with her. She vowed that if I took her by force she would kill herself out of shame for having caused the most powerful knight in Christendom to violate the Code of Chivalry."

He stood and stumbled over to the bed in the corner and fell upon it. Weeks of eating and sleeping intermittently, as well as his consumption of beer had taken its toll. He was soon in a deep sleep, his body twitched in response to the memories that haunted his dreams.

Orlando stood in a forest holding a hare by the ears. He was bringing it back to share with Angelica, when he saw Renaud standing before her.

"I beg your forgiveness, for rejecting your entreaties for love," said Renaud. "Madness covered my heart." He knelt and grasped her hands in his. "I am your servant."

"Unhand my lady," Orlando snarled.

Renaud turned. There was defiance in his eyes.

"Your lady?" he said. "That has yet to be determined. I believe that she has not yielded herself to any man's advances."

Angelica snatched her hands out of Renaud's.

"It is time we finish the duel we started in Cathay," said Orlando, as he dropped the hare and drew Durindana.

"I shall hate to spill the blood of a kinsman," said Renaud, as he drew his sword, "but

182

you leave me no choice."

"I command you to stop this fight!" roared Charlemagne. "I need both of you in our battle against the Saracens."

The emperor and his troops emerged from the forest. Renaud and Orlando glared at one another before slowly lowering and sheathing their swords.

"On the morrow," said Charlemagne, "whichever of you proves to be the more valiant in battle shall win the right to claim her as your own."

Orlando thrashed in the bed as he relived the sight of Angelica being led away by soldiers. His dreams followed the same predictable path from memory to nightmare. He now saw images of Angelica running from the battlefield as her tent was attacked by Saracens. She ran through the fields until she came to a forest where the branches scratched her delicate face. He sat up screaming as his beloved Angelica was ravished by multiple attackers.

Orlando was startled when he awoke and did not recognize his surroundings. As his eyes focused upon the faces of the peasants, he remembered where he was. He swung his legs off the bed, swayed as he stood, gave a gesture of gratitude to the couple for their hospitality and left.

The warm summer breeze helped clear his mind as he continued on his journey, this time riding on Brigliodoro's back. He had not followed the emperor to Paris for he felt the overwhelming need to find and protect Angelica. Orlando had been Charlemagne's most loyal and steadfast paladin, but now he was the most errant knight; all due to the love of a woman.

He looked down at his shield. In his grief, he changed his standard from white and crimson quartering to pitch black because he did not want to be recognized. He was unworthy of respect. He had failed his lady, his sovereign, and himself.

The sound of laughter broke through Orlando's gloom. He lifted his head. Across the field, a man and woman were walking hand in hand together. At first, he thought he recognized them. Orlando squinted. His heart sank as he realized that it was not his dear friend Brandimart, nor Brandimart's wife Flordelis, even though the two women's laughs were similar. A knot grew in his throat as he realized he had lost not only his lady but his best friend as well. He would have valued Brandimart's company during this search, but he no longer deserved such pleasure.

Orlando continued berating himself as his horse plodded onward. As he came upon an encampment of Saracens, Orlando was lifted out of his stupor. The visions from his nightmares of Angelica being ravished by Saracen soldiers flashed before his eyes. He was convinced she was being held captive in one of these tents and that God led him to this location to liberate her.

He dismounted Brigliodoro, tying him securely to a tree.

"Angelica!" he bellowed as he strode toward the encampment. "Where are you?"

Immediately soldiers came forward in response to his voice. Orlando struck at them, using Durindana to vent his fury and frustration. Heads and limbs flew as soldier after soldier was hacked to death. Still more warriors came forward to defend their encampment and they suffered a similar fate.

"Angelica?" He searched every tent to no avail. She was not there. Saracens kept coming at him, and he killed them. Being surrounded by his enemies meant only that he had more men to kill. He was fearless in the face of the odds.

"My child," spoke his mother's voice. *"What you lack in beauty you make up for in strength. Never fear being cut by arrows or swords, for your midwife used a magic salve on you when you were a baby. Your skin is charmed impenetrable."*

The Saracens fought valiantly against him with their arrows, lances, and swords. None had any effect. None drew any blood. None stopped Orlando from brutally killing every man, save one survivor.

~ ~ ~

The Muslim army was camped outside the fortified city of Paris. Inside the royal tent, Amir Akramont and his wazirs were huddled over a map of Paris.

"My lord," said his chamberlain. "There is a messenger from Governor Manilard who seeks permission to speak."

"Send him in," said Akramont glancing up from the map.

A young bedraggled man was ushered inside and he bowed low, "My lord, I bear bad news."

"What is it?"

"Governors Manilard and al-Zahira are dead. All their troops have been killed."

"All of them?" said Akramont as he turned and gave the man his full attention. "How could that happen? Who led the attack? Where?"

"Half a day's ride west of here, and it was not the work of an army," said the man. "It was a single knight."

"One man?" asked Mandricardo, showing sudden interest. "Do you know who?"

"No, my lord."

"Tell me his standard," Mandricardo pressed.

"His shield was draped in black. He bore no crest on his helmet."

"A man in black," Mandricardo mused. "I will go in search of this man who has caused so much damage to our forces. He shall pay with his own blood."

Akramont nodded his assent.

CHAPTER 50

Ruggiero awoke to children's laughter. Boys and girls chased each other as they ran between the rows of sleeping adults.

He had not slept well the previous night due to the multitude of noises coming from hundreds of other people. One man snored so loudly that Aistulf finally threatened the man with great bodily harm if he did not move to the other end of the encampment. Other sounds were distracting in a different manner, including those of copulation between many of the new couples. Thankfully, the children had been kept in an area far away from them.

Try as he might to ignore them, Ruggiero was aroused at the sounds of couples having sex, but it was laced with a sense of guilt as well. He had been reassured by Melissa that Bradamante did not blame him for his infidelity with Alcina because she understood it was due to magical spells. However, if he had succumbed to the temptations of Rangada, Malha, or any of Alcina's courtesans, it would represent a willful betrayal of Bradamante's love.

Soon the morning air was filled with a heady mixture of onion, green chilies, ginger, and curry. During breakfast Logistilla's attendants surveyed the hundreds of refugees about their intended destinations. Many came from diverse parts of Asia including Sericana, Cathay, Circassia, Tartary, and all over India.

Ruggiero and Aistulf were invited inside the palace. They sat down at a table laden with tropical fruit and were soon joined by Logistilla and Melissa.

"This afternoon Melissa will show you how to control that magical creature of yours," Logistilla said to Ruggiero as she handed him cakes made from lychees. "Then you shall be free to leave on the morrow."

"That is kind of you," said Ruggiero. He paused and thought about how best to pose the question that had been bothering him. "I wondered why you did not help these people before now."

The enchantress gave him a rueful smile. "Though my life has been dedicated to opposing Alcina, unfortunately my powers are limited. Over the course of my entire life I was not able to accomplish what you and Melissa did in one day's time."

"I do not understand," said Ruggiero.

"My father was one of Alcina's victims," Logistilla explained. "I was only a girl when he was taken prisoner. He had been sent on a fool's errand to procure a charm to make our village leader invincible. There were rumors such an amulet could be bought at a neighboring coastal town. My father was afraid to return with a worthless trinket, so he asked for a demonstration. Once the amulet was around his neck, he was under Alcina's spell and taken back to this island. Unlike the rest of her prisoners my father did not seek invulnerability for himself, but was commanded to do so by someone else. Most of her prisoners were vainglorious men who sought power by any means. They share many selfish qualities with Alcina. Those are the men who disturb your sensibilities with their lascivious acts."

Ruggiero nodded, grateful that she understood.

The aged enchantress idly drew circles on the surface of the table. "I began having nightmares about my father the day he disappeared. My mother was worried and took me to the village healer named Anasuya. The healer used her magical skills to divine what happened to my father. Once I knew where he was, I became obsessed with rescuing him. I studied magical arts for nearly a year from that wise woman. Then my mother died of a broken heart. I never told her about Alcina, or the true fate of my father, but my mother somehow knew he was never coming back."

Logistilla took a long drink of water. "After my mother's death, I had no family left and no reason to remain in the village. Anasuya begged me to wait. She said I was not ready to challenge Alcina. She warned that I would never return should I set out on my quest, but I knew he was still alive and being held prisoner. I could not wait any longer. Anasuya was right. I have been bound to this island ever since I set foot here over one hundred years ago."

"Did you free your father?" asked Aistulf.

"Sadly no. I stowed away on a ship bound for this island, and in the dead of night I crept onto Alcina's palace grounds. There were no guards then; there had never been a need for them before. I quickly set about breaking the magical bonds of the first men that I found. Those angry men set off to seek revenge against Alcina and did not use stealth. She heard their approach and killed them. I tried in vain to find my father and when I heard her bell ringing, I retreated to the forest. I hoped to return later, but I never got the chance. That night at the center of the island, Alcina and I had our one and only confrontation. She tried killing me by magic, but her spells had a different effect. Some of her powers were transferred to me, because she committed a heinous act that night."

Aistulf took one of her hands in his, "What did she do?"

Logistilla wiped the tears from her face, pausing to regain her voice. "When she learned of my identity and purpose for coming, she ordered my father's tree to be chopped down and burned. Although your enchanted form had been attacked by the hippogriff, your soul was still intact and your body unharmed until the magic spell was broken. My father was murdered. This changed my cause from rescue to one of vengeance. During my battle with Alcina the island split into two and created the narrow isthmus. A magical barrier was created which neither one of us can cross, nor leave this island. I am yin to her yang, but as her powers are destroyed, my powers are also weakened."

"The memory of that fateful night lived on among the imprisoned men," said Aistulf. "Your name was whispered amongst the trees. We knew that if anyone breached the barrier, there was the promise of freedom."

Logistilla smiled and patted his hand. "Her evil reign has finally ended."

Many new lines were etched into the enchantress' face, and her hands appeared bonier than before.

"Is Alcina dead?" Ruggiero asked.

"No," said Logistilla. "Not yet, but she will not last much longer. I fear that I will die as well, for our lives have been linked for so long. I only hope to live long enough to oversee the safe passage of all of her former slaves and prisoners to their destinations. Then, I will happily pass into the Afterlife."

Ruggiero marveled at her calmness at discussing her imminent death. He wondered if he would ever have such strength and peace of mind.

"What will happen to the children?" asked Aistulf.

"Some will either be adopted by my attendants and others will be adopted by the men and women leaving here. Unfortunately, we cannot know with any certainty the parentage of the children, or how they are related to one another."

"Why is that?" asked Ruggiero.

"Alcina never allowed mothers to bond with their children. After giving birth, the women nursed multiple babies and only stayed long enough to regain a comely figure. Those women who were not as attractive were left to care for the children or work in the kitchens. Children grew up not knowing who their parents were or how they were related to one another. This meant that many of the women engaged in sex with whatever male they chose, never knowing if they might be coupling with a brother, father, uncle or cousin."

Ruggiero pushed away his plate of food at this information.

"The strong boys were sent to apprentice with the sailors, while the handsome ones were destined to serve at Alcina's palace," said Logistilla.

"What of the weak or homely?" asked Aistulf.

"They were classified as 'excess children' and they were sold into slavery. However, children born with deformities were taken to Erifilla for disposal."

Ruggiero hit the table with his fist.

"Why are there no elderly people, except for your attendants?" asked Aistulf. "Did she kill them off when they got too old?"

"No," said Logistilla. "They were sold off as well. Alcina is cruel and heartless. She created her own private world of beautiful people designed to provide her with future generations of slaves. She oversaw the deflowering of every maiden. As her slaves aged and became obsolete, their sale provided her with luxurious comforts."

Tears fell down Ruggiero's cheeks.

"You must not hold it against the women who seek a chance for a new life with different men," Logistilla said. "They have been raised in a perverse sheltered world and are terrified of what the future holds for them. Alcina worked to suppress motherly instincts in them. However, some are showing interest in the children."

She gestured to a few women in the distance who laughed and played with children they held in their arms.

"How can we be sure none of these people will be sold into slavery?" asked Aistulf.

"I shall examine everyone's souls before their departure," said Logistilla. "I will see if they harbor thoughts of selling anyone into slavery. Those with such intentions will be put on a special ship whose destination is a small, uninhabited island one hundred leagues southeast of here. They will be left there with a few days' provisions and to their own devices. Otherwise, everyone else will be taken to their chosen destination. The sailors are welcome to join my crew or they can set out with Alcina's old rigs and seek their fortunes. Of all Alcina's people, the sailors will find their transition to freedom the easiest."

After finishing their meal, Ruggiero and Aistulf were taken to a clearing far away from the crowds of people. The hippogriff was brought forward, fitted with a bridle. Ruggiero felt apprehensive at the sight of the strange flying beast.

Melissa climbed on the hippogriff's back and gestured for the two knights to come near. All morning long she demonstrated how to command the animal. She swooped in the air, climbed high and landed before them. Both men watched with keen interest and afterward, Ruggiero mounted the beast with confidence. After an hour of flying over Logistilla's half of the island he landed while smiling broadly. On the morrow he would set off for Francia and reclaim his life.

Aistulf asked to try his hand at riding the hippogriff. Ruggiero handed him the reins and laughed while his friend shouted with delight as he took off to the sky.

CHAPTER 51

Mandricardo felt exhilarated leaving the confines of the Muslim encampment outside Paris. The massacre of two battalions of Muslim soldiers was the first hint that Orlando might be nearby. He had been waiting for such news.

After parting ways with Ruggiero and Gradasso, and their foolish decision to help a follower of Charlemagne, Mandricardo joined Akramont's forces and suffered through the long march to Paris. Pillaging was the only diversion on that insufferable journey. Upon reaching their destination, Mandricardo was angered to learn that Orlando had abandoned his station once more. His only solace was hearing that Charlemagne was furious with the famed paladin. Rumors flew of Orlando being stripped of his lands and title.

Mandricardo had no interest in fighting a war with the Franks. Siding with Akramont was a means to an end. Once he finished his goals in Francia, he would be free to return to Tartary. Then he could continue his own war of expansion by annexing Circassia. He had abandoned that effort when an old man shamed him for not avenging his father's death.

It was midday when they arrived at the site where the soldiers had been slaughtered. Limbs were strewn about and dried blood painted the ground a brownish black. The lone survivor, who had been their guide, stumbled as he knelt down before a decapitated body wearing an overcoat of red with a golden claw.

The youth retched.

"That was Governor Manilard," he said wiping his mouth.

Governor Sabri touched the lad on his shoulder. "They shall all have proper burials."

190

The corners of Mandricardo's mouth twitched as he surveyed the devastation surrounding him. He was eager to meet and challenge the man responsible, for he would be a man worth fighting. If the black knight was not Orlando, he would still be a formidable opponent. Mandricardo had grown weary waiting outside the walls of Paris. Archery was for cowards. The glory of war came from killing men in hand-to-hand combat. The black knight would have felt the warm blood of his enemies wash over his body. Mandricardo wanted the fame and glory that would come by defeating such a knight.

"Once the burials are finished," Sabri said to Mandricardo, "I will organize an expedition to join you in the hunt for this villain."

"Perhaps you misunderstood," said Mandricardo. "*I* will search for the black knight. Others would only slow down my quest. I have never lost a duel, nor have any of my duels ever ended with anything less than a dead opponent. I do not take hostages or prisoners." *The only exception to that rule is Gradasso, but that will be remedied one day.*

Sabri eyed him carefully. "As you wish. May Allah be with you."

CHAPTER 52

Ruggiero found this night more peaceful than the previous one. The number of people sleeping outdoors decreased dramatically as hundreds had left for the mainland. He lay on blankets next to Aistulf who was staring at the waning half-moon.

"Where are we going on the morrow?" asked Aistulf. "For as I said before, I owe you my life and am now bound to you."

Ruggiero shook his head. "Are you not previously sworn to serve Charlemagne and to rule the kingdom of Essex one day?"

"Yes."

"Then those loyalties take precedence over your fidelity to me."

"Who are you, Ruggiero? All I know about you is that you are the bravest and most virtuous knight I have ever met. What brought you here?"

"I had been engaged in war, but was captured by the Sufi mystic Atallah. He was my mentor and raised me after the deaths of my parents. In one form or another, he has kept me a prisoner for all of my life."

Aistulf sat up. "Why would he try to keep you from the world? Your strength and valor are unparalleled."

"He does not think I am ready," said Ruggiero. "I was knighted by Akramont and served him for less than a month. We had been battling in Francia for only a week's time when Atallah imprisoned me again. Only this time he imprisoned others to keep me company. The bravery of a single knight released me and all the other captives. I had just begun to offer my gratitude to our rescuer when Atallah tricked me into mounting the hippogriff. I was then brought to Alcina's domain."

"Your guardian caused you to be brought *here*?" Aistulf said.

"Yes. An unforgivable act."

"And you said that you fought against the Franks?"

192

"Yes, even though my late father had served Charlemagne. I was raised a Muslim."

"That makes us enemies," said Aistulf, his brow furrowed. "Yet I refuse to think in those terms for there is no knight whom I respect as much as you. On the morrow we shall part ways, but should we ever meet on the field of battle I will not fight against you. Not only would I not want to test my mettle against yours, but more importantly I do not wish to see you perish from this earth. I would be loath to extinguish a light such as yours."

Ruggiero shook Aistulf's hand. "Should we meet again on the battlefield, I would find it discourteous to engage in combat with someone I consider a friend."

He turned away from his friend, settled down on his bedroll, and tried concentrating on thoughts other than war. He relived his kiss with Bradamante in his dreams, where they were never disrupted by the hippogriff.

CHAPTER 53

Ruggiero rose to the cheerful sound of birds singing and eagerly anticipated the start of his journey back to Francia. After breaking his fast, Melissa brought forth the hippogriff and Rabican from the stables. Aistulf clapped and whistled to see his horse fully outfitted with his personal saddle. Attendants came forward and helped dress him in his own armor. Aistulf's helmet and shield were gold plated, adorned with pearls, and had a leopard emblazon. His horse was draped with leopard skins, covered by an ornate jewel encrusted saddle, and he bore a gold-dipped lance. Ruggiero stared at his friend, for he had never seen anyone sport ornate and expensive weaponry that relied more on fashion and aesthetics than functionality.

"It is doubtful that you could ever be confused with another warrior," Ruggiero said.

Aistulf laughed. "True. This is my style. I had no worries because I knew Logistilla would bring about the return of my belongings."

"She wishes an audience with you in her chambers," Melissa said to Aistulf.

He nodded and left for the palace.

"Ruggiero, I have gifts for your journey." The enchantress gave a large woolen blanket and a sheep skin. "Here is bedding for you, so that you will not have to seek out lodging with your unusual mount. I have packed your saddlebags with dried fruit, flat bread, and smoked fish. Enough food for a few days travel and to get you back to Francia."

"Thank you. Where is Bradamante?" he asked.

"Marseille. She is leading the troops there and is looking forward to your return."

Ruggiero smiled at the thought, but the smile quickly left his face. "I cannot go there."

"Why not?" asked Melissa.

"She is commanding. She cannot be seen with an enemy soldier. It would be impossible for us to be together privately, and we cannot risk anyone overhearing our conversation. I doubt that she is ever alone in a closed room with a man. It would be injurious to her reputation as a virtuous maid." He paced. "If I went to Marseille, there is the danger that I would be compelled to take up arms for Akramont's forces. I never want to fight against her. I could not live with myself should I cause her harm."

"Would you like to write her a letter?" asked Melissa. "I will deliver it personally."

"Can she read Latin?" he asked.

Melissa smiled. "Yes. She can read and write Latin. She struggles with Greek, but if you prefer that language…"

He shook his head. Ruggiero did not want to put anything down on parchment that might prove embarrassing to Bradamante if someone else had to read it to her. He gratefully accepted the parchment, ink, and a quill and sat down at a desk. His hand was poised to write when he became seized with panic. There was so much he wanted to convey, but he did not know where to start or where to end. Every line he thought of seemed too small and too inadequate to encompass his feelings for her. Paralyzed with fear, he chewed on a thumbnail, then the other. He stopped when he realized he had destroyed all of his fingernails by the agony of indecision. Ruggiero rolled up the parchment.

"I cannot. My heart is bursting with news for her, but I do not know how to put my love for her into words. I fear that I am a man of action rather than poetry. Instead, I shall beg Duke Aymon to grant me an audience and ask for her hand in marriage. Pray tell me where I may find him."

Melissa embraced Ruggiero. "He is in Montauban."

~~~

Aistulf sat by Logistilla's bedside. She was deathly pale, her breathing labored.

"Come closer," she said, in a bare whisper, "I have two gifts for you. This book will help break any magical spells and enchantments you may encounter."

She handed him a tan, leather-bound book without markings on its cover.

"The other gift is a horn. It causes fright in everyone who hears it, including your allies, so use it wisely. Keep these tools with you at all times. Do not pass them to others."

Aistulf took the ram's horn from her and slung its strap over his shoulder. He squeezed her ice cold hands in his as tears welled in his eyes. "I shall cherish these gifts forever."

She smiled as she touched his cheek. "You are meant for great things, Aistulf. Do not hurry back to be a mere soldier of war; you must use your tools and gifts, and set off for the skies."

Ruggiero and Melissa entered the room. Logistilla gave them a wan smile, beckoning Ruggiero forward. He knelt next to her as she grasped his hand.

"Ruggiero, with you rests the hope of generations. You must follow your heart," she whispered. "Melissa, you must see to the needs of my people."

Then the aged enchantress closed her eyes and drifted off to sleep.

~~~

In Greece, Atropos used her scissors to cut an overly long scarlet thread which years before had somehow enveloped a white thread. In so doing, two lives were ended simultaneously; one beautiful and virtuous, the other hideous and evil.

CHAPTER 54

Mandricardo began his quest for the black knight by following the tracks of bloodstained hoof prints that led away from Paris. He thought it strange that a knight capable of killing scores of men did not go forward to fight the larger army. He followed the tracks westward until the droplets of blood were no longer visible. Mandricardo visited every hovel in the area and finally came upon a village. Talking with the locals required Mandricardo summoning upon all his linguistic skills to speak rudimentary Frankish.

"Warrior in black. Seen him?" Mandricardo asked an old man with white whiskers.

The man babbled in return and conferred with others who nodded and joined in the speaking with great enthusiasm. Mandricardo had difficulty following their words and asked for their statements to be repeated several times. The interactions with Frankish peasants were frustrating, but he gleaned a direction to follow. And if he was not mistaken, they had said the black knight had been tearfully seeking a blonde woman. A violent man being brought to tears over a woman? The thought made him laugh.

As the sun hung low in the sky on his second day of searching, he came upon a large encampment of soldiers. Men were still pounding tent stakes in the ground. A few words in Arabic reached Mandricardo's ears. He smiled. Arabic was not his mother language, but he knew it well as opposed to the guttural Frankish tongue. It also meant that the warriors were reinforcements for Akramont.

Mandricardo rode over to where the horses were being fed and he dismounted.

"I am Mandricardo, Khan of Tartary. I come from Paris on a mission from Amir Akramont. Please take me to your commander."

He handed the reins to his horse over to a young man, while another scrambled to his feet.

"Follow me."

They passed a man butchering a goat. It would be awhile before a warm meal was ready. A soldier wearing a plumed helmet stood at the center of the camp.

"Sir," said the young man, "This is Mandricardo, Khan of Tartary. He serves Amir Akramont and asked to speak with you."

The commander nodded and dismissed the soldier while looking Mandricardo over from head to toe.

"I came from Paris," said Mandricardo. "There was an attack on two battalions of Muslim soldiers two days ago. Have you had any troubles on your journey?"

"No. We have not encountered any resistance at all," said the commander.

"Have you seen any lone soldiers? A knight in black, perhaps?"

"You are the only lone soldier we have come across."

Mandricardo sensed disbelief and hostility in the tone of the commander's voice. And why had this man not offered him food and drink already? "I have been searching all day and would like to rest for awhile. Please direct me to a tent where I may wait until supper is ready."

The commander's eyes made a quick scan of the campground. The decision of where to house a guest seemed a difficult one for the man to make.

The peal of a woman's laugh rang out, followed by another woman's laugh.

"You have women with you," smiled Mandricardo. "I could use a woman's company more than sleep. Fetch me your prettiest whore."

The commander's face turned to stone. "There are no whores here."

Mandricardo laughed. "Whatever you wish to call them. A woman's looks makes no real difference, as long as she is warm and wet."

"You must leave," said the man as he placed his hand on the pommel of his sword.

"Are you or are you not sworn to serve Amir Akramont?" asked Mandricardo.

"We serve Governor Stordilano of Granada, who serves Amir Marsilio."

"And Marsilio is sworn to Akramont. I am an ally of Akramont. Your hospitality to me is mandatory."

Other soldiers gathered around them.

"We cannot provide what you seek," said the commander. "We are escorting the governor's daughter to Paris where she will be married to Governor Rodomont of Sarza."

"Ahh, Doralice of Granada," said Mandricardo. "I have seen her beautiful image adorning Rodomont's standard. I have wondered if it did her justice. I should like to judge for myself."

"I cannot allow that sir," said the commander. "I am charged with safeguarding her passage and you pose a threat to her."

Mandricardo was infuriated. How dare they deny him anything? He was a monarch and these were mere soldiers. Two spears were pointed at him. Mandricardo grabbed the shaft of one spear, wrenched it free and swung the weapon at the commander's head, shattering his temple. The man fell to the ground in agony. Another soldier was tripped as he raced forward. Mandricardo stomped on the man's exposed neck, crushing his windpipe and then picked up a shield and bashed it over the skull of a third soldier.

The commotion brought more men. Mandricardo grabbed a discarded sword and dispatched the others with similar ease. Killing men in battle was a pleasurable act, better than any sport. None of these soldiers provided him with any real challenge, and the act of killing all these men without any help solidified his confidence that he was up to the task of challenging the black knight.

However that confrontation would have to wait for another time. Now that all the obstacles were cleared from his path, Mandricardo was on another mission. He was determined to find and possess Doralice of Granada.

CHAPTER 55

"Has he been stopped yet?" asked Doralice.

Her manservant, a dwarf named Devante, carefully lifted the flap on the tent and peered outside. Standing on the tips of his toes, he bobbed his head trying to see across the camp. He winced before closing the tent flap.

"No milady, the madman continues his rampage. More lay dead."

Doralice's attendants Fidelia and Roana clasped her hands. Terror filled their eyes.

"What am I to do?" wailed Doralice.

"We must leave this place," Devante said yanking her by the arm.

Once outside the tent, the reality of the carnage struck her. Near the campfire were five mangled bodies. The distance across the camp to where the horses were tethered looked impossibly far. Doralice began shaking but could not move.

"We must leave milady," said Devante trying to pull her forward. "We have no choice."

"I - I cannot," she said wrenching her arm free and retreating back in the tent.

Fidelia threw a blanket around Doralice's shoulders and stroked her hair. "If only Rodomont were here. He would put things right."

At the sound of Rodomont's name Doralice lifted her head. "Yes, I would be safe if he were here."

"I will send word to him," said Devante.

Doralice gave him a quick embrace before the diminutive man left the tent. She wanted to watch him escape safely, but she could not bring herself to look outside again. Listening intently, she heard the sounds of swords clinking, the moans of wounded men, and then the sound of a horse galloping away. A small wave of relief allowed her stomach to unclench a little. Devante had escaped and would send word to her father. A rescue party would be dispatched on her behalf.

Another scream rang out, dashing her hopes for survival. At least her father would know how she died. He would see that she was buried properly. Tears ran down her face as she braced herself for the inevitable. Earlier in the day she had felt nervous about her impending wedding, now she dreaded her impending death.

"Do you think he is after riches?" asked Fidelia.

The question startled Doralice. She turned and faced the elderly woman who had taken care of her since infancy. "Riches? Of course, riches. That must be what he wants. He will leave us alone if I give him my dowry."

She scurried about and brought forth a small casket containing jewelry. Opening the lid, she retrieved a handful of gold coins and hid them in a small bag.

"Just in case he leaves us alive," she said with a nervous laugh. She placed the box near the tent opening. "How far did they say we were? Thirty miles from Paris? Perhaps we can find our way there without an escort."

Fidelia urged Doralice into a corner and covered her with a blanket. "Make yourself as small as possible. Pray he won't find you."

Doralice hugged her knees to her chest. She could feel Fidelia piling blankets and clothes in front of where she was hidden. The air under the blanket was stifling, but the thought of dying from suffocation was preferable to dying at the hands of a maniac.

"Roana," said Fidelia. "Hide over here. I have a plan."

The camp was silent except for the sound of footsteps. A single pair of footsteps. Doralice knew then that all of her father's men had perished. That thought filled her with despair.

The footsteps stopped in front of the tent. There was a rustling noise, followed by the sound of a man chuckling.

"Doralice," said a man with a gentle voice. "Long have I wanted to meet you."

"Take the dowry and go," said Fidelia.

"I am not here for wealth, but to find Doralice. I have heard her beauty is unparalleled and wish to see it myself. Where is she?"

"Sh-she left," said Fidelia. "She was frightened by your actions. She took a horse and left."

"She did not leave on a horse. Do not try to trick me."

Doralice heard the sound of him rummaging around the tent.

"There you are. Come let me look at you."

"I am veiled until marriage," said Roana. "Please leave."

Doralice began praying silently that Fidelia's ruse would work. Then came the sound of Roana shrieking.

"You are not the lady I seek," said the man, his voice sounding irritated. "Where is she?"

"I am Doralice," insisted Roana.

"Enough of your foolishness. I have seen her likeness. Doralice has fair skin, yours is brown."

"The artist did not capture her true likeness," said Fidelia. "She is Doralice."

The man grunted as he returned to his searching the tent. Doralice felt the woolen blanket being lifted and fresh air washed over her.

"Doralice," he whispered.

In the desperate hope that the Angel of Death would pass over her, she kept her eyes closed and her face to the ground.

"Do not fear me."

His manner surprised her. She had expected to be attacked immediately. He knelt down, but did not touch her.

"I wish to see your face."

She remained still hoping he might be fooled into thinking she died under the blankets.

"I see you breathing. Show me your face."

The tenderness in his voice was disorienting. She expected him to yell and curse, not to sound amused.

"I want to see your face."

She turned her face to him, but kept her eyes closed. "Please take the gold if you like, but do not harm us."

"Harm you? I would no sooner harm a flower or the sun. To harm you would be to harm Beauty incarnate."

Why was this murderer talking of poetry?

"Look at me. I cannot truly judge your beauty otherwise."

She sat up, lifted her head, and opened her eyes, but she would not look at his face. Instead she stared at the blood dripping off his armor.

"Allow me to introduce myself. I am Mandricardo, Khan of Tartary. I was sent on a mission for Amir Akramont, when I came upon your encampment. I thought only to pass the night with a group of fellow soldiers. I was delighted to discover the purpose of this transport. Many times I heard of your beauty. I merely wished to make your acquaintance."

Her eyes shifted to the ground.

"Fools. They not only refused such an honest request, they insulted me," said Mandricardo. "They treated me as if I were your enemy, rather than your admirer. As if I was a common thief, instead of a powerful and respected monarch of a vast domain. No one insults me and lives to tell the tale. Excuse me while I wash up. I must appear frightful."

He crossed to a basin of water and splashed his face. Moistening a towel, he wiped away the blood from his armor and shield. He threw the bloodstained towel on the ground and returned to her side.

"Come," he said as he extended a hand for her. "You cannot stay here, surrounded by death. Let me see to your needs."

"What?"

"You shall come with me. Do not worry. No harm will come to you while you are with me."

CHAPTER 56

Doralice watched Mandricardo load up the saddlebags on his destrier as well as those of a chestnut colored mare. Her treasure-laden casket was packed along with a few dresses that had been in trunks. Last, he attached his shield to the palfrey's saddle and tethered its reins to those of his destrier. Doralice urged Fidelia and Roana to ready other horses, when Mandricardo shook his head.

"They are not coming with us," he said.

"We cannot leave them behind. Fidelia has been my attendant since I was a baby and Roana—"

"I cannot take a retinue of women with me. They appear resourceful enough." He tossed a few gold coins onto the ground. "They are now free to make their own mark in the world."

Doralice opened her mouth to raise an objection, but quickly closed it when Fidelia gave her a look of warning. She turned her back to avoid crying when Mandricardo lifted her onto his horse. He mounted the same horse, placing her on his lap, his arms wrapped around her, as he seized the reins.

"Why am I not riding my own horse?" she asked.

"Because you are distraught, and I cannot comfort you from a distance," he said as the horses began walking.

She turned behind and saw Roana on her knees, wailing in prayer while Fidelia embraced her. Doralice blinked back tears and felt an urge to jump off the horse's back. Just as the thought of how she might get away from him crossed her mind, his hand gripped her arm tightly.

"I have you," he said. "I will not let you fall."

Doralice was numb. She was in the arms of a murderer and had no idea where he was taking her. "Are we going to Paris then, to see my father?"

He shook his head. "As I said before, I am on a mission. Once that is over, I should like very much to take you back to Tartary as my queen."

She was stunned. He did not want to murder her; he wanted to marry her.

"You seem surprised. Do you think yourself unworthy of that honor?"

"But I am already –"

"I know. Your father has promised your hand in marriage to another. I offer you a choice. You are a beautiful noblewoman deserving the finest that life has to offer. I submit that Tartary is superior to that of Sarza. Rodomont's land is an arid desert while mine is vast and verdant. Many palaces are scattered throughout my kingdom, and you will enjoy visiting them all. You deserve a powerful warrior as your husband, and my prowess is undisputed on the field of glory. I have even beaten the dreaded Gradasso."

"Gradasso? He terrorized my land a year ago."

Mandricardo nodded. "I defeated him a few months ago in Anatolia, the same day that I won this suit of armor."

Doralice examined the cuirass by gingerly touching the raised outline of a screaming eagle.

"This armor once belonged to Hector of Troy, but now belongs to me. No other warrior had proven himself worthy, until I came along."

Doralice looked at him with awe, and for the first time noticed that he was handsome. He had a strong jaw line, clear blue eyes, and she was intrigued by his red hair. She had never seen hair that color. His full beard was trimmed, framing his face perfectly. Never having been so physically close to a man before, she was nervous to have his arms around her. Her heart was fluttering like a butterfly with a broken wing. Doralice found his strong smell of sweat surprisingly appealing.

"Does Gradasso live?" she asked.

"He does. It was merely a test of prowess, not a duel to the death."

Mandricardo removed her scarf and touched her hair. He pressed her body against his, breathing in her scent. "You deserve a husband who will be a tender, yet passionate lover."

Doralice shuddered.

"You deserve to be caressed and shown how to experience pleasure," he said, stroking her cheek. "I have seen how Rodomont treats women, and I would hate to think of you being at his mercy. He has cruelly ravished Frankish women. Why would he show any more tenderness with you than he has with them? Bedding a woman properly can sometimes take all night to ensure that she achieves ecstasy. I have seen Rodomont use a woman in less time than it takes for a horse to pass water."

"He ravishes women," she said, closing her eyes in resignation.

"Women are spoils of war. It has always been that way. Do not be surprised to hear of any warrior taking liberty with conquered women. They are plunder."

"And you?" she asked, trembling.

"I am a lover of women, I do not rape them," he said with a half-smile.

She nodded, unsure of what to think.

"You deserve better than Rodomont. You deserve a husband who will satisfy *your* needs." He brought both horses to a stop and then cupped her face in his hands. "Let me demonstrate with a kiss."

His lips brushed softly against hers and when she thought it would be over, the kiss changed its quality. It soon became a tender exploration of her mouth with his lips and tongue, then intense and demanding. He moved one hand slowly upward caressing a breast. She stiffened at the intimate touch, but her body betrayed her as she leaned into his hand. The power of his kiss elicited new sensations that were inherently pleasurable. As he broke their kiss, her eyes fluttered open.

"A good kiss can last all night long," he said. "You deserve a husband who can unlock the passion hidden deep within you. I would hate to see you married to someone ugly, coarse, and cruel. The choice is yours."

Mandricardo kicked his horse to make it start walking again. Doralice was bewildered for he had brought forth in her a jumble of conflicting emotions. Never before had she felt the overwhelming urge to be physically intimate with a man, but the feeling was laced with guilt. She was supposed to marry Rodomont, a brave and powerful governor to whom her father had given his solemn word. If she were to submit to Mandricardo's advances, both her father and Rodomont would be furious.

Doralice chastised herself. She should never have allowed herself to be taken by Mandricardo. As a chaste and proper maiden she should have kicked, screamed, and forced him to lose his temper and kill her back at the encampment. She would be lying dead, ravished or not, alongside her father's soldiers. It would have been an honorable death. Now she had to bargain with the devil to make up for her earlier lack of judgment and for abandoning Fidelia and Roana.

"After I finish my mission, I will either return to Tartary with you as my queen or I shall take you to Paris to see your father. At that point you might still be compelled to marry Rodomont; that is if he will still *accept* you as his bride."

"Why would he not?"

Mandricardo smiled. "Should you reject my offer of marriage, I shall not molest you, but we will still share a bed together."

Her jaw dropped.

"I cannot protect you if I am not near you," he said. "However, after tonight, your reputation will always be in doubt. Rodomont may not wish to marry you as rumors about your virtue and fidelity will plague him in his lands and beyond. Then again, his pride might prevent him from rescinding his offer, but he may always suspect your honor and treat you in a cruel manner. He could also marry again and your stature might suffer."

Fresh tears spilled down her cheeks.

"The choice is yours. Agree to be my wife and I shall show you pleasure beyond anything you have ever known or take your chances with Rodomont. However, I must warn you that I will not repeat my offer. Tonight I will come to our bed as a loving bridegroom or as a rejected and frustrated lover. Either way, by morning, you will no longer be thought of as a maiden. Your fate is in your hands."

Doralice sobbed. This time Mandricardo remained quiet and left her alone with her thoughts. His hand had long since returned to her waist and now there was a large gap between their bodies. He held her loosely, but she no longer felt the warmth of his arms around her. She had no idea what she should do, but she knew Mandricardo was correct about her permanently tarnished reputation. Though he swore it would be up to her to decide whether they became lovers, nothing would stop him from ravishing her.

An unmarried woman who was no longer a virgin was considered a whore even when she was a victim of rape. Without witnesses, it would be her word against his. He could violate her repeatedly and in the eyes of the law it would be no different than if she willingly gave her maidenhead to him.

Doralice also feared Rodomont's reaction once he found out she had been with Mandricardo. She had seen Rodomont's terrible temper on full display when he was tournament champion in Granada. In the mêlée, one man died, two men lost limbs and one man was crippled due to Rodomont's actions. The look on Rodomont's face as he viciously swung his sword made Doralice nervous about marrying him. Her father tried reassuring her that deaths and injuries sometimes happened in tournaments, but his voice trembled as he spoke.

Should Mandricardo return her untouched to Paris and if Rodomont rejected her as his bride, there was no telling what would become of her. For honor's sake, her father might have her put to death – even if she was still a virgin – because of her being alone with a man. Doralice covered her face in her hands. Life had been much simpler when decisions were made for her.

The horses stopped at a peasant household. Mandricardo bargained with the man to sleep in their house and have meals. He handed the farmer one silver coin as the family quickly moved into a small barn. The farmer's wife began preparing a late meal for their unexpected guests over an open fire.

"You cook outside, we rest inside," Mandricardo said in broken Frankish, as he unfastened the saddlebags.

The riches were brought inside the house, lest the poor family be tempted with monetary wealth beyond their imaginings. The house had only one room, with a dirt floor, roughly hewn wooden furniture, and a single straw bed. Doralice had barely gotten over the shock of such lowly accommodations when she realized that Mandricardo had removed his armor and gambeson. He stood before her wearing only thin breeches revealing that his desire for her was unabated.

Doralice looked at his bare chest with its rippling muscles and soft red curls. She turned her gaze upon his handsome face and decided he was far more attractive than Rodomont. There really was no choice but to submit, for she sensed he would not lie peacefully next to her as a frustrated lover. She might as well accept him as her husband, as it would probably be the best of all her possible fates.

"We should get married first," she said.

"I look to no one to sanctify my actions. If I say you are my wife, you are. Doralice, do you agree to be my wife and queen?"

"Yes."

"Then you are."

Mandricardo unfastened the back of her gown in a slow, deliberate manner. He had won. Doralice was about to surrender herself completely to his desires.

CHAPTER 57

The night sky in Marseille was filled with dense clouds. Bradamante knew there would be no better conditions to cloak their secret weapon. Guy, Duke of Burgundy insisted she retire early. He promised to wake her in the dead of night when the dangerous mission began. Geoffroi, Count of Foix and Lucien of Auch were to dress all in black and smear coal dust on their faces. Their plan was to move unseen in a rowboat to the nearby island outside the harbor where the Muslim ships docked at night. The small vessel would allow them to maneuver between the large ships and deliver their flammable cargo upon the masts and prows.

Bradamante fell into a deep sleep shortly after her head touched the pillow. In her dreams she was kissing Ruggiero, only this time they were not dressed in armor or standing on a mountain near Foix. They wore clothes fit for the royal court while standing in the gardens at her family's castle in Montauban. A sound caused the lovers to break their embrace. She was startled to see her mother and father glaring at her.

A second knock on Bradamante's door woke her.

"Arise, Bradamante," said Guy. "It has begun."

Sitting up, still groggy with sleep, she tried putting aside her dream as only her imagination. It was difficult for her to forget the hostility on her parents' faces. Nor could she dismiss the likelihood of their outrage should they learn their only daughter was in love with a Muslim.

Bradamante, dressed in doublets, called for a squire to assist with her armor. Once ready for combat, she covered herself in a black cape. Guy was similarly dressed and waiting patiently outside her chamber. The two leaders walked through the military compound to the highest tower.

Guy left the torch he had used to light their way up the winding staircase in a bracket outside the door of the upper most chamber. They stepped into the darkened room and quickly closed the door so that the light would not be seen from the outside. Bradamante closed her eyes and waited for their adjustment to the new unlit surroundings. When she opened her eyes again she was able to see dark shadows in the small lookout.

Everything seemed peaceful and still. There was no breeze or sounds, not even the cry of a seagull. Bradamante and Guy waited patiently in tense silence when a small burst of light quickly became a line of fire across the prow of a ship. A bell rang furiously, followed by men shouting as they scrambled onto the deck and tried dousing the flames. Another ship suffered the same fate and the sounds repeated themselves. Soon all the men in the Muslim fleet were awake and yelling. Buckets of water were thrown onto the fire, but instead of extinguishing the inferno, they intensified the conflagration. Bradamante now heard screams as men became engulfed in flames and burned to death. As tears fell down her face, she was glad to be in darkness where no one could witness her sympathy to their enemy.

The entire enemy fleet became consumed by fire. Some of the ships tried leaving, but without wind they were unable to sail away. In the ensuing chaos they could not work together to row their way out of the disaster. There was the sound of splashing as men jumped from their ships into the water. Throughout the long, cold night Bradamante and Guy stood in silence watching the human devastation that they granted permission to happen. Once the sun rose and light stole onto the horizon, the sight of charred and mangled bodies clinging to smoldering ships emerged from the haze. The skies were filled with plumes of black smoke and the acrid smell of burnt flesh.

The Count of Foix had found a formula capable of destroying an army in a single night. Bradamante had overseen the death of thousands of men without getting a single drop of blood on her hands or risking her own safety. She was horrified at the aftermath and wondered if such a weapon of abject cruelty should ever be used again.

CHAPTER 58

Mandricardo smiled at Doralice sleeping. The previous night had been far better than he had anticipated. The young lady from Granada had been a passionate lover, and he regarded the previous day as one of the best of his life. He brushed the hair out of her face, gently waking her.

"Good morning my queen," he said.

She yawned and looked up at him with a smile. "Good morning my husband and king."

Mandricardo leaned over and kissed her while lazily tracing circles around one of her nipples causing her to shiver. He had a beautiful nude woman in bed with him, and could not pass up an opportunity to start the day by satisfying all his appetites.

After partaking of a meal of porridge and bread, Mandricardo repacked the saddlebags. This time he allowed Doralice to ride upon her own horse for he knew she would not run away. Because of the night before, her fate and future were inextricably wed with his. They left the peasants' household on a road bearing southeast.

"Husband, where are we headed?" she asked.

"Our host told me that the man I seek was at his house a few days ago and was spotted on a road not far from here just yesterday."

"What is your mission? You never told me."

"A lone knight killed two battalions of soldiers on their way to Paris. I was sent to punish him."

Doralice shuddered.

"The only surviving witness of the massacre described the knight as being dressed all in black. He did not know who this man was, but I suspect Orlando."

"Orlando!"

"If I am right," he continued, ignoring her outburst, "then my true mission to the Frankish Empire will be complete."

"I do not understand."

"Orlando killed my father. I must avenge his death."

"But Orlando is legend."

"As am I," replied Mandricardo.

"Of course my husband," she said chastened. "I – I merely meant…"

"All the more fame and glory for me when I defeat that infidel."

"Yes," she said, smiling weakly. "Husband, why are you not carrying a sword?"

"I set out on my quest for revenge on foot, without weapons or armor, vowing to seize whatever I needed by force. When I won this suit of armor I swore that I would not bind any sword to my side except Durindana. That famous sword was once Hector's and is now wielded by Orlando."

Mandricardo saw a look of apprehension cross her face before she turned away from him. He glared at the back of her head, vowing she would regret ever doubting his prowess on the field of glory.

CHAPTER 59

All day long, blackened corpses washed upon the rocky shore in Marseille. The water renowned for its clarity and sparkling blue color had overnight become murky and brackish. Normally, the rugged white mountaintops surrounding the city were visible for miles around, but they had become obscured as the smoke and ash in the air decreased visibility to less than half a mile. It was difficult telling night from day because the sun's rays barely penetrated the thick haze. Few people could last long at gathering the dead bodies because the ash caused labored breathing and fainting. Days later, people were still sneezing soot.

Bradamante oversaw the clean up effort because she felt responsible. If the approval had not been given to test that weapon, the water would not be filled with blackened corpses. This arduous task had been going on for hours when Bradamante heard her name called.

Guy, Duke of Burgundy, waved and beckoned for her to join him inside a small building. Upon her entry, she realized that a stranger was in the room with Guy. The man stood upon her arrival and bowed. He was utterly broken and reeked of smoke. Bradamante could not tell the color of his skin or hair underneath the soot and ashes.

"Bradamante, this is Kumanda," said Guy. "He is now the leader of the Saracen forces. Out of the entire fleet, his ship is the only survivor. There was not enough room on the docks and so his ship was anchored a distance away from the others."

"That was fortunate for him," said Bradamante.

"He does not see it that way," said Guy. "How good is your Arabic?"

"I know a few phrases, but not enough to carry on a conversation."

"That is similar to his Frankish." Guy refilled the man's cup with water. "He has come to surrender all claims to Marseille. He asks only to oversee the burial of those who died last night."Kumanda's hands shook as he tried lifting the cup to his mouth. Water spilled down his front as he hacked uncontrollably. Guy thumped him on his back. The man coughed up a large black mass of phlegm onto a dirty rag.

"He must bear his dead away from here," said Bradamante as she handed the man a washbasin. "The water will take years to recover. I do not want the soil polluted by those charred bodies. He must also send a messenger to Akramont telling of the abandonment of Marseille and that his surrender stipulates there will be no further attempts to claim this city."

Guy translated Bradamante's terms to Kumanda. The man nodded and left. The next morning what was left of his crew would begin loading the dead onto their ship for transport elsewhere for burial.

As evening approached, the sea released two more badly burned corpses upon the rocky beach. This was a discovery Bradamante had been dreading. Arrows stuck out from the back of the men's necks, and their shields were still firmly clutched in their charred arms. Their standards identified them as Geoffroi, Count of Foix and Lucien of Auch.

Bradamante said a silent prayer as she heard the news. There were no tears left to shed, and she felt hollow. She retired her room and wrote letters. One was to Emperor Charlemagne telling him of the Saracens' surrender in Marseille and crediting two soldiers who bravely sacrificed their own lives. She asked they be given royal honors posthumously. Their bodies would be taken by wagon along with her second letter addressed to the count of Toulouse. She requested that he arrange funerals for the two heroes who had lived in neighboring towns.

A knock at her door announced a visitor.

"We should be the ones who pack the count's belongings," Guy said as he opened her door.

Bradamante knew what he meant. Guy wanted to assure that any notes Geoffroi made about the weapon be kept a carefully guarded secret. She followed the duke of Burgundy down the hallway to the late count's room. Guy took a large ring of keys and tried them one by one until he found a key that worked.

The room was tidied, almost as if it had not been occupied. The bed was made and the small desk had only a pot of ink, a quill, a blotter, a small oil lamp, and a wax tablet whose markings had been smoothed over. Guy lit the lamp and examined the tablet. He frowned as he ran his fingers over its surface.

"It has been wiped clean," he said.

Guy shifted his attention to the wooden trunk in the corner. He lifted the lid and began removing its contents. Bradamante took the clothes handed to her and carefully placed them on the bed.

"This might be it," Guy said as he pulled out a piece of parchment from the bottom of the trunk.

Bradamante held her breath as he began reading.

Guy shook his head. "It is only an unfinished letter."

"Who is it to?"

"Your father."

Bradamante felt her cheeks begin to burn.

"Geoffroi was to begin negotiations with your father regarding a marriage with you. There is a mention of an attempt he was leading to drive the infidels from our coastline. I believe he wanted to finish this after his weapon was tried out."

Bradamante turned her back to Guy and refolded the linen tunic on the bed. She felt Guy's comforting hand on her shoulder.

"I am sorry, Bradamante. He would have made a fine husband for you."

She nodded and busied herself by refolding other items of clothes. Guy most likely thought she felt sorrow at having lost a suitor, but instead she was relieved. Her father would have jumped at such a marital prospect for her, and that would have eliminated her chance at a marriage with Ruggiero. Her sense of relief gave way to a profound sense of guilt and shame. Here she was grateful for not having a potential romantic rival for her hand, when an honorable man was dead.

Guy resumed his search of the trunk, but found nothing that described how the liquid fire was created. The two men responsible for unleashing its hellish powers had taken their secret to the grave. Bradamante was privately grateful for that as well. Only she and the duke of Burgundy knew the existence of the weapon that caused so many to perish, and neither wanted to admit that they had allowed its formula to be lost once again. They would rather their emperor think the fires had been set in a more conventional fashion.

That night as Bradamante lay on her bed, she shivered uncontrollably. She had never felt as cold as she was that night, and no amount of blankets could warm her. She willed herself to a dreamless night's sleep; after witnessing the horrors of the past day it was unlikely her dreams would be pleasant.

CHAPTER 60

Ruggiero chose the name Kamal for the hippogriff as it meant beauty and perfection in Arabic. Once he overcame his fear that the winged creature might take him on another uncontrollable journey, he marveled at the majestic nature of the beast. Kamal's head was that of a giant eagle. The alertness in Kamal's eyes and a twitch of his golden tail brought back fond memories to Ruggiero of his beloved horse Frontino. Perhaps he could forge a similar bond with this mount.

The return journey to Francia was enjoyable as they soared above and below the clouds. They flew over mountains, lakes, and vast expanses of arid land. The first night they camped near a stream far away from any village.

As Ruggiero stoked a small fire to keep warm, he reflected on the task that lay before him. He had no idea how to approach Duke Aymon. He was a Muslim knight, who was still practically a novice, asking for the hand in marriage of the only daughter of an important Christian nobleman. And he was asking to marry a woman whom Aistulf thought of as being the finest lady in Christendom. Surely many noblemen would want her as their wife.

Ruggiero could not think of any reason why Duke Aymon would allow for such a betrothal to occur, let alone grant him an audience. His heart was now firmly lodged in his throat as he stared at the glowing embers. He was afraid that if he waited to distinguish himself in battle before asking for Bradamante's hand, another suitor would become betrothed to her. He could not bear to think of her being married to anyone else.

Then Ruggiero thought of Aistulf and rebuked himself for not confiding in his friend about his love for Bradamante. He had worried family gossip might ruin his chances, but Aistulf might have been his only hope. Had Aistulf written a letter of introduction detailing Ruggiero's recent acts of valor, then perhaps Duke Aymon would realize his daughter could not find a more loyal and upstanding husband. Even if Aymon had little respect for his nephew, Aistulf was still heir to the throne of Essex and one of twelve paladins serving Charlemagne. That had to account for something. Bringing a letter from Aistulf would have been a better strategy than arriving empty-handed to Montauban.

Ruggiero buried his head in his hands. He would rather face Erifilla or Caligorant again than Duke Aymon. Failure against monsters resulted only in a nasty and brutal death, but failing with Aymon would mean living without Bradamante's love, a fate worse than death. He slept fitfully that night, dreading what the next few days might bring.

The next morning after prayers and breakfast, he put the upcoming meeting with Duke Aymon out of his mind. He would rest that night near Montauban and then devise a strategy for approaching Bradamante's father. Until that time he needed to concentrate on the landscape and his flight. He avoided the Provence coastline. He did not want to test his resolve to refrain from seeing the Maid.

That night as he flew near a great forest north of Toulouse he spied the glow of a small campfire. The smell of roasting meat hung in the air, making his mouth water. He directed Kamal to fly in circles, but did not see anyone. He cautiously brought the winged animal down in the clearing and surveyed the site. The fire was built in front of a large hollowed out tree stump. Nearby there was a stream filled with fresh cool water. He led the hippogriff to drink while tethering it to a large oak tree.

"Hello?" he called out.

The only sound heard in reply was the rustling of leaves by a gentle gust of wind. Ruggiero sat down before the fire and turned the body of the roasting hare. The meat was turning a crispy brown on the outside. Rotating the stick caused a few drops of fat to sizzle on the flames. His stomach rumbled and his mouth watered. He could not understand why this game was abandoned, and knew that it would soon burn if not removed from the fire.

He had planned on eating his stores of dried food, but he was now faced with the irresistible opportunity to have fresh roasted meat. Ruggiero laid his blanket and sheep skin near the fire. He vowed to himself that should the hunter return, he would offer his stored food and promise to hunt for replacement game the next day. However, no one came. Ruggiero tore off a leg from the hare and tasted it. The meat was succulent and warmed him inside.

Ruggiero then noticed a small earthenware jug. Pulling the cork he drank, and was not terribly surprised to taste red wine. Alcohol was *haram*, forbidden for Muslims, but Ruggiero did not spit it out once he realized what it was. He took another swallow, justifying his consumption with the knowledge that to marry Bradamante he would have to convert to Christianity, and wine was used in Christian ceremonies. His late father and his future bride drank wine. Besides, he preferred its taste to water.

As Ruggiero stared into the flames, he felt the wine relax his nerves. Many legends featured heroes proving their worth before they were rewarded with the hand of a princess. He could offer Duke Aymon to kill any monster or creature terrorizing the neighboring villages. Surely there must be a chimera or hydra somewhere, or possibly an ogre or Cyclops. There had to be some heroic task he could perform for Duke Aymon to demonstrate his bravery and prowess. Closing his eyes, he fell into a deep sleep where he slew dozens of blood curdling monsters by his expert use of Balisarda.

~~~

A man had been waiting patiently in the shadows. Once he was certain Ruggiero was in a deep sleep, he crept forward and gently removed the magic ring from Ruggiero's finger. The man untied the hippogriff and walked the beast away. Atallah turned toward Ruggiero's sleeping form and murmured, "Forgive me, dear child. I do this out of love for you."

~~~

The sun was rising when a calamitous noise roused Ruggiero from his slumber. He sat up, grabbed his helmet, sword and the nearest shield. Running into the forest, he sought out the source of the din. He stopped as a ten-foot tall giant threw Bradamante over his shoulders.

"Help me Ruggiero!" she screamed.

The giant turned and ran into the open door of a large stone castle. Ruggiero followed close behind with his sword drawn and ready to kill.

Part IV

The Siege of Paris

CHAPTER 61

Akramont, Amir of the Maghreb, sat in the royal tent studying the map of Paris. His tapered fingers traced the city's perimeter, pausing over each gate. Different scenarios of attack and defense ran through his mind.

The keys to fame and glory were victory and expansion of an empire. The walls of his royal palace in Bizerta were decorated with mosaics depicting the many conquests by his noble ancestor, Alexander the Great. Akramont could recite every detail about that famed warrior, from his taming of the wild horse Bucephalus at the age of twelve, to the conquests of Greece, Tyre, Egypt, Persia, and India, to his mysterious death at age thirty-two. Akramont longed for his own name and exploits to rival those of his famous ancestor. Alexander had been crowned King of Macedonia at age twenty, and now Akramont at twenty-two years of age felt Alexander's legacy propelling him forward.

"Your move," said Marsilio.

Akramont's attention was diverted to a chess game with the Amir of al-Andalus. He scanned the board, noted his opponent's move and scowled. After studying the positions of the pieces, he smiled as his knight took a bishop.

"How much longer do we have to wait before striking our enemies?" demanded Rodomont.

Akramont kept his eyes focused on the map of Paris. "I am waiting to hear from spies and field commanders."

He could hear Rodomont pace in the back of the royal tent, but would not allow himself to display any reaction to the man's temper. Akramont knew that his calmness exuded a sense of power, while the governor of Sarza appeared weak by his anger and frustration. Rodomont's fury also stood in stark contrast to that of Gradasso, who sat on a cushion polishing his scimitar with aloof disinterest.

Brunello walked cautiously into the tent, falling on his knees at Akramont's feet. "Your lordship, I bring news," he said.

"What is it Brunello?"

"I fear it will displease you, my lord," he said, his face cast downward.

"What is it?"

"Our enemies have reinforcements on their way."

"How many?" asked Akramont.

"At least ten thousand, my lord," said Brunello. "They crossed the channel led by Renaud."

Gradasso stood up, suddenly interested. "How long until their arrival?"

"Soon. It could be tonight or on the morrow," said Brunello, burying his face once more.

Akramont yanked the small man to his feet, and held him in the air. "Why are you delayed in returning to me?"

"I rode my horse as fast as possible, but I drove him too hard and he died," sobbed Brunello. "It was two days before I found another horse to steal."

Akramont threw the dwarf to the ground, and returned his attention to the map.

Sabri, the elderly governor of Algocco, entered the tent and bowed as he approached Akramont. "My lord, the engineers have finished their second tower, four more are being built but they will not be ready for another day or so."

"They have been tested?" Akramont asked.

"Yes," said Sabri. "Two are ready, but there will be more soon."

"How many ladders?"

"Dozens, as well as catapults."

Marsilio peered outside the tent opening. "Tonight would be a crescent moon, but there is a thick blanket of clouds to enshroud us with darkness. The infidels will not expect us to strike tonight, so the element of surprise will be on our side."

"Darkness or light makes no difference to me," said Rodomont. "I want to raze Paris and then go to Rome. There I shall eat the beating heart of the pope himself!"

"Killing the pope will be necessary to destroy this false church," said Marsilio, as he sat back down near the chessboard and steepled his fingers. "Only then can we lead the people in these lands to the one true faith. However, committing such an act to their religious leader will only make the infidels burn with hatred toward us. They would refuse to learn the teachings of the prophet Muhammad, peace be upon him."

Rodomont's lips twitched with a slight smile. As if he did not care about the consequences of his actions.

Akramont diverted his eyes again to the map. "Gradasso, you conquered Paris last year," he said. "Tell me how you accomplished that feat."

"Charlemagne engaged us in war; he did not hide behind those walls like he is now," said Gradasso. "He was taken prisoner as well as his paladins. It was over quickly."

"He has learned from his mistakes," said Akramont. "The Franks have not left their protective confines."

His fingers lingered over two gates on the southern wall of the city.

"You should learn from a mistake I made," said Gradasso. "I showed mercy to Charlemagne, thinking he was a man of honor. However, that knave allows two of his paladins to flaunt possessions rightfully belonging to me. Since the emperor is not a man of his word, he must die." He stood and pounded a fist onto a table. "Furthermore, you must kill all his children and kinsmen who could be seen as his heirs. Leave no relative for the Christians to rally around."

"He is right," agreed Marsilio. "Charlemagne must die."

Akramont studied the small smile on the face of the silver-haired amir. He wondered if Marsilio's concurrence was due to agreement in strategy or predicated on selfish political motives. If the emperor was taken out of the game, Marsilio would have an easier time as ruler of al-Andalus and the lands north of it.

"Tell me about Charlemagne," said Akramont. "You have fought border wars with him over the years. Give me the measure of this man."

"Have you ever seen him in person?" asked Marsilio.

"Only from a distance."

"Even at the age of sixty, he still cuts an imposing figure," said Marsilio. "Beyond being the tallest man I have ever seen, he has a countenance about him that makes me think of Moses bringing the Ten Commandments down from Mount Sinai. He may appear pious, but he has a notorious weakness for food and women. However, as a military leader and strategist, there is none better. If it had not been for the Saxons keeping Charlemagne busy in the north over the years, I would have had him at my doorstep more often."

"You believe we should strike tonight?" asked Akramont.

"Yes. We cannot allow Renaud and his reinforcements to join Charlemagne," said Marsilio. "We have no walls guarding our encampment. Renaud would slaughter us in our sleep if given the chance."

"There will be a terrible storm tonight," Sabri warned. "Regardless of the darkness, our enemies will know in advance of our attack. They cannot fail to hear the siege towers being moved into place."

"They will soil themselves knowing that this is their last night alive," said Rodomont.

Akramont crossed to the tent opening and looked out at the gathering clouds and then back at the expectant faces of his wazirs. He could not permit himself to be considered weak or indecisive. Especially since many of these governors were twice his age, and were unaccustomed to taking orders from a younger man. If he waited another day to strike, the promised reinforcements might tip the balance toward the Franks.

"We attack tonight under the cloud of darkness," announced Akramont. "Ready your forces and prepare to move the towers into place."

He went back to the chess board and moved a rook.

"With any luck, tonight shall lead to the same fate for Charlemagne," Akramont smiled as Marsilio recognized the game was over. "*Shah mat.*"

CHAPTER 62

Renaud stared in the distance, hoping that by sheer force of will he could cause the reappearance of his messengers. He depended upon their report to decide how to deploy thousands of soldiers. Moreover, his future as a paladin of Charlemagne rested with the success of this mission. Being the eldest son from a famous military family and a nephew to Charlemagne, he grew up with high expectations of him. No one doubted his skills anymore. Instead, they wondered about his ability to see a mission through.

Rumors had spread throughout the land about why he had abandoned his duel with Gradasso the year before. Some tales were wilder than others, but they all shared the common theme of cowardice. Renaud likened the gossip surrounding him to the Hydra fought by Heracles, where when one head was cut off two would grow back in its place. He wanted to kill that monster by striking at its heart, and rid all doubts surrounding his courage and loyalty. Only victory in this battle would put those fears to rest.

Standing on a road a few miles north of Paris, Renaud wrestled with what to do next. Should he order his men to make camp for the night and ride out the storm, or press onward and join the besieged Franks? They had stopped to rest their horses, but he did not give the order to pitch tents. His troops had traveled fifteen miles already. They could be asked to march further or they could arrive in the morning fully rested and ready for battle. However, by entering Paris in broad daylight they would forfeit any element of surprise.

Renaud scanned the horizon again. Seeing nothing, he turned toward a few men who had built a campfire. He angrily strode toward them.

"No fires," he hissed. "We cannot risk being seen or heard."

The chastened soldier bowed his head. As Renaud turned his back, another soldier grumbled. He gave a piercing glance over his left shoulder at the four men sitting on the ground. Renaud would brook no dissent on the matter.

His last message from Charlemagne ordered a third of the troops to report directly for defense inside the city walls. The remaining troops were to attack the invading forces, and according to the last intelligence, the Saracens had concentrated their efforts on the southwestern gates.

Finally two horsemen appeared on the road. They were dressed as peasants, but under their cloaks they wore armor. Renaud smiled at their approach and he ushered them aside to speak with his commanders.

"Is the pontoon bridge ready?" Renaud asked, in a hushed tone.

"Yes, they are finishing now. By the time you get there it will be complete."

Renaud embraced the messenger, kissing him on the cheek. Startled by such an emotional reaction the man blushed and hastily left the commanders who were huddling over a map of Paris.

"Edward and Herman, you will lead your troops and all of our supplies on this road leading to Paris," said Renaud, pointing at the map. "You will approach Saint Denis' gate here and Saint Martin's gate here on the northern side of the city. Keep your banners down until you are just beyond the archers' range. Then unfurl them showing the standard of King Odo of Essex." Renaud turned to his other commanders while gesturing at the map. "We shall cross the Seine south of Paris then split our forces into three lines to divide and surround the infidels. Zerbin, you will advance closest to the walls of Paris; Leanian, you will take the middle ground; and Ariodant you will be in charge of the outside flank."

"And where will you be?" asked Zerbin.

"Leading the charge in front of all the forces."

CHAPTER 63

Charlemagne walked the Citadel's parapet overlooking the fortified city of Paris. The night air was heavy with water, like a new mother needing to nurse. Sweat dripped off his brow as he shifted his weight. His knees and ankles were alight with pain, a reliable indicator of an impending rainstorm. Charlemagne closed his eyes and imagined he was soaking in Aachen's natural hot springs. His joints ached with gout and the only relief for that pain was in those magical waters. Instead, he was stuck in Paris for he was loath to do anything that might bring war to his palace doorstep.

The dark clouds matched his dour mood. Having lived in an almost constant state of war since he was crowned king more than thirty years before, Charlemagne found himself in the unusual and uncomfortable position of defending his domain, rather than attacking his enemies. He preferred being the aggressor.

The island in the middle of the Seine River was the heart of the city, and the Citadel stood there towering over all else. It had served as the palace for the Merovingian dynasty, but now housed the Count of Paris and Charlemagne's forces. The city was bursting at its seams with people who had left their towns out of fear of the invading army. People had streamed into Paris by the thousands, doubling its population.

From the Citadel's roof, Charlemagne saw the entire island as well as the Left and Right Banks inside the thirty-foot high walls. The city was a nightmare. The Romans had designed Paris as they had all cities: straight roads that met at right angles to one another. Large stone buildings were erected from the limestone quarried beneath the city. However, once the Romans lost their hold over these lands, the people began building in ways the Roman engineers would never have permitted. Clusters of houses were built so close to one another that the streets became crooked and honeycombed with humanity.

Worse than the city's haphazard layout was the sanitation. The narrow earthen streets were never cracked and parched, even in times of drought, because the dirt was continually moistened by the contents of chamber pots. Charlemagne had a difficult time deciding which was the more oppressive: the humidity or the stench of raw sewage.

"Your Majesty," a familiar voice called to him.

Charlemagne turned and saw his old friend and closest advisor, Namo, Duke of Bavaria, standing a respectful distance away. Namo looked tired. He was a man whose age should have allowed him to be exempt from war, but Charlemagne still relied on his sage advice. Namo had served as counselor to the king since Charlemagne's ascension to the throne. Out of loyalty, Namo was still there at his side.

"When did we get so old, my friend?" said Charlemagne. "It seems like it was only a year ago when we were first conquering the Lombards and then putting down the Saxons."

"The Saxons gave us our gray hair," said Namo. "They refuse to stay conquered."

Charlemagne clapped him on the back. "Indeed they have vexed me for years. Now I have this young amir."

"May I give you my thoughts?"

"Please. I need your counsel."

"I am worried, Charles," said Namo. "I am worried about what will happen should Akramont's forces defeat us. He may order mass conversions. He must know about that day in Verdun."

"We had baptized them, but they never gave up their idolatry," said Charlemagne.

"I know," said Namo, giving a calming gesture with his hands. "They were pagans who repeatedly resisted our Lord. My fear is that Akramont may similarly order conversion by the sword. I fear he will create thousands of Christian martyrs."

Charlemagne stroked his mustache as he stared up at the sky. Namo had reminded him of the worst day of his life. He could still recall the sight and sounds of thousands of Saxon men being beheaded and the overwhelming smell of blood. He did not want his own people to suffer a similar fate at the hands of Saracens. Such thoughts consumed him, but he dared not give voice to those fears lest anyone think he harbored doubts of his ultimate victory.

"It shall not come to that, for we will not be defeated," said Charlemagne. "As long as I can mount a horse and lift a sword, I will continue leading my army into battle. Let us go inside where it may be cooler. The air is stagnant, nary a breeze all day."

Namo led him down a spiral staircase and through a hallway until they arrived at a small room where the elderly Archbishop Turpin was waiting.

"Namo, do you have any news for me?" asked Charlemagne.

"Yes, your Majesty. Our spies have told us the enemy camp has been feverishly building ladders and siege towers. The lookouts saw increased activity among their troops this evening. They are expecting an attack tonight."

"What of our readiness?"

"As you instructed, more spiked chains have been stretched across the river. We have forces stationed at each of the gates on our Left Bank. Traps are set for several gates. We are working to install similar traps inside each gate on that bank."

"They have been here for over a fortnight," said Charlemagne, "but Akramont has yet to secure our northern gates. He will likely erect bridges to span the river and then fully blockade us. How are our food supplies holding out?"

"Without further shipments and with our current rationing, it should last for thirty days. There is also news that Gradasso joined Akramont's ranks."

Charlemagne turned his back, hiding his face that burned with shame. "Gradasso has returned. What is said about his motives for joining with Akramont?"

"That he is still obsessed over seizing Bayard and Durindana. It is rumored that he seeks revenge on you as well."

"How many men did he bring with him this time?"

"None your Majesty. He came alone."

"Alone? That is odd. Then again, his entire quest was odd." Charlemagne turned back to face him. "Is there any *good* news to report?"

"Renaud is bringing close to nine thousand troops from Britain. They should arrive in the next day or so."

"And how many troops does our enemy have?"

"They invaded us with a force approaching 80,000 men," replied Namo. "We think they now have about half that many."

"Half?"

"The battle in Toulouse was fierce, and Akramont diverted some of his forces attempting to secure Provence and its coastline."

"Bradamante and Guy, Duke of Burgundy, are to be thanked for their leadership in Marseille," said Charlemagne. "Can you tell me the number of our forces inside these walls?"

"It stands at about fifteen thousand, your Majesty."

"With the addition of Renaud's troops, we shall still be outnumbered nearly two to one," said Charlemagne, shaking his head.

"There is other news which does not bode well for our enemies."

"Do tell."

"Two battalions of Saracen soldiers were on their way to Paris when they were slaughtered by a single knight."

Charlemagne raised an eyebrow. "One man vanquished two battalions of armed soldiers?"

"Yes, your Majesty."

"Do you know who was responsible?"

"There are only two paladins capable of such a feat," said Namo. "One is Renaud, the other is Orlando."

"Orlando," said Charlemagne. "Is there any word of his whereabouts?"

"No, your Majesty. I have sent messengers far and wide throughout the land, but there has been no word."

"I fear his love for Angelica will drive him mad. He abandoned me when I needed him most. Once he was my finest champion, until that accursed woman showed her face at my ill-fated tournament. At least Renaud has returned to my service." He extended his right hand to Archbishop Turpin. "Come Father, it is time we prepare."

The men knelt and bowed their heads.

"Heavenly Father, hear my prayer," said Charlemagne. "I have dedicated my life to expanding your church's reach and influence. I have fought countless battles on your behalf against those who worshipped pagan idols. Now I find myself, and the empire I rule in your name, in peril. You have blessed me far more than I deserve, but I humbly ask that you bless me once more with victory. Our enemies seek to destroy this empire. They claim to worship you as well, but they deny the divinity of your son Jesus Christ. They disavow His sacrificial death by crucifixion, and therefore the miracle of His resurrection. Without sacrifice there can be no redemption. The Saracens would have us repudiate these essential tenets of our faith in order to follow the teachings of a false prophet." He paused and cleared his throat. "I know as a man I have not lived up to your expectations. I am weak and have far too often succumbed to temptations of the flesh, but I beg of you to not forsake your people in this hour of need to punish my personal failings. I ask that you give my army the strength of purpose, and with your power of righteousness repel these invaders. In Jesus' name we pray. Amen."

"Amen," said Namo and the archbishop in unison.

Charlemagne raised his head and stood. "The archbishop will now hear my confession. Namo, you and your sons will dispatch priests to hear confessions of all our soldiers and of the people in this city. The time is at hand where everyone's souls must be prepared for the Afterlife."

Namo nodded and left. Charlemagne knelt again, this time with the archbishop's hand on his head.

"Bless me Father, for I have sinned…"

CHAPTER 64

Akramont was restless for night to fall. Supper had long been consumed, and he paced in his tent as he anxiously awaited the time to perform their night prayer. He felt it imperative for every soldier to participate before entering this battle. The governors had gathered in his tent; they all knelt on their prayer rugs, except for Rodomont who stood in the back with his arms crossed.

His vassals were watching him for signs of weakness. He did not want to confront Rodomont before beginning the prayer, but he smiled after devising a plan to reassert his dominance over the arrogant warrior while rebuking him for profane behavior.

Akramont stood in the front of the tent and began the prayer. After finishing the required recitations he added his own words in honor of the coming battle.

"Allah hear our prayer." He lifted his hands into the air, his face pointed toward Heaven. "Two generations ago, your word was stopped not far from here in Tours by Charles Martel. We are here with this great army of commanders and warriors from the Maghreb and Asia to renew our commitment to spread your glory and the teachings of your greatest prophet Muhammad, peace be upon him."

"Amen," the men responded in unison.

"Bless us as we attack our enemies."

"Amen."

"Help us put your sacred words above those of our enemies."

"Amen."

"Fill us with your glory."

"Amen."

"Bless us with your strength."

"Amen."

"Bless us with victory."

"Amen."

"We promise to serve you, and to lead these people to worship you as we have been taught by your prophets and by the Qur'an."

"Amen."

"*Allahu Akbar.*"

"Amen."

As the prayer ended, Akramont remained motionless with his hands in the air, tears streaming down his face. "Allah is with us."

Akramont slowly walked over and placed one hand on the shoulder of his cousin Daniso. "You shall have the position of honor as the first to cross over the walls into the heart of that accursed city. Your name will be sung for generations as a hero."

"I am honored," replied Daniso, bowing his head.

"I deserve that honor!" bellowed Rodomont. "I came to Francia first. I invaded while you spent months searching mountaintops for your prophesied savior, Ruggiero. Where is that fabled boy now? I have been your greatest champion from the beginning and I will not be denied my rightful place as the first to enter Paris."

Akramont calmly turned his head to Rodomont. "You did not pray. I have yet to see you pray. While I appreciate your valor and service, I cannot allow a man who is not devout to be placed in the primary role that you seek. It would be an affront to Allah. Instead that honor shall go to the son of my late Uncle Almont, a man who was known for upholding the faith of Islam against all who sought to destroy it."

Daniso gave an appreciative nod, while Rodomont's fists remained clenched.

Sabri stepped between Akramont and Rodomont. "There are two towers ready, my lord. Might I suggest Rodomont's men use the second one? It would reward them for their service in this war which has been longer than most of the soldiers here."

Akramont nodded and pointed at the map of Paris. "Daniso your troops will attack this gate, Rodomont yours will attack here…"

CHAPTER 65

Renaud led the battalions to the newly constructed pontoon bridge over the Seine River. A copse of trees obscured it so that no one in Paris would see the crossing of the troops. Thunder rumbled in the distance and Renaud no longer feared being heard by their enemies, three miles to their west. He knew the men wondered why they were continuing onward in such weather, and were likely harboring doubts about his leadership. They needed him to inspire them to victory.

Turning to the engineers who had constructed the bridge he said, "After all our men have crossed, you will destroy this bridge. Our enemies shall not avail themselves of your handiwork."

"Yes my lord."

Renaud watched until all the troops had assembled in a large mass waiting to cross the makeshift bridge. The time had come for him to summon all his charm to rally his forces onward to victory and glory. He gripped his shield, which bore a standard of a silver lion on a field of red and readjusted his golden helmet, which was adorned with a crest of a lion's head and chest. Drawing out his sword, Flamberge, he held it aloft in the sky and waited until all eyes were upon him.

"Tonight we shall make history," he began. "Our enemies have been waiting for a night such as this to destroy Paris. I could not live with myself if we rode there on the morrow and found that while we slept, the city had burned to the ground. Instead, we must press on and use this darkness to cloak our arrival. We have the advantage of surprising our enemy. They are concerned only with attacking the city walls; they are not expecting to defend themselves as well."

A murmur of excitement rippled through the mass of soldiers.

"We are here because Charles the Great and his army have been attacked by a ruthless enemy whose purpose is to utterly destroy Christendom. Your clan leaders listened to the pleas of Charlemagne and sent you here, not as a favor, but because they recognize all of Europe is in danger from the Saracen menace. Should the Frankish Empire fall, it will only be a matter of time before hordes of infidels cross the channel and invade your lands as well. Just as the Romans first conquered Gaul before invading Britain, this scourge will visit you if they are not stopped here and now."

Even in the darkness, Renaud could see the level of anger rising in the men. Faces were contorted with rage as their hands clenched weapons.

"This is not a fight between rulers over land; it is a war between faiths. My great-grandfather Charles Martel repulsed the Saracen threat in the last century at the battle of Tours. As his descendant, I must live up to his memory and fulfill his legacy. Let us press onward to victory for Charlemagne and for Jesus Christ!"

A resounding cheer rose from the soldiers as thunder boomed in the distance.

CHAPTER 66

Do you expect me to bow down and kiss your feet in gratitude for finally including me in your war, dear cousin? thought Daniso, Governor of Zumara, as he watched Akramont conferring with Sabri and Marsilio. *You have kept me outside your circle of advisors as if my input was unimportant. Yet now that you need a warrior to risk being killed you do not turn to those frail old men to lead the attack, you turn to your lowly kinsman. I shall show you, the governors, and the caliph that the wrong man was made amir. It was my title by birthright and you stole it from me, just like your father did.*

Daniso strode out of the royal tent and over to his forces. It was his duty to inform them of the battle plan and inspire them to victory. He gathered his troops around him as he gestured to a large siege tower being rolled out from the forest.

"Tonight the world will see what warriors from Zumara can accomplish," he began. "We will lead the army as the first battalion of soldiers to attack this accursed city. Let us cleanse this land by fire, purging it of its sinful legacy. We shall use our swords as agents of vengeance and send the infidels to their deaths!"

The men beat their fists on their shields as thunder rumbled.

"Let us go forth and show everyone the will of Zumara! For Allah!" he roared.

His men pushed the siege tower toward Saint Germain's gate, while Akramont's forces used a battering ram at Saint Michel's gate. They hoped by distracting the Frankish guards, Daniso's men would have an easier time. Akramont's soldiers bellowed as the door received numerous blows. Frankish archers responded by sending a hailstorm of arrows their way.

Daniso gripped his sword and shield tightly in anticipation of combat. He not only wanted to prove his own worth as a governor and as a warrior, but to avenge his father's death at the hands of Orlando seventeen years before. To demonstrate his animosity toward that famous paladin, Daniso deliberately bore the same standard as Orlando, red and white quartering, in the hopes of provoking a duel with his nemesis.

Daniso resented Orlando for not only killing his father, but for wielding Durindana; a sword which had been passed down in his family for generations. By all rights, *he* should be the one wielding that famous blade and not his father's murderer. Should he vanquish Orlando and reclaim Durindana, all the governors who had been quick to bow down to Akramont would be forced to remember they once served Almont. They would then realize they should have pledged fealty to Almont's heir and not Troiano's. Daniso smiled at the thought of Caliph Harun al-Rashid recognizing him as the true leader of the Maghreb and not Akramont.

The siege tower was heavy and awkward to move, but Daniso's soldiers were filled with fury and they soon crossed the heavy stone bridge at Saint Germain's gate. As the forty foot tall structure was pushed against the closed portcullis, the fiercest warriors entered the wooden tower and climbed to the top. They were anxious to breach the sanctity of the city walls and annihilate all who refused to surrender. Daniso was the first to jump onto the parapet. The Muslim soldiers jostled amongst themselves to have the glory of being the second warrior to enter the Parisian domain.

With one sweep of his arm, Daniso decapitated a Frankish soldier with his sword. He proudly held the severed head aloft to the cheers of his men.

CHAPTER 67

Bradamante sat at a large banquet table in Marseille. Her hands trembled when Melissa poured wine into her goblet in front of the gathered army.

"What brings you?"

Melissa smiled. "Fear not. No one can hear our words."

Bradamante's pulse quickened as she realized she could clearly discern Melissa's voice, but everything else was a soft buzzing of indistinguishable sounds. The large hall was filled with soldiers eating their supper while engaged in conversation with their tablemates. None were paying the two women any attention.

"As you cannot hear anyone else, neither can they hear us."

"Is he free of that witch?" asked Bradamante.

"Yes, he secured his freedom as well as hundreds of others from Alcina's evil reign."

"Thank you," Bradamante said, remembering to breathe. "Is he here?"

"No. He thought it unwise. He felt it dangerous for your reputation to have a Saracen soldier meet with you in private or even in public."

"But you could have disguised him."

"He would never agree to use deception."

"Where is he now?" Bradamante asked before taking a long drink of wine.

"He set out to meet with your father in Montauban. He planned on asking for your hand in marriage."

Bradamante's heart skipped a beat. "And?"

"He never arrived," said the enchantress, lowering her head.

"What happened?"

"Atallah tricked him and took him prisoner."

"Again? Why did you not stop this from happening?"

"You had the chance to stop Atallah, but you did not listen to my warning."

"You are right. I did not murder a broken old man when I had the chance. I worried that my intended bridegroom might never forgive me if I committed such an unholy act. Tell me why you did not ensure Ruggiero's safe passage back."

Melissa sighed. "I was engaged in other matters at the time."

"Other matters? You were the one who told me of my great destiny. How could you be distracted from delivering my future husband to me?"

"I had a funeral to arrange. The woman who spent her life fighting Alcina's evil reign passed away after Ruggiero's liberation. I was charged with the disposition of her estate."

Bradamante hung her head in shame. "Please, forgive my selfishness."

Melissa wiped away a single tear. "It does not matter. Our only concern now is Ruggiero. Atallah tricked him by using your likeness and made Ruggiero believe you were in mortal danger. The wizard will attempt to imprison you as well, but you must not fall for his deception."

"How will he try to deceive me?"

"As you enter the Gresigne Forest and venture near the enchanted castle, you will see what will appear to be Ruggiero in a deadly struggle with monsters. Do not believe your eyes, it will be sorcery. You must remain strong, and run your blade through the false Ruggiero without pause or delay. Do not flinch from your duty, or you will lose your chance for a future with the real Ruggiero." Melissa removed a small drawstring bag from around her neck and handed it to Bradamante. "Inside are magic herbs from the Far East. Feed them to your horse as you set off in the morning and you will arrive at your destination before the sun sets."

"I will not fail this time," said Bradamante as she clutched the leather bag.

As Melissa walked away carrying the pitcher of wine, the sounds in the hall slowly returned to normal.

CHAPTER 68

A messenger alerted Charlemagne that reinforcements from Britain were approaching two of the northern gates.

"Thank you, Lord," Charlemagne said as he clasped his hands.

Once he arrived at Saint Martin's gate, he ordered the raising of the portcullis as the soldiers waited for entry. Charlemagne strode over to their leader.

"Edward," he said as they embraced. "You are truly Heaven sent."

"Herman and I brought the keenest archers from the isles."

"The attack has begun," said Charlemagne. "Your men are needed to guard the southern gates."

"Your Majesty," Edward said, "Renaud is leading thousands of men across the Seine. They will strike the infidels tonight."

Charlemagne smiled.

CHAPTER 69

Daniso felt vindicated as he held the head of a Frankish soldier high in the air. He was the first Muslim to cross into Paris, and knew this moment would be remembered for years to come. He had drawn the first blood that would lead to their victory. Later, when historians recorded this battle, he would see to it that the soldier he killed was a famous knight. He would not settle for the fallen man to be a commoner. No, if need be, the deceased would be transformed into a famous duke or count; someone of noble birth whose death would be notable. Daniso raised his sword high into the air warning the Franks they were facing his mighty blade. He was confident that he would soon reclaim his birthright, and prove that he, not Akramont, was the rightful heir to Almont's legacy.

~~~

The dark storm clouds over the city erupted into a flash of lightning that sought out the highest metal object. The thunderbolt struck Daniso's sword and the current coursed through his body, killing him instantly. As the charge sought its way to the ground, it ricocheted on the armor clad soldiers in the tower, jumping from one to another. The wood of the structure ignited and flames lit the night sky. Screams of the dying men carried for miles in the oppressively humid night air as well as the smell of their burning flesh.

The Franks guarding the wall where Daniso had stood ran away fearing they might also be caught up in the chain reaction of death. Rodomont recognized that all attention was directed toward the area Daniso attacked. He barked orders to his men to continue moving the second tower into place at the gate nearest the banks of the Seine River.

Rodomont scrambled up the tower and leaped upon the rampart, followed by his most loyal subjects. He slashed and killed any Frankish soldier he came across. His sword became stained with the blood of his enemies. His forces spilled over the walls, ran down the stairs, and opened the gate allowing hundreds more soldiers to pour into the city.

He wanted the streets of Paris to run red with blood, but Rodomont quickly came upon a large trench isolating the area in front of the gate. The wide ditch was lined with pointed branches and sharpened wooden spikes, designed to impale anyone who fell on them. A single bridge traversed the distance, and the Franks were already destroying it. This would leave his men on an island surrounded by archers. Several arrows bounced off his thick dragon-hide armor, but they easily penetrated the leather armor of his foot soldiers.

"Ladders!" Rodomont commanded. "Get ladders!"

With that order, his men grabbed ladders from inside the fortified walls and also retrieved ones the Muslim army had constructed. Hundreds of soldiers climbed down into the ditch and tried walking over the dangerous wooden stakes. Some men carried ladders above their heads for use on the other side.

Not wanting to be slowed down by such tedium, Rodomont decided on another way to cross the barrier. Throwing his shield to the ground, he chose a Frankish archer to target. He leaned back and hurled his heavy sword into the air as if it was a light spear. The flying weapon hit its mark, piercing the man's chest. Then Rodomont went as far back as the wall and made a running jump, barely clearing the distance over the divide. His teeth collided with the earth and his hands and knees landed in a splayed position. He knew if he had worn traditional heavy mail armor rather than the hide of a dragon, he could not have accomplished that arduous jump.

Rodomont spat dirt, blood, and a broken tooth out of his mouth feeling angrier for having suffered the indignity of falling on his face. As he turned behind to assess the progress of his men, he witnessed Frankish soldiers throwing torches into the trench. The flames lit the pitch-soaked wood, quickly spreading a conflagration throughout the length and breadth of the culvert. The screams of men dying by fire once again filled the night, as well as the acrid smell of burning flesh.

He was the only invader who had penetrated the inner sanctum of Paris. Rodomont was infuriated and determined to destroy the city and all its residents single-handedly. Yanking his sword loose from the dead soldier's chest, he slaughtered the archers surrounding him one by one. Once his path was cleared, he set out to find and kill Charlemagne.

CHAPTER 70

Renaud waited impatiently for the thousands of soldiers to cross the pontoon bridge across the Seine River. His nerves were on edge, and he found it more difficult with each passing moment to resist starting the attack. Traveling with thousands of men was difficult logistically, but it was imperative he demonstrate sound leadership. As he faced Paris, a tremendous lightning bolt illuminated the night sky. A few moments later, thunder reverberated so loudly that many horses reared on their hind legs in fright. He had to calm Bayard, likewise the other knights had to settle the nerves of their mounts.

As the thunder dissipated a new sound rose in the distance. Renaud swore it was the shrieks of the damned in Hell. Flames shot high into the sky outside the Paris walls. He could wait no longer. Paris needed his strong arm and sword to defend her honor.

The commanders, Zerbin, Leanian, and Ariodant exchanged looks with Renaud. The time had come. Renaud touched his belt to assure himself his sword Flamberge was properly attached. He bowed his head in a silent prayer before he grabbed the lance offered to him by a squire. Then he galloped off into the night ready to face his enemies.

CHAPTER 71

Akramont watched in horror as his cousin was struck by lightning and the siege tower became engulfed with flames. Men shrieked in agony as they burned to death. He wondered if this was a sign from Heaven, but immediately dismissed the thought. Fear could not be allowed to enter into his heart or mind. Allah was on his side, of that he was certain. His forces had the advantage in numbers, so he would press onward. This would be the night of his final victory over Charlemagne.

His troops continued battering on the gate. They brought out ladders and the soldiers climbed them in numbers designed to overwhelm the Frankish defenders. The ladders were quickly pushed away from the wall and the Muslim soldiers fell backward on their compatriots. The attackers were then pelted with bottles that exploded on impact, showering the area with scorching hot sand. The Franks also poured scalding liquid onto the Muslim warriors, eliciting more screams of pain and agony.

Akramont's will was not deterred. He was determined this gate would fall and his men would gain entry. He gave the signal for more men to advance against the walls.

CHAPTER 72

Bradamante gathered her thoughts about how to leave her station with honor as Melissa's retreating form became lost in the crowd. Leaving her seat at the banquet table, Bradamante came to the side of Guy, Duke of Burgundy.

"You were speaking with that old woman again," he said, concern etched on his face. "Did she bear bad news?"

Bradamante nodded. "I am leaving at dawn. It is an urgent family matter."

"Shall I send a message to Charlemagne?"

"No, he has far more important concerns right now. I also do not wish to put a messenger's life at risk to deliver such a missive through a battlefield on my behalf. Once this matter is resolved, I shall seek further orders. Until then, I leave this city's protection in your hands."

"You will be sorely missed," said Guy.

She gave him a rueful smile before retiring to her private chambers. There she tried calming herself, but found it impossible to sleep. After endless tossing and turning, she lit a lamp, and sharpened her sword. With each stroke she envisioned Atallah suffering from her blade.

CHAPTER 73

Rodomont strode through the narrow dirt streets of Paris slaughtering anyone in his path, leaving a trail of limbs behind him. As he came upon a row of houses, he grabbed a torch and aimed it at the dry thatched roofs. The flames spread quickly. The house was soon burning and the fire spread from rooftop to rooftop. Soon entire sections of the city were ablaze. He laughed at the sight of people running and screaming in the streets. This was only the start in settling the score for the deaths of his men.

He snarled as he came upon a small church. Rodomont wanted the Christians to know how much disdain he had for them and their god. The doors were shut and barricaded from the inside, but it could not withstand his powerful kicks. The priest at the altar halted his Latin prayer when Rodomont entered the sacred space of the chapel.

The decorated rounded arches, the high ceiling, murals adorning the walls, and marble statues of saints all helped raise bile in the back of his throat. He regarded all religions as a sign of weakness. He wanted to destroy this house of superstition and all the pitiful people who bowed their head in prayer. The peasants were improperly armed to fight against a knight, and he quickly dispatched them with ease. Their pleas for mercy only emboldened him to kill with greater viciousness. Rodomont saved the priest for last. Taking the man's severed head, he mounted it on the altar's crucifix.

He stood at the front of the church surveying the scene of carnage and was unsatisfied. Yanking a tapestry off the wall, he threw it onto the ground and added linens from the altar onto the pile. He poured lamp oil upon the heap and ignited the fabric with a candle. Rodomont smiled as the faces in the tapestry became blackened by flames. He then left the church to wreak more havoc on the city.

CHAPTER 74

Renaud's horse galloped out in front of the Christian soldiers. The sound of Bayard's hoof beats were drowned out by the battering rams and the screams of those burning to death. As he drew near the Saracen army, Renaud let out a battle cry announcing his presence and allowing his enemies to defend themselves. Even from a distance, Renaud recognized the gigantic African who turned and charged at him. Puliano was a large, heavy man who required the strongest of mares to support his bulk. His girth had benefited him in the past for with it came immense power, but his brawn had never been tested by a paladin. Renaud's lance broke as it struck the giant man's trunk, piercing his armor. A large thump announced the fall of Puliano's lifeless body.

Renaud drew his sword Flamberge, then slashed and killed the soldiers surrounding him. Zerbin and his men arrived, joining in the slaughter. The Saracens greatly outnumbered the Christians, but the flanks of the newly arrived forces divided and conquered them. The walls of Paris were soon stacked with piles of corpses.

CHAPTER 75

A small girl dared peek outside of her hiding place. She had hidden behind a statue in an apse. Once she was sure that the bad man who had broken into the church had left she ran toward the fire and threw the woolen blanket from her shoulders onto the flames. She laid her body upon the blanket hoping to smother the fire as tears streamed down her cheeks.

The Saracen army had attacked and burned the village near her home. Her parents fled in terror, joining the hundreds of others on their way to Paris. Her family arrived to an overcrowded city that was rationing food. That night as the rumors of invasion swept through the people, her family fled again. This time they sought sanctuary in the Lord's house.

Geneviève sobbed because she knew her parents were dead, but she could not bring herself to look for their lifeless bodies. The events in the church forged a bond with her to the city of Paris. Her destiny lay here. She had never dreamed of any life other than being a peasant, but she now knew that she must dedicate her life to serving God by joining a convent.

Clutching her rosary, she knelt and prayed to every saint she knew. She prayed to Saint Julien who the church was named after, then to Saint Martin, Saint James, Saint Mary and the patron saints of Paris: Saints Denis and Geneviève. Finally she prayed to Jesus.

"My Lord, do not turn your eyes from Paris. Please save your people."

She crossed herself in gratitude as the rain began to beat down on the roof in answer to her prayers.

CHAPTER 76

Rodomont's dragon-hide armor repelled rain, but water still fell on his exposed face and neck. It then trickled inside his leather suit causing his sweat soaked gambeson to become water logged. The thick hide clung to him as if it was a natural extension of his own skin.

He trudged through the muddy streets of Paris, crossed a bridge over the Seine River, and walked onto an island. It was difficult to see, but even in the darkness the outline of the tallest building on the western edge of the island was still visible. As he turned towards the towers, he tripped and fell into a deep mud puddle. Cursing the city, he spat out mud and quickly resumed his mission.

Frankish soldiers stood guard outside the Citadel pelting Rodomont with arrows, but their missiles bounced harmlessly off his charmed armor. Rodomont forced his way inside the gates, and found himself surrounded by eight knights on horseback in the stone courtyard. One of the warriors towered over the others and had a fierce demeanor. Rodomont's pulse quickened as he recognized that warrior was Charlemagne himself.

"Surrender!" yelled a mounted knight whose spear was pointed at Rodomont's heart.

Rodomont grabbed the weapon, and in a single move yanked it out of the knight's hand. Swinging it wildly in the air like a cudgel, Rodomont struck the young man in the head. A dozen or more mounted knights appeared, cornering Rodomont. He cursed them in Arabic, accusing them of cowardice for fighting him on horseback when he was on foot. Jabbing the broken pole at the horses' legs caused them to rear.

Taking advantage of the momentary chaos, Rodomont climbed the outside of the building to the rooftop. Panting from exhaustion, he wondered how much longer he could continue. The night had been a failure for he had not killed Charlemagne when he had the chance. He vacillated on whether to continue single-handedly destroying the Citadel and all its occupants or if he should somehow seek retreat.

A flash of lightning lit up the sky and struck a tree south of the city. In an instant he could see thousands of soldiers engaged in battle outside the walls of Paris. On a hilltop, a diminutive man stood alone. Rodomont squinted hoping to see the man again. A few more flashes of lightning followed and he realized the man was not a figment of his imagination, but flesh and blood. The man was frantically waving Rodomont's standard that bore the face of Doralice.

CHAPTER 77

Akramont's brow was bathed in sweat and his arms ached from swinging his heavy sword. He had lost count of the number of men in this battle he had killed and wondered how much longer this night and this battle would last. A chill wind cooled him off. A moment later came torrential rains, destroying all visibility. The torches on the castle walls were extinguished leaving everyone in utter darkness.

He then heard the sound of a horn signaling retreat, followed by another horn. Akramont's hands shook with rage. Who dared give such an order? Only he had that power. His anger increased as he watched his turning away from the walls and heading back toward their encampment. The night sky was once again illuminated with a flash of lightning and with it, the outline of thousands of Christian soldiers in the distance. The reinforcements for the Frankish army had arrived and were destroying Marsilio's troops. He was no closer to conquering Paris than before this accursed night began, but now his forces were vulnerable to their enemies who were surrounding them.

Retreat was the only wise course of action. Akramont could not fathom how things had gone so terribly wrong, and wished by sheer force of will to reverse the events of that night. Daniso's death weighed heavily on his mind. Had he not insisted on attacking when a storm was imminent, his cousin might still be alive. Akramont uttered a curse under his breath before giving his own belated order to disengage from battle.

CHAPTER 78

Rodomont could not believe his eyes. Doralice's manservant was waving to him. He had seen the eunuch many times in Granada during his negotiations with her father regarding marriage. All thoughts of battle left him as Rodomont sought out the dwarf. Leaping down the exterior of the Citadel, he slid down its walls, and jumped from one level to another without concern for safety. Once on the ground, he dispatched anyone in his way with a blow of his sword. A short time later, he was outside the walls of Paris and standing in front of the little man.

"Doralice…where is she?" Rodomont asked as he gasped for breath.

"Far from here," said the dwarf. "She needs your help. Now."

Without waiting to hear more, Rodomont searched for a horse. He threw the nearest soldier from his saddle and struck down a second knight who tried resisting.

"Here is a fresh horse," Rodomont said, as he hoisted the servant onto the saddle. He mounted the other steed and commanded, "Take me to her. Tell me what happened on the way."

They galloped away into the cold, dark, wet night. Once they were a few miles down the road, Rodomont demanded, "Tell me what happened!"

"A lone warrior came to our camp and killed all her escorts."

"Describe the bastard responsible."

"He has red hair and wore old-fashioned armor with a silver screaming eagle on a field of blue."

"Mandricardo," Rodomont said through clenched teeth.

CHAPTER 79

Renaud was drenched by the deluge, but his spirits rose at the sound of horns signaling retreat by his enemies. This was fortuitous as Bayard resisted going forth into the thicket of soldiers. Several times his horse had almost tripped over the dead and fallen. The ground itself had become treacherously slick with mud. He worried about the likelihood of accidentally killing his own men due to poor visibility and the changed landscape. Renaud issued his own signal for the Christian soldiers to regroup away from the Saracen forces. It was a slow process to disentangle themselves from their enemies and gather before the easternmost gate on the left bank.

"Guardians of the gate!" he shouted. "I am Renaud, Count of Montauban. I have brought thousands of reinforcements from Britain. The Saracen army has fled the field. I ask that you open up and let us in."

"I do not recognize you," said the guardian. "How can I know this is not a trick?"

"Bring Charlemagne here. My uncle will vouch for me!"

The rain fell unabated as they waited for what seemed like an eternity outside the city walls. The men were exhausted, ravenous, and numb from the cold rain.

"Announce yourself again," came a booming voice from the parapet at last.

"Your Majesty, it is I, your humble servant Renaud. I ask your gates be opened to allow several thousand cold, tired, and hungry soldiers to enter."

A few moments later the portcullis was raised allowing the army to enter the city of Paris. Renaud led the procession and dismounted as he approached his uncle.

He knelt before Charlemagne, bowing his head. "I have fulfilled your orders, your Majesty."

"Rise dear nephew," said Charlemagne. He embraced Renaud as if he were a long lost son. "It is good to have you back by my side. Tonight was horrible, but this battle is over." The emperor turned toward Namo. "Instruct the kitchens to make a banquet for our soldiers, so that they may live to fight another day!" He placed an arm around Renaud's shoulders. "We shall find a place for you to rest until the meal is ready. Then you shall sit at my right hand."

CHAPTER 80

Dawn had barely broken when Bradamante was dressed and ready to leave. She took out the leather bag from Melissa. Bradamante cut a hole inside an apple, poured the herbal mixture inside, and fed the fruit to Nikephoros. The charger eagerly ate the offered food. He snorted and pawed the ground showing he was ready to leave.

Bradamante left Marseille with its skies still filled with smoke and ash. She was finally able to breathe fresh air as she skirted the southern boundaries of Arles to avoid being seen by the Muslim forces. Riding past the marshy delta of the Camargue, she was grateful to pass through there before the heat of the day set in when the flies and mosquitoes would be out in full force.

The marshland gave way to more solid ground as she followed the rugged coastline rather than attempt to traverse through mountains at the base of the Alps. The cypress trees changed in shape from tall wisps near Beziers to those with upswept branches with flat tops near Narbonne. As she left the coastline and rode inland she followed the Aude River valley with Alaric's Mountain looming in the southern skies. Thick clouds clung to the mountaintops, named after a Visigothic king, reminding Bradamante of the old folk saying that King Alaric was wearing a hat.

She had ridden her horse harder that day than she had ever dared, but Nikephoros showed no difficulty with the breakneck pace. They stopped only once at midday when she was overcome with hunger. She hobbled her horse, which was the only thing that kept the restless beast from galloping away. Nikephoros drank from the Aude River and grazed on its banks while Bradamante ate bread, apples, and dried fish. The walled city of Carcassonne towered above them in the distance. During her journey she focused on finding the shortest path and did not allow herself to enjoy the vistas or landscapes she rode past. After passing the town of Albi, she knew her destination was not far and doubts crept into her mind.

The previous night when she spoke with Melissa, Bradamante felt as if something had been forgotten and unsaid. As Nikephoros galloped past a large tree stump, Bradamante saw its circular form and realized what bothered her. The ring! Ruggiero should have been protected from Atallah's spells if he had been wearing the magic ring. If he no longer had it, who did?

She suddenly doubted Melissa's intentions. Bradamante had been warned since childhood to avoid witches and wizards. Miracles by holy men and women were revered, but other magic was considered the work of the Devil. The idea that her cousin Maugis was trained in the magical arts was of great concern to her mother. Bradamante wondered if anything Melissa had shown or told her was the truth. The enchantress obviously knew how to read her heart and mind, but what was Melissa's true purpose? Perhaps Melissa was only interested in obtaining the magic ring and Bradamante was an unwitting fool in a selfish scheme.

Melissa had offered no proof that Ruggiero had actually flown to an island east of India. After a short conversation, Bradamante willingly gave the enchantress the ring. Perhaps Melissa wanted competitors such as Atallah eliminated and had used Bradamante to try and kill him. Brunello's death would have prevented him from laying claim to the stolen ring. Now she was once again being told to kill Atallah, only this time he would be in the guise of Ruggiero. How could Melissa be so certain of what Bradamante would see upon her arrival unless the enchantress staged the scene herself?

Furthermore, it would be difficult for Bradamante to attack the form of Ruggiero, even if only an illusion. However, if Melissa was evil and wanted to harm the reputation of the house of Lyon this would be the perfect plot. Bradamante would be disgraced if she murdered a man who would later be revealed to have a romantic link with her. It would be a larger scandal when it became known he was a sworn enemy of Charlemagne.

If I killed Ruggiero…if I killed Ruggiero. She had trouble finishing the thought. *If I killed Ruggiero, I would have to kill myself. And that would be the greatest disgrace of all for my family to suffer.*

Melissa's words alone were not enough. Bradamante needed proof before killing anyone. Instead, she would have to subdue any monsters or attackers. Perhaps Melissa's insistence that Bradamante rush to Ruggiero's rescue was to prevent her from the realization that the ring should have protected him from magical spells.

Bradamante's mind leapt to the opposite extreme. What if Melissa had told her the truth? What would happen should she become Atallah's prisoner and held with Ruggiero? She remembered their kiss and how Ruggiero's lips made her body tremble. She broke out in a sweat considering the temptations she might face if she were alone with him.

Any consummation of their relationship without their union first being consecrated by a priest would be a cardinal sin. Even if they were living in a magical place without worries of war or differences of faith, they would never be beyond God's laws. She could not allow herself to submit to her passions. To do so would condemn their souls to everlasting, burning Hell. Her jaw clenched at the thought.

Bradamante then willed herself to forget about such worries, because she had arrived at the outskirts of the forest. Her only concern was finding Ruggiero.

CHAPTER 81

Akramont stared at his reflection in a bowl of water. He hardly recognized himself. His eyes were bloodshot, his cheeks were sunken, and he looked as if he had aged twenty years in a single night. Splashing his face with water, he girded himself to confront his two most trusted advisors. He turned and towered over Sabri and Marsilio who waited for him on the cushions he had insisted they sit upon.

"Tell me what happened last night," said Akramont. "Tell me why you were the one to give the signal to retreat."

Both men moved to stand, but Akramont motioned for them to remain on the ground. He wanted them to feel like children, even though they were old enough to be his father.

Marsilio bowed his head. "My lord, it was with a heavy heart that I blew my horn. I am a veteran of countless battles, and have lost my share of them. I not only have responsibilities to you, but to my own countrymen. My men were the first ones attacked by Renaud's forces. They were destroying us. There was no time to confer with you or anyone on strategy. Had I waited any longer, my men would all be dead."

"And Sabri, what have you to say?" asked Akramont.

Sabri closed his eyes and took a deep breath. "I failed you my lord and for that I beg your forgiveness."

Akramont nodded, happy that at least one of them had shown enough respect to apologize.

"I did not serve you as I should have," said Sabri. "I held my tongue when I should have spoken out against the attack. I was afraid you might dismiss my concerns as being nothing more than an old man's fear of battle. My fear of losing my stature as a wazir caused me to keep my reservations to myself. If you will still have me, I vow to give you my honest opinions regardless of how they will be received. You deserve the benefit of my years of experience, even if it upsets you or contradicts your other advisors."

Sabri knelt before Akramont, his head bowed. Akramont stared at the white hair on the man's head. He wondered what would have happened if Sabri had spoken forcefully against the attack last night. Would he have made a different decision? Or would he still have succumbed to the urgings of Marsilio and Rodomont?

"I forgive you Sabri, as I also forgive Marsilio," said Akramont. "I should have been the one to order the retreat. I did not because in the darkness, I was unaware of the dangers to all of our men. The lightning strikes provided the only light to show why you were retreating."

He knew that the real reason was his stubborn pride that prevented him from recognizing and admitting defeat. "Come with me as I review the fallen."

Marsilio and Sabri walked on either side of Akramont as they left the camp and ventured to the scene of the previous night's battle. The overcast sky reflected Akramont's dour mood. He cautiously walked over the soggy ground torn apart by hoof prints and reviewed the myriad corpses of men and horses strewn about. Imams wailed their prayers.

He had performed this onerous task after every battle, but never had he felt sorrow like this. Previously he had justified casualties as a sacrifice necessary to assure victory. This battle had been a terrible defeat and he could find no solace in their deaths. He already regretted ordering the attack. In retrospect, he realized how foolhardy it had been to risk the safety of his army in such inclement weather. Thousands died because of his impatience and his fear of ridicule by vassals who swore allegiance to him.

A small cadre of men toiled in the shadow of the walls surrounding Paris. Yet, on this morning there had not been any hostile acts from the city's defenders. The archers lowered their weapons and did not attack the Muslim soldiers who moved about retrieving their dead well within firing range of the archers' arrows.

Surgeons walked amongst the fallen finding the wounded. They assessed the injuries to determine if there was any chance for recovery or if it would only be a matter of time before they succumbed. The wounded were taken to medical tents, while the dead Muslim soldiers were laid next to each other awaiting burial preparations. The few dead Christian soldiers were put in a separate area to be dealt with later.

Various governors came forward throughout the morning giving Akramont reports of the previous evening. He was apprised of the number and readiness of the remaining troops. Through the long night there had not only been many casualties, but many desertions as well, depleting the overall ranks.

Akramont continued his solemn duty of surveying the dead when he came upon the charred remains of the contingent led by his cousin. The acrid smell of their burnt bodies hung oppressively in the air. A lump welled in his throat as he recognized a jeweled sword clutched in a blackened hand. Daniso's corpse. Tears stung Akramont's eyes as he stared at Daniso's empty eye sockets. He thought of Daniso as more like a brother than an older cousin.

Daniso had been orphaned as a small child and Akramont's father adopted him. Tradition would have passed the leadership role of amir onto Daniso, but such a vast territory was too dangerous to be left in the hands of an eight year old. Instead that responsibility went to Troiano.

Akramont sighed. Daniso's family legacy of tragedy had been repeated, this time a five-year old son was left behind. Akramont faced a similar dilemma as his father had before him. This time it was *his* responsibility to oversee the protection of a young child and widow. He would follow in his father's footsteps and annex Zumara, until Daniso's son was old enough to assume the responsibility of being heir to the throne.

Akramont pried the sword out of the dead man's hand and gave it to his chamberlain. "See that his body is kept separate from the rest. Daniso shall have his own service and his own grave. After we finish here, I shall deliver the news of his martyrdom to his widow."

He thought of the beautiful young widow and considered making her his third wife. As his wife, she would be provided for and secure from harm. Of course, he would have to wait until after the mourning period of four months and ten days had passed before broaching the topic of remarriage with her.

Governor Stordilano of Granada fell to his knees in front of Akramont. "I bear heartrending news. Rodomont's forces are without a single survivor. He breached a gate last night and his men followed him inside. The cruel Franks had a trap waiting for them. They all perished in a ditch consumed with fire."

Akramont lifted the elderly man to his feet and embraced him.

"My daughter, Doralice, was to marry him," said Stordilano through tears. "Rodomont wanted to distinguish himself in battle last night, to prove his worth as a warrior for his bride. It was his fervent wish that their marriage no longer be delayed, so I sent for her. She is to arrive here today or on the morrow at the latest. Rather than wearing festive clothes for a wedding, she shall wear mourning clothes."

"Doralice will have a husband," comforted Akramont. "We shall find her another man to marry. Perhaps Mandricardo, he has a vast kingdom and has yet to wed."

Stordilano nodded. "Thank you for your concern about my daughter's welfare."

"Pardon me," interrupted the chamberlain, "but two of Governor Brunello's soldiers wish to report a theft to you."

"I do not wish to hear about petty thefts at this time," said Akramont.

"The matter concerns Governor Rodomont."

Stordilano appeared startled, while Akramont's brow furrowed. "I shall hear them."

Two soldiers stepped forward. "Last night, Governor Rodomont stole both our horses."

"When did this happen?" asked Akramont.

"Around the time the retreat was sounded. He left with a dwarf."

"Brunello?"

"No," the soldier insisted. "That man was not our leader. Rodomont and the dwarf spoke of a woman before heading westward."

"I have a servant who is a dwarf," said Stordilano. "He serves my daughter. They must have been talking of Doralice! She is in trouble. I will send a team of my finest knights."

"There is no need for that," said Akramont. "Rodomont is on his way. You could find no greater champion for her honor. Mark my words, you shall see your daughter and Rodomont again, safe and sound."

"But if —"

"Far too many of our men were sacrificed last night, and our enemies have fresh troops. I am gratified to hear Rodomont did not perish, but am saddened he is not here with us. However, he is on a mission to defend the virtue of your daughter and that is also of importance. Unfortunately, I cannot afford to lose any more men from this campaign."

Stordilano nodded and stumbled as he turned to leave. The two soldiers caught him and supported the elderly man back to his tent.

Sabri cleared his throat. "Might I suggest sending messengers to locate those who have left your side and call for their return? Mandricardo left on a mission. There is also the disappearance of Ruggiero to the skies as reported by Gradasso and Brunello. Perhaps messengers will find those men as well as others who have pledged loyalty to your cause and persuade them to return to battle out of a sense of honor and duty."

"I agree," said Marsilio. "I would also suggest sending envoys to the Saxons."

Akramont raised an eyebrow.

"It is true the Saxons are pagans who worship strange gods," said Marsilio. "They have also vexed Charlemagne for decades. They refuse to stay conquered or to convert to worshipping the one god. For years I worried that the spring thaw would bring Frankish troops through the Pyrenees, but Charlemagne repeatedly had to put down Saxon rebellions leaving little time for expansion into my domain."

Akramont nodded. "Should the Saxons learn their enemy is hiding behind the walls of Paris, they might rise up again in hopes of throwing off their Frankish overlords."

"Exactly," said Marsilio.

Akramont gestured to his chamberlain. "Have a list of the soldiers who are missing drawn up. Then send ten messengers throughout the land searching for them and command them to return to my service. I also need an envoy to send to the Saxons."

"I will have that done before sundown tonight."

The chamberlain left as a group of soldiers approached Akramont.

"We have a messenger from Charlemagne," announced the lead warrior.

A small man dressed with a Jewish prayer shawl and a yarmulke bowed towards Marsilio. He spoke in perfect Arabic. "Good day your lordship, Amir Marsilio. My name is Nachman and Charlemagne bade that I speak with you. He requests safe passage of our soldiers to release your dead for burial and asks for the return of our fallen warriors."

"I am in command here," snapped Akramont. "You shall address me."

Nachman bowed toward him. "Charlemagne and Amir Marsilio have extended that courtesy to each other in the past. The emperor wanted to appeal to an old friend and rival out of respect to their long history together."

Marsilio smiled. "We have always recognized a cessation of hostilities for burials."

"Tell your emperor all courtesy will be extended as is custom in this matter," said Akramont.

Nachman blanched and opened his mouth to speak, but stopped.

"You doubt my integrity?" asked Akramont.

The messenger took a deep breath. "Sir, are you aware of what transpired last night within the walls of Paris?"

"Hundreds of my men burned to death."

The small Jewish man hesitated, and then appeared to be studying the look on Akramont's face. "That did happen, but did you know that the church of *Saint Julien le Pauvre* was desecrated?"

Sabri closed his eyes.

"Rodomont massacred everyone inside and defiled the altar," said Nachman.

Sabri bowed his head and began reciting a prayer.

"I was unaware of this," said Akramont. "I swear to you that Rodomont's actions went against my express orders. Please relay my apology to Charlemagne. Tell the emperor that I share his revulsion over a place of worship being treated in a sacrilegious manner. Allah would not approve."

Nachman stared at him.

"You disbelieve my sincerity," said Akramont.

The messenger remained silent.

"I have expressly forbidden that any harm shall come to churches in your land," Akramont said as he pointed to various structures outside the Paris walls. "Inspect them if you wish. On my orders, none of my soldiers have stepped foot inside them."

Nachman's expression changed from skepticism to relief as he turned and saw *Saint-Germaine-des-Pres* standing untouched. "I shall convey your message to my sovereign as well as your agreement to a truce for this day to honor the dead."

Akramont turned and made his way through a field of corpses. He was saddened to see several horse carcasses for they could be of no further use for his army. Dietary rules forbade the eating of any animal that had not been slaughtered properly. Then he came upon one grievously wounded, but still alive.

"Bismallah," announced Akramont as he took his sword and severed the horse's neck. He spoke to one of his servants. "Have the butcher finish this. I wish to have it for my dinner. I have grown tired of mutton."

CHAPTER 82

Renaud and his men had been taken to the Citadel. The men were brought to the barracks, while Renaud was led to a private chamber. There a barber shaved off his beard and trimmed his shoulder length hair while a large wooden bathtub was filled. A loaf of bread, some cheeses, and wine staved off Renaud's fierce hunger.

The only light in the room came from the fire and a few oil lamps. Renaud appreciated the large bed waiting for him and welcomed his squire's assistance in removing his armor before entering the bath. The young man took Renaud's sweat soaked gambeson and breeches away to be laundered.

Renaud soaked in the warm water removing the chill from his bones and washed away the blood of his enemies. He felt as if years of torment had been lifted from his shoulders. He was weary and needed rest, but lingered in the bath.

A washerwoman entered the room and hung his laundered clothes near the hearth to dry. Renaud's interest in sleep disappeared when she gave him an appraising smile. She bore the same look on her face other women gave him after his triumphs in tournaments. Women loved winners. She gave him a smile that made it clear she was his for the taking. The woman was not a remarkable beauty, but she was receptive and available.

The laundress held out a towel for him as he stepped out of the tub and she wrapped it around his body. The towel soon fell to the floor alongside the woman's clothes.

Renaud had suffered from a long period of abstinence, and he did not like the drought. As he caressed the woman's curves, he fantasized that she was the fair Angelica who possessed his thoughts and dreams. He hoped he would soon be with Angelica, but at that moment he was content satisfying his own needs.

Hours later he was woken by a squire. "Sir, it is time for the banquet." Renaud rolled over. His bedmate had left while he slept, but her heady smell still lingered on the bedding. He smiled at the pleasant memory. She had required no seduction, and had likely vied with other women for the opportunity to be alone with the hero of the battle.

Renaud was dressed by his squire and led downstairs to the great hall, a large room with many pillars supporting the arched ceiling. Torches on the walls shined over thousands of men who waited at the numerous long tables and benches to be fed. Heads turned following his progress as he strode through the middle of the room to the high table. As promised, a seat at the right hand of Charlemagne was waiting for him.

Archbishop Turpin stood and said a prayer, followed by servants bustling about bringing food. The sovereign was always served first, but this time Charlemagne deferred to his nephew who gratefully complied and filled his plate with herring.

"Fortune smiled on us last night," Charlemagne said, as he broke off a large chunk of warm brown bread and spread honey over it. "We were almost overrun by our enemies, but you delivered unto me needed reinforcements."

Renaud nodded and smiled at the emperor. He took another bite of herring and closed his eyes to savor its taste. After subsisting for months on food made in makeshift campsites, he gained a new appreciation for meals prepared in real kitchens.

"I was given a report on the devastation you wrought last night among the Saracen ranks," Charlemagne continued. "They are hurting today, far worse than the good people of Paris. While many Parisians lost their homes to fire last night, it pales in comparison to the number of infidels who perished. Your surprise attack struck terror in their hearts, and made them retreat. I am grateful to have you back by my side."

"It is my honor, your majesty."

"If only your cousin Orlando was here. Then we would be assured of ultimate victory over our enemies."

"Where is he?" asked Renaud, startled.

"No one knows; he flew off in a rage when he learned Angelica escaped from Duke Namo's protective guard. He has not been seen since Toulouse."

Renaud raised his mug of beer and took a long drink. "And he has sent no word to you?"

"Nothing," said Charlemagne. "If it were not for my sister Bertha, I would strip him of his title and lands for this desertion. However, there is some hope he might be nearby. Last night I was told of a lone knight destroying two battalions of Saracens a few days ago on a road west of here. I can only hope it was my errant nephew."

Renaud paused for a moment. "Dearest uncle, with your permission I would go and search for our kinsman. I brought you thousands of troops as reinforcements, but none are the peer to the Count of Anglant. If after a fortnight, I have failed in my mission to find him, then I shall return."

The emperor studied Renaud's face. "I trust whatever bad blood you had with him has passed."

"Yes, sir, it has."

"Bring Orlando back to me and you shall be richly rewarded," Charlemagne promised. He then signaled for his seneschal. "Have Renaud and Guichard's horses readied for a long journey. They shall depart after finishing their meal."

"Guichard?" asked Renaud.

"Yes, I thought you might enjoy having a brother keep you company."

CHAPTER 83

Bradamante brought her horse to a canter as she entered the Gresigne Forest. She was somewhat familiar with the woods because she had joined her father and brothers on hunting expeditions there. The forest was east of Montauban and filled with deer, wild boar, foxes, hare, and other game. However, she generally avoided traveling within its boundaries because it was easy to get lost within the four thousand hectares laced with scores of crisscrossing trails.

She held her shield tightly as she left the bright sunlight and rode into the darkened forest. The woods were alive with the sounds of songbirds, crickets, squirrels and chipmunks. The shadows of trees danced on the dirt path as filtered sunlight streamed through the canopy. She was unsure where she would find Ruggiero, but trusted she would find a sign to show her the way.

An immense oak tree loomed in front of her. The tree stretched to the sky and looked old enough to have been growing since the time of Christ. Its trunk was at least six feet across and its mighty limbs were gnarled like an old man stricken by a lifetime of hard labor. A flash of white caught Bradamante's eye as a dove took flight from that oak and briefly landed on a neighboring cherry tree. Intrigued, she led her horse away from the trail and followed the bird as it made its way from tree to tree deeper into the wood. As a silence fell over the forest, Bradamante's senses were heightened. Something was about to happen.

Drawing her sword, she sniffed the air, and caught a whiff of a foul smell, like rotting meat. Closing her eyes, she concentrated on listening for signs of trouble. Soon she heard heavy footsteps, followed by a crash. Bradamante urged her horse through the dense underbrush in the direction of the sounds and came upon a gruesome ten-foot giant toppling trees as he ran. Pursuing him she came upon another giant with large gashes on his thighs and blood coursing down his legs. The wounded giant gave a fearsome snarl at a man – Ruggiero – whose sword seemed to have caused the injuries.

Her stomach clenched. This was the scene Melissa had warned her about. The man looked like Ruggiero. How could she be certain this was all an illusion?

With a back-handed swing, one of the monsters sent Ruggiero flying through the air. His back hit a large chestnut tree and he slumped over.

A giant picked up the unconscious Ruggiero by one foot and dangled him upside down. The other one grabbed the warrior's wrists and pulled. Bradamante gritted her teeth as she rode towards the two monsters, targeting the wounded one. She intended on severing his hand with her sword before they killed Ruggiero by a crude drawing and quartering.

As her sword connected with the giant's forearm the earth seemed to melt under her feet. Nikephoros reared on his hind legs and Bradamante reined him in. They were suddenly no longer in the forest, but instead inside a stone building. She dismounted and the horse galloped away from her.

"Bradamante, where are you?" came Ruggiero's faraway voice.

Bradamante knew then that Melissa had been truthful. She stood in a spacious room in an elaborately furnished castle. Ornate tapestries of knights in battle and paintings of nobility adorned each wall, with multiple staircases leading to various wings of the castle. With sword and shield in hand she began her search.

She went through numerous bedrooms, private chambers, kitchens, and dozens of other lavishly appointed rooms that were magically illuminated without lamp, torch or candle. Eventually, she was back in the main hall where she started. Ruggiero's voice had called to her many times, but never once had she caught a glimpse of him. She collapsed into a chair and wept. She was Atallah's prisoner and there was no door or window to the outside world. Bradamante feared she might never escape this enchanted castle or find her beloved.

CHAPTER 84

The clouds broke up by midday, but Akramont's mood was still overcast. He sat alone in his tent, absentmindedly staring at a pattern on his prayer rug. After watching wagonload after wagonload of dead soldiers being brought to the makeshift burial grounds, he lost all appetite for food. He vowed to remain fasting until sundown as a way of demonstrating penitence to Allah.

In the distance, Akramont's two wives could be heard consoling Daniso's widow. The wail that pierced the air when she heard the news of her husband's death would forever haunt Akramont's soul. As he sat brooding, the sound of her anguished cries reverberated in his ears. He tried thinking of what to say at the funeral service later that day, for all eyes would be upon him. His heart felt as if it was made of lead and he could think of nothing to inspire his forces.

Akramont winced as harsh sunlight flooded into the tent as his chamberlain entered. "Sorry to bother you my lord, but a king from Asia has arrived to join our ranks. He has five thousand soldiers with him."

Akramont knelt, raised his hands above his head and cupped them as if to catch water from a pitcher. "Thank you Allah. I knew you would not forsake me."

He rose and followed his servant to greet the new king. "Who is he and where is his kingdom?"

"King Sacripant of Circassia."

Akramont nodded, recognizing the name. He surveyed the rows and rows of soldiers marching toward his encampment and hope rose inside his chest. A banner flapped in the wind showing a black wild boar on a field of crimson. Akramont stepped forward to welcome the newest king to his campaign, but was surprised when the monarch remained on horseback.

"What happened here?" Sacripant asked as a wagon filled with corpses passed.

"The battle did not go well last night."

"You fought last night? Were you ignorant that a massive storm was due?"

"I knew there would be rain."

"Rain," Sacripant snorted. "That was not a mere sprinkling of water, it was a torrential downpour. The most violent thunderstorm I have ever seen. I knew enough to have my soldiers pitch camp early yesterday. After all, we walk around wearing iron on our bodies, why deliberately tempt lightning?"

Akramont gritted his teeth, wishing he could send this insolent man away, but he needed the spiritual lift for his troops that would come with the addition of five thousand new soldiers. He could not refuse this man's help and would therefore have to accept all that went with it, including insults to his manhood. "I hoped the clouds would obscure our attack and help us take our enemies by surprise."

"If that is the case, why did you not wait five days?" countered Sacripant. "Your attack would have been under the dark of the new moon."

"They would have expected that."

Sacripant laughed loudly as he dismounted. "Are you in such haste for glory and fame that you thought victory could be won in a single night? Did you honestly think you could surprise Charlemagne in war? He has led armies into battle longer than you have been alive. Any fortified city under siege knows their enemy will attack; the only question is when. There is no element of surprise."

Akramont's cheeks burned with anger, but he held his tongue.

"You needlessly sent men to their deaths," Sacripant continued. "And yet the perimeter of Paris is still not secured. Sieges require time and patience. Your impatience has allowed and continues to allow your enemies to receive food and supplies. Today you bury thousands of men who should still be alive. Your lust for victory and bad advice from your wazirs allowed an ill-conceived attack to go forward."

"You have condemned my strategies with great ease," Akramont said. "Tell me, what you would advise."

"Let us retire to your tent, bring me food and drink, then I shall tell you."

Akramont escorted the King of Circassia through the camp. A servant hurriedly set a goblet of fresh drawn water and a plate of food before Sacripant who sat down on an embroidered cushion.

"Have you no wine?" Sacripant asked.

Akramont waved a hand at the servant to retrieve the contraband liquid obtained by sacking Frankish towns.

The Circassian king made a show of washing his hands in a water bowl while waiting for his preferred beverage. Akramont took that time to survey his guest. Sacripant was short and stout with a barrel chest and a thick neck. The top of his head was bald, but the rest of his body was matted with a dense layer of hair. His eyebrows were bushy and wild, while his beard was a tangled mess.

The servant returned with the wine and received a curt nod. Sacripant took a long drink, closed his eyes, and a smile came over his face. Akramont remained calm throughout this demonstration. He knew that his temperament was being tested and he fell back upon a relaxation technique of internally reciting the generations of descendants from his ancestor Alexander the Great.

Sacripant drained his goblet, grunted for a refill, and attacked a roasted leg of mutton. He had not finished chewing the mouthful of food when he began speaking. "How many troops on this campaign were sent by your commander, Caliph Harun al-Rashid?"

Akramont gave him a cold stare and said nothing.

"As I suspected." Bits of food fell from Sacripant's mouth onto his beard. "Harun will not be pleased by you embarking on such an expedition without his orders. Especially since he and the emperor have exchanged diplomatic envoys and gifts. How many of your wazirs know your mission lacks the Caliph's approval?"

Akramont said nothing.

"You should be careful," said Sacripant as he took another swig of wine. "On my journey to Francia, I heard rumors of the Caliph amassing armies to send to Bizerta to quash your rebellion against his authority."

"Tell me what brings you here," said Akramont. "Francia is far from your home and you did not bring enough troops to conquer an empire."

"I came west in search of Angelica," said Sacripant. "Rumors say she left Cathay with Orlando. She will be mine. I will join your ranks while seeking her whereabouts."

Akramont suppressed a smirk for he had heard tales of Angelica's famed beauty and he knew that the man sitting before him with food in his beard had as much chance as Brunello of winning that maiden's heart.

"Beyond the woman, I am also seeking revenge," said Sacripant. "While I was in Cathay, defending Angelica in a bloody siege, my brother Olibandro was left in charge of my kingdom. He was killed by a bastard who dared invade my country in my absence. I have heard reports that he is now in Francia as well."

Akramont winced as the king casually dropped food onto a rug. "You have been fed, now it is time for you to share your advice."

"Starvation and disease is how you win a siege," Sacripant said, while gnawing at the remaining meat on a bone. "Start by building pontoon bridges across the Seine to transport your troops around the city. Then secure all the gates; do not allow anyone in or out of them. Soon their food supplies will dwindle and the people inside will suffer. Go to nearby villages and find some women to entertain your troops. After a few days when they have been worn out, kill the women, then carve up their bodies into small pieces suitable for the catapult. Bury those parts for about a week until they start rotting. At that point you will have weapons ready to launch over the walls and into the city itself. Disease and death will follow."

Sacripant wiped his mouth with the back of his hand. The Asian king's eyes were cold, leaving Akramont no doubt that this advice came from first hand experience.

CHAPTER 85

Renaud waited patiently for another caravan of wagons to leave the walled city of Paris carrying burned corpses to the Saracen encampment. He, his brother Guichard, and a squire slipped out quietly among the cortège. They wore heavy cloaks over their armor, hoping this disguise would allow them to pass in front of their enemies unquestioned. The seeming endless stream of grisly corpses had taken its toll. So when the three Franks rode quietly out of Paris, no one tried stopping them as their path deviated from the procession of wagons toward a road heading west.

They rode in silence until they were several miles away from Paris, well out of the sight and sound of their enemies. The three men dismounted and removed their cloaks. Renaud donned the distinctive gold helmet he claimed after killing the famed warrior Mambrino.

The sun had finally broken through the gloom. Renaud closed his eyes and smiled. He welcomed the feel of warm sunshine upon his face. The weather had been overcast and gloomy in the preceding days and with the change in climate came a change in attitude.

"Our fair sister increased her fame in your absence," Guichard announced, breaking the silence.

"Do tell," Renaud urged.

"She has valiantly led our defense of Marseille. The infidels have been unable to claim that port city."

"Wonderful. It has been ages since I have seen Bradamante."

"She has grown to be a great beauty, and a fierce warrior. Likewise, your family has grown in your prolonged absence."

"Bernard is tall now, is he?"

"He is, but I was speaking of the birth of your newest son."

"What?" asked Renaud. "I have another son?"

"Clarice gave birth five months ago. She named the boy Aymon."

"Why did no one tell me this before?"

"You have been gone a long time, brother. Messages from family are hard to deliver to someone on the other side of the world."

"Yes, but –"

"Perhaps you expected Charlemagne to inform you of this?" asked Guichard. "I believe he has more important things on his mind right now."

Renaud was stunned. The enormity of the time he had been away from his family finally hit him. He had not even known that Clarice conceived the last night they had been together.

It was another mile before Guichard broke the silence again. "I am pleased to see you have reclaimed Bayard. Aistulf found you then?"

"Yes, in the east. I was grateful to see our kinsman, and for the return of such a fine steed."

"Tell me brother, I long to hear from your own lips what transpired the day you disappeared. I refuse to believe you ran away from a duel with Gradasso."

Renaud's temper flared. "I did not leave of my own accord."

"I believe you. I have never known you to avoid a fight. I bear new scars defending your name." Guichard pointed to a small, raised pink patch of skin on his left cheek in the shape of a signet ring.

"Who dared question my honor?"

"The Maganzas of course. Ganelon insisted both you and Orlando be stripped of your titles as paladins. He wanted Bertolai and Pinabel elevated as replacements."

Renaud snarled, "Traitors."

"Pinabel has yet to report for duty. Charlemagne would sooner hang him than reward him."

"That is reassuring."

"Tell me what happened that fateful day with Gradasso," Guichard pressed.

"I reported to the dueling site at the appointed time, and fought with what I thought was my opponent. Later I realized it was not Gradasso, but a demon. I was tricked into boarding an enchanted vessel and taken to faraway lands. The ship itself was enveloped by magic. I passed through storms, but the waters surrounding the ship were placid and I remained dry. Other times, when the seas were calm and the sails should have been slack, a peculiar wind kept the ship going forward. Within a few days, the ship had sailed itself around the horn of Africa and docked near Cathay."

"Angelica's kingdom," whispered Guichard.

"Yes. Angelica. The first time I saw her at that accursed tournament I was like every other man and fell in love with her instantly. I was outraged when Feraguto slew Argalia. I was to have been the third man to joust, and he destroyed my chance to win her outright. When she fled for her life, I, like many other love struck knights, pursued her. My only concern was to find her and make her my own. I rode until I could ride no more, then when I awoke I saw her beautiful face smiling down at me. She begged me to be her lover."

"And so you…"

"Then comes something I cannot explain. After waking, I found that I loathed her more than anyone in the world. All the hatred I have toward the Maganzas would be a mere drop in the ocean of vitriol I felt the moment I saw her face. I spurned her in a coarse and cruel manner. No lady should ever endure the treatment I bestowed upon her. I returned immediately to the service of Charlemagne and fought Gradasso. Later when I arrived in Cathay, Angelica was waiting for me. She was still passionately in love with me, and threw herself at my feet."

Guichard stared at him.

"I still hated her," said Renaud. "I even joined forces with the fierce Queen Marfisa who took over the siege outside Angelica's castle after Orlando killed Agrikhan of Tartary. It was only when Charlemagne's messengers came and announced the impending invasion by Saracen forces that I was able to think clearly enough to return to my sovereign and my duty."

"What became of Aistulf?" asked Guichard.

"I cannot say for certain, but I believe he is dead."

"What happened?"

"He was swallowed by a whale," said Renaud.

"A whale?"

"Just as the ship I was lured on that brought me to Cathay was no ordinary ship, I fear that the whale that swallowed him was no ordinary sea creature. I believe it was due to sorcery. I tried rescuing him, but failed."

Guichard bowed his head and said a silent prayer. Renault felt guilt. He had rescued many strangers from magical prisons, but was unable to save a kinsman.

"There is something else I must ask you," said Guichard. "I heard that you and Orlando fought over Angelica. How can that be true if you hate her?"

Renaud sighed. "It is true, I have fought Orlando. Twice, in fact. Once in Cathay when I hated her and he was her greatest defender. The second time, and more recently, after we both returned to Francia and after I had fallen back in love with her."

Guichard stopped his horse. "Just like that? You love her, then you hate her, then you love her again?"

"Yes, another thing I cannot explain," said Renaud, who stopped his horse as well. "As soon as I experienced my change of heart, she spurned me. She treated me as if I was her greatest nightmare, but back in Cathay she implored me in ways that would make eunuchs feel desire. I do not understand what happened to me or her."

"So you fought Orlando over a woman who despises you and Charlemagne stopped the fight?"

"Yes. He needed both of us in battle the next day in Toulouse. He placed Angelica in Duke Namo's safekeeping. She was to be presented either to Orlando or me, whoever proved more valiant in battle."

"Who won the prize?" asked Guichard.

"No one, because we lost that battle and she escaped during the chaos."

"Now I understand. You offered to find Orlando because you think he will lead you to Angelica."

Renaud remained silent, but nudged Bayard to start walking again.

"But of course, you merely wish to love Angelica from afar," said Guichard, his voice sarcastic.

"Afar?"

"Yes, courtly love, for that is the only love you can show a woman who is not your wife," replied Guichard. "Or need I remind you of your duty to Clarice? The woman who bore you a son in your absence?"

"Tell me Guichard, what is your experience with love?"

"I have none, for I am a soldier without lands or title. I have a salary for my services to our emperor, but it is not enough to support a wife or children. I follow in our father's footsteps, hoping to distinguish myself in battle, and be rewarded for my acts of bravery. Until that time, I cannot pledge my heart to any woman for it would surely be broken."

"You do not understand love."

"I understand that you and Aistulf were raised in the royal palace and exposed to our king with his concubines. Your first knowledge of a woman was not on your bridal bed, but in a bordello."

Renaud's cheeks burned.

"I was trained in a different household," continued Guichard. "One where the Code of Chivalry was taken seriously, especially as it pertains to women."

Renaud could not believe how insufferable his brother was. He was worse than Clarice and her nagging.

"When you had your sudden change of heart, were there any fountains around by any chance?" asked Guichard.

"Fountains?"

"Yes, a fountain where none should be. Did you come across a fountain say in a wood, and by chance did you drink of it?"

Renaud thought back to that day when he had followed Angelica, and was parched with thirst. He stumbled upon a golden fountain with the most refreshing cool, clear water. After drinking his fill he had fallen asleep, and awoke to find Angelica kneeling next to him. "Yes, I did drink of one, what of it?"

"And did you come upon it again on your return journey?"

Renaud nodded. "I saw it again, but it was after I quenched my thirst in a nearby stream. However, Angelica was standing in front of that same fountain when I came upon her."

"As I suspected," said Guichard. "Our cousin Maugis warned me about drinking from fountains. He said Merlin scattered several magical fountains throughout our land. One was made with the intent of saving the noble knight Tristan from ruining his uncle's kingdom. Merlin wanted to remove Isolde from Tristan's heart, but the valorous knight never drank its magical waters. Yet the fountain remains and anyone who drinks of it will have their ardor chilled. However, nearby is the Stream of Love which causes its drinkers to fall passionately in love with whomever they see first. I believe that you and Angelica twice drank of opposing waters, causing you both to feel opposing emotions toward one another."

Renaud thought for a moment. "So if I could get her to drink from that stream again, she would love me?"

"You would be playing with sorcery," warned Guichard. "It is bad enough our cousin Maugis has dedicated his life to wizardry; I will not aid you in a quest to use magic. The love you hold for Angelica is based on witchcraft and lust. She will be your downfall should you continue to pursue her. Devastation surrounds that woman. If there is any magical remedy to be pursued, it should be to completely remove her from your heart so you might once again show the proper love and respect that is due Clarice. Your wife is virtuous and respectable; you cannot say the same of Angelica."

Renaud knew what his brother said was true. His obsession with Angelica had overpowered his judgment. Even as he served as ambassador for Charlemagne seeking troops from the various tribes in Britain, he felt a constant urge to find and possess her. He would have killed Orlando that day had their fight not been stopped. His eagerness to seek out his famed cousin was not to serve the emperor and return a wayward paladin to the fold but to eliminate a romantic rival and renew his pursuit of Angelica.

"I understand the passion she stirs in you," said Guichard. "I was also overcome with desire when she walked into that hall. But, I am no longer under her spell. The power of Angelica's beauty is due to sorcery. I will help you in your quest to find Orlando and bring him back to serve Charlemagne. I will not help you pursue a woman who is cursed."

CHAPTER 86

Rodomont rode relentlessly throughout the night and the next day to reach Doralice as quickly as possible. His horse was exhausted, but he would not allow it to rest. He whipped the beast whenever it dared move at less than a canter. The dwarf likewise was exhausted, but Rodomont would not allow him to rest either. Nothing would cause him to stop before he reached Doralice.

By morning they came upon an area where fresh mounds of tilled earth indicated large graves. A foreboding silence and the smell of death and despair hung in the air.

"Is this where you were?" asked Rodomont.

"No," replied the dwarf. "It is still further down this road. I wonder what happened here."

"This must be where Manilard and al-Zahira's men were killed," said Rodomont. His lip curled; this was the reason Mandricardo left Akramont's camp. If that bastard had never gone on a mission, Rodomont would be looking upon the face of his blushing bride rather than dried blood upon the ground. His impatience flared again as he struck his horse, urging it onward.

They rounded a curve as the setting sun turned the landscape to vivid shades of red and orange. A few tents remained standing where two women were digging graves.

"Devante!" shrieked a young woman.

The dwarf fell out of his saddle and onto the ground.

"Where is Doralice?" Rodomont demanded.

The young woman's eyes filled with tears. "Alas milord, my lady was abducted by the murderer. She pleaded, but he would not listen. They rode down that road."

"Rodomont will find Doralice," said the dwarf. "All will be set right."

Rodomont dismounted, grabbed his silk standard from the back of his horse and an unadorned shield from the ground before mounting a fresh horse to ride. He left without saying another word. He was on a mad, desperate race to find his lady.

~~~

Renaud's quest for Orlando went at a comfortable pace. He stopped and asked the few travelers on the road if they knew of any recent massacres of soldiers. One elderly man told him that such a thing happened seven miles further down the road near a large oak tree and a stream. The man did not know who was responsible nor had he seen anyone who fit Orlando's description.

As Renaud's party approached those landmarks, they came upon a field with trampled grass, black bloodstains, and dotted with fresh mounds of earth. It had been several days since the slaughter and undoubtedly the Saracen army had sent an expedition to bury their dead.

Renaud dismounted and handed the reins of his horse to his squire. He scanned the area. All the supplies of the army had been removed. He could make out where some tents and campfires had been. There were also tracks from wagon wheels that led back to the road to Paris. It was likely that those tracks had been made by the burial party.

He frowned. The site had been disturbed so much that it complicated tracking the culprit.

"Renaud, over here," called Guichard.

His brother was standing near the road at the far end of the field and pointing to bloodstained hoof prints leading away from Paris.

The squire looked puzzled. "Why would a soldier capable of this kind of violence not head toward the war in Paris?"

"Maybe because that knight had another mission in mind," said Renaud.

They followed the road westward even after the hoof prints faded away. A couple miles further along they came across a village where the people were rebuilding after being sacked. A carpenter was making planks from logs. The man soon paused from his laboring and drank from an earthenware jug.

"Pardon me," said Renaud. "I am with Charlemagne's forces. Do you know anything about a recent massacre of Saracen forces around here?"

"Which one?" said the man as he wiped his brow.

"Which one?" Renaud repeated. "I was asking about the massacre a week ago not four miles east of here."

"And there was another massacre of Saracen soldiers a few days ago twenty miles west of here."

Renaud's spirits rose. Orlando must be on a killing spree. At least he had a direction to set off in which to find him. "Do you know anything about the party or parties responsible?"

"No, but I sleep better at night knowing that someone's killing the Saracen invaders."

Renaud wondered if anyone in the village might know something that would be helpful. He did not want to spend all day asking questions, so he climbed upon a mounting block and cleared his throat. "Attention. I am Renaud, Count of Montauban and paladin to Charlemagne. I am on a mission from your emperor and am in search of the knight responsible for massacres at Saracen encampments. Has anyone here seen or talked with any lone knights?"

An elderly woman stepped forward. "I have milord. A few days ago a soldier came up to me and his armor was coated in blood."

"Did he say anything?"

"Yes, milord. He was looking for a beautiful blonde woman. He was quite broken up about her."

"Had you seen the woman?"

"No, milord."

"Can you tell me what the man looked like? Did he bear a standard?" asked Renaud.

"He was fearsome," said the woman. "Tall, dark hair, beard. No real standard to speak of, just a shield of black."

~~~

Mandricardo still tracked Orlando, but he no longer had the same level of obsession for finding the paladin. Originally he had wanted no one with him on this mission. Doralice's company had been a pleasant surprise. Not only did she provide him sensual pleasures, but she had also proved adept at helping him track the Black Knight. She was able to converse far more readily than he was with the Frankish peasants. Normally he never liked others to assert themselves when he was supposed to lead, but she was tremendously helpful. She even helped tutor him in that guttural tongue.

His mood improved so much that he found himself marveling at the mountains and scenic vistas they passed. Mandricardo soon found that he had greater interest in identifying a suitable place for their nightly amorous activities than he had in seeking revenge.

~~~

Doralice caught herself repeatedly looking over her shoulder each day. Nightmares haunted her with scenes of Mandricardo dying at the hands of the notorious Black Knight. However, when the helmet was removed, Rodomont was staring at her with rage and hatred in his eyes. She hid her worries from her new husband, who was oblivious to her increasingly dour mood. As long as she had sex with him multiple times a day, nothing else mattered to him. Doralice tried focusing her thoughts on his steady litany of promises regarding the realm of Tartary, and ignoring the mounting fear she had about impending duels with Orlando or Rodomont.

~~~

Nearly a fortnight passed since Orlando had savagely killed a campsite full of soldiers. He had lost all sense of direction and had no idea where he was. He was simply following his heart. He sensed Angelica was nearby. Orlando knew he would soon learn what happened to his beloved. His wanderings had brought him outside the boundary of a vast forest. He came to rest near an apple orchard, ate his fill, and fell into a deep sleep.

~~~

Bradamante had come to the realization that Atallah had no intention of ever letting her see Ruggiero while they were both inside the enchanted dwelling. She could search all day long and never find him. She could remain in one place and Ruggiero could walk past her, but neither would see the other because magic rendered them invisible to one another. Bradamante repeatedly railed against Atallah's cruelty.

For the first few days she refused to eat any of the food magically appearing before her, fearing it was poisoned. She also suspected the wizard might strike while she slept. Once her hunger and exhaustion could no longer be denied, she challenged him directly.

"Atallah," she shouted. "Once again you demonstrate your cowardice by using deception. Are you going to compound your sins by poisoning or attacking a resting captive? Prove to me you have some honor and swear no harm shall come to me via food, drink, or rest."

A single white feather floated down from the ceiling settling at her feet. Then platters of food appeared upon a banquet table. Her mouth watered at the warm bread, roasted beef, honey-dipped pastries, and wine. She quietly ate her fill, and walked into the next room where a large bed invited her to rest. As long as her mind did not focus on Ruggiero she slept in peace, but as soon as she thought of him, phantom voices urged her forward into searches. As the days dragged into weeks she could see no way out of the hopeless situation or the castle.

"Atallah," she said one day. "What do you want from me?"

Silence.

"Shall I renounce my love for Ruggiero? Swear an oath I will never seek him again?"

A door appeared in the stone wall. Slowly it opened and for the first time since she was imprisoned, she saw the outdoors. Bright sunshine blinded her as it flooded into the castle, birds chirped in the distance, and a warm breeze blew across her face. She was tempted to walk outside and end her suffering, but to do so she would surrender any future she had with Ruggiero. Bradamante suspected Atallah would remove her memory from Ruggiero's heart allowing the young knight to rejoin Akramont's forces and fulfill his other possible destiny.

She closed her eyes and saw the image of her future child's face. If she left the castle, the child would never be born. Her sovereign would suffer defeat and Christendom would be devastated.

"My freedom can be won by denying my heart?" she said. "That is too costly a price. I would rather you tear the beating heart from my chest than tell me I must deny my love for Ruggiero. As long as I live, I shall love him and only him."

The door closed and its outline melted, leaving a blank stone wall. Bradamante uttered a low curse against the wizard, and returned to berating herself for having doubted Melissa.

~~~

Melissa had not given up on helping Bradamante and Ruggiero, but she turned to another for help. Rather than speak to him directly, once again she used her powers and directed a horse to bear its rider off course. This horseman was returning home after a long overland journey from Asia. He had been on his way to Paris, but while in southern Francia was brought inside a vast forest and before an ominous looking castle. The warrior appeared agitated as he stared at the stone structure. Aistulf removed a golden lance from the side of his saddle, couched it under his right arm, and prepared for battle.

Part V
Rescues and Duels

CHAPTER 87

Aistulf stared in disbelief as an ogre ran outside the castle, picked up a buxom red-haired woman and threw her over his shoulder.

"Help me, Aistulf!" she screamed.

He squinted to see the woman more clearly and was puzzled when he recognized her. Over the years, he had seen many fantastic sights, but he could not understand how he was looking upon the face and figure of Berthild the barmaid. She had lavished attention on him and Renaud when they were squires in the royal court at Aachen. Her image had been the source of many vivid, erotic dreams and Aistulf fancied her to be his first love. However, she had died in childbirth many years before.

"Sorcery," he muttered.

Shifting his lance, he grabbed the magical horn Logistilla gave him. He blew into the instrument with all his might. The blare was as loud as a thousand trumpeting elephants. The image of the woman and ogre disappeared, and was replaced by a frightened old wizard. Aistulf urged his horse forward as the old man stumbled and fell.

Aistulf leapt off his horse and jumped the old magician. Using the fabric from the wizard's turban he bound the old man's hands together. As he did so, Aistulf noticed the ring worn by his prisoner.

"That belongs to Ruggiero," he said, tearing it off the wizard's finger. He clasped the ring tightly in one hand hoping it could tell him where his friend was. Sensing nothing he slipped it on for safe keeping until he could return it to Ruggiero.

"You must be Atallah, the man who was afraid to allow a paragon of bravery and uncommon courtesy to face his destiny." Aistulf spat in Atallah's face. "That was for the abuse Ruggiero suffered at the hands of Alcina. How dare you send such a noble soul into that hag's clutches."

A single tear rolled down the wizened old man's cheek.

"Tell me what has befallen him," demanded Aistulf.

Atallah's eyes were unfocused as he stared into the distance.

Aistulf grabbed him roughly by the collar, nearly choking the elderly man. "I owe Ruggiero my life. Tell me where he is."

As the old man gasped for breath, Aistulf glanced over his shoulder at the castle and knew the answer. Hoping to prevent Atallah from casting spells by verbal incantations alone, Aistulf tore strips of fabric off the bottom of the wizard's cloak.

"This will teach you not to answer me," said Aistulf, as he gagged his captive.

Retrieving Logistilla's book from his horse's saddlebags, it magically opened to a page with a drawing of a stone fortress in the margin along with an image of a wizard. The words all ran together in a cramped hand making it difficult to read. He squinted and reread the passage several times to make out the meaning.

castellas beset by magic require necromancers to enslave evil spirits whose entrapment is locked by a powerful spell placed on a magical surface to lift the enchantment one must utterly destroy the magical object taking care to first invoke divine protection lest the demons possess you upon their release

Aistulf scanned the forest ground. After a few false starts, he spied a large slate rock with engravings on its surface.

"Dear Lord," Aistulf prayed. "Help me break the spell that imprisons Ruggiero and protect me from the evil that haunts this site."

He made another sharp blast on his horn and then raised the flat rock above his head dashing it against a boulder with all his might. It smashed into three large pieces. Green smoke shot through the air as if launched by a catapult. As the magic spell ended, the massive stone walls disappeared like a fine mist under harsh sunlight. A flash of gold and feathers caught Aistulf's eye. The hippogriff flew high into the air, circled once, and landed at Atallah's feet.

"Kamal, Ruggiero's steed," Aistulf whispered.

He tried creeping forward to seize the reins of the beast, but the hippogriff flew off despite his cries of protest. He felt obligated to return Kamal to Ruggiero, so he ran after the winged beast. He resented being bound to the earth, while the animal traveled in the sky. Rabican joined the chase and Aistulf was grateful to remount his own magical horse. Together they pursued the hippogriff.

~~~

Bradamante had heard the deafening noise of a horn being sounded. Terror filled her veins. Immediately she drew out her sword and held her shield in a defensive posture. Moments passed as she remained in one place and waited. The only sound was her labored breathing while fear clung fast to her heart. Then there was another blast of the horn followed by the dissolving of the stone walls. She was standing on the forest floor. Ruggiero held his sword in the air poised to strike.

CHAPTER 88

Ruggiero did not believe his eyes. Bradamante's form appeared before him. This had to be another cruel trick by Atallah. He was tempted to strike his sword through the magical mist, hoping to break the mystic's evil spell.

"Ruggiero?" Bradamante asked.

The fresh breeze upon his face made him realize he was no longer inside a castle. Tears welled in his eyes as he understood she was not a phantom. They sheathed their swords in unison as Ruggiero rushed to cradle her face in his hands. His tears mingled with hers as they kissed.

The distant sound of a horse crashing through the forest interrupted them.

"Atallah!" said Ruggiero. "We must stop him before he separates us again."

He was surprised that there was no clearing in the forest where the vast castle once stood. Ruggiero knew every one of those one hundred rooms by heart after having searched each one repeatedly for Bradamante. Now he held her hand as they set out in search of Atallah.

Their search was short as the sound of whimpering drew them to the old man's side. The Sufi mystic was bound, gagged, and lying near a clump of trees. Ruggiero drew out his sword and looked around to see if the Atallah's assailant was nearby. A search of the surrounding area did not reveal anyone, so he returned to the mystic's side and propped him up against the trunk of a large oak tree.

As he stared at Atallah, Ruggiero found that he was in no hurry to release him. The anger he had felt when Melissa returned his memories to him rose again within him. He might never get another chance to confront his guardian without interruption.

"Atallah you must stop this madness," said Ruggiero. "My destiny lies with this fair maid, you know that. I owe you my life but you have violated my trust. I no longer think of you as my adopted father, instead you are my jailer who would keep me imprisoned for the rest of my life. I am a man, and must be allowed to live my life free of your interference." He took Bradamante's hand and kissed it. "This is the woman of my dreams. You knew that and yet you delivered me to the clutches of an old hag. How could you do that to someone you profess to love?"

Atallah shut his eyes.

"You knew my heart and yet you harmed me in that dishonorable manner. Alcina was a cruel, selfish, and evil old witch. She removed all memory of Bradamante from my heart, making me forget my sense of honor. My conduct while under her spell was shameful, but you are responsible for that. Swear you will never cast another spell over me again, nor ask anyone else to use magic against me."

Ruggiero untied the gag from Atallah's mouth. Tears streamed down the old man's face. He tried speaking, but no words came out.

"Swear it," Ruggiero demanded, grabbing him by the collar.

"I swear," Atallah rasped, "upon your mother's grave. I swear that I shall no longer use magic to try and protect you."

"Swear that you will leave Bradamante and her family alone as well."

"I swear," he said sobbing. "Please find it in your heart to forgive me. I only wanted to protect you from harm."

"Yet, because of you, I have suffered grievously."

"Her family has many enemies," warned Atallah. "Beware. They will scheme to cut you down in the prime of your life."

"You have told me that before, but it does not matter. I would rather die having spent one night in her arms than live an entire lifetime without her love."

Bradamante broke down in tears. Ruggiero held her while she sobbed on his shoulder. Stroking her hair he murmured, "No other woman could ever captivate my heart."

She clung to him as he breathed in her scent. As her sobbing subsided, he kissed the tears away from her cheeks. Bradamante rewarded him with a smile that made his heart soar.

"Even if we had only one night together?" she asked.

"My life will have served a purpose. I could never love another woman, and I cannot live without your love."

He placed an arm around her back and turned toward Atallah who now bore acceptance on his face.

"Please untie me," said Atallah. "I swear by all I hold as holy that I shall do nothing to interfere with your union ever again. I wish to give you my blessing."

"If you break that vow," said Ruggiero, "I shall run you through for dishonor."

Atallah nodded. Ruggiero loosened the knots and helped lift up Atallah as the old man struggled to stand.

"Who bound you?" asked Ruggiero.

"A knight. He left in pursuit of the hippogriff and is far away from here by now." Atallah leaned on Ruggiero as he smiled at Bradamante. "How could Ruggiero not fall in love with you? You have the face of an angel and the spirit of a lioness."

The mystic led her to the encampment on the banks of a stream where Ruggiero had stayed. The blanket and sheep skin used were still there near a hollowed out tree stump.

"You two will embark upon a new journey. To prove that I harbor no resentment or ill feelings, I wish to give you some gifts," said Atallah. "First you will need horses."

He lifted his hands and two horses walked out of the woods. One was a dappled gray, the other a black stallion. Atallah tied their reins to a nearby tree.

"I apologize, but the hippogriff took to flight when the spell was broken. You may use my horse Deimos," said Atallah.

Ruggiero admired his new destrier while Bradamante stroked the nose of the gray horse.

"You cannot start on a journey without a proper meal." Atallah waved his arms. A large cloth appeared on the ground covered with food. There were succulent beef roasts, baked pheasant, stewed carrots and onions, various cheeses, baked breads with honey, as well as bowls filled with cherries, blackberries, raspberries, and cream. "And you cannot sit down to a feast without being properly attired," continued the mystic, as he waved his arms again.

Their armor hung on a nearby beech tree. Ruggiero wore a white linen tunic and breeches, while Bradamante was dressed in a light blue gown made of pure silk. It clung to her curves as if sewn by an expert tailor. She smiled as she touched the fabric of her dress. Ruggiero could not help but stare. He had always thought her beautiful, but seeing her in a dress made him desire her even more. She brought her hands up to her head which was once again draped in long tresses.

"My hair," she laughed. "I had forgotten how it felt to have long hair."

"And now, I shall take my leave," said Atallah.

"Wait!" said Bradamante. "I do not wish to appear ungrateful, but could you return my hair back to the way it was?"

"You wish to remain looking like a boy?"

"That does not matter to me, but my family saw me with cropped hair. I fear their reaction if it returns to its former length too quickly. They would suspect magic, and I do not wish to alarm them. If you would please, make a wig for me? I could wear that until my own locks grow back."

With a small wave of his hand, he made her wish come true. Atallah turned to Ruggiero, kissed him on the cheek, and walked away into the forest.

Ruggiero took Bradamante by the hand and they sat down before the sumptuous spread. Taking turns feeding each other, he relished being with the woman he loved. After eating his fill, Ruggiero reclined on the sheepskin blanket. Bradamante lay down next to him. He traced the contours of her delicate face, leaned forward and kissed her.

Bradamante had dreamt many times of being in Ruggiero's arms and kissing him, but it was hard for her to believe her dreams had finally become reality. Pulling herself away from him, she gazed at his face. She marveled at the way the sunlight picked up different shades of color in his eyes. There were flecks of green, gold, and brown, and she decided she would love nothing better than to look into his eyes forever. Her fingers stroked the stubble of whiskers that had grown on his cheeks. In a few months time, she surmised, he would have the start of a nice growth of beard. She touched the curls on his head, something she had yearned to do the first time she met him.

"What happened to the ring I gave you?" she asked, when she glanced at his hands.

"I believe Atallah took it from me the night I slept here," he replied. "That is why he fooled me into believing his magic. That is behind us now. All I care about is that you and I are finally together."

Bradamante blushed as Ruggiero's eyes drank in the curves of her body, from the swell of her bosom to her small waist, past her full hips to the ends of her long legs. She dared not give his body such an appraisal. It was enough for her to be next to him, feeling the warmth of his body. His gaze returned to her eyes and he smiled at her appreciatively.

"Bradamante, I wish this was our wedding night. Then there would be nothing to stop us from consummating our love for one another. For now, I pledge my eternal love for you with a kiss."

As he pressed his body against hers, Bradamante felt overwhelmed by the flood of new sensations. With every breath, her chest rose and fell against his. Her fingers touched the soft linen of his tunic, feeling the taut muscles of his back and arms. His hands roamed over her backside, slowly making their way toward the front of her bodice. Ruggiero's lips slid down her neck as Bradamante's breathing became ragged.

She then felt something that brought her back to her senses. It was a scabbard pressing into her thigh. Reaching down to remove the belt on his waist, she was startled to discover he was not wearing one. The top of his breeches were secured with a drawstring. Her face burned as she realized what she felt was not a foreign object, but the weapon of love that no proper maiden should feel until her bridal bed.

Bradamante pushed herself away. "I love you Ruggiero, but I cannot give you what you desire. Not until we are properly wed."

"I understand," said Ruggiero. "There is nothing I want more than to be your lawful husband."

She sat up, smoothing the wrinkles from her dress. "My father will never accept our marriage, unless you are baptized a Christian. And I cannot marry you without his permission and blessing."

"I would submit to baptism by fire for you if necessary. Christianity was the faith of my father, and it shall be the faith of our children," said Ruggiero as he tenderly wiped a tear from her face. "Atallah taught me that God is in everything that surrounds us. Besides, there is not as much difference between Islam and Christianity as you would think. There is no god but God. We have a shared heritage with stories of Abraham, Moses, David, and Jesus. I will celebrate new holidays and change my outward expressions of worship for you, but I cannot change my heart or my beliefs because we worship the same one god. Let us depart and find a place for me to be baptized today. This will fulfill my late father's wish for me to be a Christian. Then we shall speak with your father about our marriage. Love has brought us together and we *shall* be married."

She kissed him. "There is an abbey not too far from here. You can be baptized before the sun sets today."

They packed their saddlebags with their weapons and armor and any food that would keep during their travel. After making their way to a road an elderly peasant woman riding horseback called out to them.

"What ails thee?" asked Bradamante.

"Oh milady, milord," the peasant wailed. "Please stop a tragedy if you can. A young man is to be put to death at sundown for loving a young woman."

CHAPTER 89

"A man is to be killed?" asked Bradamante.

"He is to be burned to death in the center square," said the peasant. "Over a lady."

"Was she married?"

"No, but she was a noblewoman. They were secret lovers, until caught in bed together."

"Why did they not marry?" asked Ruggiero.

"Her father is off at war, and the young man has no land or title. He is also of a different faith from the lady."

Bradamante and Ruggiero exchanged a look.

"What will happen to the lady?" asked Bradamante.

"No one knows," said the woman, shaking her head. "After they were found together naked, she was taken away."

"We must help this young man," announced Bradamante.

Ruggiero dismounted and helped Bradamante out of her saddle. Each unpacked their armor and went in opposite directions to dress for battle. The peasant seemed surprised when Bradamante motioned for her to follow behind some tall brush. She wanted help getting out of her fine clothes and into a gambeson and hauberk. The old woman raised her eyebrows as she watched Bradamante transform from a lady with long beautiful tresses into a warrior.

"You look like – "

"A boy," finished Bradamante, as she put her helmet upon her cropped hair, "but verily I assure you there are few men who are my peers."

The peasant stared as Bradamante packed her wig and gown into her saddlebags.

"Where is this barbaric act to occur?" asked Bradamante once all three were mounted on their horses.

"East of here in Cordes."

Bradamante suddenly felt as if she were punched in her stomach. "Pray tell me the lady's name in question."

"Fiordespina."

Tears stung her eyes, as Bradamante's fears were confirmed.

"Do you know her?" Ruggiero asked.

"Yes," she said, fighting to keep her composure. "She is my friend. We must stop this madness from happening!"

She galloped off into the distance. Ruggiero followed closely behind, but the peasant's horse was tired and could not keep up. They rode as fast as the rough path would allow until they approached a fork in the road.

"Wait my lady!" yelled the peasant from behind. "You must not go that way."

"But this is the shortest route," protested Bradamante.

"It is fraught with danger. The other way is longer, but safer."

"We will not get there in time if we take that road," said Bradamante.

The old lady nodded, then shook her head in frustration.

"What danger lies in the shorter path?" asked Ruggiero.

"The castle of Altaripa," said the peasant. "Count Ansel's horrid son is there with his new wife. That vile couple has forced every nobleman and every lady who passed their way to be stripped of clothes and horses. I beg of you, do not go that way."

"I have never avoided a fight, nor will I bow down to villains," said Ruggiero.

"Did you pass that way earlier?" asked Bradamante.

"Yes, but they do not notice people like me," said the peasant, gesturing at her tattered garments and tired horse. "That evil man coerced four knights to enforce his unjust rule. In this past month, my town has seen a steady stream of disgraced noblemen and ladies come to our doorsteps naked, shamed, and begging for help."

"Altaripa," Bradamante said, through clenched teeth. "My father has spoken that accursed name. No Lyon will ever pay tribute to the house of the Maganza, nor shall we vary our paths to avoid them."

With that, she galloped forward, leading the way. An intense anger simmered within Bradamante. All the frustration she had felt since she had first been separated from Ruggiero rose to the surface. Her hatred toward Atallah was gone. It was replaced by desire to assail anyone who would harm Fiordespina. Altaripa and the Maganzas stood in her way. They would feel the wrath of her sword if they dared try to impede her progress.

Bradamante pulled on the reins to stop her horse as she neared the castle. A grand stone edifice stood above crossroads in the mountainous area. The entire region would soon be afflicted by this guile, either by forcing lengthy detours or by humiliating scores of people. She knew the Maganzas possessed great wealth, but had never considered how it was amassed. Now she knew: treachery.

A bell sounded in the tower as four knights rode out of the castle gates. The leader wore a surcoat of crimson bedecked with white flowers.

"I will handle this," said Ruggiero as he selected Atallah's shield.

"We shall do this together," she replied.

"No. It would break my heart if I lost you. I have single-handedly beaten scores of monsters while freeing myself from Alcina; I can handle four knights."

Bradamante bit her tongue. She hated when her brothers tried protecting her from harm, and now her future husband was treating her in the same patronizing manner. Her brothers had realized she could hold her own, and grew to depend upon her fighting by their sides. She would respect Ruggiero's wishes and allow him to enter this fight alone, but should he have trouble she would come to his aid.

"Baron!" called out the first knight. "Have you heard of the tribute demanded by the lord of this castle?"

"We do not require hospitality," replied Ruggiero. "Our day's journey is not over. We are merely using the road and passing by the castle."

"A toll is required nonetheless," said the knight. "You may pass, but first you must forfeit your armor and your horses."

"And if I refuse?"

"Then you shall have to earn your right of passage. Should you defeat me, there are three more knights you will have to vanquish."

"Pray tell me your names," said Ruggiero, "so that I may know who I have defeated."

"I am Sansonetto," replied the knight and gestured to a trio of knights behind him who nodded as their names were called. "My compatriots are Guidone Selvaggio and the famed brothers, Aquilant and Grifon. Since you refuse to comply with the required tribute, we must duel. Do you prefer swords or the joust?"

A cart came forward filled with dozens of lances made from oak and tipped with iron. Ruggiero nodded at it, and two squires began readying the knights with weapons. Bradamante knew that Ruggiero was eager to demonstrate his military prowess in the full light of day for her benefit.

A crowd from within the castle gathered outside to view the spectacle. A well-dressed woman walked onto the parapet. Ruggiero's demeanor abruptly changed. No longer did he appear calm and focused, instead his face was contorted with rage as he glared at a man who rode out of the castle on a white horse.

"Pinabel!" shouted Ruggiero. "Is this how you repay your debts? I set out to rescue your wife and now you dare to deny me my right of passage unless I strip myself of dignity? You are as shameless as your harlot wife."

Bradamante's anger rose at the mention of Pinabel's name. She had vowed that he would pay for his treachery, and now that day had arrived.

Pinabel's face colored, but he said nothing. He gave a curt nod at a squire who dropped a scarf signaling the riders to begin the joust. Two horses thundered at each other while both knights landed fierce blows upon the other's shield. Ruggiero's shield absorbed the strike, whereas Sansonetto's cleaved in half at the brutal impact. Sansonetto's shoulder was pierced by the lance. He screamed while falling on the ground.

Pinabel sounded a call for his servants to tend to the knight's wounds. Bradamante lost interest in the jousting match. Ruggiero had insisted on challenging the four knights himself to gain the right to travel to Cordes, but she had a new goal in mind: revenge. Her entire focus was centered on the man who betrayed her in the Pyrenees. The vile coward had ridden to higher ground in an apparent effort to improve his vantage point. Bradamante gripped her sword and followed him, blocking his return to the castle.

Her pulse quickened when he turned and stared at her shield. She gave Pinabel a wicked smile and his face registered shock. His eyes shifted from her to his men and then to a small trail. He galloped off into a thicket, but Bradamante was determined not to lose her quarry. She followed him through deep and treacherous ravines.

The trees grew close together, but she could still see flashes of the white horse ahead in the distance. He had unwittingly ridden into a trap. A hill with a sheer face of rock stood in his forward path with two steep slopes on either side. Bradamante's desire for vengeance was stoked as Pinabel was cornered. His face drained of all color.

"Have you never seen a ghost before?" taunted Bradamante. "Have you never looked into the eyes of someone who died after falling to the bottom of a cold, dark cave?"

Pinabel trembled as he looked at her sword and frantically cast around for anyone or anything, to help him.

"You dare flaunt your heinous crime by riding on the back of my mare," she said, as anger pounded in her ears. "Eos was a gift from Charlemagne, and your mere touch defiles her."

Bradamante moved her own horse closer. Stalking him, her eyes were focused solely upon her prey.

"You begged for my help as well as Ruggiero's, because you were too weak to protect your lady and too cowardly to rescue her. After I agreed to champion your cause, your true nature came forth. Your villainy not only betrayed me, but betrayed Charlemagne as well. I survived your attempted murder. Due to my acts of bravery, your lady was released from her prison. How did you react to such good fortune? You oppressed others into servitude and imposed tolls counter to the rules of hospitality. Your vile acts are an affront to our emperor, to the laws of this empire, and to Christendom. I cannot allow your besmirching of my faith and my sovereign to continue. Pray that your latest confession is current for you shall soon be accounting for your life in the Hereafter."

She thrust her sword deep into his side, piercing his armor.

"This absolves you from your humiliation for being indebted to the house of Lyon."

She stabbed him repeatedly until he fell from her bloodstained white horse and was undeniably dead.

CHAPTER 90

Another knight came forward to challenge Ruggiero. He bore a black shield with a white diagonal line. "It is my honor to defend the rules of Altaripa," he announced. "My name is Guidone Selvaggio."

"It is your honor to uphold the rule of a tyrant?" asked Ruggiero. "If you are an honorable knight, pray tell me why you swore fealty to such a dishonorable man."

"It was not of our own accord," he said, "but we are men of our word and we must therefore live up to our vows."

The two other mounted knights nodded in agreement. One held a shield with a white rose on a field of black; the other's had a black rose on a field of white.

"This man forced you to swear an oath superseding your previous oaths to a sovereign," said Ruggiero. "If your vow was not sworn voluntarily, then you are not bound by the rules of chivalry to its covenant. Your integrity should require upholding your previously sworn duties."

"You speak the truth," said Guidone. "Verily we do wish to break these unjust bonds which hold us to this man. However, we have not discovered a way to accomplish such a feat without being dishonorable in the process. Do you choose the joust again?"

"No. I have urgent need to continue my journey, so my preference is to use my sword against all of you at once. Pray forgive me if I should maim or kill any of you, for truly there is no quarrel amongst us," said Ruggiero, as he drew out Balisarda.

The three knights followed suit and withdrew their swords. Guidone struck first and his blade connected hard with Ruggiero's shield. Ruggiero lifted his arm to return the blow and was shocked when both his opponent and his opponent's horse were on the ground unconscious. With his sword still held high in the air, Ruggiero saw that Aquilant and Grifon and their mounts were also rendered senseless and lying on the ground. He was baffled by the sight and soon realized that every other human and animal was similarly struck down. His face burned with shame when he saw the torn drape hanging from his shield.

Magic had defeated his opponents. The laudable words he used earlier to question their integrity as knights now rang hollow. He had won this fight without honor. There was only one thing he could do to restore his honor, he must rid himself of the shield. He was disheartened to not see Bradamante anywhere. Frantically he searched the grounds.

"She must have grown anxious and gone on ahead to rescue the young man," he muttered to himself.

Shaking his head, he picked up the old peasant and slung her unconscious form over the back of Deimos. Ruggiero rode off in search of a place to discard the accursed shield where no one would ever find it. After crossing a bridge, he saw an old abandoned well on a hillside. Using the silk covering to bind a large stone to the shield, he hurled the bundle over the edge. A splash echoed up the walls of the black abyss announcing it had struck bottom. He remounted Deimos as the old woman regained her senses.

"Wh-what happened?" she said.

"We are free of that accursed castle and shall soon arrive at Cordes."

"And your lady? Where is she?"

"I think she rode on ahead."

"Yes," said the peasant. "Pray that she waits for us before attempting the rescue. There are many guards."

Ruggiero shared her worries about Bradamante's safety. He knew the Maid was a powerful warrior, but it only took one misstep to die in battle. Urging Deimos to go faster, they rode up a steep hill where another rider accosted them.

"My lord!" said the man who was looking at his shield adorned with a silver eagle. "Are you Ruggiero?"

"Yes."

"I finally found you. I was sent by Amir Akramont. He bade me remind you of the solemn oath you swore to him. His forces are outside Paris. They are in desperate need of your return."

"Thank you," said Ruggiero.

"I must be off, I have others to notify," said the messenger as he continued on his way.

Ruggiero was grateful Bradamante had not heard those orders. He had no choice, but to delay their marriage. Honor and duty superseded his own needs, including his love and devotion for a fair maiden. His oath to her would be postponed until the war was over. He wondered how he was going to tell her this without breaking her heart.

As he grabbed the reins he saw a small bouquet of wild flowers braided into his horse's mane. The bluebell colored flowers had wilted in the hot sun. Ruggiero felt guilt at the token of love his lady had left for him while he had packed.

"My lord," said the peasant. "The sun has begun setting. We must hurry."

He kicked his heels in the horse's flanks again. As they reached the castle the peasant waved to the guards who allowed her to cross through the gates. A large crowd of people had gathered around the fountain in the center of the fortified city. It had been converted that morning into a funeral pyre awaiting the flame to be lit. The spectators pushed and shoved vying to get a better look at the condemned prisoner tied securely to a tall pole and standing upon a large pile of pitch soaked wood. Dozens of soldiers armed with spears were stationed around the perimeter to assure no one came too close.

Ruggiero helped the peasant down from his horse and desperately looked around the crowded square for Bradamante. His heart stopped when he saw her face on the soldier set to die by fire.

CHAPTER 91

Belle woke with a terrible headache. She touched her scalp and screamed when she saw blood on her fingers. As she sat up on the stone walkway of the castle ramparts, others woke. They too, suffered from similar injuries. She scanned the grounds and saw her three remaining champions and their horses lying unconscious. Panic seized her as she desperately searched for her husband Pinabel. He was not on the ground, nor were the two knights and the peasant woman who had trespassed earlier.

Vultures swooped in a large circle overhead before descending in an area over a ridge. Belle raced through the castle yelling for servants to grab weapons and follow her. She came outside just as Grifon, Aquilant, and Guidone Selvaggio were beginning to rouse.

"Get up!" she yelled as she mounted a palfrey. "My lord is in danger. You must ride to his defense."

Belle led the expedition of more than twenty men to the area marked by scavenger birds. Branches tore at her clothes and face as she forced her mount through the thick brush. Her heart pounded as she heard the cries of the carrion birds fighting one another. As her horse edged down the embankment she was surprised to see a man carrying a black shield shooing vultures away from the corpse of her husband.

"My love," she cried.

The man raised his face and stared at her. "Angelica?"

His eyebrows were creased as if he were trying to recognize her face.

Belle screamed as she saw his hands covered in blood. "Murderer!"

"No," said the man. "He was dead when I came upon him."

"Liar! Seize him," she commanded.

Aquilant and Grifon dismounted and stepped forward, but did not touch him.

"Orlando?" asked Aquilant.

The man nodded and the brothers shared a look with each other.

"He killed my husband. You must kill him. I order you to seize him!" screamed Belle.

"He is a paladin of Charlemagne," said Grifon. "Furthermore, he is betrothed to our Aunt Alda. He is to be our kinsman. We cannot kill him."

"He is a murderer and must die for this crime. Guidone kill him."

Aquilant and Grifon blocked his path.

Guidone shook his head. "I cannot either."

Belle could not understand their refusal. Did they not realize this man had murdered Pinabel? "Someone must kill him," said Belle as she faced her servants. "No one will be allowed back into the castle unless he dies."

Reluctantly her servants stepped forward bearing swords. They were met by Orlando's blade and soon lay dead in the ravine next to their late master. Belle tore her hair as she witnessed men dying one after another while her three knights stood by and did nothing.

She turned her horse back to the castle followed by Aquilant, Grifon, and Guidone Selvaggio. They overtook her a few hundred yards outside the castle and with great effort removed her from the saddle.

"This is for coercing us to serve your husband by threatening the life of my brother," said Aquilant as he bound her hands together.

Grifon tied her feet together and gagged her. "And this is for all those nights when you forced us to pleasure you or risk seeing another in our party accused of rape and put to death. You disgust me."

The three knights carried her into the castle and placed her in a small antechamber. The door closed, leaving her alone. She tried screaming, but the sounds were muffled by the gag. Try as she might, she could not loosen the bonds that held her. Fearing what else they had planned for her, she forced herself to calm and listen to the three knights talking outside her door.

"We must find Sansonetto and leave this accursed place," said Grifon. "We are no longer bound by our oath to Pinabel and we never swore to serve his mad harlot widow."

"We should leave now," said Aquilant. "There is still hope that we may reclaim our honor by returning to Charlemagne's service."

"While you get Sansonetto, I will go to the kitchens for food," said Guidone. "I shall tell the cooks that she was restrained due to her fits of hysteria. I expect they will allow her to remain in seclusion until morning. After all, they hate her as much as we do."

CHAPTER 92

Orlando wept. For a fleeting moment he thought he had found Angelica, but instead he had found a crazed woman. He had not killed the man who lay dead at the bottom of the hill, but he had killed the man's servants. He felt no guilt, because he had defended himself when attacked.

He thought back to the day in the forest when he fought with Renaud, and how he had acquiesced to Charlemagne's orders. The emperor made a pronouncement of awarding Angelica as a spoil of war depending on the following day's performance in battle. Orlando regretted not objecting to that plan at its inception. Angelica had agreed to be his bride; she merely needed to be baptized. He should have argued with his sovereign to listen to what *she* wanted. If Charlemagne had extended that courtesy, Orlando and Angelica could have been married that night by Archbishop Turpin. She would have been kept near the emperor's women during the battle. She would have been safer there than in Duke Namo's keeping. Because he had been unwilling to challenge his liege, he had failed his lady.

Orlando hoped she had found a safe place to stay that was warm and dry. He hated thinking of Angelica living in a cave and scrounging for food, as he had done as a child when his parents lived in exile. He could not bear to think of a dainty and beautiful woman living in such misery as his mother had. Orlando wiped the sweat from his brow and staggered up the steep slope with his horse, Brigliodoro, behind him. As he emerged onto the ridge top, Orlando saw a man and woman on horseback.

"Baron!" bellowed the man in armor. "I have been searching for you. Your standard and the blood on your hands betray your guilt. You massacred two battalions of Muslim soldiers and shall pay for their deaths."

"Before we fight, pray tell me your name."

"I am Mandricardo, son of Agrikhan of Tartary."

"You seek vengeance, yet you bear no sword or weapon?"

"I will not wear a sword on my belt until I can wrest the famed Durindana from Orlando. My father was renowned for his skill and could not have died in battle, unless treachery was involved. Orlando is the fiend responsible. His valor is exaggerated. Without Durindana, he would be just another knight."

"You dare question my honor! I am Orlando and this is the sword you seek." He brandished Durindana. "Your accusation is a lie. I have killed many brave men in battle, but *never* with dishonor. I have never struck a man with his back turned nor while he slept, nor have I attacked an unarmed man. Your father fought well, but I was the victor because I was the strongest. You desire to test your prowess against mine and yet you come unprepared." Orlando gestured to the bottom of the hill. "Down there you will find unused lances. You accuse me of false acclaim due to this blade? To prove my worth I shall renounce it until our duel is over."

Orlando hung his sword on a high branch of a nearby tree while Mandricardo dismounted, and descended down the steep incline where he gathered weapons.

~~~

As the two warriors mounted their steeds and readied themselves for jousting, Doralice said a silent prayer. She had dreaded this day ever since learning of Mandricardo's quest. For years she heard the name Orlando uttered in reverent tones, for he was held in high respect and honor by her people. The fierce countenance on his face reminded her that she could become a widow in the blink of an eye. Doralice fervently hoped her husband measured up to the famed paladin's skill.

The horses thundered across the ridge top. Their lances splintered into a thousand rough wooden shards as they crashed against each other's shields. Neither warrior claimed an advantage as both shields were still intact and the riders remained in their saddles. Her husband turned his horse around and charged again. This time he aimed his broken lance with jagged points at Orlando's head. The paladin ducked and his shield protected him.

The broken shafts were thrown to the ground. Mandricardo brought his horse directly alongside Orlando's and attacked him with his bare hands. He took Orlando in a warrior's embrace and pinned his arms to his body. Mandricardo appeared to be trying to squeeze the life out of his opponent as Heracles had killed the giant Antaeus.

Doralice held her breath as the two men struggled with one another. Orlando's face was reddening, but he was not trying to break Mandricardo's grasp of him. Instead his hands were fumbling around his waist. Doralice was puzzled by his actions, until she saw the paladin holding a dagger. She wanted to call out and warn her husband, but was afraid of distracting him during a fight. Silently she prayed that Orlando would not find any opening in Mandricardo's armor to thrust his blade.

Orlando shifted in his saddle as he tried attacking Mandricardo. As he did so, his boot connected solidly in the side of Mandricardo's horse. The animal shied sideways then reared breaking her husband's grip on the paladin. Mandricardo clung desperately to his horse as it bolted from the site. She heard her husband bellowing commands to his mount, but the beast ignored him. Fearing for his safety, Doralice set off on her horse in pursuit of her husband.

~~~

Orlando gave a rueful smile as his opponent's horse galloped away uncontrolled. Their duel was far from over, but this was a welcomed momentary reprieve. As he stood waiting for his opponent's return, something on a nearby tree caught his eye.

He walked over to inspect the bark carefully and saw the name Angelica inscribed in Arabic. His heart stopped as his fingers traced the letters to assure himself it was not a trick of light. As a young man in Charlemagne's court he was taught not only to read and write in Latin, but to read Greek and Arabic as well. He was confused at the next line that read, "loves Medoro." *Angelica loves Medoro.* The words made no sense to him. Was Medoro a food? A plant? Or some pet name she devised to use instead of his real name Orlando?

For weeks he had searched for some sign of her, only to find a cryptic message, but no lady. He ambled around frantically and came upon a bower of ivy and plants forming an arch and providing shade from the hot summer sun. Underneath was a trampled grassy area. As he walked inside he saw more inscriptions written with charcoal on large rocks. Again he saw *Angelica loves Medoro* as well as *Medoro loves Angelica.* Orlando froze as he saw the message:

Here the sweet Angelica and I
the humble Medoro
rest naked in each other's arms
delighting in Nature's beauty
this blessed place provides
May future lovers discover
the pleasures of this bower

Orlando shook his head in disbelief. There must be another woman named Angelica. That crude message could not be about the princess of Cathay, for she was engaged to him. The unchaste woman described in the poem could not be his lady. Angelica could not love another man. She swore that she loved him and wanted to be his bride. Perhaps he made a bad translation. Something was wrong, terribly wrong.

He staggered from the site, desperate to explain away what he saw. A small house stood nearby.

"My lord, what brings you here?" asked a peasant as he opened the door.

"I – I am looking for a woman. Named Angelica. Seen her?"

"Yes," said the man. "The prettiest girl I ever saw. She stayed with me and my family for over a month."

"H–How did she come here?"

"I took my lambs to market in Toulouse when I was trapped by the war. I stayed there until the battle moved on. The morning they were burying their dead, I started back home. The young lady ran to my wagon and begged for my help."

"So you took her home with you?"

"Along with a wounded soldier."

Orlando swallowed hard. "A soldier?"

"He was a handsome lad, but close to death. She found him on the battlefield and her heart went out to him. She bandaged him up as best she could, but he needed tending. Two weeks she stayed at his bedside while he had the fever. When he finally woke, he saw Angelica smiling down on him. Of course he fell in love with her."

"And was he a king or a governor or a…"

"No my lord," said the shepherd. "Foot soldier. And she claimed to be a princess of a kingdom far away. Imagine, a princess and a commoner."

"Wh–where did she go?"

"They went back east to be with her father."

Orlando's hands shook. The story could not be true. He was having another nightmare. It would end as soon as he woke. The shepherd went inside his house and returned with a small wooden box.

"She gave me this as a gift when she left."

The man opened the box and handed Orlando a golden bracelet with rubies and sapphires. His throat grew tight as he recognized the bracelet that she had always worn. He lifted it to his lips and kissed the stones before it slipped from his fingers, dropping to the ground.

"My lord, is something the matter?" asked the shepherd.

Tears streamed down Orlando's face as he could no longer deny the truth. He ran from the man's house as if leaving that dwelling would change reality. Unwelcome images flooded Orlando's mind. No longer would he be plagued with scenes of Angelica being ravished; instead he saw vivid pictures of her in a joyful embrace in another man's arms. She groaned in ecstasy as her naked limbs entwined with a man thrusting himself into her while fondling her bare breasts. Orlando ran faster, but his imagination would not stop. He screamed in agony, throwing his shield and helmet into the air. Tearing the armor and padding off his body, he rid himself of all his clothes, but his mental anguish still consumed him. He ripped fistfuls of hair from his head. In a fit of fury, he tore a tree up by its roots and hurled it into the air. Orlando ran without concern of where he was going. He howled in pain, stumbling on the ground desperate to purge the demons occupying his tortured mind.

CHAPTER 93

Ruggiero gave a loud battle cry as he withdrew Balisarda and charged at the soldiers guarding the prisoner. Spectators scattered as they heard his shout, falling over each other, desperately seeking cover. He struck a soldier and sent the man's head sailing through the crowd. Guards sprang in response, attacking Ruggiero in every direction. He slashed and killed everyone his blade touched. A few villagers were trampled to death in the ensuing mêlée. One after another the soldiers all fell victim to Ruggiero. He was standing in a newly vacant courtyard. Blood was splattered everywhere and limbs were strewn about.

The townspeople sought refuge in the nearest dwellings, hiding behind closed doors, likely praying that the Angel of Death would pass over them. The peasant who had sought his aid untied the cords binding the prisoner's hands. She handed a sword and shield to the released soldier. They were the only three people left in the village square.

The peasant woman embraced Ruggiero. "You saved his life. Bless you, milord."

She left his side and ran indoors. The former prisoner knelt in front of Ruggiero.

"Thank you, sir," he began. "I shall forever be in your debt."

Ruggiero was dumbstruck for while the face before him looked like Bradamante's, the voice belonged to a man.

"Pray tell me your name so I may know my savior."

"I am Ruggiero. May I ask yours in return?"

"I am Richardet, a son of Duke Aymon of Dordogne."

CHAPTER 94

Bradamante ambled through the woods and clambered up the side of a large hill after having lost her bearings in the ravine with Pinabel. As sweat dripped down her face, she became more confused. The surrounding landscape swam before her eyes. Nothing was familiar.

She found a road, but it did not lead back to Altaripa. A stream of cool water beckoned her forward. Bradamante and her two horses gratefully drank their fill. Afterward, she washed the dried blood off of Eos. Tears flowed as she watched swirls of red discoloring the fresh water. She had never killed except in battle, but now she had committed murder.

Bradamante allowed Nikephoros and Eos to graze on the banks of the stream while she prayed for God's forgiveness. She had been overcome with rage and took the law into her own hands. Justice was reserved for Charlemagne and his vassals to mete out. Pinabel would have eventually been punished, but it was not her place to usurp enforcement of the law.

"I shall confess this crime to my uncle when I see him again and throw myself at his mercy," she said aloud. "Dear Lord, please find it in your heart to forgive my transgression."

Once she finished her prayer, she tethered her horses together and set off on her journey into the woods. Bradamante still wanted to go to the abbey with the hopes of meeting Ruggiero there, but was uncertain which way to proceed. She had not traveled far when she came upon a man bearing two mounts, one an unusual creature with wings. He turned at the sound of hoof beats and stopped while waiting for her approach.

"Cousin?" he asked.

"Aistulf?"

The two warriors dismounted and embraced each other.

"Let me look at you," said Aistulf. "You must have grown six inches since I saw you last."

He removed her helmet, and his jaw dropped.

"I suffered a blow to the head. My hair was cut to help it heal," she said.

"Tell me the name of the bastard who dared harm you. He shall taste the wrath of my sword," said Aistulf.

"Thank you, but he tasted mine that very night."

They rode together for miles telling each other what had happened since they last saw each other. Bradamante was particularly interested in what happened in Asia with her brother Renaud. Aistulf eventually related his tale of being held prisoner by Alcina. Bradamante was relieved that he did not dwell upon the details of the evil witch, but was surprised when he confessed that he had been her honored guest for many months before being imprisoned.

"I was liberated by an acquaintance of yours," he said. "A man of incredible valor by the name of Ruggiero. Do you recall meeting him?"

"Yes, he is an honorable man."

"It is a shame that he is a Saracen. Otherwise he would be a worthy candidate for your hand in marriage."

She gave a bittersweet smile at that, but did not meet his eyes.

"In fact, this winged creature belongs to him," said Aistulf as he gestured toward his other mount. "I am surprised you have not asked me about it."

"Indeed, I was waiting for an opportune time to ask you about that strange beast, but I desired more of hearing your tales."

"Kamal is a hippogriff, an offspring of an impossible love of two sworn enemies: griffins and horses. Griffins are fierce protectors of gold and avengers of evil. The legendary one-eyed Arimaspi ride on horseback while raiding gold guarded by griffins. That is the source of the long standing enmity between griffins and horses."

Bradamante gave her cousin a wan smile trying to feign interest in the origins of this magical beast. She could not help but think the hippogriff symbolized the impossible love that she and Ruggiero felt for one another.

"Ruggiero flew back to Francia on Kamal," continued Aistulf, "while I rode overland on Rabican. Earlier today I rode through this wood and happened upon a castle beset by magic. After breaking its curse, this flying creature was freed. I know Ruggiero must be around here somewhere, so I followed and tracked the hippogriff down for him. I have spent half the day searching for my friend so that I may return Kamal to him."

Bradamante felt her throat constrict and was at a loss for words. She had studiously avoided looking at the hippogriff for the sight of him was a painful reminder of Ruggiero being taken to Alcina's realm. She took a swig of water from her flask to help regain her voice.

"I saw Ruggiero earlier today," she said evenly.

"How does he fare? Do you know where he is now?"

"He is well. I do not know his current location, but he has another mount, a fine stallion. He does not need that flying beast anymore."

"Cousin," said Aistulf, "if Ruggiero is no longer in need of Kamal, then I shall claim him for myself. I was advised to not hurry back and be a mere soldier in war, but to take off to the skies. With this animal, I shall certainly have some great adventures."

"Are you certain you wish to fly on that winged beast? Do you know how to control it?"

"Do not worry, fair cousin. He has been fashioned with a bit and a bridle and I have experience flying him. However, I cannot take to the skies without finding someone to care for Rabican. Therefore I must impose upon you to take care of this marvelous horse."

Aistulf told her about Rabican's magical origins and powers. He dismounted and unpacked the steed's saddlebags of his possessions and transferred them to the hippogriff's bags.

"Do you not wish to take your famous golden saddle?" she asked.

"I cannot, for it does not fit the hippogriff properly. One day I shall ask for it as well as Rabican back, but for now, I shall leave them in your capable hands. Plus I cannot take the golden lance that has been fitted to the side of Rabican's saddle. I shall have no need for lances in the sky."

"A golden lance? Dear cousin that must weigh a ton."

He laughed. "It is only dipped in gold my dear, but the lance is strong and has brought me great luck. I have used it many times, never once losing a joust with it, nor needing repair. You may use this lucky lance until I reclaim it. May Fortune smile down on us and allow our paths to cross again soon."

They dismounted and the two embraced each other tearfully. He kissed her fondly on the forehead before tethering the three horses together. Bradamante mounted Rabican as Aistulf mounted Kamal. He waved goodbye and in a few steps became airborne. As the hippogriff flew higher and higher into the air, she could not help but recall Ruggiero's flight when he was taken against his will into the skies. Once again she was pained by the separation from her beloved and wondered what had become of him.

Bradamante approached a fork in the road where she would go northward to reach the abbey. She turned on the new road when another familiar figure appeared.

"Bradamante!" said Alard. "What brings you this way?"

"Brother, I —"

"Three horses? Such prosperity. Come let me take one of those leads while I escort you back to Montauban. Mother will be pleased to have you home again."

Bradamante smiled outwardly, but inside she was in agony. She was now unable to meet Ruggiero at the abbey, because she would be held captive at her family's home instead.

CHAPTER 95

Mandricardo's horse galloped at breakneck speed. The reins had fallen during his wrestling with Orlando and now dragged on the ground as the horse ran away. He tried and failed to grasp the reins. Verbal commands and yanking on the mane did not slow the animal. The horse did not respond to his attempts of control, but instead ran faster and traveled overland on uneven ground.

The stallion tripped as it attempted to jump over a ditch and Mandricardo flew through the air. His outspread arms broke his fall, but his face planted on the ground. He spat grass and dirt out of his mouth as he stood. His body screamed out in pain, but he needed to finish off Orlando.

"Husband," cried Doralice as she brought her horse to a halt. "Are you hurt?"

Mandricardo went over to his fallen horse and grabbed the reins. "Get up, you worthless beast. Get up!"

The horse whimpered, but did not move. He realized from the head's odd angle to the body that his horse's neck was broken.

"Damn this nag to hell!" Mandricardo kicked the dying animal.

He snatched his belongings from the saddlebags and stuffed what would fit into the bags on Doralice's palfrey. Scowling he walked back to the dueling site without saying another word. With each stride his anger increased. He had fantasized killing Orlando for months, and somehow had been outwitted by that treacherous infidel.

As Mandricardo approached the area where they had fought, he was surprised Orlando was not there waiting for him. There were signs of destruction in the area – an uprooted tree, and armor strewn about. He smiled to see a black stallion grazing nearby and Durindana still hanging off a tree branch, its blade reflecting light from the setting sun.

"It appears the famous Orlando abandoned the field." He grabbed the prized sword and strapped it to his belt.

Mandricardo mounted Orlando's horse, turned to his wife and smiled. "Let us find somewhere to spend the night, for my quest is over."

After traveling overland they came upon a road leading them to a castle. As they entered the unguarded gates, they were surprised to find the entrance deserted. They tied their horses and entered the building. Once inside, they found a handful of servants feasting in the dining hall. The last fortnight Doralice had tutored Mandricardo in regional dialects making him more confident in conversing with Franks.

"Hello," said Mandricardo. "Where is your lord?"

"He died earlier this day," said an old man wiping his mouth.

"But – uh – there is still a lady of the castle," confessed a woman.

"Where is she? I wish to speak with her," said Mandricardo.

The servants exchanged glances. "She is in mourning and refuses visitors," said the old man.

"I must pay her my respects," Mandricardo insisted.

"Very well, I shall bring you to her."

Mandricardo motioned for Doralice to be seated. "Remain here. This will not take long."

She gave him a faltering smile and sat down as instructed. He kissed the top of her head before following the old man. As they stood outside a door, the servant told Mandricardo about a tribute which his late master had required of travelers. He also relayed castle gossip about the lady of the house having cuckolded her husband with the four knights who left earlier that day.

"You are free to spend the night, but there are more members of the family due to arrive here on the morrow. Take what you will, but be sure to leave before the morning is over. All losses will be blamed on the four knights."

Mandricardo nodded and opened the door to reveal a woman lying on the floor, bound and gagged. He set the oil lamp on the floor as the feeble light cast a warm glow in the room. The woman wore an expensive gown and jewelry and had a curvaceous figure and pleasing face. Her cheeks bore scratches, her clothes torn, but her beauty was still evident. He knelt down and lifted her up, leaning her against his chest as he whispered soothing sounds into her ear while untying her gag.

"My husband was murdered," she rasped. "His murderer got away. You must help me."

"Who bound you?" he said, reaching down to untie her feet. He massaged her ankles and calves relieving the deep marks left in her skin.

"Three knights. Aquilant, Grifon, and Guidone Selvaggio. You must find and kill them. They refused to avenge the murder of an honorable man."

"Is that so?" Mandricardo said, with a cold smile as he untied her hands. "Maybe they refused because your husband was a dishonorable man, just as you are a dishonorable woman."

"How dare you," she said as she raised a hand to slap him.

He grabbed her by the wrists. His anger no longer allowed him to attempt conversing in a foreign tongue. He reverted to his own language not caring that she would not understand anything he said.

"You are merely the wife of a petty nobleman, whereas I am a powerful monarch. Your husband's rule superseded those of your own emperor. Such arrogance would eventually be punished, but I am about to do something I have never done before. I am going to perform an unsolicited favor for another king. In my country such acts of treachery would earn you a trip to the gallows. However, there is no time for that."

Her eyes grew wide as he took the sash that had gagged her mouth and wrapped it securely around her throat. As he squeezed and began crushing her windpipe, her hands clawed frantically at him. He held the fabric taut until all life left her body. Draping the silken fabric around her bruised neck, he carefully positioned her body to appear as if she were sleeping peacefully.

"That is your reward for placing yourself above a king."

Mandricardo walked out of the room and told the old man, "Pity, she died of a broken heart."

CHAPTER 96

Ruggiero stared at Richardet. His likeness to Bradamante was uncanny. Ruggiero would have remained frozen in place had Richardet not acted. The young man raced to the stables and brought forth a beautiful stallion.

"Come, I know a castle nearby where we can stay the night," he said.

The first mile or so Richardet kept looking over his shoulder, when it became apparent that no one was coming in pursuit, he wept.

"Sir Ruggiero, I am overwhelmed by your valorous acts on my behalf. Why though? I am but a stranger to you."

"A woman came and pleaded your case. She said a man would die for being in love. To me, love can never be considered a crime. Love is the greatest power on the face of the earth, especially when the love is returned." Richardet closed his eyes as more tears streamed down his face. "She returned my love, but ours was a forbidden love. In her father's eyes, it was a crime for I knew her as a man does his wife."

"Tell me about your lady," said Ruggiero.

"Fiordespina," he said, choking on her name, "is the daughter of Amir Marsilio of Hispania. I had seen her in Saragossa and was in awe of her beauty. I marveled at her long black hair, large brown eyes, the curve of her face, and the way she moved with the grace of a dancer. It hurt to look upon her. She was a lady beyond my wildest aspirations. She is not only royalty, but a Saracen as well. Amir Marsilio would never consider me as a suitor for his daughter, even if I were a Saracen. He could marry her off to a governor. In my heart I was willing to settle for a lesser woman to love, until…"

"Until what?"

"I overheard my parents discussing my brother Alard's future. My mother wants him to enter a monastery. I knew then it would only be a matter of time before she insisted I follow that path as well."

316

"A monastery?" asked Ruggiero.

"Yes, it would prevent my father's lands from being divided between too many of his sons upon his death. I learned then that my parents would never permit me to marry; instead I would be condemned to live a life without love."

Richardet became sullen. They rode for several miles before Ruggiero dared break the silence. "Forgive me. I recognize your face, but your name is unfamiliar."

"Perhaps you have confused me with my twin sister, Bradamante. She is an accomplished warrior and we share a strong resemblance to one another. All our lives people have had difficulty telling us apart. This was a source of great amusement in our childhood for we played tricks on our family. We switched clothes and passed ourselves off as one another. She wore a boy's cap and I, a maid's hat and gown. Later after we changed back to our regular clothes, no one noticed the difference."

"Indeed," said Ruggiero, "that must be the source of my confusion. I have made her acquaintance. Please, tell me how you and your lady became lovers."

"It was due to my close resemblance with my fair sister," said Richardet.

He regaled a story of Bradamante suffering a head wound, followed by her hair being shorn, and Fiordespina mistaking her for a handsome young man.

"I could not help wonder if Fiordespina might have fallen for me had she spied me resting. A flicker of hope seized my heart as my sister unwittingly gave me the tools to craft a plan. She gave me a surcoat and this fine horse which were gifts from Fiordespina. I shaved to remove any stubble from my face, and to make the illusion complete, I cropped my hair to mimic my sister's cut. I left home the next morning, riding all day to Fiordespina's castle."

"How did she react when she saw you?"

"Overjoyed," Richardet said, with a wistful smile. "I appeared in the same guise my sister wore when she left. Fiordespina thought her friend had returned. I was welcomed with open arms. A gown was brought forth for me to wear and I was soon walking arm in arm with the woman I loved. I altered my voice to disguise my true sex, but I said very little. I was afraid I might reveal ignorance of things my sister would know. My reluctance to speak proved helpful in my deception. Fiordespina poured her heart out to me. She yearned to be in love and was terrified of being in a loveless marriage. Her desire was to find a man who understood her as well as I did."

"When did she discover you were a man?"

"That night in bed. Bradamante had stayed with Fiordespina in her chambers, so I expected to be brought there as well. I was careful to not reveal my true form too early. I discreetly changed into bed clothes and waited under the covers for her to join me. I lay there wrestling with my conscience. I considered telling my lady the truth that I was not Bradamante, but her brother instead. That I had loved her from afar, but I feared her reaction. So after Fiordespina climbed into bed, I spun a tale of magic. I told her while on my journey home I came upon a lake where I saw a beautiful damsel being attacked by a foul creature. I drew my sword, fell into the water, and slew the monster. After her rescue, I discovered the lady was a water fairy. She granted me a single wish. I said that my wish was to become a man to fulfill Fiordespina's greatest desire."

Ruggiero laughed, and cast him a knowing look. "And she believed you?"

"I do not know, but my story was never mentioned again. After completing my tale, I placed her hand under the covers, proving I was no maid. No other words were spoken the rest of the night, yet we had not a moment's rest. The next morning she insisted I continue dressing as a woman, for she would never be allowed to bring a man to her bedroom. By day we appeared to be two girls strolling about, and by night we were lovers."

"Did you think that arrangement would last forever?"

"In her arms I was in Heaven. We could not wait for nightfall to experience such bliss, but we worried how long it would last. We talked of various plots for leaving and starting a new life together, but the perimeter of the villa was surrounded by guards. We never devised a good plan. Each night we were in ecstasy, and promised ourselves that the next day we would discover a way to escape."

"What caused your condemnation?"

"One night her servant, Neron, burst into her room. We were caught in the act. I was put into chains until today when I was to be killed."

"And your lady, what has become of her?"

"I do not know," said Richardet, wiping the tears from his face. "I believe she was sent to her father."

The two men started a slow climb up the side of a steep hill. The sun had already set, but some light was left in the sky.

"My Uncle Beuve has a castle not much farther from here. His son, Aldigier, is the caretaker, something my sister is not too happy about," said Richardet.

"Why is that?"

"Because he is a bastard."

Ruggiero was startled at that pronouncement.

"My sister," Richardet continued, "I love her dearly, but she lives by a strict moral code. She has no sympathy for those who fail to live up to her standards. Our uncle had a child with a commoner before he married. It had been a family secret until Beuve's wife died in childbirth; afterwards he brought forth Aldigier, claiming him as his son. My sister has never truly accepted Aldigier as part of our family, as if he were somehow responsible for his father's indiscretions."

Ruggiero once again felt grateful that he had resisted the temptation of Malha. "I am curious as to how your sister became a warrior."

"That all stems from Bradamante and I being inseparable as children. We could not fall asleep without being next to each other. I think we were five when they finally got us to sleep in separate beds. It was another year before we could sleep in separate rooms. We could not bear to be apart. Our mother became infuriated, but the more she railed the harder we clung to one another."

They continued climbing the hill and as they turned around a bend, a stone tower appeared in the distance.

"One day when we were only three, our family went to Aachen to celebrate Orlando's knighthood ceremony. All of our extended family was on hand and Renaud, having just been made a squire, thought it high time I started sword play. He fashioned a big wooden sword and shield for me, but when they tried taking Bradamante away to play with our girl cousins, we both cried. Neither of us would allow the other to be out of our sight. Mother kept telling her that girls did not fight; only boys used swords and shields. Nothing calmed Bradamante, and both of us were distraught. Finally, my father suggested they make another sword and shield for my sister. He predicted she would become scared the first time her shield was hit and run crying to Mother."

"What happened?"

"She did not become scared, she became mad," laughed Richardet. "Renaud loves telling the story of how this little girl had fierce determination in her eyes. As if she wanted to prove she was worthy of being a Lyon. Charlemagne laughed at our mother and said it was clear Bradamante was destined to be a warrior for it was in her blood. He ordered my father to have her trained in the martial arts. Mother refers to this as 'The Day I Lost My Only Daughter to War.'"

Ruggiero and Richardet shared a laugh.

"Mother has blamed our father ever since for turning my sister against her own feminine nature. As if Bradamante could ever be an ordinary woman."

Ruggiero gave a wistful smile. "I wish I had a brother or a sister. My father was murdered before I was born, and my mother died giving birth to me. The only person I knew growing up was my guardian. As a small child I desperately wanted someone my own age to play with, so I created an imaginary friend."

"Did that help?"

"A little. You may find this strange, but my imaginary friend was a sister. She seemed real to me at the time. All these years later I still half-believe she was flesh and blood. Atallah said I stopped that game once he started training me in the hunt. Pray tell me when your sister joined the battlefield."

"That happened when Renaud was knighted," said Richardet. "A day before the ceremony there was a large family gathering. We had not seen our brother in several years, and Bradamante was determined to impress Renaud. She snuck away from our mother, stripped out of her beautiful raiment, and donned her armor. She challenged Renaud, which he found amusing at first. He quickly changed his mind when she scored against him. Our father had been walking in the gardens with King Charles when they came upon the duel. Soon a large crowd gathered watching Renaud and Bradamante engaged in fierce swordplay. They were better than many exhibitions in tournaments. Charlemagne was so impressed that he named Renaud as one of his paladins and insisted Bradamante join his forces that very day."

"How old was she?" asked Ruggiero.

"Thirteen. Within a year, she was commanding troops. She has an instinct for strategy in battle. Charlemagne has never knighted her because she is a woman, but he gives her far more responsibility than knights twice or three times her age. Our mother hates it. The day Bradamante dueled with Renaud, our mother had been trying to secure a husband for her. Mother's plans were ruined when King Charles commanded Bradamante to be his soldier. All her marital prospects were scared off by Bradamante's military skills. None could match her."

They approached the castle as the sky was turning purple. Richardet waved to the guard in the tower.

"Hello! Tell Algidier that his youngest kinsman is at the gate."

After a short while, another man appeared in the tower and called down, "Richardet, what brings you here?"

"I was hoping for a warm meal and a place to spend the night."

"Done," said the man.

The portcullis was soon opened and the man awaited them in the courtyard. The cousins embraced each other warmly, and Richardet performed introductions. Aldigier had black hair with streaks of silver. He brought Richardet and Ruggiero to a room to wash up before supper. Ruggiero lingered behind them, performing belated prayers once he was alone.

It was the first time that Ruggiero had been in a castle not created by magic. He was surprised to find the stone floor cold and damp, even though it was summer. The wind picked up and howled, causing a draft to blow on his face through the chinks in the wall. After finishing his prayers, he stood and left to find his host.

A servant showed him to a seat next to Richardet at a large dining table. Ruggiero marveled at an elaborate tapestry hanging on the wall depicting knights in armor.

As his goblet was almost filled with wine, Ruggiero covered it with his hand. "Water, please."

The servant nodded and left for the kitchens, returning with a new pitcher. Ruggiero dipped his bread into warm lamb stew and savored the taste of garlic and rosemary.

"Tell me about the story on the walls," he said to Richardet, who had already devoured his meal.

"The man with the regal bearing is Charlemagne, of course," Richardet said, pointing at the distinguished looking man on horseback in the center of the tapestry. All the figures were facing him. "This is our grandfather, Bernard of Lyon." Richardet gestured to an elderly soldier holding a sword in the sky. "He was a famous knight and had been a counselor to King Pepin and later to King Charles. The four knights kneeling behind him are his sons."

Richardet stood and walked over to the wall and pointed at the figures. "Odo is the eldest. He married the maiden queen of Essex when she was but a child. They were without any children for many years, but she finally produced an heir to the throne when she bore Aistulf."

Ruggiero smiled at the image of Odo, for the face in the tapestry bore a strong resemblance to that of his friend.

"Next to him is my father Beuve," interjected Aldigier, "the second son."

"The third son is Milon," said Richardet. "He eloped with Bertha, a sister of King Charles, causing a royal scandal. Our family suffered the wrath of Charlemagne until our grandfather publicly disavowed his own son."

"I remember when Orlando and his mother were discovered in Italy," said Aldigier. "He was a bedraggled urchin who survived by his wits and petty thefts. Charlemagne and his entourage were on a visit to the pope when they stopped in the village of Sutri for a banquet. Orlando stole food from the king's own plate! Guards chased him back to the cave where he lived. Orlando and his mother were brought back in chains to the royal party. The mood changed when Charlemagne recognized his sister and was overjoyed because he thought she had died years before."

"Where was Orlando's father?"

Aldigier shook his head. "Milon had died in battle years before when the Saracens attacked Italy; he went to the aid of the Frankish army. The Saracens had aided the Lombards in their insurrection against Charlemagne. Almonte killed Milon the same day he killed Bernard of Lyon."

Ruggiero looked away in shame. He served Akramont and Akramont's uncle had killed the grandfather and uncle of his host. Yet, he reminded himself, his own father and grandfather would have fought in that same battle on behalf of Charlemagne.

"Orlando and his mother were welcomed to the royal court in Aachen," Aldigier resumed his story. "From that day onward, he was trained as a knight. To remember his humble beginnings he fashioned his standard in red and white quartering to reflect the colors of the ragged clothing he wore the day he met King Charles. My father tells the most marvelous stories about Orlando's training, where the young man was desperate to prove that he came from a noble line of warriors. During another invasion of Saracens in Italy, and at the age of fifteen, Orlando avenged the death of his father and grandfather by slaying Almonte and seizing Durindana."

"He was a knight at that age?"

"No, just a squire. But when the knights around him died, Orlando grabbed a sword and fought," replied Aldigier. "His heroic actions are credited with the Franks' victory that day. He became even more beloved by Charlemagne. His formal knighting ceremony was not held, however, until he turned eighteen."

Richardet and Ruggiero exchanged a knowing look.

"And that was the day my mother lost her only daughter to war,'" laughed Richardet. "Here is my father Aymon." He indicated the fourth son on the wall hanging. "His many acts of bravery helped restore the house of Lyon back into royal favor."

Ruggiero marveled at the entire tapestry and the stories revealed by his companions. He turned and was surprised when his host appeared forlorn.

"Pardon, but does something vex you?" Ruggiero asked.

"Yes," said Aldigier as he sighed and sat back down. "I am overcome with worry over the fate of my half-brothers, Vivien and Maugis. They are hostages of the evil Lanfusa. For weeks now I have been trying to gather enough ransom to secure their release."

"Lanfusa? Feraguto's mother?" asked Richardet.

"Yes. Just yesterday I learned from a trusted source that their ransom has been gathered by another party," said Aldigier, as he took a long drink of wine. "Bertolai."

A look of terror passed over Richardet's face.

"Who is Bertolai?" asked Ruggiero.

"A traitor. Born of the house of Maganza," answered Richardet. "We Lyons have had a blood feud for generations with the Maganzas. If they are willing to pay ransom for my kinsmen, it can only mean they plan to enslave or kill them."

Ruggiero remembered Bradamante speaking harshly about the Maganzas before their arrival at Altaripa. These had to be her family's enemies that Atallah had repeatedly warned him about. If Bertolai was anything like the treacherous Pinabel, he could not allow Bradamante's kinsmen to suffer if he had the power to stop it.

"When is the exchange?" asked Ruggiero.

"On the morrow at midday in Saint Antonin, but I lack enough men to mount a rescue attempt," Aldigier said. "I sent a message to Renaud, but there is no real hope the messenger will find him in time."

"I shall go and liberate your brothers," vowed Ruggiero. "I do not require an army, only my sword."

Aldigier shook his head. "That is a kind offer, but it will take more than a single knight to secure their release."

"Cousin," interrupted Richardet. "This is not an idle boast made by a braggart. If it were not for him, my bones would be cinders and ash."

"What do you mean?" asked Aldigier.

"Today at sundown, I was to be publicly executed, until this brave, valorous man came to my rescue. Alone, he fought off at least twenty armed Saracen guards. In the morning we shall all go, but allow Ruggiero to lead us. Tomorrow night we shall all drink to the liberation of Vivien and Maugis."

Aldigier wiped a tear from his face. "We leave at dawn."

Ruggiero was shown to a small private chamber. It was sparsely furnished with only a bed, a small table, a stool, and an oil lamp. After being left alone, he said his night prayers and asked for Divine guidance. He was torn between following his heart and his moral obligation to his sovereign. Earlier that day, a messenger delivered orders for him to return to Akramont's side, and yet here he was planning another rescue expedition. He had no choice. The only honorable act was to return to battle. And yet, he had also sworn to be baptized. He wondered if Bradamante was at the abbey waiting for him. If he never showed, would she ever forgive him?

He knew that somehow he needed to get a letter to her. Servants responded to his call, bringing him parchment, ink, and a quill. Tears filled his eyes as he sat at the table staring at the blank writing surface. Whatever he wrote would break her heart.

From the knight Ruggiero to the lady Bradamante

CHAPTER 97

"What brings you home this time sister?" Alard asked as their horses journeyed onward to Montauban.

Bradamante found herself at a loss for words. There was not a ready excuse for why she left her post in Marseille. She could not tell him that she had been sent on a rescue mission for a Muslim soldier.

"I - I…"

"I must ask," he interrupted, "have you heard anything of Richardet's whereabouts?"

"What do you mean?"

"He has not been seen since the morning you left Montauban," he said. "Mother was upset when both of you left home without saying goodbye. But Father and Hippalca knew of your intention to return to duty. There was no such honorable excuse for Richardet. He merely said he was going for a long ride without saying where he was going or when he would return."

Bradamante's heart sank. "No reports of him at all?"

"None. Mother began fretting and pacing the halls that afternoon. She imagined him being ambushed with his corpse lying on the side of the road. Or that he was grievously wounded and trapped under the body of his horse. I have searched the countryside every day since then, with nothing to show for it."

"I had no idea," said Bradamante.

"Today I scoured the roads in the forest again," he said. "The letter you sent asking him to join you in Marseille drove Mother to tears."

Bradamante nodded, but did not respond. She wondered if the events earlier that day with Fiordespina might be linked with her brother's disappearance. She said a silent prayer hoping Ruggiero had found his way to the square and rescued the condemned man in time.

The sky was dark and the half moon had risen when they arrived home in Montauban. Once again the castle sprang to life when word of Bradamante's return was announced. Her parents embraced her, quickly ushering her inside for a late supper.

Bradamante was happy to be surrounded by her family again, but all she could think about was Ruggiero. She wanted to know where he was, if he was safe, and how she could get a message to him.

As Hippalca set down Bradamante's trencher, the two young women's eyes met. "Come to my chamber in the morning," whispered Bradamante. "I must speak with you."

Hippalca nodded and resumed her serving duties. Bradamante knew their talk have to wait until morning. It would be ungrateful to her family if she left the meal early again.

That night, Bradamante slept fitfully. Memories of her prolonged kiss with Ruggiero and the desire he stirred kept her awake. Finally she devised a plan for the morrow and fell asleep remembering his loving embrace.

The sun rose in a clear blue sky. Bradamante crept out of bed early so she could find and speak with Hippalca alone. As the two maids walked in the small courtyard, Bradamante told her handmaid of events transpiring since they had last spoken. Hippalca eagerly listened as she was told of Bradamante's reunion with Ruggiero and pledging their undying love to one other.

"Why did he not escort you last night?" asked Hippalca.

"We were separated again. It was my fault this time. We had left on our journey to the abbey when we were approached and asked to save the life of a condemned man. On our way to the rescue, we came across Pinabel."

Hippalca's fists clenched. "What a horrible man. Did you seek revenge?"

"That was when I became separated from Ruggiero," said Bradamante as she brushed dirt off her dress. "Tell me, did Frontino arrive here safely?"

"Yes milady."

"And is the surcoat finished?"

"I tied the last knot yesterday."

"Good," said Bradamante. "After breaking your fast, you will leave for the abbey. Ruggiero and I were to go there yesterday for his baptism, but our plans were disrupted. Dress Frontino in his surcoat and deliver him to my beloved, as a token of my love and devotion. Afterwards, bring Ruggiero back here straight away, so he may begin talks with my father. Should anyone accost you on the journey tell them that this horse belongs to the pride of Reggio, the famed warrior Ruggiero."

CHAPTER 98

Doralice woke covered in a cold sweat. While falling asleep the night before, she hoped Orlando's defeat meant the end of her recurring nightmares. Yet her dreams were more violent than ever. In this dream, Mandricardo's challenger was Rodomont. Theirs was a brutal duel, and as her husband lay dying, Rodomont ravished her. His revenge was complete when he bludgeoned her to death with his enormous sword.

Light had entered the darkened chamber announcing that dawn had broken. Mandricardo lay next to her, snoring loudly, oblivious to her fears. Afraid of falling back asleep and returning to such a vivid nightmare, she eased herself out of bed careful to not wake her husband. After splashing her face with water, she dressed for the day. Doralice considered kneeling and performing a morning prayer, but could not. Since becoming Mandricardo's wife, she followed his example and no longer prayed. This disconnection to her previous spiritual life led her to doubt whether or not Allah cared about her.

Doralice sat down at a woman's dressing table. There was an ornate ivory casket with an engraved image of a lady holding a rope and gently leading the Wild Man of the Woods. She smiled as her fingers gingerly traced the carving. It had been a favorite tale of hers from childhood. The tale was that a pure and virtuous lady was capable of taming a wild beast, in this case, a feral man. She shook her head at her naïveté at ever believing such noble expectations of womanhood. A Virgin taming the Wild Man. Mandricardo had not been tamed by her pure nature and heart. He had controlled her from the very beginning.

She wiped a tear away thinking how her husband had been a gentle and generous lover. Had been. Until the previous night. The door to the lord and lady's chamber had not even closed when Mandricardo forced himself upon her with no warning. He lifted her skirts and thrust himself inside her. She was nothing more than a vessel where he unloaded his lust.

What happened to his pledge to satisfy her needs? Or making a kiss last all night? He had not even bothered to kiss her. More tears fell down her cheeks. What did this new behavior of his portend for her as his wife?

Doralice removed the lid of the ivory casket and found beautiful gold necklaces adorned with pearls, rubies, and sapphires. She lifted them out and held them against her neck, admiring them in the mirror. She lost all interest in jewelry when she saw a jeweled dagger lying on the bottom of the box. Picking up the small weapon, she drew it out of its elaborate leather tooled scabbard. The blade came to a sharp point, and as she idly touched its surface, she imagined how things would have been different had she owned such an object when Mandricardo attacked her camp. She could have died a virtuous death.

Mandricardo began stirring. Doralice stiffened. He would want to start the day like he did every morning. With sex. She had never dared refused him, but having sex was the last thing she wanted to do.

Fearing that her husband might think she was plotting his demise, she slipped the dagger into its sheath and sat on it.

"Ah, there is my queen," he said. "Come back to bed so we may properly start our day as husband and wife."

He patted the bed next to him while giving her a rakish smile.

"I cannot," she said. "I am sore from last night."

"Pardon?"

"Husband," she began slowly, afraid his anger would flare. "You should plow the soil first before planting your seed. I was not prepared. You caused me great pain."

She bowed her head, afraid to see his reaction to her defiance. There was silence for a few moments then the rustling of Mandricardo getting out of bed and putting on some clothing. He knelt in front of her, wearing only breeches. His hair was tousled and he wore a concerned look on his face. Her heart pounded as Mandricardo gently wiped away her tears.

"Forgive me, my love," he said as he kissed her hands. "I was flush with the excitement of victory. I promise I shall never behave so beastly toward you again."

She wanted to believe him. She wanted to forgive him.

Then she thought about his choice of words. He only promised he would never behave so beastly toward *her* again. Not that he vowed to never behave so beastly again. Did that mean in the future he would use someone else when he felt the overwhelming need to rut? She almost laughed at the realization, but knew she could not laugh at Mandricardo – that would be dangerous.

"Our life in Tartary awaits us," he said. "We can leave for there today, or should you wish to view some of the beautiful countryside, we may do that as well."

His voice was tender, that of a lover who wanted forgiveness. If she did not respond well to his gentle entreaties, she might see his cold demanding side.

"Let us leave today," she said looking into his eyes and forcing a smile on her face.

He kissed her softly on the mouth. As he stood, he saw the jumble of jewelry on the table. He chose a necklace with sapphires and fastened it around her neck.

"The lady of this castle will not need this anymore," he said, his fingers lingering at the nape of her neck.

He then left her side so he could finish dressing. She breathed a sigh of relief. She had avoided sex with him without provoking his temper. Perhaps he was remorseful. Perhaps he actually loved her. Perhaps. She hoped those things were true since her life was bound to him.

They left the chamber in search of food before setting off on their journey. Mandricardo quietly slipped the casket of jewels into his saddlebags without notice of the castle's servants.

Doralice was determined to put the events of the previous night behind her and enjoy herself. The bright morning sunshine helped lift her spirits.

As they approached a fork in the road, Doralice froze at the sight of a rider in the distance. He wore dark green armor and held a flag aloft.

Rodomont.

"I changed my mind," she announced. "There is a village nearby I would like to visit." Her horse galloped onto the road in the forest and left Mandricardo behind.

CHAPTER 99

Ruggiero, Richardet, and Aldigier left Agrismont at daybreak. The rendezvous point for the exchange of the hostages was to be outside the village of Saint Antonin. There were over twelve miles to cover by midday. Ruggiero did not want to waste any time, lest they arrive too late. The party headed west and followed the gorges of the Aveyron River. The rolling green hills were covered with trees and rugged cliffs of striated rock. The colors of the rocky crags changed every mile or so from bright white with dark gray streaks to a dullish gray with patches of orange.

The seriousness of their mission cast a pall over the trio and they spoke few words. Richardet tried striking up a conversation a few times, but nothing worked to lighten the somber mood of the day. Ruggiero sensed that Aldigier blamed himself for being unable to arrange the release of his brothers. This proud man would probably rather die attempting to liberate them than live to see his kinsmen enslaved or killed.

After reaching the halfway mark to their destination, Ruggiero suggested resting their horses. While the mounts drank from the river, Ruggiero performed one of his daily prayers and asked Allah's blessing in this endeavor. After finishing, he raised his head, and saw his companions staring at him.

"You are Saracen?" asked Richardet.

"I am a Muslim," said Ruggiero.

"But, you speak our language so well," blurted Richardet.

"I am fluent in many languages."

"Wh–why should you want to help us?" stammered Richardet, his face reddening. "You will be fighting other Saracens."

"Hostages help finance wars, but bargaining with the enemies of your prisoners is dishonorable," said Ruggiero. "I have learned of dishonorable conduct. Should I do nothing, I would be made an accomplice."

Richardet gaped at him. "You are the most honorable knight I have ever met."

Aldigier's eyes filled with tears as he knelt in front of Ruggiero. "My family shall be forever in your debt for your selfless actions on our behalf."

Ruggiero found their stares discomfiting. He could feel his cheeks becoming warm. "Let us carry on."

They remounted their horses and Richardet assailed Ruggiero with questions. He asked about Ruggiero's family, where he had spent his youth, how and when he became a knight. Ruggiero wanted to appear respectful, even though the barrage of questions made him uneasy. This was after all, the brother of his beloved. The better impression he made on her kin, the more likely her father would grant permission on marriage.

As Ruggiero told the story of his descent from Hector of Troy, a knight entered the road in the distance. The soldier stopped in an aggressive pose. As they drew near the soldier's standard was finally discernable – a golden phoenix on a field of green.

"Three soldiers dressed for battle," announced the knight in halting Frankish. "But are you skilled in the art of war?"

"All of us are," said Richardet.

"Prove it. Duel with me or show your skill is only in the art of dress."

Ruggiero motioned to Richardet to remain still.

"Baron," said Ruggiero. "Ordinarily a challenge made would be a challenge accepted otherwise our honor would be tarnished with the stain of cowardice. However, your challenge shall have to be delayed, lest our current mission be made in vain. My companions have kinsmen who have been held prisoner for over a month, but their captors bargained in bad faith. Today those hostages are to be ransomed to a family with long standing enmity against their house. Should we not arrive at the place of exchange in time, they will be met with enslavement or death."

"I hate slavery," spat the soldier. "I was sold into slavery as a child. I remove my challenge and offer my sword instead. Honor shall be on our side!"

The foursome rode in silence with a quickened pace. A palpable nervous energy coursed between them. Ruggiero chose a small copse of trees for them to hide behind where they could watch the three roads converging in the valley just north of the village. After a short while, a column of over two dozen foot soldiers marched southward on the road following a small river. They carried two men bound and gagged on the backs of donkeys. Aldigier fumed at the sight.

"There they are," said Richardet, "let us rescue them."

"Not yet," said Ruggiero. "Our hosts have arrived bringing the guests of honor, but there will be more guests at this party. Some will be bearing gifts. If we strike too soon, not everyone will learn their lesson regarding treachery."

Soon another line of armed foot soldiers marched around the bend coming from the west. In the center of their line was a wagon loaded down with ransom. Ruggiero could make out brass urns, golden candlesticks, bolts of fabric, furs and leather goods. He was certain there were more luxury items in the closed burlap sacks.

Richardet and Aldigier uttered curses at the sight of the Maganzans.

Ruggiero turned to their new companion, "You speak Arabic, do you not?"

"That is my mother tongue," replied the green knight in Arabic.

"You and I will attack the Christians while shouting in Arabic," Ruggiero announced, "and they shall attack the line of Muslim soldiers shouting in Frankish."

"But I want to stain the ground with the blood of the Maganzas," argued Richardet.

"Yes," said Ruggiero, "but by splitting up and attacking the lines at the same time and using foreign tongues at them, we will confuse them. Both sides will likely think they were betrayed. They might even aid us by killing the other party. We have only to worry about not killing each other or your kinsmen. These rats may flee from their sinking ships, for I will not cage any of them."

Aldigier nodded his assent and the foursome split up as Ruggiero directed. Their sudden appearance upon the scene shocked the marching armies. The Maganzas fled as two fierce warriors slaughtered their soldiers. Indeed, Ruggiero felt as if the green knight was his mirror image. They hacked their way down the line of Maganza soldiers as if competing with one another. Out of the corner of Ruggiero's eye, he watched in admiration at his fellow warrior's skill.

It is a good thing we did not fight this man earlier. He is a formidable swordsman.

A few Christian soldiers fled in the direction of the village, while others scrambled up the rocky hillside. After the Maganza party was either slaughtered or dispersed, Ruggiero left to assist Bradamante's kinsmen. The Muslim soldiers held spears at the throats of Richardet and Aldigier. Ruggiero regretted not staying with Richardet stay with him and sending the green knight with Aldigier. Alas, Bradamante's twin was in danger again.

"Die, infidels!" yelled Ruggiero as he charged his horse at them.

His sword severed the man's arm that had held a spear at Richardet's neck. Blood spurted like a pulsing fountain as the man screamed. The others surrounding him scattered at the sight. The enemies were gone and Ruggiero was alone with his companions and their kinsmen.

Richardet massaged his neck in a likely attempt at reassuring himself there were no wounds. Aldigier's hands fumbled while undoing his brothers' fetters.

"I will go get two more horses for our party," said Richardet after tying his own stallion to a tree. "Perhaps you can help Aldigier untie them."

Ruggiero removed the dagger from his belt and cut through the rope binding a skinny man with greasy black hair. The man grabbed Ruggiero's hand.

"Thank you for saving us and my kinsmen," he said.

Ruggiero felt a tingling sensation as the man touched him. His years of living with Atallah led him to recognize that this man was not only magical, but was trying to read his mind.

"You are welcome," said Ruggiero. He wrenched his hand free and began cutting the bindings of the other prisoner, a well-built man with a mane of light brown hair.

"I beg your forgiveness my brothers," said Aldigier. "I did my best to arrange a ransom for you, but I could not satisfy Lanfusa. She bargained in bad faith."

"We are rid of her," said the man Ruggiero was freeing, "and we are with you. That is all that matters now."

"This is my friend, Ruggiero," said Richardet as he returned holding the reins to two new horses. "He saved my life yesterday and your lives today. The house of Lyon owes him a great debt."

Ruggiero nodded modestly. The fourth soldier in the rescue party led the wagon loaded with treasure toward them.

"There is gold, jewelry, and food," announced the green knight. "Let us find a place to enjoy a feast."

"I am Vivien," said the larger of the two men, "and this is my brother, Maugis."

The skinny man bowed. "Pray tell us your name for we are indebted to you as well."

The soldier removed his helmet to the surprise of all. Ruggiero saw the shock he felt reflected on the other men's faces. They had all expected their fierce companion to be a man, but as raven colored hair fell over her shoulders and the softness of her facial features were revealed, it was unmistakable that she was a woman.

"I am Queen Marfisa."

CHAPTER 100

Rodomont was furious. For over a fortnight he had pursued Mandricardo. He slept only when he could no longer keep his eyes open, and ate only when he found food that could be easily snatched on his journey. He was tired, hungry and filled with anger. That morning he had seen Doralice in the distance, of that he was certain. She had looked straight at him. She saw his wave. Yet she galloped away on her horse.

As if she was afraid of him.

Only then did his eyes stray to her companion. The antique armor and red hair confirmed the bastard's identity as Mandricardo.

Rodomont stared at the image of Doralice on his silk banner. She had sent for him to rescue her, and now she ran from him. Why? This maid had occupied his mind and heart for over a year while he held repeated negotiations with her father. Those talks had been tedious, but Doralice had many suitors. The wily Stordilano played them off one another. In the end, Rodomont earned the right to her hand in marriage. He had opened his heart to Doralice and professed his love to her. His standard proclaimed his ardor for her to the entire world. For Doralice to turn her back on him now was not only a betrayal, but an insult to his manhood.

How could he face Akramont and others, when it became known that the woman he venerated was a disloyal whore? First he needed to ascertain the truth from her own lips before deciding if she deserved any mercy.

His horse was tired and weary. It was the latest in a string of horses he had ridden during his pursuit. One after another they died from exhaustion. Rodomont had continued on foot until he found another horse to steal. Sometimes he had to fight or kill the owners, but he was never long without a mount. He seethed as he rode around the southern boundary of the forest. Doralice and Mandricardo were far ahead of him for they rode on fresh horses; his could barely stand, let alone gallop.

The chirping of a bird irritated Rodomont and he beat his charger. The horse's knees buckled and collapsed. He whipped the beast with his stick, with no response. No amount of striking could make the animal rise from the dead. Rodomont grabbed his standard and started walking. He would not stop until he claimed what was rightfully his.

As he came upon various forks in the road he scrutinized the area for two sets of horseshoe tracks, one larger than the other. He had been following those tracks for days, but he finally knew for certain they belonged to those he sought. Rodomont trudged along under the midday sun, his face dripping with sweat and approached a bridge spanning a river.

He perked up when he heard the sound of hoof beats. A sneer crossed his face when he thought he might have finally caught up with Doralice. Instead, at the crossroads was a young woman riding a palfrey while leading a warhorse dressed in a richly embroidered surcoat. Such a steed deserved to be ridden by a nobleman, not led by a mere woman. Striding over to the horse, he grabbed it by the reins.

"Unhand him," cried the woman. "This horse belongs to the pride of Reggio, the famed warrior Ruggiero."

Rodomont laughed. For the first time in weeks something amused him.

"Ruggiero? The young whelp lacking facial hair? Am I to tremble at the sound of his name?" He mounted the horse, feeling suddenly calm. "If anyone should tremble it is he. Tell him Governor Rodomont of Sarza has his horse."

Across the wide plain covered with peach and apple orchards were two figures riding in the distance. They were the same figures he had seen earlier that day but now they rode tired horses, while his was relatively fresh. He galloped off with a burning desire to retrieve his lady and restore his dignity.

"Stop! Come back here!" yelled the woman, as she urged her horse to gallop in pursuit.

Her palfrey was no match for his stolen destrier. Soon Rodomont had left her far behind. With each cadence of the hoof beats, confidence grew inside him. He would soon vanquish his greatest foe and reclaim his bride-to-be.

~~~

Doralice looked over her shoulder repeatedly that day, and had not seen Rodomont since the morning. She hoped the circuitous route she took around the vast forest would lead him astray. Once confident she had shaken him from their trail, she settled her horse into a comfortable walk. Soon she was swept up in Mandricardo's tales of his childhood in Tartary. She laughed and turned once again to check the road behind them. Her laughter stopped as she saw the rider in the distance bearing down on them.

"What is it?" asked Mandricardo.

"Rodomont is after us. He will try to kill you, let us ride far away," she pleaded.

"Kings do not run."

"He has filled my nightmares ever since we have been together."

"Those dreams will end with his death. I have bested Gradasso, and I have bested Orlando. Surely I can beat this miserable wretch of a man," he said drawing out Durindana.

Mandricardo waited in a defensive pose while Rodomont continued his charge. Orlando's old horse pawed the ground in anticipation. As Rodomont passed a line of trees, her husband began his attack. The two warriors' swords clashed in midair.

"Doralice is mine!" roared Rodomont. "You shall die for touching her."

"She is my wife and queen," shouted Mandricardo. "She belongs to me."

He brought Durindana down directly upon Rodomont's helmet. Doralice gave a sigh of relief as she watched Rodomont slump forward onto his horse's neck. Mandricardo lifted his sword again when Rodomont's horse jumped sideways. Her husband swung wildly in the air but missed his target completely.

A woman on a small horse galloped up to them from where Rodomont had come. She stared at Mandricardo with a puzzled look on her face.

"Ruggiero?" she asked.

Mandricardo did not respond to her because Rodomont was recovering.

"Her father promised Doralice to me," said Rodomont. "You have no claim to her."

"She gave herself willingly to me," said Mandricardo.

"LIAR!" Rodomont lifted his heavy sword above his head with both hands and crashed it down upon Mandricardo's helmet.

"Stop this fight. I beg of you," the woman pleaded. "That horse belongs to my master. You must give it back."

Rodomont bared his yellowed teeth, "The horse is mine now. After I finish humbling this bastard, I shall humble you as well."

She quailed from the look on his face. Tears filled her eyes. She hurriedly urged her horse off on a path through the hills.

Doralice sat on the back of her palfrey chewing a thumbnail. The duel was directly from her nightmares. How much longer would this fight last? Who would be the victor?

Their swords clanged on the shields again and again; her horse jumped each time at the sound.

A man on horseback galloped up to them, and came to a stop near Doralice. "My lady. Are these Muslim warriors?"

"They are."

"I bear news from Amir Akramont."

"How do things fare in the war?" she asked.

"Not well. He bades all those who are sworn to serve him to return to Paris immediately. Otherwise all shall be for naught and another generation of Muslims will suffer shame and defeat at the hands of infidels here in Francia."

"My father is Governor Stordilano of Granada. Do you have any word of him?"

"He still lived when I left the city, but things were dire then. I cannot say what has happened since my departure."

"Thank you. I will stop their fight and deliver your message," she said.

He nodded and rode away.

Doralice sobbed. For all the plans she had made with Mandricardo, she had never considered her father might be in danger. She assumed Akramont's forces would be victorious because Mandricardo never expressed any doubts. Then again, he never cared about the war her father was fighting. Or her father. Mandricardo only cared about himself. He was fighting with Rodomont because she had become Mandricardo's possession. She turned to watch the two men fighting over her, and made her decision. There was only one honorable thing to do. Dismounting, she retrieved an item from her saddlebags.

"You will stop this fight now," she yelled.

The men held their swords in midair, surprised at her outburst.

"A messenger from Amir Akramont has commanded both of you to return to Paris immediately," she said, with a strong voice that surprised even her.

"Only one of us will survive this day," said Mandricardo.

"No! You will both return," said Doralice. "Akramont's campaign is in trouble, and my father is there. The amir needs as many strong warriors as possible. He needs both of you."

"I cannot allow this bastard to continue living," said Rodomont.

"You will both return," she warned, "or you shall be fighting over my dead body."

She brought out the jeweled dagger she had been holding behind her back and withdrew it from its sheath. She pointed it over her heart.

"You will cease this fight, you will return to save my father, or I will kill myself."

Rodomont and Mandricardo looked at her and then at each other. With nods, the two men put away their swords. For the first time in her life, Doralice had won.

CHAPTER 101

"Queen Marfisa," said Vivien with awe. "Warrior queen of the Amazons?"

"No," she said while lifting the reins of the wagon team. "I have no army of women, but I have conquered seven kingdoms. The first king I slew without an army."

The wagon worked its way down the narrow streets of Saint Antonin and stopped in front of a fountain in the center of the village square. It was a round marble fountain with water pouring out of a whale's mouth while it swallowed the Biblical figure of Jonah. Behind was a large building built of gray and orange stones with a tiled roof and closed iron gates. This rest of the village was comprised of wooden buildings with shingled roofs. The closed doors and shutters gave it an abandoned look.

Ruggiero realized that the town was devoid of people except for those in his party. He suspected the townsfolk must have heard about the massacre by some of the men who had escaped with their lives. The wagonload of riches would have announced to the villagers that the culprits of the bloodbath were now in their midst. He reasoned that they chose to stay indoors to prevent becoming victims themselves.

Marfisa and Ruggiero worked together to spread a red linen cloth on the ground while the others set out golden platters laden with smoked fish, dried meat, cheeses, and breads for their picnic.

"How did you go from being a slave to a queen?" asked Richardet as he handed her a plate.

All eyes were upon her, eager to hear her story.

"The first king I killed was my master. He tried forcing himself on me, but I was ready. I used the knife strapped to my leg," said Marfisa, as she cut the end off a length of sausage. "I did not want to be put to death, so I donned his armor, opened the doors, and shouted, 'the king is dead, long live Queen Marfisa!'"

"What happened then?" asked Aldigier, as he piled herring on his plate.

"His guards were good warriors and fought well, but I had nothing to lose," she said with a smile. "I killed ten men before the rest surrendered."

Vivien rummaged through the wagon and extracted a purple silk gown with small beads and golden threads decorating the bodice. He presented the elegant garment to Marfisa.

"This is clearly meant for royalty. I can think of no woman more deserving to wear such finery. Please, I beg of you to grant me the honor of wearing this. I wish to see the woman who was my savior in her full glory," he said, bowing and kissing her hand.

Marfisa blushed, held the dress in her hands, and nodded her assent. Richardet sprang forward offering to be her squire and helped remove her armor and gambeson. He carefully held the gown above Marfisa's head before it fell gracefully onto her full figure.

Vivien placed a string of pearls around her neck and handed her a silver filigree hand mirror. Marfisa seemed puzzled as she gazed at her own image. Her hands kept touching the silk sleeves in wonderment as her face became fixed in a permanent smile.

"I have never worn anything like this," she said. "I have worn armor since the day I named myself queen."

She smiled and appeared to be fighting back tears as she sat down next to Ruggiero.

"Allow me to get your drink," said Richardet. He walked over to the fountain and held a golden goblet in front of one of its spouts.

"Do not drink from that fountain!" Ruggiero cried.

"Why not?" asked Richardet. "The water seems pure."

"I do not trust waters from fountains," he said. "I came across one that was bewitched."

"But our horses do not seem to have suffered any ill consequences," Richardet argued. He gestured to the horses drinking their fill from the bottom of the fountain surrounding the sculpture.

"It may be difficult to tell if they have been put under a spell," said Maugis. "Ruggiero is right. It is dangerous to drink of fountains. Years ago, Merlin constructed several fountains throughout the lands with enchanted waters. There is no telling what powers they may hold, so it is prudent to avoid fountains whenever possible. There is a well across this courtyard. I shall go and fetch water for our companions' dinners."

Ruggiero and Marfisa took the offered goblets of freshly drawn water, while Bradamante's kinsmen drank wine found in the wagonload of ransom. The party reveled in each other's company. Laughter soon rang out as the cousins regaled stories of their recent adventures. Ruggiero was surprised when he noticed Marfisa stealing glances at him while they ate.

His attention shifted to a young woman who rode into the courtyard. She wore a plain brown dress and was on the back of a small palfrey. The woman's eyes became fixed on Ruggiero's shield leaning against the fountain. She looked at him, ignoring all the others. Tears were in her eyes.

Richardet's laugh ended abruptly when he looked up and saw the woman. His kinsmen followed his gaze at the woman who was dismounting her horse. All the men stood as she walked toward Richardet.

"Hippalca, what brings you here?" Richardet asked taking her hand in his.

"My lord, it is your sister," she said bowing her head. "Bradamante returned to Montauban last night. She bade me to bring a horse to this village on her behalf. It was a fine destrier named Frontino, an animal she dearly loved. Alas, on my journey here, I was accosted. It was taken from me by force."

"Allow me to assist this young lady," said Ruggiero.

"Thank you for your generous offer Ruggiero," said Richardet, "but this pertains to my sister and her handmaid. It is my responsibility."

"I insist. You have only now been reunited with your kinsmen. You should enjoy your time with them. I have no family left. It would be my honor and privilege to once again be of service to the house of Lyon."

"I will not fight you over this matter," said Richardet. "If you are so determined…"

Ruggiero and Hippalca remounted their horses and set out retracing her path. As soon as they were outside the village boundaries and alone together, he broke their silence.

"She is safe?" asked Ruggiero.

"Yes. Bradamante arrived home late last night. She knew her parents would be upset if she left this morning, so she sent me in her stead. I was to deliver Frontino as a sign of her love and devotion to you. After your baptism, you are to come back with me to Montauban. Her father is there now. You can begin your discussion with him tonight about marriage."

Ruggiero hung his head. He then told Hippalca about the messenger commanding his return to battle. Honor required that he follow Akramont's orders, but he also remained committed to Bradamante's love. He pressed his letter to Bradamante into Hippalca's hand.

"Swear to me that you will deliver this in private."

"I swear, milord."

Ruggiero wanted Bradamante to be reassured that his love for her was eternal and unwavering. He and Hippalca spoke of nothing else until reaching the site of where she had last seen Frontino.

"He is not here," Hippalca said sounding frustrated. "I was certain we would pass him on the road here. The knave must have taken the lowland path rather than the direct route."

"What did he look like?" he asked.

"I can do better than that. I can tell you his name."

"Who is he?"

"Rodomont."

CHAPTER 102

Mandricardo and Rodomont rode side by side on the lower road following the northward. Neither trusted turning their back on the other. Doralice rode behind them and all three were silent. Nothing could be said without shattering their fragile truce.

Mandricardo resented having to go back to Paris. He had never cared about Akramont's campaign and never formally swore allegiance to the cause. His mission to humiliate Orlando and wield Durindana had been completed. It was time to return to his own realm, but he would not relinquish Doralice without a fight. She was a beautiful woman of noble blood, which he required for his queen. She was also a willing and satisfying lover who should bear many strong legitimate sons. His own mother was of royal blood, but she treated her conjugal duties as a distasteful obligatory function and was therefore held in low regard by his late father. That was a royal marriage he did not want to emulate. He would bring Doralice back to Tartary and they would tour their country in grand style.

But first he must be rid of Rodomont.

He cast surreptitious glances at his rival. The Sarzan was covered with dark green scaly dragon armor from the top of his head to the top of his feet where he wore metal shoes. The suit was cinched closed in the back making his chest and abdomen seamless and without weakness. Rodomont was utterly dependent upon squires to assist in donning and doffing that armor. Therefore, he would have worn his armor without fail for the past fortnight; during the sweltering hot days and the muggy or rain filled nights. Rodomont exuded a foul stench matching his foul personality. Another glance allowed him to note the only vulnerable spots were the feet, the groin, the neck, and the face. Mandricardo smiled. A short blade would work. A fatal strike could be delivered through the underside of Rodomont's jaw and into the skull.

~~~

Rodomont was seething. During his pursuit he banished any thoughts of Doralice and Mandricardo as lovers. That bastard had boasted she was his queen and willingly took him to her bed. She did not deny such a blasphemous statement, so it must be true.

But it was a truth he could not bear.

He gritted his teeth in anger and for the first time the image of Mandricardo undressing Doralice entered his mind. He clenched the pommel of his sword and the image disappeared. As he looked at the haughty profile of the Tartar, a low growl escaped Rodomont's throat. There had never been a man he wanted to kill more than Mandricardo.

The three riders made their way onto the paved streets of a small village by mid-afternoon. Rodomont felt the full effects of his relentless pursuit. He ached from head to toe, he needed rest, a bath, and above all else, a good meal. As they entered the courtyard of the village, he spied four knights and a lady wearing a purple gown eating a leisurely dinner. There was still plenty of food left on platters before them. Rodomont dismounted his horse, grabbed a smoked leg of lamb, and began devouring it.

The lady stood and uttered an obscenity in Arabic at him.

"Pardon my companion, dear lady," Mandricardo said soothingly in Arabic to her. "He has not had a proper meal in weeks. While I admit his manners are clearly lacking, a lady such as yourself could not begrudge a starving man food when you have it in such abundance."

Her companions started to stand when she motioned for them to remain seated. "He may eat his fill, but he must stand downwind of us," she replied while holding her nose.

Rodomont moved without protest. He had resolved to keep his vow to Doralice and refrain from any fights until they returned to Paris. It was his way of showing his love and devotion to his lady, a woman he would punish later for her infidelity. He would wait until her father mediated the dispute on claims to her. Stordilano promised his daughter's hand in marriage to him, and unless the Governor of Granada wanted an invasion by the Sarzan army, he would not renege on the deal. However, should he discover upon arrival in Paris that Stordilano had died in battle, he would kill Mandricardo before spilling any more Frankish blood.

"My companion not only requires a meal, but a bride as well," stated Mandricardo. "You, my lady, shall belong to him. Unless one of your companions can prove they are my superior in battle."

"I will never consent to marrying that man!" she cried.

The four men rose and spoke in agitated tones in Frankish as they donned armor. Two of the men mounted horses while the other two brought forth lances from the back of a cart filled with riches. One of the men offered him a lance, but Rodomont shook his head and continued eating.

"I am Vivien, son of Beuve of Agrismont," announced one of the mounted warriors in Frankish. "And you are…"

"Khan Mandricardo of Tartary and son of Agrikhan."

The two men exchanged nods and couched their lances. A signal was given and their horses charged. The Tartar landed a perfect hit upon Vivien's shield, knocking him to the ground. Mandricardo faced his second opponent, a dark-haired skinny man who soon landed on the dirt as well.

"Hand me a lance," demanded a silver-haired man as he mounted a horse.

The fourth man, a blond youth, handed the weapon to him. Rodomont stared at the blond soldier who stood watching the duel. He felt as if he should know this young man, but had difficulty placing him.

The two horsemen charged at one another. The Frank's shield was cleaved in two. Mandricardo's lance pierced his opponent's arm causing a torrent of blood to flow. The two defeated men helped the wounded man off his horse.

The blond was Mandricardo's last challenger. He jumped upon a large horse and was handed a lance by the staggering Vivien. The young man couched his lance, appearing eager to prove his worth. His stallion snorted as the charge began. The youth bore down and readied for impact when one of his horse's hooves slipped in a large rut in the earthen road. The rider lost his balance and fell out of the saddle.

Mandricardo laughed as he looked at the four defeated men. "My lady," he announced with a wave of his hand, "none of your lords proved themselves worthy against me. Therefore, you must consent to my earlier decree. You are my possession and you shall become Rodomont's wife."

The woman's face turned purple with rage. "You are just like your late father. You treat women as barter, as if we were nothing more than trinkets. No man owns me, nor shall any man. These men championed my cause, but that was a rarity. Defending my honor has, until today, been my own province."

She stripped herself out of her dress, revealing a thin tunic and tights. Mandricardo leered while looking upon her muscular figure unadorned by billowy skirts. One of the Franks stepped forward and helped her don a quilted gambeson and armor. She was soon seated upon a horse, armed with a lance.

"I am Queen Marfisa. You shall pay for insulting my honor," she snarled as she cast a scathing look at Doralice. "And for insulting the honor of all women."

Mandricardo laughed again, "A girl thinks she can best the Khan of Tartary."

As Vivien gave the signal the two charged, their lances shattered upon impact, but both riders remained upright in their saddles. Marfisa railed when she saw her opponent was unharmed. She drew her sword and attacked him with a shocking ferocity. Mandricardo in return showered her with blows from his blade.

Rodomont no longer found humor in this display. The duel between Marfisa and Mandricardo was real. Mandricardo had sworn an oath that he would not fight until Paris.

Rodomont stepped forward and bellowed, "Stop! I command both of you to stop!"

Marfisa and Mandricardo held their swords in mid-air, each watching the other carefully.

"Mandricardo, if you want to fight someone, I will restate my challenge," Rodomont said. "Doralice is the only woman I desire as my bride. We made a truce. We swore to not lift up swords in anger until after coming to the aid of Amir Akramont. That is where our honor lies, not in fighting with a girl or these insignificant children."

"Akramont?" asked Marfisa. "He is the commander in the campaign against Charlemagne, is he not?"

"Yes," said Rodomont. "A messenger found us earlier imploring us to return to his side in Paris."

"That is the kind of adventure I sought by coming to Francia," Marfisa said. "I will not marry you or any man. Upon your insistence, I shall put aside my quarrel with this louse-ridden bastard until victory over the Franks is assured."

Mandricardo's lip curled as he glowered at her. She snarled back at him. He then gave her a curt nod. Mandricardo and Marfisa sheathed their weapons having formed their own fragile truce.

CHAPTER 103

Ruggiero had not spent much time thinking about Rodomont since that fateful night when he first met Bradamante. He remembered the outrage he felt when she told him about the Sarzan governor killing her horse in battle and leaving her for dead trapped under its carcass. Ruggiero had never been so ashamed of a fellow knight's actions. Her testimony also elicited an instinctive protectiveness toward Frontino.

Just thinking of Frontino caused a pang of sadness inside his heart. Ruggiero loved that destrier and sorely missed his company. They had developed a strong bond as horse and rider. Frontino anticipated Ruggiero's needs in battle, responding to the lightest touch as if reading his mind.

Bradamante must have claimed Frontino after he was taken away by the hippogriff. He could think of no finer caretaker for his treasured steed. And now, out of love she tried returning his horse as a sign of her troth. Nothing could have been deemed a more precious gift to him and there could be no one more objectionable to have stolen his destrier than Rodomont.

An old Arabic proverb held that a horse was attached to its master's honor. Rodomont had no honor. The mere thought of that foul man touching his horse filled Ruggiero with anger. He vowed to rectify this situation immediately, lest by his inaction, he would be perceived as being indifferent to the gift his bride had bestowed upon him. Ruggiero would never insult his beloved, and therefore could not allow Rodomont's heinous crime to go unchallenged and unpunished.

Ruggiero and Hippalca returned to Saint Antonin by taking the longer but easier path alongside the western banks of the Aveyron River. The two riders made their way to the courtyard where they had left Richardet's kinsmen with Queen Marfisa. A horse in a beautiful surcoat was drinking from the fountain, its reins held by Rodomont. It was difficult to recognize Frontino covered by the embroidered fabric, but Ruggiero knew that was his destrier.

"Only a coward would steal a horse from an unarmed maid," thundered Ruggiero in Arabic. "I am claiming what is rightfully mine."

Rodomont turned around and sneered. "The youngest and most celebrated of all Akramont's knights is gracing us yet again with his presence. What brought you out of hiding this time?"

"Unhand that horse."

"Were you aware that the fate of Akramont's army rests on your tiny shoulders?" said Rodomont. "The amir delayed his invasion on your behalf. A superstitious old fool prophesied that you would be the key to victory. Akramont sent legions of soldiers throughout the Maghreb searching for you, while I began the war in Francia. He made you his knight and you were by his side how long? A week? Then you abandoned him. He still holds out hope for your return. Tell me, child, does swearing loyalty mean anything to you?"

Rodomont cast a glance at a woman on a small horse before she turned her head away. Ruggiero's blood boiled at the insults by Rodomont, but he held his tongue.

"Akramont's army struggles to survive," said Rodomont. "Yet the hope of his entire campaign is here arguing over an animal. It is my turn to remind you that the way of the knight is to serve his sovereign. The amir's forces are in peril and we are commanded to return to his side. I swore an oath to Akramont on his quest to defeat Charlemagne. I swerved from that service only once to defend the honor of my lady, Doralice." He gestured toward the blushing woman. "We both require steeds, you have one and now I have one as well. If you wish to fight over this horse, let it be in Paris after we have returned to the service of our liege."

Rodomont defiantly mounted Frontino.

"Dismount that horse," said Ruggiero. "You wish to defer our fight? You must first relinquish Frontino, for I cannot allow you to despoil such a noble steed. You may have this horse instead."

"This one suits me," said Rodomont, casting a sideways look at Mandricardo. "I do not exchange mounts as if they were mere trinkets."

Mandricardo's face twisted as Ruggiero lifted his shield, "You still dare carry my standard? I warned you once to renounce that eagle or die."

Ruggiero drew Balisarda. "I bear the standard of my noble ancestors. This is my birthright, not yours. For me to renounce my standard would be to disown my heritage and bring dishonor upon myself. I refused to fight an unarmed opponent, but now I see you have claimed a sword. You must either yield Hector's standard or earn that right through me."

Marfisa rode her horse in front of Ruggiero's while Rodomont blocked Mandricardo.

"Twice you have broken your vow today," spat Rodomont. "First you fought over a girl, now you are willing to die over a bird. Akramont's mission is in jeopardy, and yet you spend your time quarreling over vanities. If you wish to fight an opponent today, then fight me. After I have finished with you, Marfisa and Ruggiero can argue amongst themselves and the carrion birds as to how best to divvy up your entrails."

Mandricardo turned his sword toward Rodomont when Marfisa came between them.

"You will cease!" she roared. "Akramont needs every warrior. We must subdue the Franks first. Then we can resume our fights." She looked Mandricardo coldly in the eye. "You shall regret insulting my honor."

"I will only defer my fight with Rodomont if he returns my horse," said Ruggiero. "He has no regard for animals. I cannot allow him to retain control of Frontino. He will either relinquish my horse or I shall die here defending my honor."

"Then it shall be the latter," said Rodomont, "but I will not accept blame for your death. Let it be remembered that you were the one to exalt petty pride over an oath of fealty."

Ruggiero drove his horse past Marfisa's and attacked Rodomont. A vendor's cart overturned and spilled plums all over the ground.

"Defer this fight, or you shall fight me as well," Mandricardo bellowed while attacking Ruggiero from behind.

Rodomont followed suit and struck more blows upon Ruggiero. He slumped forward and Balisarda fell to the ground. Slowly Ruggiero came to his senses and realized that Deimos had borne him away from his enemies.

Marfisa struck Mandricardo repeatedly with her blade. Vivien handed Ruggiero a new sword as Rodomont came forward and renewed his attack. This time, the Sarzan suffered numerous blows to his helmet by Ruggiero. Rodomont slumped forward onto Frontino's neck, and would have dropped his ancestor's heavy weapon had it not been securely tied to his wrist.

Ruggiero turned his attention to Marfisa. She fell as her horse slipped on the fruit strewn ground. He charged forward to defend the warrior queen by engaging Mandricardo in battle, allowing her time to recover.

"Now I remember you," croaked Rodomont in broken Frankish, "I thought you wanted to die with your emperor. This will be the last time you ever interfere with my duels."

Ruggiero turned in time to see Rodomont raise his sword high over Richardet's head. He was horrified at the sight, but was too far away to intervene. Then Maugis raised his hands and uttered a few words. It was a gesture that Ruggiero recognized from Atallah's casting of spells. Ruggiero's suspicion of Maugis being a wizard was confirmed when a gust of wind blew, knocking Rodomont backward in his saddle. Frontino reared as a black cloud suddenly appeared.

Maugis pointed a finger and drew a line in the sky that went from the ominous cloud to Doralice's palfrey. A gigantic horsefly, the size of a small bird, emerged from the cloud. It followed the arc that Maugis drew in the air with his finger and it dived at Doralice's horse burrowing under the saddle. Doralice screamed as her animal jumped high into the air and bolted from the site. Mandricardo and Rodomont sheathed their swords and galloped off in pursuit of her.

Marfisa scrambled to her feet and stood open mouthed. Her hands shook as she helped her horse stand. "Bastard. He left a fight. I will kill him."

Vivien stepped forward and carefully folded the silken gown she had worn earlier and packed it in her horse's saddlebags. "Are you injured my lady?"

"No. I am fine."

"You helped save my life and that of my brother. I shall never forget your heroism," Vivien said as he kissed her hand.

Marfisa smiled at him and remounted her horse. "And I am honored that you and your kinsmen defended my virtue."

Richardet went over to Ruggiero and spoke to him quietly. "I do not understand much Arabic, but I thought I heard Paris mentioned. Is that where you are headed?"

"Yes," said Ruggiero. "Those are my orders. I am to return to Akramont's service."

"Please, if you can, find out what has befallen Fiordespina. Save her if possible."

"I promise. Please give my regards to your sister. Tell her I will recover the horse stolen from her maid."

"Godspeed, Ruggiero," said Richardet.

Ruggiero saluted the others. He exchanged a look with Hippalca before riding off with Marfisa in pursuit of Rodomont and Mandricardo.

CHAPTER 104

Richardet shook his head as he surveyed the courtyard in Saint Antonin. Trampled fruit and splinters of wood were strewn about. The villagers who had stayed inside would emerge soon, and when they did they would be livid. He gestured to his kinsmen to pack the wagon and leave.

Hippalca had been tending Aldigier's wounds and bandaged him up as best she could. Aldigier sat next to her on the wagon as she drove the team of horses, while their horses were led by Richardet and Vivien. They quietly left the village without speaking, hoping not to raise the ire of the villagers. There would soon be a clamor about the deaths of numerous soldiers at the crossroads outside of the town. It was best for them to leave before any fingers of blame were pointed in their direction.

"Hippalca must have safe passage back to Montauban," said Richardet once they were outside of the village. "I will not allow her to be accosted again."

"Thank you my lord," she said.

"We cannot make it to Montauban before nightfall," said Vivien, "especially with a wagon slowing our pace. My father has a dear friend in Bruniquel. I am certain he will offer us hospitality for the night."

The road they chose avoided following the serpentine Averyon River. Instead, they traveled southwest over a road flanked by wheat fields and apple orchards. Upon crossing a bridge over the river, they turned southeast and headed toward Bruniquel, a town resting on a hilltop high above the valley floor. The stones used in the fortified village looked orange from the rays of the setting sun. The horses had difficulty pulling the wagon up the steep climb leading to the town.

The guardsmen at the ramparts waited until their lord gave approval to admit the travelers. The wagon slowly made its way through the village until they arrived at a villa at the summit overlooking the Aveyron valley. An elderly man with white hair was waiting for them at the gates.

"Vivien!" said the man. "Such a delightful surprise. Tonight we shall make merry, celebrate life and good company. But first —" he snapped his fingers toward a servant, "we must have the surgeon summoned to tend to your brother's wounds."

A servant nodded and left. Two other servants carried Aldigier indoors. The old man embraced Vivien.

"Geron," said Vivien, "you look well."

"You are kinder to me than the years have been. Come let us enjoy this warm evening. You will make the introductions, and then tell me what has happened to my old friend Beuve as well as what brings you my way."

The party sat down at a large wooden trestle table and benches on the terrace. Geron smiled at Hippalca and took her by the hand, sitting her next to him. Servants brought forth pitchers of wine, loaves of bread, cheeses, fresh fruit and pastries. Richardet regaled his part in the rescue and told of the various duels earlier that day. Maugis and Vivien then told their host about the circumstances of their being taken prisoner and held for ransom.

Richardet was feeling a warm glow from the wine and the company, but his jubilant mood was dampened when he noticed Hippalca ate with her head bowed.

"I must apologize, young lady," said Geron. "My kitchen did not have much on hand to provide a proper meal for such august company on short notice."

"It is I who should apologize," she said. "I do not deserve to be seated here, as I am not a lady."

"Pardon?"

"This is not my station. I am but a servant for Master Richardet's family."

"Your heritage is unimportant to me," said Geron as he patted her hand. "Tonight you are my guest. You shall be afforded the same courtesy I would show a daughter of Charlemagne."

Hippalca blushed.

"Ah, there is a smile," he said. "Come, I wish to show you the statue of the most famous lady who ever lived in this villa."

He struggled to stand upright. He put an arm around her as he led Hippalca past a large reflecting pond in the center of the courtyard. They stopped in front of a statue of a beautiful woman with long hair standing beneath a vine-covered trellis.

"Bruniquel was named after Queen Brunehaut. She was a Visigothic princess and married Sigebert, King of Austrasia and a grandson of the great Clovis. The land from Cahors to Albi was part of her dowry, but this hilltop village was her favorite home. Sadly the villa has gone into decline since her time." He pointed to areas where the stone had begun crumbling with age. "Brunehaut was a powerful woman who ruled as regent three times when Sigebert's heirs were too young to rule in their own right."

"There was a woman ruler?" asked Hippalca.

"Yes," said Geron. "Another woman, Queen Frédégonde, ruled the kingdom of Nuestria as regent for a time as well. However, those two women were bitter enemies for decades."

"Why?" asked Hippalca.

"Palace intrigue," he said with a dismissive wave of a hand. "Brunehaut's sister married Sigebert's brother, Chilperic, King of Nuestria. Brunehaut was upset when her sister died suddenly. Some say she was strangled. Brunehaut believed Chilperic's mistress Frédégonde was behind it. Later Frédégonde was made his queen, which strengthened her suspicions. Brunehaut and Frédégonde conspired against each other for years. Many wars were fought on their behest, but Brunehaut always survived. That is until Clotaire the Second finally fulfilled his late mother's wishes."

"Did he have Queen Brunehaut murdered?" asked Hippalca.

"No. She was executed. The Frankish nobles met and voted in favor of Frédégonde son Clotaire and against the succession of Brunehaut's great-grandson. Brunehaut and the small boy were put to death while Clotaire consolidated the kingdoms and proclaimed himself king of all the Franks. She was tortured for three days before being tied to the back of a horse and dragged to her death."

Hippalca covered her face with her hands and broke away from Geron's grasp.

"Why did you tell her such a story?" asked Richardet.

"It is history," Geron said with a shrug. "Queen Brunehaut was praised for her beauty, charm and intelligence, as well as for building many churches. However, despite all the good she did over the years, she fell out of favor with the court and was put to death at the hands of a kinsman."

"You would tell that kind of a story to a daughter of Charlemagne?" asked Richardet.

"His daughters would know this tale, as well as intrigues involving their own family." Geron returned to the table and took a long drink of wine.

"Hippalca, do not worry," said Richardet as he put a consoling arm around her. "Nothing like that will happen to my mother or Bradamante. Especially my sister; I cannot think of anything she could do that would cause her to lose Charlemagne's favor."

Hippalca nodded as she wiped away tears.

CHAPTER 105

Bradamante awoke feeling nervous. The night before, she went to bed anticipating dreams of Ruggiero. Drifting off to sleep, she imagined Hippalca handing him the reins to Frontino outside the abbey. She had wanted to see how grateful Ruggiero would be at the return of his horse as well as hear new professions of love from him during the night. Instead, she awoke without recalling a single dream and that troubled her.

Near midday, she became anxious for Hippalca's return. Wanting to see outside without obstruction, Bradamante removed the fenestral windows from her chamber. She was careful not to puncture the linen stretched over the wooden frames. Bradamante paced as she kept vigil for any sightings on the road outside their castle.

Beatrice entered the room. "Come to my chamber and join me in weaving."

"I am sorry Mother, I cannot."

"Would you rather have an easel set up so you could paint?"

"Not today. I am out of sorts from my journey," she said as she massaged her temples. "I have no patience for the domestic arts today. I promise on the morrow to weave by your side."

Her mother sat down on the bed and began sewing beads onto the bodice of a dress. A look of satisfaction spread on her mother's face for having extracted a promise for the following day.

As the time for her family's dinner approached, Bradamante finally spied Hippalca and a party of men rounding the bend. Her excitement faded as she realized her handmaid's companions did not include Ruggiero.

"Mother, Richardet has returned."

"Richardet?"

Beatrice dropped her sewing, ran to the window, and said a prayer at the sight of her lost son. She left and her voice could be heard up and down the halls of the castle barking orders to the servants.

Aymon and Beatrice joyfully kissed their son as he dismounted from his horse, and they embraced Vivien and Maugis. Alard happily greeted his kinsman as a party atmosphere sprung up in the household.

Bradamante was disturbed when Hippalca avoided her gaze. Her servant was soon ushered away from the wagon to assist serving the dinner. Bradamante stared at the retreating form of her handmaid and wished for nothing more than to be alone with her closest confidant.

She ate her meal in silence while the hall rang with laughter and revelry. Richardet spun a tale of getting lost, coming down with a fever and then being tended by a peasant family. He had somehow found his way to Agrismont where he heard about the attempt by the Maganzas to claim Vivien and Maugis from Lanfusa. The three men punctuated the story of the rescue by gesturing with their knives and spewing bits of roasted lamb through the air.

"And now, my mother and lovely sister shall wear jewels once worn by the Maganzas," bragged Richardet as he raised his goblet of wine. "May death rain down upon that whole accursed house."

The men heartily raised their glasses in a toast, yet Bradamante's unease grew. She left her seat and whispered in her twin's ear, "I need to speak with you."

"Of course, as soon as I finish my wine."

Bradamante excused herself and retired to her chambers to wait for Richardet. She found herself pacing yet again, this time in anger.

"What is wrong?" he asked as he entered the room. "You have been morose all day."

"I am grateful you all are safe and sound, however I have questions about details in your story. Please tell me how you and Aldigier met up with the two others who helped rescue our kinsmen."

"Helped us? Ruggiero and Marfisa did more than help. Without them, Vivien and Maugis would not be alive."

"How did you meet Ruggiero?" she pressed.

"We met two days ago. Nightfall was coming and I suggested we stay at Agrismont. During dinner, Aldigier told us of the planned hostage exchange. We came upon Marfisa on the way there."

"You avoided my question," Bradamante said. "Two days ago, I heard of a young man condemned to die for the crime of fornication. The execution was to take place outside Fiordespina's villa. I want to know if she was accused of being unchaste and if you were her lover."

Richardet studied the floor, his cheeks aflame. "Yes, to all of it."

"Ruggiero rescued you."

"Yes."

"Tell me how you became Fiordespina's lover. I know how strict that household was run."

"I, uh, I—"

"Well?" she demanded.

"I pretended I was you."

"After she discovered you were not female, what happened then?"

"She was delighted. It was our secret. By day, I looked like a woman, and by night I acted like a man."

"How did you tell her that you were my brother and not me?"

"She never knew the truth," he said, blanching under Bradamante's glare. "I told her a story about a magic wish being granted. That I wished to become a man rather than remain a maid, and that I did it with her in mind."

Bradamante slapped him. "You lied to her. You used my good name to bear false witness to a virtuous maid to satisfy your own lust."

Richardet touched his cheek. "It started out that way, I grant you. I feared her rejection if she knew the truth. Then after becoming lovers, my fears went away."

"You deceived her."

"Yes, but I also love her. What I could not say with words, I showed her with deeds. She returned my love. Whether or not she knew my real name, Fiordespina knew my heart."

"You love her, but not enough to tell her the truth. She deserved your honesty, not your deception. She lost her maidenhood based on lies."

"Oh, like you never lie," he spat back. "You lied to Mother when you told her you cut your hair because it was too hot in the summer sun."

"I lied to protect Mother."

"You lied because you were afraid she might interfere with your ability to make war. Tell me why you left your post at Marseille."

"Do not change the subject," she warned. "You were the one who thought only of himself, without any care of who might be hurt along the way."

"I am no different than most men."

"Our father – "

"Yes, our father. Have you heard he is like Uncle Beuve and fathered a bastard?"

"Lies!"

"Who knows how many bastards Renaud has fathered?"

Her cheeks burned with anger.

"Ah, but then, we have our own emperor to look up to for moral leadership." Richardet paced the room. "He has wives as well as concubines. His bastards are all to be treated as royalty. Meanwhile, his daughters have never married, but they have made him a grandfather more than once. Yes, King Charles *the Great* has certainly set the high moral standard for how Christian men should treat women."

Bradamante closed her eyes. Richardet had struck several nerves. She had heard the rumors surrounding their father, but dismissed them as malicious gossip. Aymon maintained that fidelity was a virtue. She wanted to believe her father had remained faithful to her mother throughout their marriage. Bradamante knew from being in battle with Renaud that rumors of his infidelities were true. It had always bothered her, but she turned a blind eye toward his indiscretions. Similarly, she tried ignoring the behavior of her emperor which ran counter to church teachings. She justified it as a current extension of Biblical customs where kings such as David and Solomon had multiple wives and concubines. The hardest part for her was reconciling the children born of Charlemagne's unmarried daughters. Upon opening her eyes, she saw a smug look on Richardet's face. He had successfully distracted her from his transgressions.

"Did you ever consider asking for her hand in marriage?" she asked.

"Are you mad? Amir Marsilio would never allow his daughter to marry the fourth son of a Christian nobleman."

"Our father is the fourth son of a Christian nobleman, and he married a sister of Charlemagne."

Richardet laughed. "Do you know how that came about, dear sister? King Charles did not intend for her to marry anyone, Mother was supposed to take the veil."

"Did they…?"

"No, the first time Father met her was on their wedding day," he said. "Father seized the opportunity to marry well. Our father saved the life of King Charles in battle. Later, after our king was in a fit of drunken revelry, and in front of an assembly of nobles, he asked our father to name his reward. He could ask for anything: land, riches, or a title. All those were his for the mere asking. Instead, Father asked for the hand of the king's youngest sister. King Charles could not turn down the request without losing face, but he was unhappy with the turn of events. That is why our mother did not have an appropriate dowry and why we live so far from the royal court. It is also why our emperor is opposed to drunkenness; that night was the last time he drank heavily."

Bradamante was stunned. Never had she questioned the rationale behind Charlemagne's agreement to her parents' marriage. Now, as she thought about it, she could not see any political advantage that her sovereign would have reaped from being aligned with her family.

Richardet sat down on the bed and held his head in his hands. "For me to have followed in our father's footsteps, I would have to betray Charlemagne and save the life of his enemy, Amir Marsilio. I cannot do that."

"Brother, did you *ever* stop to think what would happen to Fiordespina when it was discovered she was no longer a virgin?"

"I will not go to my grave regretting that I passed up a chance to be with the woman I loved. I seized Fortune's forelock with both hands; something you cannot understand, because you have never loved anyone. You have no idea what it is like to burn in love."

Bradamante wanted to scream that she knew all about being in love and being unable to declare her love openly. She wanted him to know she was not only furious with him, but envious that he and Fiordespina had expressed their love physically together. It was something she and Ruggiero denied themselves out of a sense of propriety.

"A maid's virtue and reputation is all that she has," Bradamante said evenly. "When that is stripped from her, she is no longer marriageable. All you could think about was your own pleasure. Tell me the circumstances of when you were discovered."

"Neron sent word to Marsilio that the great Bradamante was in his daughter's villa, and he intended to hold her hostage. He expected Marsilio to demand a large ransom from Charlemagne. However, those plans changed when Neron received a letter back from Marsilio telling him about your exploits in Marseille. The amir questioned the identity of Fiordespina's guest, for he knew you could not be in two places at the same time. That night Neron broke into her chambers. I was taken away and forced to tell who I was."

"What happened to her?"

"Neron said he was taking her to Paris to see her father."

Bradamante pinched the bridge of her nose. "Marsilio might order her execution for having disgraced her family."

Richardet absentmindedly ripped the petals off a rose.

"You are lucky to have escaped with your life," she continued. "If Ruggiero had not saved your miserable neck—"

"He sends his regards to you by the way," he said, interrupting her tirade. "He vowed that he would retrieve your horse from the thief."

"Ruggiero is an honorable man. It is a shame he is not a Christian, for Charlemagne could use a few more *virtuous* knights."

Richardet appeared stung by her remark.

"Please leave me," she said turning her back on him. "Go see to our kinsmen. I have not the heart to engage in frivolity, something that appears to suit you."

Richardet turned on his heel and left without saying another word.

Bradamante ushered in Hippalca who had been waiting silently outside in the hallway. She closed the door behind her. "My brother's attitude toward women is reproachable. He is unworthy of your affection. Come sit with me and relay what transpired yesterday with Ruggiero."

The two young women sat on the edge of the bed.

"I am sorry milady. I failed you," said Hippalca.

"How so?"

Hippalca bowed her head. "I was accosted on my journey and Frontino was stolen. I warned the brigand that the horse belonged to Ruggiero. He was not dissuaded. He laughed scornfully at me. I pleaded to no avail."

"Do you know his name?"

"Rodomont."

Bradamante closed her eyes.

"He threatened to ravish me if I did not leave his side."

"There is nothing you could have said or done. He is evil," said Bradamante.

"All hope is not lost milady," said Hippalca. "Ruggiero vowed to reclaim Frontino and left in pursuit of that scoundrel."

Bradamante bit her lip with worry.

Hippalca drew out a letter from the folds of her dress. "Ruggiero gave me this and bade me give it to you in private."

Bradamante seized the parchment.

From the knight Ruggiero to the lady Bradamante
My beloved Bradamante

It is with a heavy heart that I write this letter. I know not how this will find its way to you but I have faith God will provide a trusted messenger. Today after our cruel separation a messenger from Amir Akramont found me. His campaign is in desperate straights and has given urgent orders for me to report to Paris. I have sworn fealty to him and my honor as a knight rests on that vow. If I were to refuse to return to his side in his hour of need it will be looked upon as the mark of a disloyal coward. The plans we made earlier today were done in ignorance of the current state of the war. I cannot marry you at this juncture in time for it would be seen as an attempt to circumvent my sacred oath to my sovereign. As if my vow to serve Akramont was proffered only to secure knighthood without any sense of loyalty and that I abandoned him when defeat appeared imminent. Your reputation would be equally subject to ridicule for you would be considered an unwitting partner in deception and dishonor. I cannot allow our love and our marriage to be looked at in such a disrespectful manner. Therefore I must delay my pledge of marriage to you. Akramont is depending upon his knights to liberate him. Once that is accomplished and after I have secured the severance of the bonds of service to him I shall spend the rest of my life serving you and our love. I ask that you grant me a month to accomplish this task. Then I pledge to you my loyalty and devotion as your husband for the rest of my days.

Your servant in love
Ruggiero

Tears fell onto the parchment smearing the ink as Melissa's words from Merlin's cave rang in Bradamante's ears.

"Should Ruggiero remain a Saracen, he shall bring about the defeat of Charlemagne and the fall of the Frankish Empire."

There was still a small thread of hope from which to cling.

"Tell me Hippalca, was he baptized?"

"No, milady. As I first came upon him, Ruggiero was leaning against a fountain in the courtyard. He was resting in the shadows of the abbey."

Bradamante threw her arms around Hippalca. "I have failed everyone."

END OF VOLUME ONE

APPENDICES

MAPS

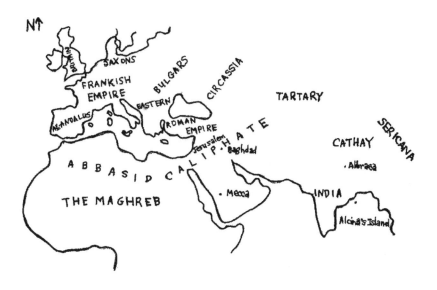

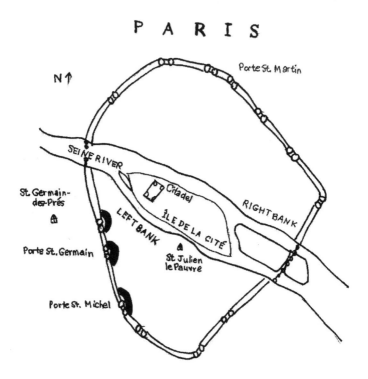

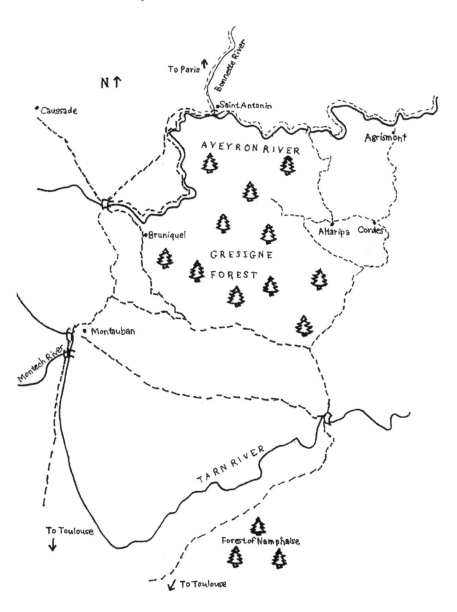

Alphabetical List of Characters and Story Elements

Here are some aids to assist in the pronunciation of character names. Like many words, there are variations and the reader should feel free to choose whichever pronunciation she or he prefers. The parentheses demonstrate the variety of names for these characters used by the poets Ariosto and Boiardo and some of the more popular versions used by various translators.

Aegisthus /Ah-JEES-thoose/ Greek warrior who betrayed and slew Astyanax.

Agrikhan /a-GRI-kahn/ (Agricane, Agrican) Asian warrior. King of Tartary, father of Mandricardo. Led siege in Cathay when Angelica refused to marry him. Killed by Orlando.

Agrismont /a-griz-MAHNT/ (Agrismonte) Castle owned by Duke Aymon's brother Beuve and guarded by his bastard son Aldigiero.

Aistulf /AY-stoolff/ (Astolfo) Christian warrior. One of twelve paladins of Charlemagne. Son of King Odo of Essex. Cousin to Orlando, Renaud, Alard, Guichard, Bradamante, Richardet, Vivien, Maugis and Aldigiero. Good looking young man who loves fashion and boasts of his prowess, but is not well respected by his peers. Had been imprisoned by Alcina. Claimed the golden lance after Argalia's death.

Akramont /AKRAH-mahnt/ (Agramant, Agramante) Amir of the Maghreb (North Africa). His palace is in Bizerta, Tunisia. Commander of Muslim forces in the invasion of the Frankish Empire. Son of Troiano. Descendant of Alexander the Great.

al-Andalus /al ANDA loose/ Muslim name for the area that is now modern day Spain. The name in Latin was Hispania. Historical maps from that period also refer to it as the Umayyad Emirate or the Emirate of Córdoba.

Alard /ah LARD/ (Alardo) Christian warrior. Third son of Duke Aymon and Beatrice. Brother to Renaud, Guichard, Bradamante and Richardet. Cousin to Orlando, Aistulf, Vivien, Maugis and Aldigier.

Alcina - /al SEE nah/ or /al CHEE nah/ Evil sorceress. Has an island east of India and has had many men as her lovers, she turns them into trees, rocks or statues when she is through with them.

Alda /ALL duh/ (Aude) Betrothed to Orlando. Sister to Oliver.

Aldigier /al DEE jee ay/ (Aldigiero) Bastard son of Beuve, caretaker for Agrismont. Half-brother to Vivien and Maugis. Cousin to Aistulf, Orlando, Renaud, Guichard, Alard, Bradamante and Richardet.

Ali /AH-lee/ Historical figure (600?-661) Cousin and son-in-law to the Prophet Muhammad. Warrior. Caliph between 656-661. Owner of a legendary sword Dhul Fiqar with a bifurcated blade.

Almont /all MAHNT/ (Almonte) Deceased Muslim warrior. Became Amir of the Maghreb at the death of his father. Older brother to Troiano. Father to Daniso. Uncle to Akramont. Killed Bernard of Lyon and Milon. Slain by a young Orlando. Previous owner of Durindana.

Altaripa /al tah REE pah/ Castle owned by Count Ansel of the Maganza house.

al-Zahira /al zah HE rah/ (Alzirdo) African commander killed by Orlando.

Anasuya /a nah SOO yah/ Mentor to Logistilla.

Ansel /an SELL/ (Anselmo) Elderly Christian Count of Altaripa. House of Maganza. Father of Pinabel.

Andromache /an DRA MAH kah/ Wife of Hector of Troy, mother to Astyanax. Killed by the Greeks after the fall of Troy.

Angelica /ahn JELL i kah/ Muslim princess of Cathay. Loved by many men. She owned a powerful magical ring that nullified enchantments. Daughter of Galafron, sister to Argalia.

Aquilant /ah qui LAHNT/ (Aquilante) Christian knight. Son of Oliver, brother to Grifon.

Ariège /a REE ejj/ A region at the base of the Pyrenees mountains named after the Ariège River.

Ariodant /a REE oh dahnt/ (Ariodante) Christian knight. Originally an Italian knight who moved to Scotland. Duke of Albany, a commander of Scottish forces in defense of Paris.

Argalia /ar GAH lee ah/ Son of King Galafron of Cathay. Brother to Angelica. Owned a golden lance. Killed by Feraguto.

Astyanax /a STY ah nax/ Son of Hector, survived the fall of Troy. Widely thought to have been killed by the Greeks with his mother Andromache, but was secretly spirited out of the city. He was raised in Sicily and married a warrior queen from Siracusa. Betrayed and killed by Aegisthus. His wife escaped the Greeks, and bore their son Polidoro in Reggio.

Atallah /a TAHL ah/ (Atalante, Atlante, Atlantes, Atlas) - Muslim wizard who raised Ruggiero from infancy on Mount Carena in Tunisia.

Atropos /a TRAH pohs/ The Fate sister who cuts the thread of life.

Aymon /AY mohn/ (Amone) Christian warrior. Duke of Dordogne. Fourth son of Bernard of Lyon. Brother King Odo of Essex, Beuve of Agrismont and Milon. Married to Beatrice, sister of Charlemagne. Father of Renaud, Guichard, Alard, Bradamante and Richardet. Uncle to Orlando, Aistulf, Maugis, Vivien and Aldigiero.

Aymon /AY mohn/ Infant son to Renaud and Clarice.

Balisarda /bah li SAR duh/ Sword Brunello gave to Ruggiero.

Bardulasto /bar dew LAH stow/ Muslim warrior. Governor of Alcazar. Ambushed and tried to kill Ruggiero at the tournament on Mount Carena. Slain by Ruggiero.

Barigano /bar i GAH no/ Muslim warrior. Cousin of Bardulasto. He tried avenging Behram's death by attacking Ruggiero on the plains of Toulouse. Died at the hands of Bradamante.

Bayard /bay ARD/ (Bayardo) Enchanted horse owned by Renaud. Powerful, swift with near-human intelligence. Coveted by Gradasso.

Beatrice /BEE ah triss/ Wife of Duke Aymon. Mother to Renaud, Guichard, Alard, Bradamante and Richardet. Sister to Charlemagne.

Belle /bell/ Pinabel's wife.

Beltramo /bell TRAH moh/ Son of Rampaldo, brother to Ruggiero II. Jealous of his brother's wife, and betrayed his father and brother which caused their deaths.

Bernard of Lyon /ber NARD of LEE ohn/ (Clairmont in the poems) - Late Christian warrior. Father to Odo, Beuve, Milon and Aymon. Killed by Almont.

Bernard /ber NARD/ Eldest son of Renaud and Clarice, named after Duke Aymon's father.

Bertha /BURR thah/ (Bertrada) Sister of Charlemagne. Eloped with Milon. Mother of Orlando. Bertha was also the name of Charlemagne's mother, who was known as Bertha of the Big Foot or Goosefoot.

Berthild /BURR tilled/ Barmaid of Aistulf's youth.

Bertolai /burr toe LIE/ Christian warrior. Member of the Maganza house. Offered to pay the ransom of Vivien and Maugis from Lanfusa.

Beuve /BWEV/ (Buovo) Christian soldier and lord of Agrismont. Second son of Bernard of Lyon. Brother to Odo, Milon, and Aymon. Father to Maugis, Vivien, and has a bastard son Aldigier.

Bizerta /bi ZURR tah/ Home of Akramont's palace. Site of where his war council decided to invade Francia. City in modern day Tunisia.

Bradamante /brah dah MAHNT/ or /brah dah MAHN tay/ (Bradamant) Christian warrior. Daughter of Duke Aymon and Beatrice. Sister of Renaud, Guichard, Alard, and twin to Richardet. Niece of Charlemagne. Cousin to Orlando, Aistulf, Vivien, Maugis and Aldigier. Loved by Ruggiero.

Brandimart /BRAN di mart/ (Brandimarte, Florismart) Noble warrior who became Orlando's close friend. Married to Flordelis.

Brigliodoro /brig lee oh DOOR oh/ Orlando's renowned horse.

Brunehaut /broon HOAT/ Historical figure, also known as Brunhilda, (534-613). Daughter of Visigothic King Athanagild. Married to King Sigebert of Austrasia. Regent three times for underage male heirs. Put to death by her nephew Clothaire II.

Brunello /BREW nell oh/ Thief who stole Angelica's ring. Akramont rewarded the theft by making Brunello the governor of Tingitana. The ring allowed the enchanted castle on Mount Carena hiding Ruggiero to be revealed.

Bruniquel /brew ni KELL/ Small hilltop village that dates back to the time of the Romans. Queen Brunehaut once lived there.

Burgundy /BURR gun dee/ Region in the north of France. Guy is the Duke of Burgundy.

Caligorant /CAH li go ruhnt/ Cyclops on Alcina's island.

Calliope /cah lie OH pee/ Muse of Epic Poetry from Greek mythology.

Carloman /CAR lo man/ Historical figure. (751-771). Younger brother to Charlemagne, son of Pepin the Short. Inherited half of his father's kingdom along with his brother. Carloman's untimely death led Charlemagne to become king of all the Franks.

Charlemagne /SHAR le mane/ Historical figure, (742-814). King Charles the Great of the Frankish Empire, Emperor of the Western Roman Empire. Son of Pepin the Short, grandson to Charles Martel. Brother to Carloman, Gisela, Bertha and Beatrice. Uncle to Orlando, Renaud, Guichard, Alard, Bradamante, and Richardet. There was no historical Beatrice, therefore her five children are fictional. There was an historical Orlando or Roland, but he was not a nephew to Charlemagne as the only sister to King Charles, Gisela, never married and entered a convent.

Charles Martel /charlz mar TELL/ Historical figure, (686-741). Grandfather to King Charles the Great. Father to King Pepin. Mayor of the Palace. Repulsed invasion of Saracens at the Battle of Poitiers (Tours) in 732. Also known as Charles the Hammer.

Clarice /clah REESE/ Wife of Renaud, mother to his children.

Clodovaco /kloh dah VAH koh/- Son of Floviano. Brother to Constante. Ancestor to Ruggiero.

Clotaire /KLOH tair/ Historical figure, (570-629). King of Nuestria and later of all the Franks. He had his aunt, Queen Brunehaut executed.

Clotho /KLOH thoh/ The Fate from Greek mythology who spun the thread of life.

Constante /CON stant/ Son of Floviano. Brother to Clodovaco. Ancestor to King Charles.

Cordes /cord/ A mountaintop village in the Midi-Pyrenees. The modern name is Cordes-sur-Ciel. It dates back to the 13th century, which is technically outside the time frame of this story, but it is situated in an area where a village is needed thus its inclusion.

Cyllarus /SILL ah russ/ Andalusian stallion given to Bradamante by Fiordespina. Later given to Richardet.

Daniforte /DAN i fort/ Muslim warrior. Tried to stop Ruggiero from defending Bradamante. Killed.

Daniso /duh NEE so/ (Dardinello) - Muslim warrior. Governor of Zumara. Son of Almont, nephew to Troiano, cousin to Akramont.

Deimos /DAY mohs/ Atallah's horse given to Ruggiero.

Devante /deh VAHNT/- Dwarf sent by Doralice to seek help by Rodomont.

Dhul Fiqar /DOOL fi car/ a sword used by Ali during the time of the Prophet Muhammad. It was bifurcated and was thought to have magical abilities. Current whereabouts are a mystery.

Doralice /DOR ah leese/ Daughter of Governor Stordilano of Granada. Famed beauty betrothed to Rodomont.

Dordogne /DOR doh nya/ River and region in Southwest France. Duke Aymon is the Duke of Dordogne.

Durindana /dur in DAH nah/ sword once owned by Hector of Troy. Thought to be the finest sword next to King Arthur's Excalibur. Owned by Orlando and coveted by Gradasso and Mandricardo.

Edward /ED ward/ Earl of Shrewsbury. A commander of Christian forces in defense of Paris.

Eos /AY ohss/ Bradamante's snow white mare.

Erebus /AIR eh buss/ Richardet's horse that Bradamante borrowed. Died in the battle near Toulouse.

Erifilla /AIR uh fill ah/ Ogress on Alcina's island.

Erinyes /ee RIHN ih eez/ Also known as the Avenging Furies. Three sisters who were avenging goddesses in Greek mythology. They tormented the living and the dead who had committed acts of evil.

Falerina /fa le REE nah/ Sorceress who created an enchanted garden that ensnared many knights. Defeated by Orlando.

Fates /FATES/ Three sisters in Greek mythology who determined the length of mortals' lives. Clotho, Lachesis and Atropos.

Feraguto /fair uh GOO toh/ (Feragu, Ferraù) - Muslim soldier, nephew to Marsilio, Amir of al-Andalus. Killed Argalia.

Fidelia /fi DELL ee ah/ Attendant to Doralice.

Fiordespina /fee OR deh spee nah/ Muslim maiden. Daughter of Marsilio, Amir of al-Andalus. Sister to Matalista.

Flamberge /FLAM berj/ (Floberge, Flamborge, Fusberta) Renaud's sword.

Flordelis /FLOR deh lee/ (Fiordelisa, Fiordeli, Fiordigili) Wife of Brandimart.

Foix /FWAH/ A town at the base of the Pyrenees mountains.

Frédégonde /FRAY day gond/- Historical figure, (550-597). Married King Chilperic of Nuestria. Bitter enemy of Queen Brunehaut.

Frédélas /FRAY day less/ A town north of the Pyrenees mountains. The town's modern name is Pamiers.

Frontino /FRON tee noh/ Horse ridden by Ruggiero.

Furies /FUHR eez/ Also known as the Erinyes. Three sisters who were avenging goddesses in Roman mythology. They tormented the living and the dead who had committed acts of evil.

Galafron /gal AH frahn/ Khan of Cathay. Father to Angelica and Argalia.

Galiziella /gal ah zee ELL ah/ (Galaciella) - Wife of Ruggiero II, mother to Ruggiero III. Muslim warrior who converted to Christianity before marriage. Escaped the pillage of Reggio and died as she gave birth.

Ganelon /GAN eh lon/ Count in the house of Maganza. Christian warrior, but enemy to the house of Lyon.

Garamanta /gare ah MAHN tah/ Old African governor had used divination to determine the existence and whereabouts of Ruggiero. Died shortly after making a pronouncement regarding Ruggiero, and did not join in the invasion of the Frankish Empire.

Geneviève /zhon VEE ev/ Young girl who survived the attack on the church Saint Julien le Pauvre.

Geoffroi /JEFF wah/ Christian knight. Count of Foix. Former captive of Atallah. Helped organize freed knights on a mission to Marseilles.

Geron /GARE on/ Lord of Bruniquel.

Gradasso /grah DAH so/ Asian warrior. King of Sericana. Obsessed with obtaining Bayard and Durindana. Invaded al-Andalus (Hispania) with one hundred and fifty thousand troops to obtain Bayard and Durindana those. Briefly held King Charles prisoner, humiliated by Aistulf.

Grifon /GRIFF on/ (Grifone) Christian knight. Son of Oliver, brother to Aquilant.

Guichard /GWEE shard/ Christian knight. Second son of Duke Aymon and Beatrice. Brother to Renaud, Bradamante and Richardet. Cousin to Orlando, Aistulf, Vivien, Maugis and Aldigier.

Guidone Selvaggio /GWEE dohn sel VAJJ ee oh/ Christian knight from the Black Sea area, met up with Aquilant, Grifon and Sansonetto. Forced to serve Pinabel at Altaripa.

Guillaume /GEE ohm/ Duke of Orléans. Died in the battle of Toulouse.

Guy /GEE/ Christian knight. Duke of Burgundy, peer of Charlemagne. Stationed in Marseille with Bradamante.

Hector /heck TOR/ Acclaimed warrior of the legendary city of Troy. Noble ancestor to Ruggiero. Original owner of Durindana.

Herman /HER mun/ Earl of Abergavenny. A commander of Christian forces in defense of Paris.

Hippalca /hip PALL kah/ Handmaid and confidante to Bradamante.

Hispania /hiss SPAHN ee ah/ The Latin name for Spain. The Muslim name for the area during the time of Charlemagne was al-Andalus. Historical maps from that period also refer to it as the Umayyad Emirate or the Emirate of Córdoba.

Kamal /kah MALL/ Name Ruggiero gave to the hippogriff.

Kumanda /koo MAHN dah/ A commander of the Muslim fleet in Marseille.

Lachesis /lah KEE siss/ The Fate who measured the length of someone's life thread.

Lanfusa /lan FOO sah/ Muslim noblewoman. Mother of Feraguto. Held Vivien and Maugis hostage.

Leanian /lee AHN nee ahn/ (Leonetto) - Duke of Lancaster, a commander of Christian forces in defense of Paris.

Lethe /LEETH/ Magical river of forgetfulness in Greek mythology.

Logistilla /LOH ji still ah/ Good sorceress who opposes Alcina. They reside on opposite ends of the same island.

Lucien /LOO see en/ Christian foot soldier from Auch who helped develop a secret weapon with the Count of Foix.

Lyon house /LEE ohn/ The house of Bernard of Lyon, blood enemies to the house of Maganza. The city of Lyon was known as Lugdunum at the time of the Romans. (The poets used Clairmont and Mongrana for Bradamante's family. The city associated with Bernard was changed to avoid recalling the historical echo of the Crusades as the First Crusade was called by Pope Urban II at the Council of Clermont in 1095.)

Maganza house /mah GAHN zah/ Wealthy Christian warriors. Longstanding blood feud with the Lyon house. A few of its members are Ansel, Bertolai, Ganelon, and Pinabel.

Malha /MAHL ha/ Female slave to Alcina.

Mambrino /MAM bree noh/ Famed Muslim warrior who was killed by Renaud in previous legends. He had owned a charmed golden helmet, which is now worn proudly by Renaud.

Mandricardo /man dri CAR doh/ Asian warrior. Khan of Tartary, son of Agrikhan. Wears arms once belonging to Hector of Troy. Seeks to avenge his father's death, and vowed to not bind any sword until he wields Durindana.

Manilard /man i LARD/ Muslim commander killed by Orlando.

Marfisa /mar FEE sah/ Muslim warrior queen from the East. She besieged Angelica in Cathay.

Marie de Foix /MAH ree deh FWAH/ daughter of innkeeper that became one of Atallah's captives.

Marsilio /mar SEE lee oh/ (Marsil, Marsilies, Marsilione) Amir of al-Andalus. Muslim. Ally of Akramont's invasion of Francia. Father of Matalista and Fiordespina. Uncle to Feraguto.

Martisino /MAR teh see noh/ Muslim governor of Garamanta. Attacked Bradamante near Toulouse. Killed by Bradamante.

Matalista /ma TAH lee stah/ Muslim warrior. Son of Amir Marsilio of al-Andalus. Brother to Fiordespina.

Maugis /MOH jee/ (Malagi, Malagigi, Malagise) Son of Beuve. Brother to Vivien. Half brother to Aldigier. Wizard. Cousin to Aistulf, Orlando, Renaud, Guichard, Alard, Bradamante and Richardet.

Melissa /muh LISS uh/ Enchantress who aids Bradamante and Ruggiero.

Merlin /MURR linn/ legendary sorcerer from King Arthur's time. His bones rest in a cave in the Pyrenees and will answer questions about the future. Placed magical fountains around the Frankish Empire.

Milon /mee LOHN/ (Melone, Milone) Christian warrior. Third son of Bernard of Lyon. Brother to Odo, Beuve and Aymon. Eloped with Bertha, the sister of King Charles. Lived in exile with Bertha in Sutri, Italy. Father of Orlando. Died in battle when Orlando was a small boy.

Mnemosyne /NEM oh seen/ Titaness from Greek Mythology. Goddess of memory. Mother to the Nine Muses who were fathered by Zeus sleeping with Mnemosyne nine nights in a row. A spring or river is named after her that restores or enhances memory.

Montauban /MOHN toh bohn/ (Montalbano) the ancestral home to Bradamante and her brothers. Renaud is now the Count of Montauban. The real city in France was founded in the twelfth century, but this location could not be changed for sake of historical accuracy because Renaud de Montauban is a strong part of the legends.

Mount Carena /mount cah RAY nuh/ Mountain that Atallah raised Ruggiero. Somewhere in Tunisia

Muhammad /moo HAH med/ Historical figure. Prophet and founder of Islam. (570-632).

Nachman /NAHK man/ Jewish messenger sent by Charlemagne to speak with Akramont.

Namo /NAH moh/ Christian warrior. Duke of Bavaria and counselor to Charlemagne. Father of four sons.

Namphaise /NAM fayz/ Frankish hermit who tended to Bradamante's head wound, named after obscure saint who once was a soldier of Charlemagne.

Nemesis /NEM eh siss/ Goddess of retribution from Greek Mythology.

Neron /NAIR on/ Eunuch. Chief attendant to Fiordespina.

Nikephoros /ni KEE for ohs/ Bradamante's gelding she obtained in Foix.

Odo /OH doh/ (Otto, Otone) Christian soldier. King of Essex. Eldest son of Bernard of Lyon. Brother to Beuve, Milon, and Aymon. Father to Aistulf. (King of England in poem).

Olibandro /oh li BAHN droh/ Asian warrior. Brother to King Sacripant of Circassia. Killed by Mandricardo.

Oliver /ah LIV er/ (Olivier, Oliviero) Christian warrior. Paladin of Charlemagne. Brother to Alda. Father to Aquilant and Grifon.

Orlando /or LAN doh/ (Roland) Christian soldier. Son of Milon and Bertha. Nephew to King Charles. Count of Anglante. One of Charlemagne's twelve paladins. Cousin to Renaud, Guichard, Alard, Bradamante, Richardet, Aistulf, Vivien, Maugis and Aldigiero. In love with Angelica. Has enchanted skin which cannot be penetrated by any normal sword or weapon.

Ottino /ah TEE noh/ Count of Toulouse.

Pepin /PEP in/ Historical figure (714-768). Nickname was Pepin le Bref or Pepin the Short. Father to Charlemagne, Carloman, Gisela. This story includes him being father to Bertha and Beatrice.

Pinabel /PIN eh bell/ (Pinabello) - Christian warrior. Knight in the house of Maganza. He is wealthy and treacherous. His wife Belle was abducted while he was en route to bring fresh troops for Charlemagne to the battle in Toulouse.

Polidoro /poh li DOR oh/ Son of Astyanax. Ancestor of Ruggiero.

Rabican /RAB i can/ Horse created by magic of smoke and fire. Won by Renaud after dueling with a giant. Given to Aistulf. Ruggiero rode this horse on Alcina's island.

Rampaldo /ram PALL doh/ Christian. Ruler of Reggio Italy. Son of Ruggiero I, father to Ruggiero II and Beltramo. Grandfather to Ruggiero III. Betrayed by his son Beltramo and murdered.

Rangada /ran GAH dah/ Female slave to Alcina.

Renaud /ren OH/ (Rinaldo, Ranaldo, Reynaud) Christian soldier. Count of Montauban, eldest son of Duke Aymon and Beatrice. Esteemed warrior. Nephew and paladin to Charlemagne. Husband to Clarice. Brother to Guichard, Alard, Bradamante, Richardet. Father to Bernard and Aymon. Cousin to Orlando, Aistulf, Maugis, Vivien and Aldigiero. In love with Angelica. Owns the coveted destrier Bayard.

Richardet /ree shar DAY/ (Ricciardetto) Christian soldier. Fourth son of Duke Aymon and Beatrice. Nephew to Charlemagne. Brother to Renaud, Guichard, Alard, and twin to Bradamante.

Roana /roh AH nah/ Attendant to Doralice.

Rodomont /roh duh MAHNT/ (Rodamonte, Rodomonte) African soldier. Atheist. Governor of Sarza. Sworn to Akramont. Descendant of Nimrod. Owns enchanted dragon hide armor. Betrothed to Doralice of Granada.

Ruggiero II /ruh JAIR oh/ (Rogero) Christian warrior. Son of Rampaldo. Brother to Beltramo. Husband to Galaziella. Father to Ruggiero III. Served King Charles as a knight. Betrayed by Beltramo and murdered.

Ruggiero III or Ruggiero Tazeem /ruh JAIR oh/ (Rogero) Muslim warrior and descendant of Hector of Troy. Son of Ruggiero II and Galiziella. Raised on Mount Carena by wizard Atallah. Loved by Bradamante.

Sabri /SAH bree/ (Sobrino) - Devout Muslim. Elderly African governor of Algocco and Garbo. Serves as wazir to Akramont, as he had done previously for Troiano. He warned against invasion of Frankish Empire.

Sacripant /sa kri PAHNT/ (Sacripante) Asian warrior. King of Circassia. In love with Angelica. Helped defend Angelica's castle in Cathay against Agrican's army. His brother Olibandro was killed defending Circassia while Sacripant was in Cathay.

Saint Antonin /SAINT AN toh nin/ Town on the Aveyron River in France. It dates back to the time of the Romans and had a monastery dedicated to the martyred Saint Antonin. Modern name is Saint-Antonin-Noble-Val.

Sansonetto /san soh NET oh/ Christian soldier coerced to fulfill harsh tributes of all knights and ladies to the castle Altaripa. Fought with Ruggiero.

Sarza /SAR zuh/ Area ruled by Governor Rodomont which would be modern day Algeria.

Sigebert /SEE guh burt/ Historical figure (535-575). King of Austrasia. Married Brunehaut. Assassinated when he was at war with his brother Chilperic, King of Nuestria.

Stordilano /stor de LAH noh/ Muslim warrior. Governor of Granada who serves Marsilio, Amir of al-Andalus. Father to Doralice.

Tingitana /tin ji TAHN nah/ Area that Governor Brunello ruled. It is situated in modern day Morocco.

Toulouse /too LOOZ/ A town in southern France that is north of the Pyrenees Mountains and dates back to the time of the Romans.

Troiano /troy AH noh/ Deceased African warrior. Brother of Almont. King of Tunisia. Became amir at the death of his brother. Father of Akramont. Killed by Orlando.

Vivien /VIV ee ahn/ (Viviano) Christian warrior. Son of Beuve. Brother to Maugis, half brother to Aldigiero. Cousin to Aistulf, Orlando, Renaud, Guichard, Alard, Bradamante and Richardet.

Zerbin /ZER bin/ (Zerbino) Prince of Scotland, leads the Scots in defense of Paris.

AUTHOR'S NOTE

Quest of the Warrior Maiden is an adaptation of two classic epic poems that were written during the Italian Renaissance: *Orlando inamorato* by Matteo Maria Boiardo and *Orlando furioso* by Ludovico Ariosto. I first read *Orlando furioso* in 2003 when I was participating in online debates about the Harry Potter series. There was a suggestion that hippogriffs were a symbol of love and as part of my research, I decided to read the poem because it was the first time that a hippogriff was used as a character in literature. I wanted to see how it was used in context of the story.

After I finished reading the poem I decided to introduce the Bradamante/Ruggiero love story to modern audiences in the hopes that the couple could be recognized as part of the pantheon of classic romantic couples from legend such as Guinevere/Lancelot, Tristan/Isolde, and Robin Hood/Maid Marion.

Historical events:

The first thing I want to mention is that the war depicted in the story did not take place. There was no invasion of the Frankish Empire by North African forces during the time of Charlemagne. I do mention the battle of Tours (Poitiers) that was a decisive win for his grandfather Charles Martel, but there was no similar invasion during Charlemagne's reign.

Settings:

The poets, Boiardo and Ariosto, were skilled at creating a rich tapestry of characters and interwoven plot lines, but they were not skilled historians or geographers. I chose to set the story in the year 802, which is after Charlemagne had been crowned emperor. The poets were vague about when their stories took place as well as the length of time for the various events. Because Charlemagne gave the months different names than we are accustomed, I chose not to use that naming system. I did not want to confuse people. Therefore, I decided to use the longest day of the year to start my story. Do not waste your time trying to calculate when that would have landed on the calendar, I simply chose the date Wednesday, June 22, 802 to start my story.

I also moved several events in the poems to locations I thought made more logical sense. For example, the climax of the first novel takes place in a village in the Midi-Pyrenees region rather than the city of Bayonne. I could not understand why these characters would have independently all gone to that location. Instead it seemed to me as if Ariosto just wanted to include another area of France in his epic story. So I moved it to the village of Saint Antonin where there is an abbey reputed to have been founded by Charlemagne's father *Pepin le Bref.*

I tried very hard to only use locations that would have existed in the ninth century, but there are some exceptions. One good example is the town of Montauban. The city of Montauban was founded in 1144 and Charlemagne died in 814. However, Renaud de Montauban is a well-known character from the Carolingian legend cycle. Trying to divorce Renaud from Montauban would be like trying to take Robin Hood out of Sherwood Forest. It would not be right. I could no more change Renaud's hometown than I would try to use another Italian city's name for Leonardo da Vinci, say Leonardo da Napolitano.

Montauban is also known in legend for being made of white stone. I could not change it to be a wooden fortress even though it might be a more accurate historical depiction.

Using Montauban as the centerpiece for many of the locales, I tried using those landmarks around it that made logical sense. The "palace of illusions" needed to be in a forest and the great *Forêt de Gresigne* is east of Montauban.

There is a village named *Cordes-sur-Ciel* that I use as the home for Fiordespina. It was not founded until the year 1222, but I needed a town nearby and decided to use what was available. The town was named Cordes until 1993 when sur-Ciel was appended to reflect its lofty appearance to the valley below.

The distances between Montauban, Cordes, and Saint Antonin are not difficult for modern day travelers by car, but it would be difficult to traverse all those distances by horseback. I stretched it a little, but it is not as if I had chose towns fifty miles away from each other and expected my characters to make it there in an afternoon without magical help.

Both poems use Spain as the name of the area south of Francia. The Muslims at the time referred to it as al-Andalus. In Latin texts from the time it was referred to as Hispania. So I use both names to describe the same area, depending on the perspective of the character at the time in the narrative.

I am not exactly sure where the kingdoms of Cathay and Sericana were supposed to be. Cathay is commonly thought of as China, but Sericana is described by the poets as being a vast kingdom east of Cathay. I chose to place Cathay as east of India and Sericana as east of Cathay.

Medieval Paris:

Ariosto's siege on Paris was predicated on the town being heavily fortified. That is not what it was like in the ninth century. The fortifications as described by Ariosto and what I chose to use were in fact the work of Philippe Auguste built from 1190-1210.

I considered removing the fortifications, but as soon as I did the consequences of that action made the siege on Paris become far more complicated than I wanted. The Vikings raided and sacked Paris several times in the ninth century after the time of Charlemagne. I decided after a series of "what if?" questions that became a nightmare, that I would instead just to admit to my readers that the wall was not there at the time when this fictional war would have taken place. None of these events happened anyway, so just realize that and enjoy the story.

Historical characters:

Most of the characters in the story are fictional. However, Charlemagne is an historical figure. Historians know when he lived, when he died, the battles he fought and the lands he conquered. He is not a mythical king like King Arthur whose existence is debated.

The character Orlando (Roland) is based on an historical figure of Hroaldus mentioned by Charlemagne's biographer Einhard. He died in 778 at the battle of Roncesvalles (Roncevaux) which became immortalized in the famous poem *Chanson de Roland* or Song of Roland. Orlando in the role of hero captured many poets' imaginations and he was used repeatedly in many legends in ways the historical figure could not have done in real life.

Caliph Harun-al-Rashid was an historical figure and he is mentioned briefly in my novel, but was not a part of *Orlando furioso*.

Saint Namphaise was a hermit who at one timed served in Charlemagne's army. I was looking on the Catholic.org website for the perfect name for the character of a hermit and came upon his story. He also lived in the general area, so I used him in my story. I hope that my story will help spur interest in a saint who is not widely known outside the Quercy region of France. I discovered a website (www.quercy.net) which dedicated a page to the Legend of Saint Namphaise. This led to my favorite day of sightseeing France, namely finding sacred sites associated with an obscure saint.

Character Names:

Boiardo and Ariosto gave their immense cast of characters names that are difficult for modern audiences to wrap their minds and tongues around. Most of them were Italian names, even for non-Italian characters. I wrestled with what kind of naming scheme I wanted to use in my story. My first impulse was to use those names I was used to seeing in the English translations: Bradamante, Ruggiero, Rinaldo, Astolfo, Orlando, etc. Then a friend of mine made the suggestion to have the names better reflect the origins of the characters. Astolfo was from Britain, so why should he have an Italian name? It would be better to have him named Aistulf. Similarly, Rinaldo was French and so he should have the French name Renaud. Because I am incorporating another legend of Orlando where he was raised in exile in Sutri, Italy, I am keeping the Italian version of his name Orlando rather than Roland.

I then chose to alter some of the North African names to ones that sounded less Italian. Hence Agramante became Akramont, Sobrino became Sabri, and Dardinello became Daniso to name a few. Unfortunately I could not find adequate cognates for all North African characters, so the Italian sounding Brunello remained the same.

Charles the Great, or Charlemagne, might never have been called that during his lifetime. I, however, chose to use the name Charlemagne throughout my story because that is how we think of him. In addition, his family repeatedly used a few names over the generations, such as: Pepin, Charles, Carloman and Louis. Confusion would abound unless there was some way to designate which one you were referring. Charlemagne's grandfather was known as Charles the Hammer (Charles Martel) and succeeding generations of Charleses were given other nicknames such as: Charles the Bald, Charles the Simple and Charles the Fat. With the sheer military conquests and expansion of land under Charlemagne's rule, I find it justifiable that people might have called him "Charles the Great" during his lifetime. If not, at least I have one name that should be recognizable for my readers.

Military titles of Muslim characters:

The poets used the title king for Agramante, his thirty-two vassals, as well as Marsilio the leader of Spain. That would not be accurate for the time period when North Africa (the Maghreb) was a part of the Abbasid Caliphate and Spain remained under the Umayyad Caliphate and known as al-Andalus. After consultation with several scholars specializing in Medieval Middle Eastern History, I chose to use the title of amir to describe both Akramont (Agramante) and Marsilio. Their subordinates were governors and their advisors were wazirs.

Religion:

Obviously the clash between religions is a source of conflict and tension. One only needs to read the newspaper to see examples in our real world. The war depicted in the poems, and in my story never took place. However, there have been wars between Christian and Muslim forces, most notoriously the Crusades. The poems were written centuries after the Crusades and it appears there were influences in the name choices of Christian characters. For example, Bradamante's paternal grandfather was Bernard of Clairmont. Or Clermont. The call for the first crusade was made by Pope Urban II in 1095 at the Council of Clermont.

I find that echo to be disturbing. Even if I were to use the Anglicized spelling of Clairmont in my story, there is no such town in France. The city is now Clermont-Ferrand, and any translation would likely change the spelling to reflect the place where the Crusades were called.

There is enough tension and conflict between Christianity and Islam in the Real World without trying to include subtle (or not so subtle) reminders of bloody historical events. Therefore, after much consideration, I decided to change the name of Bradamante's house from Clairmont to Lyon. The city of Lyon was founded by the Romans, so it is old enough, and in *Orlando innamorato* Renaud's standard was described as being the head and chest of a lion. (OI, Book 2, Canto XXX, Verses 35-36.)

Another aspect of my source material that bothered me was that both poets showed open hostility toward Islam and Muslims. The poets accused Muslims of being idol worshippers and pagans as if Islam were a polytheistic religion rather than being a monotheistic religion. I know this is a reflection of the attitudes of the times, but I do not wish to antagonize any of my potential readers by keeping that kind of attitude in my version.

I use the word Saracen in my book description to quickly evoke the time period of my story. It is an archaic term that is no longer used. The origins of the word go back to describing the children of Abraham who were descended from Ishmael and not of his son Isaac. Ishmael was born of Hagar and not of Sarah, so he was a Saracen. Saracen = Not of Sarah. It denotes ethnicity and not religious faith, but it became synonymous with Muslims. Saracen is a term that Muslims would not have used to describe themselves.

The poets also had the habit of having any sympathetic Muslim character be converted to Christianity. I found that to be offensive. I wanted to show that both sides of this fictional war had devout followers as well as those who did not have God in their hearts. The villains specifically are without faith. Some are depicted as going through the motions of religious customs when there is an audience. However, the most explicit example of an anti-religious antagonist is Rodomont an atheist who refuses to even put on an act of being a man of faith. That is because he would never bow or submit to any god.

I added a scene of Rodomont desecrating a church in Paris to demonstrate his antipathy toward religion. This type of sacrilegious act would then add fuel to the fire of the Franks against the invaders, without their realizing that this abhorrent action went against the explicit orders of the leader of the North African army.

It should be noted that there are unsympathetic characters on the Frankish side who are not devout Christians. Not all characters have the same level of religious devotion, which reflects reality. Both leaders, Charlemagne and Akramont, are depicted as devout leaders who suffer from the sins of pride and ambition.

The poets did not depict Ruggiero as being a devout Muslim. As I set about writing my story, that did not feel right. How could my hero not be devout? I sought advice from a few different Muslims to add the layer of religious acts and devotion to Islam to my story. I hope that any mistakes that I made in this area are minor.

Overall notes on the plot:

Boiardo and Ariosto wove an immense tapestry of imaginative episodes involving a myriad of knights performing feats of bravery. I harken back to the scene in the movie Karate Kid where Mr. Miyagi tells Daniel how to prune a bonsai tree by picturing the tree in your mind down to the last needle.

I look at the two poems *Orlando innamorato* or *Orlando furioso* and think of them as a wild tree with numerous branches going every which way. My inner picture of the perfect bonsai tree focuses on the love story of Bradamante and Ruggiero. Anything that does not serve that plot line has been cut away. Likewise, if I felt dissatisfied by any portion of the story, I added supplements. So there are some new characters I created to flesh out my story. I hope that the fans of these epic poems will like my adaptation and I hope those unfamiliar with the poems might become inspired to read the source material. After all, they are classics.

READING CLUB DISCUSSION GUIDE

Here are a few questions to help stimulate conversation for reading clubs. If you would like to schedule a time for the author to join your club by either Skype or speakerphone, please visit **www.LindaCMcCabe.com** and click on the link for reading groups.

1. How different was it for you to read of a woman receiving a quest in a story rather than a man?

2. Have you ever known someone who fell in love at first sight? Why do you think Bradamante did not question her love for Ruggiero when she had only met him for a brief time before they were first separated?

3. Do you think it was right for Melissa to tell Bradamante to murder Brunello and Atallah? Was Bradamante right for not following Melissa's orders? What were the consequences of her choice?

4. Did your feelings about the character of Atallah change through the course of the story?

5. Beyond the inclusion of Merlin as a character and a few brief mentions, how do you feel these legends of Charlemagne compare to Arthurian legends?

6. Ruggiero had great pride in his noble ancestor Hector of Troy and sought to live up to the image of the perfect knight. Give some examples of how Ruggiero's actions differed from the other knights in the story.

7. Doralice witnessed the murder of dozens of her armed escorts and was expecting Mandricardo to ravish and then murder her. Instead, she was surprised by his calm demeanor when he uncovered her in the tent. How else could Doralice have responded to Mandricardo's advances if she wanted to live?

8. Would Rodomont have been a better husband for Doralice?

9. What consequences, if any, do you think Bradamante will face if she admits to Charlemagne that she murdered Pinabel?

10. The clash of religious faith is prominent in this story. Give some examples of how adherents to Christianity and Islam demonstrated their piety and defense of their faith. Give some examples of how irreligious characters demonstrated their lack of faith.

11. Would your opinion of Ruggiero be different if he ignored Amir Akramont's summons to report to Paris?

12. Having a double prophecy is unusual. Describe your thoughts on how this difference sets this story apart from traditional quest stories of a prophesied youth raised in obscurity saving the world.

ACKNOWLEDGMENTS

I want to first thank my husband and son for bearing with me over these last six years of my writing and rewriting this novel. I swear the sequel will not take as long. Your patience and good humor about my newfound love of all things French and medieval is a testament of what a supportive family looks like.

I would like to thank other family members who also gave feedback and support for this project: my father Donald McCabe, my mother Ann McCabe, my uncle Charlie Kroell, and my nephew Brian McCabe.

My college Humanities professor, William G. Kilbourne, Jr., helped inspire a love of classic literature in me and offered some useful suggestions for an early draft. I would like to thank the translators of the epic poems that this story is based upon. I do not read Italian, and without their work I would not understand this incredible source material. Charles Stanley Ross has translated the entire poem of *Orlando inamorato* and is available through Parlor Press. There are a few translations of *Orlando furioso* to choose from. There are verse translations by Barbara Reynolds and David R. Slavitt and a prose translation by Guido Waldman. I hope that my series will help spur a resurgence of interest in the poems themselves. Michael Wyatt is helping to lead the way by having organized a symposium at Stanford University in April 2010 of "Mad Orlando's Legacy" and all of its cultural manifestations from opera to paintings, sculptures and the popular puppet shows being staged in Sicily.

I belong to a wonderful writers club, Redwood Writers, a branch of the California Writers Club. Through my club I have had some incredible critique partners who read early (painful) drafts and helped me craft the story into something readable. I subsequently had other critique partners who massaged the text into what it is today. I wish to acknowledge all of these marvelous writers: Rob Loughran, Kate Farrell, Karen Hart, Patrice Garrett, Catherine Keegan, Cindy Pavlinac, Liane Manso Betton, Ellen Boneparth, Carol Collier, Alla Crone, Monique Lessan, Vicka Surovtsov, Cynthia Weissbein and Persia Woolley.

Several Muslims served as consultants in the drafting of several scenes that dealt with Islamic culture and practices. I hope that the end product is something they will be proud of and enjoy reading. Those fine people who assisted me in that aspect of writing were: Tamim Ansary, Raed Jarrar, Soraya Miré, Imran Nappa, Kamran Pasha, and Ari Siletz.

I also wish to thank various scholars who responded to my questions on the H-Net list serv for Middle East Medievalists. Those who responded to my queries about specific questions on terminology were: Mushegh Asatryan, Fred Astren, Ann Chamberlin, Dr. Nicola Clarke, Mustafah Dhada, Dr. S.M. Ghazanfar, Avraham Hakim, V. Kerry Inman, Julie Meisami, Khaleel Mohammed, Alastair Northedge, Hamida Riahi, Dagmar Riedel, Dr. Mariam Rosser-Owen, Walid Saleh, Geoffrey D. Schad, Marina Tolmacheva, Dr. Cengiz Tomar and a special thank you to Letizia Osti for her moderation of the list serv which can be found at http://www.h-net.org/~midmed. In addition, I owe a debt of gratitude to both Ibrahim Al-Marashi, professor of history at IE University in Spain and Munir Shaikh for reviewing my entire manuscript for errors in regard to Islamic culture and history.

Others who read and gave me feedback on either portions or the full manuscript include: Loree Angel, Nathaela Budoc, Batja Cates, Kathi Force, Yanina Gotsulsky, John Granger, Beth Grimes, Marghi Hagan, Cara Hicks, Cindy Miller, Layla Musselwhite, Juliana LeRoy, Gil Ligad, Jacques and Jodi Ropert, Lynn Samples, Ransom Stephens, Laura Wambach, and Mike Wilson.

I attended the marvelous Break Out Novel Intensive (BONI) Workshop in February 2009 organized by Lorin Oberweger and Free-Expressions.com with the following faculty members: Donald Maass, Lisa Rector-Maass, Kimberly Frost and Jason Sitzes. The instruction was incredible, but so was the brainstorming with my fellow students. They were also tremendously helpful for me to bring my story up to a higher level. I want to mention a few of those students that I remember from that BONI workshop: Fred Campagnoli, Monica Kaufer, Lia Keyes, Birgitte Necessary, Claudine Rogers, Priscilla Blair Strapp, and Terri Thayer. Lucien Nanton helped me recognize that my first page was begging for dialogue and that Ruggiero needed to challenge Rodomont forcefully from the beginning. Those urgings helped breathe life and necessary conflict into the first chapter. For that I shall always be grateful to him.

Darrend King Brown, Anne Mini, and Vicki Weiland saw small portions of my work and gave me their professional editorial advice to help guide me in improving my storytelling. Jordan Rosenfeld served as both a developmental and copyeditor for me and I am thrilled to have had someone of her talent and expertise serve in that capacity for my story. Her gentle nudging in portions of my manuscript helped me to re-write and expand scenes that I had tried to skirt by with narrative summary. She also helped me focus the POV on one character at a time.

Jeff Sypeck reviewed an early draft of my manuscript and offered advice in regard to the historical record as it related to Charlemagne and the Medieval period as well.

I want to thank the following writers for inspiring me: Donna Woolfolk Cross, Patricia Volonakis Davis, Tess Gerritsen, Christopher Gortner, Lee Lofland, Erika Mailman, Katherine Neville, Christi Phillips, Joe Quirk, J.K. Rowling, and Richard Zimler.

I am most grateful to my dear friend José Lúcio who has been my biggest fan. He read every chapter as soon as it was written and it is he, more than anyone else, who helped shape this story. I am indebted to him for his unwavering support and encouragement.

SNEAK PEEK AT VOLUME TWO

CHAPTER 1

"May Mandricardo's manhood shrivel to match the size of his brain," said Marfisa.

The warrior queen flashed a smile at Ruggiero, signaling it was his turn.

Again.

Ruggiero shifted in his saddle. He had given up trying to be clever and instead resorted to uttering statements of what he wanted to happen. "May I sheathe my dagger in Rodomont's blackened heart."

She nodded, indicating that his salvo was considered adequate.

"May Mandricardo's manhood maintain the stiffness of boiled octopus," said Marfisa with a throaty laugh.

Ruggiero shook his head. He had endured over one hundred such rounds of this game of hers since they left the village of Saint Antonin on horseback and while he was weary of it, her enthusiasm had never waned. If anything, her curses were flying faster than at the start. Marfisa had described a wide variety of ways she desired emasculating Mandricardo including chopping, burning, mangling, and feeding body parts to farm animals. Ruggiero would have preferred paying closer attention to his riding than coming up with new curses for the two warriors they followed at breakneck speed. Concentrating on the rhythmic clattering of hooves over the well-worn stones of the old Roman road soothed his frazzled nerves. He hoped she would take a hint by the lull in the conversation.

"Well? Have you nothing more?"

Ruggiero groaned. This game would end only when they caught up with their adversaries or arrived in Paris. "May my loyal horse Frontino throw Rodomont off his back breaking the cretin's neck."

"That was as lame as a three legged horse. Have you lost your anger against that foul smelling miscreant?"

"No. My hatred toward him is a bottomless well. I want to see him dead, but I am ill suited for cursing. I prefer action over words. How is it that you have an endless supply of curses?"

"I have been cursing men ever since I can remember," she laughed. "I knew enough as a slave girl to keep them to myself, but those dark thoughts kept me from going mad. The first curse I said aloud was as I plunged my knife into the heart of the drunken king who tried ravishing me."

"Why do you bear so much hatred toward men? Did someone succeed where that king failed?"

"No. Others tried to take my maidenhead, but they sing the songs of eunuchs — at least those who are still alive," she said with a twisted smile. "My first memory is when I was a little girl and passed from man to man in a caravan of bandits. They did nothing to damage my sale price, but they destroyed my innocence."

"I am sorry you were treated thus."

"Thank you," said Marfisa. "You are the first man to ever say such a thing to me. Men do not consider a slave girl's virtue as sacrosanct as a noble woman's."

"What does class have to do with it? No one should be forced to commit lewd acts," said Ruggiero.

"Are you mocking me?"

"Why would I mock you?"

Marfisa grit her teeth. "I have never met a man who espoused such beliefs or who regarded me with respect. Most men scoff when they discover I am a woman-in-arms and realize too late that my skills are no jest."

"I do not think of women warriors as a joke," said Ruggiero. "Neither did our companions earlier."

"Why is that?"

"I never knew my mother, but she was in the Caliph's army. She died giving birth to me, and I am proud she was a respected warrior. As for our previous companions, they were grateful for your help. They also have a kinswoman whose military skills are renowned."

Marfisa's face lit up. "Another warrior maiden? What is her name?"

"Bradamante."

Ruggiero found it painful to say the Maid's name aloud. He did not want to talk about the woman he loved with Marfisa or anyone else until it was safe to do so. Their engagement was made in secret and would be scandalous if it became known. Once the war was over, they could openly declare their love for each other and be married. Until then, discretion was required.

The momentary quiet allowed for him to appreciate the beauty of the rural countryside in Francia. The road they were following had been a minor Roman road and was ill suited to accommodate the large Muslim army and therefore this area had been untouched by the ravages of the war. Oak trees dotting the hillsides cast long shadows by the setting sun while tinges of yellow and peach lingered in the sky. The three riders they chased disappeared over the crest of a hill in the distance. Temporarily losing sight of their quarry was a consequence of riding in the rolling terrain west of the Central Massif mountains. Ruggiero wondered how well they would be able to see them once there was only moonlight to guide the way.

"Have you fought against her?" asked Marfisa.

"No and I hope I never will," said Ruggiero. "I have seen her in battle though, she is formidable."

"Afraid to fight her?" taunted Marfisa. "I would love to test my skills against any warrior held in great esteem. Especially a warrior maid."

"It is out to respect that I would not want to fight her. She is honorable and for that reason, I do not wish to see her harmed," said Ruggiero. "Likewise, I consider you honorable. It would be tragic if the two of you fought. Whereas, Rodomont and Mandricardo are without honor. They deserve to die at our hands. Even if we all serve the same sovereign. My hatred of Rodomont, goes beyond today's insult. He fought against Bradamante and could not win. So he killed her horse."

"He killed a horse in battle? You are right. He deserves to die."

"Rodomont has no respect for man nor beast. It is intolerable for him to ride my horse."

"And yet you risk all our mounts dying from exhaustion during this never ending chase," said Marfisa. All four of us vowed to go to Paris and serve Akramont. Such a journey cannot be completed in a single night, so let us cease this reckless pursuit and make camp or find a place to spend the night. We shall duel with them in Paris."

"No. We cannot risk stopping. Our horses might drop down dead or even turn to dust."

"Pardon?"

"Our horses have been at full gallop since this afternoon," said Ruggiero. "Neither their horses nor ours have slowed down, stopped to graze or even take a drink of water. They are not panting or foaming at the mouth and none have made water or dropped anything during our journey. There can only be one reason: magic. I warned about drinking from that fountain and yet all the horses drank their fill."

"If our horses die once they stop, would that end your quarrel with Rodomont?"

"Of course not. I am honor bound to fight him. Else I would be accepting his insult to my integrity as a knight."

The light of the half moon made their journey more treacherous than it had been during the day, but the three riders they were chasing had not stopped. Ruggiero vowed that he would match them stride for stride. He did not trust either Rodomont or Mandricardo and was unsure if he lost their trail if they would return to Paris as they promised. There was also the concern that either or both of those men might try and kill Ruggiero in his sleep. Resting near Marfisa and the appearance of impropriety was another cause for worry. For Bradamante's sake, he did not want to do anything that might cause her heartache or doubt his fidelity. Undoubtedly Bradamante would hear about Marfisa, her role in the rescue of Vivien and Maugis and that he left for Paris with her. It was likely that Marfisa's beauty would be mentioned at the same time, although in Ruggiero's eyes no woman could outshine Bradamante.

As they passed over a crest in the road the three riders were once again in view. Ruggiero chuckled as he realized that he had nothing to fear from either Rodomont or Mandricardo that night. They were locked in a struggle trying to outdistance the other and overtake the rider who led this expedition to Paris.

Both men wanted desperately to claim Doralice of Granada as their own.

ABOUT THE AUTHOR

Photo by Cindy A. Pavlinac

Linda C. McCabe lives in the Northern California Wine Country with her college sweetheart and teenaged son. She received a master's degree as an historian of science from Sonoma State University, and loves to travel. To aid in the research of her writing, she spent a month in France scouring museums in Paris and trekking through medieval hilltop villages in the Midi-Pyrenees. She has been a member of the California Writers Club for more than a decade and is past-president of the local branch, Redwood Writers. She has had opinion/editorials published in the Santa Rosa Press Democrat, the Los Angeles Times and essays published in several of the Redwood Writers' Vintage Voices anthologies as well as the Centennial Edition of the California Writers Club Anthology West Winds. More of her writing can be found at her literary blog: lcmccabe.blogspot.com where she posts about writing, travel, medievalism and whatever strikes her interest. She also has a website at www.LindaCMcCabe.com where she invites book clubs to contact her for visits by speakerphone or Skype chats.

Made in the USA
San Bernardino, CA
26 July 2018